THE GILDA STORIES

A NOVEL BY JEWELLE GOMEZ

Other books by the author
Flamingoes and Bears
The Lipstick Papers
Oral Tradition
Forty-Three Septembers
Don't Explain

*Learn more about the work of Jewelle Gomez
at* www.JewelleGomez.com.

THE GILDA STORIES

A NOVEL BY JEWELLE GOMEZ

Firebrand
Books

Sections of this novel have appeared in the following books and magazines: *The American Voice, Lesbian Fiction* (Persephone Press/Alyson Publications), *The Village Voice Literary Supplement* and *Worlds Apart* (Alyson Publications).

The quotation from "Prologue" by Audre Lorde is taken from her book of poetry, *A Land Where Other People Live* (Broadside Press, Detroit, 1973).

Book and Cover Design by Jonathan Bruns
Typesetting by Bets Ltd.
Additional typesetting by Jonathan Bruns
Cover photos © Photonica
Author photo by Ann Chapman

Printed in Canada

Library of Congress Cataloging-in-Publication Data

Gomez, Jewelle, 1948–
    The Gilda Stories: A Novel / by Jewelle Gomez
        p.   cm
    ISBN 0-932379-95-8 (acid-free paper)
    ISBN 0-932379-94-X (pbk. : acid-free paper)
    I. Title
    PS3557.0457G5   1991
    813'.54–dc20

ACKNOWLEDGMENTS

A sincere thanks to those who have encouraged and assisted me during this long process that has traversed many lifetimes: Cheryl Clarke, Dorothy Allison, Elly Bulkin, Marianne Brown, Sandra Lara, Leslie Kahn, Evelynn Hammonds, Audre Lorde, Gregory Kolovakos, Michael Albano, Ana Oakes, Clayton Riley, Gwendolyn Henderson Smith, Katie Roberts, Babara Smith, Nancy Musgrave, Lucy Loyd, Jonathan Leiter, Robin Hirsch, Marilyn Hacker, Maria Lachina, Eric Garber, Arlene Wysong, Morgan Freeman, Gloria Stein, Eric Ashworth, Zuri McKie, Nancy Bereano, and Marty Pottenger. My family in Pawtucket and at 146 West Newton Street. The Beard's Fund and the Barbara Denning/Money for Women Fund. And Linda Nelson.

As always, my work is dedicated Gracias Archelina Sportsman Morandus, Lydia Mae Morandus, and Duke Gomes.

At night sleep locks me into an echoless coffin
sometimes at noon I dream
there is nothing to fear. . .

Audre Lorde

Chapter One
Louisiana: 1850

The Girl slept restlessly, feeling the prickly straw as if it were teasing pinches from her mother. The stiff moldy odor transformed itself into her mother's starchy dough smell. The rustling of the Girl's body in the barn hay was sometimes like the sound of fatback frying in the cooking shed behind the plantation's main house. At other moments in her dream it was the crackling of the brush as her mother raked the bristles through the Girl's thicket of dark hair before beginning the intricate pattern of braided rows.

She had traveled by night for fifteen hours before daring to stop. Her body held out until a deserted farmhouse, where it surrendered to this demanding sleep hemmed by fear.

Then the sound of walking, a man moving stealthily through the dawn light toward her. In the dream it remained what it was: danger. A white man wearing the clothes of an overseer. In the dream the Girl clutched tightly at her mother's large black hand, praying the sound of the steps would stop, that she would wake up curled around her mother's body on the straw and cornhusk mattress next to the big, old stove, grown cold with the night. In sleep she clutched the hand of her mother, which turned into the warm, wooden handle of the knife she had stolen when she ran away the day before. It pulsed beside her heart, beneath the rough shirt that hung loosely from her thin, young frame. The knife, crushed into the cotton folds near her breast, was invisible to the red-faced man who stood laughing over her, pulling her by one leg from beneath the pile of hay.

The Girl did not scream but buried herself in the beating of her heart alongside the hidden knife. She refused to believe that the hours of indecision and, finally, the act of escape were over. The walking, hiding, running through the Mississippi and Louisiana woods had quickly settled into an almost enjoyable rhythm; she was not ready to give in to those whom her mother had sworn were not fully human.

The Girl tried to remember some of the stories that her mother, now dead, had pieced together from many different languages to describe the journey to this land. The legends sketched a picture of the Fulani past—a natural rhythm of life without bondage. It was a memory that receded more with each passing year.

"Come on. Get up, gal, time now, get up!" The urgent voice of her mother was a sharp buzz in her dream. She opened her eyes to the streaking sun which slipped in through the shuttered-window opening. She hopped up, rolled the pallet to the wall, then dipped her hands quickly in the warm water in the basin on the counter. Her mother poured a bit more bubbling water from the enormous kettle. The Girl watched the steam caught by the half-light of the predawn morning rise toward the low ceiling. She slowly started to wash the hard bits of moisture from her eyes as her mother turned back to the large, black stove.

"I'ma put these biscuits out, girl, and you watch this cereal. I got to go out back. I didn't beg them folks to let you in from the fields to work with me to watch you sleepin' all day. So get busy."

Her mother left through the door quickly, pulling her skirts up around her legs as she went. The Girl ran to the stove, took the ladle in her hand, and moved the thick gruel around in the iron pot. She grinned proudly at her mother when she walked back in: no sign of sticking in the pot. Her mother returned the smile as she swept the ladle up in her large hand and set the Girl onto her next task—turning out the biscuits.

"If you lay the butter cross 'em while they hot, they like that. If they's not enough butter, lay on the lard, make 'em shine. They can't tell and they take it as generous."

"Mama, how it come they cain't tell butter from fat? Baby

Minerva can smell butter 'fore it clears the top of the churn. She won't drink no pig fat. Why they cain't tell how butter taste?"

"They ain't been here long 'nough. They just barely human. Maybe not even. They suck up the world, don't taste it."

The Girl rubbed butter over the tray of hot bread, then dumped the thick, doughy biscuits into the basket used for morning service. She loved that smell and always thought of bread when she dreamed of better times. Whenever her mother wanted to offer comfort she promised the first biscuit with real butter. The Girl imagined the home across the water that her mother sometimes spoke of as having fresh bread baking for everyone, even for those who worked in the fields. She tried to remember what her mother had said about the world as it had lived before this time but could not. The lost empires were a dream to the Girl, like the one she was having now.

She looked up at the beast from this other land, as he dragged her by her leg from the concealing straw. His face lost the laugh that had split it and became creased with lust. He untied the length of rope holding his pants, and his smile returned as he became thick with anticipation of her submission to him, his head swelling with power at the thought of invading her. He dropped to his knees before the girl whose eyes were wide, seeing into both the past and the future. He bent forward on his knees, stiff for conquest, already counting the bounty fee and savoring the stories he would tell. He felt a warmth at the pit of his belly. The girl was young, probably a virgin he thought, and she didn't appear able to resist him. He smiled at her open, unseeing eyes, interpreting their unswerving gaze as neither resignation nor loathing but desire. The flash-fire in him became hotter.

His center was bright and blinding as he placed his arms—one on each side of the Girl's head—and lowered himself. She closed her eyes. He rubbed his body against her brown skin and imagined the closing of her eyes was a need for him and his power. He started to enter her, but before his hand finished pulling her open, while it still tingled with the softness of her insides, she entered him with her heart which was now a wood-handled knife.

He made a small sound as his last breath hurried to leave him. Then he dropped softly. Warmth spread from his center of power to his chest as the blood left his body. The Girl lay still beneath him until her breath became the only sign of life in the pile of hay. She felt the blood draining from him, comfortably warm against her now cool skin.

It was like the first time her mother had been able to give her a real bath. She'd heated water in the cauldron for what seemed like hours on a night that the family was away, then filled a wooden barrel whose staves had been packed with sealing wax. She lowered the Girl, small and narrow, into the luxuriant warmth of the tub and lathered her with soap as she sang an unnamed tune.

The intimacy of her mother's hands and the warmth of the water lulled the Girl into a trance of sensuality she never forgot. Now the blood washing slowly down her breastbone and soaking into the floor below was like that bath—a cleansing. She lay still, letting the life flow over her, then slid gently from beneath the red-faced man whose cheeks had paled. The Girl moved quietly, as if he had really been her lover and she was afraid to wake him.

Looking down at the blood soaking her shirt and trousers she felt no disgust. It was the blood signaling the death of a beast and her continued life. The Girl held the slippery wood of the knife in her hand as her body began to shake in the dream/memory. She sobbed, trying to understand what she should do next. How to hide the blood and still move on. She was young and had never killed anyone.

She trembled, unable to tell if this was really happening to her all over again or if she was dreaming it—again. She held one dirty hand up to her broad, brown face and cried heartily.

That was how Gilda found her, huddled in the root cellar of her small farmhouse on the road outside of New Orleans in 1850. The Girl clutched the knife to her breast and struggled to escape her dream.

"Wake up, gal!" Gilda shook the thin shoulder gently, as if afraid to pull loose one of the shuddering limbs. Her voice was whiskey rough, her rouged face seemed young as she raised the smoky lantern.

The Girl woke with her heart pounding, desperate to leave the dream behind but seized with white fear. The pale face above her was a woman's, but the Girl had learned that they, too, could be as dangerous as their men.

Gilda shook the Girl whose eyes were now open but unseeing. The night was long, and Gilda did not have time for a hysterical child. The brown of her eyes darkened in impatience.

"Come on, gal, what you doin' in my root cellar?" The Girl's silence deepened. Gilda looked at the stained, torn shirt, the too-big pants tied tightly at her waist, and the wood-handled knife in the Girl's grip. Gilda saw in her eyes the impulse to use it.

"You don't have to do that. I'm not going to hurt you. Come on." With that Gilda pulled the Girl to her feet, careful not to be too rough; she could see the Girl was weak with hunger and wound tight around her fear. Gilda had seen a runaway slave only once. Before she'd recognized the look and smell of terror, the runaway had been captured and hauled off. Alone with the Girl, and that look bouncing around the low-ceilinged cellar, Gilda almost felt she should duck. She stared deeply into the Girl's dark eyes and said silently, *You needn't be afraid. I'll take care of you. The night hides many things.*

The Girl loosened her grip on the knife under the persuasive touch of Gilda's thoughts. She had heard of people who could talk without speaking but never expected a white to be able to do it. This one was a puzzlement to her: the dark eyes and pale skin. Her face was painted in colors like a mask, but she wore men's breeches and a heavy jacket.

Gilda moved in her small-boned frame like a team of horses pulling a load on a sodden road: gentle and relentless. "I could use you, gal, come on!" was all Gilda said as she lifted the Girl and carried her out to the buggy. She wrapped a thick shawl around the Girl's shoulders and held tightly to her with one hand as she drew the horse back onto the dark road.

After almost an hour they pulled up to a large building on the edge of the city—not a plantation house, but with the look of a hotel. The Girl blinked in surprise at the light which glowed in every room as if there were a great party. Several buggies stood at the side of the house with liveried men in attendance. A small open shed at the left held a few single, saddled horses that munched hay. They inclined their heads toward Gilda's horse. The swiftness of its approach was urgent, and the smell the buggy left behind was a perfumed wake of fear. The horses all shifted slightly, then snorted, unconcerned. They were eating, rested and unburdened for the moment. Gilda held the Girl's arm firmly as she moved around to the back of the house past the satisfied, sentient horses. She entered a huge kitchen in which two women—one black, one white—prepared platters of sliced ham and turkey.

Gilda spoke quietly to the cook's assistant. "Macey, please bring a tray to my room. Warm wine, too. Hot water first though." Not breaking her stride, she tugged the Girl up the back stairs to the two rooms that were hers. They entered a thickly furnished sitting room with books lining the small bookshelf on the north wall. Paintings and a few line drawings hung on the south wall. In front of them sat a deep couch, surrounded by a richly colored hanging fabric.

This room did not have the urgency of those below it. Few of the patrons who visited the Woodard place—as it was still known although that family had not owned it in years—had ever been invited into the private domain of its mistress. This was where Gilda retreated at the end of the night, where she spent most of the day reading, alone except for a few of the girls or Bird. Woodard's was the most prosperous establishment in the area and enjoyed the patronage of some of the most esteemed men and women of the county. The gambling, musical divertissements, and the private rooms were all well attended. Gilda employed eight girls, none yet twenty, who lived in the house and worked hard hours being what others imagined women should be. After running Woodard's for fifteen years, Gilda loved her home and her girls. It had been a wonderfully comfortable and relatively tiny segment of the 300 years she'd lived. Her private rooms held the treasures of several lifetimes.

She raised the lid of a chest and pulled out a towel and nightshirt. The Girl's open stare brushed over her, nudging at the weight of the years on her shoulders. Under that puzzled gaze the years didn't seem so grotesque. Gilda listened a moment to the throaty laughter floating up from the rooms below, where the musical entertainment had begun without her, and could just barely hear Bird introducing the evening in her deep voice. Woodard's was the only house with an "Indian girl," as her loyal patrons bragged. Although Bird now only helped to manage the house, many came just to see her, dressed in the soft cotton, sparely adorned dress that most of the women at Woodard's wore. Thin strips of leather bearing beading or quill were sometimes braided into her hair or sewn onto her dress. Townsmen ranked her among their local curiosities.

Gilda was laying out clothes when Macey entered the room lugging two buckets of water—one warm and one hot. While stealing glances at the Girl, she poured the water into a tin tub that sat in a corner of the room next to an ornate folding screen.

Gilda said, "Take off those clothes and wash. Put those others on." She spoke slowly, deliberately, knowing she was breaking through one reality into another. The words she did not speak were more important: _Rest. Trust. Home._

The Girl dropped her dusty, blood-encrusted clothes by the couch. Before climbing into the warm water, she looked up at Gilda, who gazed discreetly somewhere above her head. Gilda then picked up the clothes, ignoring the filth, and clasped them to her as she left the room. When the Girl emerged she dressed in the nightshirt and curled up on the settee, pulling a fringed shawl from its back down around her shoulders. She'd unbraided and washed the thickness of her hair and wrapped it tightly in the damp towel.

Curling her legs underneath her to keep off the night chill, she listened to the piano below and stared into the still shadows cast by the lamp. Soon Gilda entered, with Macey following sullenly behind holding a tray of food. Gilda pulled a large, overstuffed chair close to the settee while Macey put the tray on a small table. She lit another lamp near them, glancing backward over her shoulder at the strange, thin black girl with the African look to her. Macey made it her business to mind her own business, particularly when it came to Miss Gilda, but she knew the look in Gilda's eyes. It was something she saw too rarely: living in the present, or maybe just curiosity. Macey and the laundress, neither of whom lived in the house with the others, spoke many times of the anxious look weighing in Gilda's eyes. It was as if she saw something that existed only in her own head. But Macey, who dealt mostly with Bernice and some with Bird, left her imagination at home. Besides, she had no belief in voodoo magic and just barely held on to her Catholicism.

Of course there was talk around most dinner tables in the parish, especially after Bird had come to stay at the house. Macey was certain that if there was a faith Gilda held, it was not one she knew. The lively look that filled her employer's eyes now usually only appeared when she and Bird spent their evenings talking and writing together.

Some things were best not pondered, so Macey turned and hurried back down to her card game with Bernice, the cook. Gilda prepared a plate and poured from the decanter of red wine. The Girl looked furtively in her direction but was preoccupied with the cleanliness of the room and the spicy smell of the food. Her body relaxed while her mind still raced, filled with the unknowns: how far she was from the plantation, who this woman might be, how she could get away from her.

Gilda was barely able to draw her excitement back inside herself as she watched the girl. It was the clear purpose in the Girl's dark eyes that first caught her. A child's single-mindedness shone through. Deeper still was an adult perseverance. Gilda remembered that look many years before in Bird's eyes when she had returned from her one visit to her people, the Lakota. There was an intensity, curiosity, and vulnerability blended together behind a tight mask of resolve.

More importantly, Gilda saw herself behind those eyes—a younger self she barely remembered, one who would never be comfortable with having decisions made for her. Or with following a path she'd not laid herself. Gilda also saw a need for family that matched her own. She closed her eyes, and in her mind the musky smell of her mother's garments rose. She almost reached out to the phantom of her past there in the lamplit room but caught her breath and shook her head slightly. Gilda knew then she wanted the Girl to stay.

Answers to her questions slipped in among her thoughts as the Girl ate. She was startled to discover the understanding of where she was and who this woman might be. She set her glass down abruptly and stared at Gilda's narrow face which glowed with excitement even in the shadows of the lamplight. Her dark brown hair was wound low at the back of her neck leaving her tiny features exposed. Even within the tight bodice of the blue beaded dress she now wore, Gilda moved in her own deliberate way. The brown cigar she lit seemed too delicate for her broad gestures.

The Girl thought for a moment: *This is a man! A little man!*

Gilda laughed out loud at the idea in the Girl's head and said, "No, I'm a woman." Then without speaking aloud she said, *I am a woman, you know that. And you know I am a woman as no other you have known, nor has your mother known, in life or death. I am a woman as you are, and more.*

The Girl opened her mouth to speak, but her throat was too raw, her nerves too tight. She bent her mouth in recognition and puzzlement. This was a woman, and her face was not unlike her mother's despite the colors painted on it.

Its unwavering gaze was hard-edged yet full of concern. But behind the dark brown of Gilda's eyes the Girl recognized forests, ancient roots and arrows, images she had never seen before. She blinked quickly and looked again through the lamplight. There she simply saw a small woman who did not eat, who sipped slowly from a glass of wine and watched with a piercing gaze through eyes that seemed both dark and light at the same time.

When the Girl finished eating and sat back again on the settee, Gilda spoke aloud. "You don't have to tell me anything. I'll tell you. You just listen and remember when anyone asks: You're new in the house. My sister sent you over here to me as a present. You've been living in Mississippi. Now you live here and work for me. Nothing else, do you understand?" The Girl remained silent but understood the words and the reasons behind them. She didn't question. She was tired, and the more she saw of this white world, the more afraid she became that she could no longer hide from the plantation owners and the bounty hunters.

"There is linen in that chest against the wall. The chaise longue is quite comfortable. Go to sleep. We will rise early, my girl." With that, Gilda's thin face radiated an abundant smile as youthful as the Girl's. She turned out one of the lamps and left the room quickly. The Girl unfolded a clean sheet and thick blanket and spread them out smoothly, marveling at their freshness and the comforting way they clung to the bowed and carved wood of the chaise's legs. She disturbed the placid surface almost regretfully and slipped in between the covers, trying to settle into sleep.

This woman, Gilda, could see into her mind. That was clear. The Girl was not frightened though, because it seemed she could see into Gilda's as well. That made them even.

The Girl thought a little about what she had seen when the woman opened herself to her, what had made her trust her: an expanse of road stretching narrowly into the horizon, curving gently away from her; the lulling noise of rushing wind and the rustling of leaves that sounded like the soft brush of the hem of a dress on carpet. She stared down the road with her eyes closed until she lost the dream in deep sleep.

Gilda stood outside the door, listening for a moment to the Girl's restless movement. She easily quieted the Girl's turmoil with the energy of her thoughts. The music and talking from below intruded on Gilda, but she resisted, searching out the glimmerings of her past instead. How unnerving to have stumbled upon them in that moment of recognition while watching the Girl eat her supper. The memory was vague, more like a fog than a tide after so many years in which Gilda had deliberately turned away from the past.

With her eyes closed she could slip backward to the place whose name she had long since forgotten, to when she was a girl. She saw a gathering of people with burnished skin. She was among them. The spiced scent of their bodies was an aura moving alongside them as they crossed an arid expanse of land. She couldn't see much beyond the curved backs and dust-covered sandals of those walking in front of her. She held the hand of a woman she knew was her mother, and somewhere ahead was her father. Where were they all now? Dead, of course. Less than ashes, and Gilda could not remember their faces. She couldn't remember when their eyes and mouths had slipped away from her. Where had the sound of their voices gone? All that seemed left was the memory of a scented passage that had dragged her along in its wake and the dark color of blood as it seeped into sand.

She grimaced at the sense of movement, the thing she most longed to be free of. Even there, in that mythical past she could no longer see clearly, she had moved nomadically from one home to another. Through first one war then another. Which sovereign? Whose nation? She had left those things behind sometime in the past three hundred years—perhaps even longer.

She opened her eyes and looked back toward the door to the room where the Girl slept, smiling as her own past dissolved. She no longer needed those diaphanous memories. She wanted to look only forward, to the future of the Girl and Bird, and to her own resting place where she would finally have stillness.

Again the music broke into her thoughts. For the first time in a long while she was eager to join the girls in the downstairs parlor for the evening, to watch Bird moving quickly among the rooms, and to listen to the languidly told stories the girls perfected to entertain the gentlemen and make the time pass for themselves. And when the night was edged by dawn she would gratefully lie down next to Bird, welcoming the weight of her limbs stretched across her body and the smell of her hair permeating her day of rest.

During her first few months at Woodard's the Girl barely spoke but did the chores she was directed to in the house. She began to accompany Bird or Gilda some months after, to shop for the house or buy presents for members of the household, which Gilda did quite frequently. The Girl carried the packages and straightened up Gilda's suite of rooms, carefully dusting the tiny vases and figurines, the shelves of books, and rearranging fresh flowers, which she picked from the garden once she became comfortable enough to venture outside alone.

Sometimes she would sit in the pantry while the girls were around the table in the kitchen eating, talking over previous evenings, laughing at stories, or discussing their problems.

"Don't tell me I'm ungrateful. I'm grown. I want what I want and I ain't nobody's mama!" Rachel shouted at Fanny, who always had an opinion.

"Not that we know of," was Fanny's vinegary retort. Rachel only stared at her coldly, so Fanny went on. "You always want something, Rachel, and you ain't coming to nothing with this dream stuff. Running off, leavin' everythin' just 'cause you had a dream to do something you don't know nothin' 'bout."

"It's my dream an' my life, ain't it Miss Bird? You know 'bout dreams an' such."

Bird became the center of their attention as she tried to remember what would mean the most to these girls, who were really women, who had made their home with her and Gilda.

"Dreaming is not something to be ignored."

"But going to a place like that, next to the water—ready to fall in 'cording to her dream, mind you, not mine—is just foolish," Fanny insisted.

"It's a dream, not a fact. Maybe the dream just means change, change for the better. If Rachel has a dream, she reads it. Nobody else here can do that for her," Bird said.

"Anyway, I ain't packed nothin'. I'm just tellin' you my dream, is all. Damn you, Fanny, you a stone in my soup every time!"

The women laughed because Rachel always had a way with words when they got her excited.

Occasionally Gilda sat with them, as if they did not work for her, chiming in with stories and laughter just the same as Bernice, the dark, wary cook, or Rachel, the one full of ambition. There were also Rose, kind to a fault; Minta, the youngest; and the unlikely pair who were inseparable—Fanny, the opinionated, and Sarah, the appeaser. Mostly the Girl kept apart from them. She had never seen white women such as these before, and it was frightening not to know where she fit in. She had heard of bawdy houses from her mother who had heard from the men who sipped brandy in the library after dinner. But the picture had never added up to what she saw now.

These women embodied the innocence of children the Girl had known back on the plantation, yet they were also hard, speaking of the act of sex casually, sometimes with humor. And even more puzzling was their debate of topics the Girl had heard spoken of only by men. The women eagerly expressed their views on politics and economics: what slavery was doing to the South, who was dominating politics, and the local agitation against the Galatain Street "houses."

Located further from the center of activity, Gilda's house was run with brisk efficiency. She watched over the health of the women and protected them. But her presence was usually more presumed than actual. Most often she locked herself in her room until six in the evening. There she slept, read, and wrote in the voluminous journals she kept secured in a chest.

Bird managed the everyday affairs, supervising most of the marketing and arbitrating disputes with tradesmen or between the girls. She also directed the Girl in doing the sundry tasks assigned to her. And it was Bird who decided that she would teach the Girl to read. Every afternoon they sat down in Bird's shaded room with the Bible and a newspaper, going over letters and words relentlessly.

The Girl sat patiently as Bird told a story in her own words, then picked out each syllable on paper until they came together in the story she had just recited. At first the Girl did not see the sense of the lessons. No one she knew ever had need of reading, except the black preacher who came over on Saturday nights to deliver a sermon under the watchful gaze of the overseer. Even he was more likely to thwack the Bible with his rusty hand than read from it.

But soon the Girl began to enjoy the lessons. She liked knowing what Fanny was talking about when she exclaimed that Rachel was "as hard headed as Lot's wife," or recognizing the name of the Louisiana governor when she heard it cursed around the kitchen table. Another reason she enjoyed the lessons was that she liked the way Bird smelled. When they sat on the soft cushions of the couch in Bird's room, bending over the books and papers, the Girl was comforted by the pungent earthiness of the Lakota woman. She did not cover herself with the cosmetics and perfumes her housemates enjoyed. The soft scent of brown soap mixed with the leather of her headband and necklace created a familiar aura. It reminded the Girl of her mother and the strong smell of her sweat dropping onto the logs under the burning cauldrons. The Girl rarely allowed herself to miss her mother or her sisters, preferring to leave the past alone for a while, at least until she felt safe in this new world.

Sitting in the room with the Girl, Bird was no longer aloof. She was tender and patient, savoring memories of herself she found within the Girl. Bird gazed into the African eyes which struggled to see a white world through words on a page. Bird wondered what creatures, as invisible as she and the Girl were, did with their pasts.

Was she to slip it off of her shoulders and fold it into a chest to be locked away for some unknown future? And what to do with that future, the one that Gilda had given Bird with its vast expanse of road? Where would she look to read that future? What oracle could she lay on her lap to pick out the words that would frame it?

Bird taught the Girl first from the Bible and the newspaper. Neither of them could see themselves reflected there. Then she told the Girl stories of her own childhood, using them to teach her to write. She spoke each letter aloud, then the word, her own hand drawing the Girl's across the worn paper. And soon there'd be a sentence and a legend or memory of who she was. And the African girl then read it back to her. Bird enjoyed these lessons almost as much as her evenings spent alone with Gilda. And with the restlessness that agitated Gilda more each year, those times together had grown less frequent.

Gilda and Bird sometimes retreated to the farmhouse for a day or more, spending most of the time walking in the evening, riding, or reading together silently, rarely raising questions. Sometimes Gilda went to the farmhouse alone, leaving Bird anxious and irritable. This afternoon Bird prolonged the lesson with the Girl a bit. Uncertainty hung in the air around her, and she was reluctant to leave the security of the Girl's eagerness to learn. She asked her to read aloud again from the sheets of paper on which they'd just printed words. The halting sound of the Girl's voice opened a space inside of Bird. She stood quickly, walking to the curtained window.

"Go on if you understand the words, stop if you do not," Bird said with her back to the room.

She pulled the curtain aside and tied it with a sash, then fingered the small bits of pearlized quill stitched onto the leather band around her neck. Outside, the stableman was raking out hay for the horses of the evening visitors. Bird was pleased with the comfort she felt at the normal movements around the house and at the sound of the Girl's voice, which in the past year had lightened to seem more like a child's than when she'd first come. Bird turned when she heard a question.

"Tell me again of this *pox* please?" the Girl asked, pointing at the word on the paper.

"It came with the traders. They stole many things and breathed the disease into my people and sold it to us in their cloth. It makes the body feverish and causes spots over the body and many deaths."

"Why did you not die?" the Girl asked, carefully matching her words to the rhythm she had heard in Gilda's voice, just as she often imitated her walk when no one watched. She wondered if Bird's escape from the pox was connected to the rumors that she and Gilda were conjure women. She had seen many oddities since coming to the house, but none of them seemed near to conjuring to the Girl so she generally dismissed the talk.

Bird stared at her silently, startled for a moment to hear the familiar inflections from the Girl. "When the deaths came, some members of my clan moved away from the others. My mother and her brothers thought we could escape the air that was killing us. We came south to the warmth to burn away the disease from our spirits. I was sick for a time as we traveled, but we left it on the trail behind us." Bird ached as she spoke, remembering the brothers who'd become fearful of her when she'd fallen ill with the disease and then suspicious when she recovered.

In the end they were convinced she was a witch because she had survived. They chased her away from their small band into the night that had become her friend.

"Do you still have the spots?"

Bird laughed, and the small scar that lanced her eyebrow rose slightly. "Yes, there are some on my back. There is no more infection, simply the mark. Did you not have this disease before. . ." Bird's voice trailed off. She did not want to remind the Girl of past sadness.

"No disease with spots. Some fevers came, through the waters my mother said. Can I see your spots?"

Bird undid the tiny buttons at her wrists and down the front of her shirtwaist, shrugged her shoulders from the cotton dress, then turned her back toward the lamp. The Girl's eyes widened at the small raised circles that sprayed across the brown skin. She let her fingers brush the places where disease had come and placed a small finger gently atop one spot, fitting it into the indentation at its center.

"Your skin is smooth like a baby's," she said.

"Gilda has a lotion she used to rub into my back when I first came here. It makes the skin soft."

"Can I have some for my hands?"

Bird reached down and took the Girl's two hands in her own. Their fingertips were calloused in a way that Bird knew was not the result of the light cleaning and washing done at the house. She nodded and pressed the small hard hands to her face quickly, then let them go.

"Why white people feel they got to mark us?" the Girl asked, slipping back into her own vocal rhythm. Bird pushed her arms back into her sleeves as she thought for a moment.

"Maybe they're afraid they'll be forgotten." She gathered the papers from the table, then added, "They don't know that we easily forget them, who they might be. All we ever remember is their scars."

The Girl saw the deeply etched whip marks that had striped her mother's legs as she looked down at her own thin, hardened fingers. She remained silent as Bird put the papers into the wooden box holding all their lessons.

Bird wanted to tell just one more story, a happy one, but saw that the Girl, a meticulous worker, was becoming anxious. Her chores for the evening still lay ahead of her, and guests would be arriving in several hours. Or, Bird thought, anxiety might be her natural state.

The Girl left and Bird followed, locking her door behind her. Upstairs at Gilda's door she used the same key to enter. She opened the drapes slightly once inside its blackness, to let the twilight seep in, and then lay down beside the still figure. Even at its cool temperature Gilda's body had warmed the satin that lay over the soft earth. Bird didn't sleep. She watched the shadows, enjoying the familiar quiet of the room, thinking about the Girl and Gilda.

Bird enjoyed the days more since the Girl's arrival. She was grateful for her earnest curiosity and she saw Gilda responding similarly. Yet Bird was uneasy with the new way of things. Gilda was, indeed, more open and relaxed, but she was also less fully present, as if her mind were in a future none of them would know. When she tried to draw her back, Gilda only talked of the true death, how soon her time might come. Then they argued.

Even after their new routine had become old and their futures seemed secure, Bird was certain Gilda still held thoughts of true death but would speak of them to her only obliquely. When Bird asked her about the Girl and what might become of her should they decide to leave Woodard's, Gilda remained cryptic.

"She will always be with us, just as I'll always be with you," Gilda answered with a smile.

"How can that be so?" Bird asked, certain Gilda was making a joke.

"She is as strong as either of us and knows our ways."

"She's a child; she can't make the decision you'd ask of her!" Bird said with alarm when she realized it was no jest.

"We were all children at one time. And time passes. I expect she will be ready when I am."

"Ready?" Bird responded, still not able to grasp the idea of the Girl becoming one of them.

Gilda understood Bird's reluctance and lightened her voice. "Yes, ready to challenge you, my dear one. She'll be the best student you've ever had, perhaps even a scholar. We will then turn Woodard's into a college for girls!" Gilda laughed loudly, steering the conversation away from anything Bird might pursue.

In remembering that talk, Bird decided not to broach the questions now, even with herself. She simply wanted to feel Gilda near, listen to the sound of her heart as she awakened. They would go out to find their share of the blood later, perhaps together, when there was darkness.

After her second year at Woodard's the Girl began to look upon it as a home. She had grown three inches by the end of her third year and had the rounded calves and breasts of a woman. Each morning she scrubbed herself clean with cool water before coming down to the kitchen and to Bernice, who had become accustomed to her solemn, shining face. She watched the Girl closely until it seemed to her that she had gained enough weight. And the women of the house teased her gently and asked her about her lessons. Most of them were, in spite of their paint, simple farm girls and sometimes liked having a younger one to look after.

When the Girl was not doing chores or studying with Bird she stayed to herself, working in the garden. Minta sometimes joined her there, her thin, pale skin hidden under a large hat. She was only two years older than the Girl, although she had been at Woodard's for several years and carried herself as if she had always lived in a brothel.

On Minta's twentieth birthday Gilda took her into town to buy her a new dress. Not an unusual event, but the party Gilda and Bird planned was. Everyone at Woodard's dressed for dinner that evening. The kitchen was filled with teasing laughter which continued in the salon late that evening. A few of the clients who came brought Minta flowers or small trinkets, but Minta was most pleased by the simple cotton blouse the Girl had sewn especially for her.

Pride suffused Gilda's smile as she watched the girls, all of whom were women now. Even her young foundling had become Bird's assistant in the management of the house. They all had the manners of ladies, could read, write, and shoot. Rachel, to whom Minta had been closest, left for California just before Minta's birthday, hoping to start a fresh life and find a husband. The talk heard most often in the salon now was about abolition and the rising temperatures of the North and South. Even at Minta's party the passion of politics couldn't be resisted.

An older Creole man, a frequent visitor to the house, was pounding the piano ineptly but with enthusiasm as a circle of women cheered him on. The Girl served a tray of champagne and stood by the settee near the door in order to listen for Bernice calling her to the kitchen. She placed herself so she would be able to overhear the many conversations in the salon.

But it was Gilda's voice, raised slightly at the other side of the room, that came to her. "I'll say this just once tonight. The years of bartering in human flesh are near their end. And any civilized man will be grateful for it." She peered sternly at a pinched-faced man standing against the window. "You may discuss Lincoln's election in your own parlors, but I will listen to no talk of war in my house tonight."

Fanny tried to turn the conversation to horses, a subject she was most familiar with, but two men cut her off. "Horses! Nigras! It's the same damn thing, more trouble than they're worth. I say we just ship. . ."

The man at the piano stopped playing.

"As I've said gentlemen, the only name on the deed to this place is mine." After a beat of deep silence, the piano music started again and the Girl began to gather empty glasses. She backed out of the room with a full tray.

In the kitchen Bernice asked, "What that ruckus 'bout in there?"

"War talk."

"Umph, men got nothin' but war talk. Like it more'n they like hoppin' on top 'a these girls." She sucked the air through her teeth as she poured more wine into the glasses. She passed one to the Girl, and they both drank quickly.

Bernice looked more like her mother than anyone the Girl had met since running away, but she seemed like a sister too.

"What you think... if they get freedom?" Bernice asked as she slid her tongue around the rim of the champagne glass.

"We free already, Bernice. Won't mean so much over here, you think?"

"Gal, they's whole lot of us ain't free, just down the road!"

"Think they gonna come here?" the Girl asked, having a difficult time making the full picture of the world take shape in her head. The memory of the women and men, her sisters still at the plantation, made her feel slightly faint.

"Who know what they do. If they got no work, who know. With nobody to take care 'bout and nobody to pay them like Miss Gilda do us. Who know." Bernice poured more champagne into their glittering crystal.

A surge of fear welled up in the Girl. "We gotta keep this place safe, Bernice, no matter how the war goes. They'll be people needin' to come here I 'spect," the Girl said, remembering the smell of the dark earth of the root cellar where she'd taken refuge.

"Umph," Bernice said, letting her voice drop slightly, "we keep our eye out, maybe some folks need to take to root, if you knows what I mean. Me an' you can do that. I been figurin' on something like that. It's not the war, it's the freedom we got to keep our eye on."

"I remember how to do that," the Girl said, taking the last sip from her glass.

As the Girl hurried back into the salon Minta stopped her at the door, taking two glasses from the tray and setting one behind her on the mantle. She whispered in the Girl's ear conspiratorially, "You'd think these gents would give up arguin' with Miss Gilda. She's stubborner than a crow. I can't says I blame her."

"Why you say that? Don't you think there's gonna be war?"

"Sure, for certain sure. Just ain't no need talkin' it up. Be here soon enough. They always got to spoil somethin'. I'll be goddamned if one of 'em is gonna spoil my birthday!"

The Girl was full of questions but was afraid to ask them here. Sarah and Fanny came over to them, Fanny saying, "You gonna drink 'em all just cause it's your birthday?"

"If that's my desire," Minta said, draining her glass with a flourish.

She turned on her heel, picked up her other drink from the mantle, and strode to the far side of the room.

"She's a terrible slut. I can't understand why Miss Gilda keeps her here," Fanny said.

"Oh, she's alright," Sarah responded, tickling Fanny under her breast. "You jes' jealous 'cause she got a special handmade blouse for her birthday." Fanny refused to smile as she took a glass from the tray.

The Girl smiled shyly. "Aw, Miss Fanny ain't got nothin' to worry 'bout. She gets presents everyday." Fanny tried to look remote and superior, but a tiny smile turned up the corners of her mouth.

Sarah threw her arm around Fanny's waist and pulled her away saying, "Yes, and if she's lucky I'll get to wear her new brooch this Saturday." The two women, who seemed to the Girl not much more than girls themselves, made their way to the piano. Gilda and Bird stood apart at the far end of the room.

The Girl approached them with the last two glasses on her tray. "Miss Gilda?" she said in a low voice.

Gilda took a glass and gave it to Bird. Then she said, "You have that one, child."

Bird tapped the rim of the Girl's glass with her own before sipping. She turned to Gilda. "I think we're ready to move on to French."

"So soon!" Gilda was surprised and pleased.

"If we're learning one grammar, it might as well be two."

The Girl's head buzzed with excitement. She was still shocked that she could put letters and words together and make sense of them in English and that Bird had been able to teach her to understand the words of her nation. Sometimes when they were shopping in town she and Bird confused the shopkeepers along Rue Bourbon by switching back and forth between languages.

Their arrival was inevitably met by either bold, disdainful smirks or surreptitious glances. Everyone knew of the Indian from Woodard's place and now found the addition of the "dark one" a further curiosity they couldn't resist. Bird and the Girl were self-consciously erect as they meandered from one shop to the next, making their way easily among the creamy-colored quadroons who, with mighty effort, pretended they did not see them. It was some time before the Girl understood that these graceful, cold women shared her African blood. She had been so confused and upset by it that she cried as Bird tried to explain the social system of New Orleans, the levels of deceit and manners that afforded the fairer-skinned their privileges and banished the darker ones from society.

For many weeks the Girl could not bring herself to return to town to shop with Bird. First she feigned illness, then begged off because of duties with Bernice. She didn't understand her own fear of these people who tried to look through Bird as if she were glass and simply dismissed her as a slave. Only after an afternoon of making an effort to help Bernice in exchange for being excused from the shopping trip did the Girl find it possible to resume her routine. Bernice had asked her, directly, to explain herself. The Girl found the words for the shame she felt in front of those women, although she could not say why she thought this was so.

"I'll tell you what the problem is. . .you shamed alright," Bernice said in her now familiarly blunt manner, "but it's them you shamed of. Know how I knows? 'Cause long as you been here you ain't never looked shamed about nothin'. Even that first night when she dragged you in here like a sack. You was your mama's daughter and that was that. What you shamed about is them folks thinkin' they white and they ain't. Thinkin' being nasty to dark folks is gonna help make them white. That's a shame alright. Not yours. . .theirs, so just go on 'bout your business."

The Girl resumed her shopping with Bird from that afternoon on. Soon they started to speak the languages as often as they could and watched the shopkeepers' and customers' discomfort. Then they would leave the store choking back their giggles. Now to add French! She would be able to understand what she'd been certain were remarks being made about her and speak as well as they did, for Bird had said her facility with languages was excellent. The Girl was even happier than when she'd constructed her first sentence on paper. Gilda was pleased that she'd been correct; the Girl was the one who would give Bird her connection to life. Bird had opened herself to her as she had with no one else at the house except Gilda.

"So Français it is, *ma chère*."

Gilda's unwavering gaze both excited and discomfited the Girl.

She sensed some question being answered in Gilda's mind.

"Can I take that Miss Bird?" the Girl said, lifting her tray. She was relieved to have a reason to leave the room for a moment. She needed to think about what had been raised this evening: war, French, as well as the look of satisfaction in Gilda's eyes. She had tried to read Gilda's thoughts as she had been able to do on occasions in the past but was not completely successful now. She perceived a sense of completion that was certainly focused on her, but the pictures that sometimes formed in her mind when she had questions did not appear this time. She left the glasses and tray in the kitchen and stepped into the small den that was used for coats, wanting to sit quietly for a moment. The bubbling wine and excitement had given her a slight headache, and she waited for it to recede so she could rejoin the others when Minta played the piano. She rose as a gentleman entered looking for his coat.

"May I help you, sir?" she inquired.

"You sure can, little gal," he said, smiling blandly. "I've been over here to New Orleans more than a couple of times now. And I got to say this is the best house west of Chicago."

His look appraised her although he was speaking of Woodard's. She continued to meet his almost-translucent eyes, as if she might hold his gaze and keep it from traveling over her body.

"Thank you, sir. I'll be sure and tell Miss Gilda you said so." The Girl waited for the man to point toward his coat, but he stood silently with his eyes on her. The Girl had not known the auction block. She had never stood upon one and had never had any occasion to see the one used regularly in the center of the city. His look, however, made her know it intimately. The gaze from his hazel eyes seared her skin, but her face remained impassive as she spoke.

"Your coat, sir?"

"Not just yet. How old would you say you were, little gal?" The Girl's eyes were almost on a level with his.

"About seventeen. Miss Gilda gave me a birthday party last year. She said she figured I was about seventeen."

"How's it come you don't remember how old you are?" Even after the uneventful years that had passed since her arrival at the house, the Girl was still wary of white men asking questions. The talk of abolition and maybe a war meant little to her. Any of these men could capture her and take her back to the plantation.

"I was really sick for a while when I was little. My mistress, Miss

Gilda's sister, died before she could tell Miss Gilda the exact information."

"Well, you don't look more'n fourteen to me."

She wondered why he told such a foolish lie. "Could be, sir, but I don't think so."

"Come over here and let me get a closer look at you."

The Girl took two steps nearer, not sure what to expect. He reached out and rubbed her breast. The Girl jumped back, startled. "Aw come on, little gal, let me just get a little somethin' here."

"No, sir!"

"Then we'll go up to your room. I'll pay the regular price."

"No, sir! I just do housekeeping for Miss Gilda. If you want I'll call one of the other girls in."

"I don't want one of the other gals. I'm looking to get to you right now. Come on upstairs."

The Girl recognized the look in his eye. It came back to her from a place far away. She had the dream only rarely now, but whenever she did she awoke crying in terror. Here, not sleeping, the nightmare stood before her, and instead of fear she felt an icy anger. Her hands clenched and unclenched fitfully, as she thought how she would distract his attention and run from the room. She did not want to cause a fuss and spoil Minta's birthday. She closed her eyes, and her mother's face was pictured clearly. Often it had been hard to remember what her mother looked like, but now here was the African face that had comforted her so often. The Girl was awash with tears.

The girls talked often of the gentlemen, usually with a tinge of indulgence as if they were children being kept busily playing while the women did important things. Never had they indicated any fear of the men who visited Woodard's. Whatever gossip she had heard about violence seemed to come from town, frequently about the haughty, fair-skinned ones and their white lovers. Mistreatment was something she knew Gilda would never tolerate, and the Girl realized just then that neither could she.

When she opened her eyes the moisture spilled out and she said, "Please sir, Miss Gilda will be looking for me in the kitchen. I got chores now."

"This won't take long," he said and took her wrist.

"Sir, I've explained—"

She stopped short as Gilda opened the door.

"May I help you, sir?" Gilda's voice was sweet, her anger concealed under the syrup of manners. He loosened his grip on the Girl and gave a deep bow in Gilda's direction.

"Just thought I'd have a little entertainment here."

"I'm sorry, sir. The Girl works only in the kitchen. I'm sure there are others you'd like to meet."

"Don't you think it's about time you broke this one in?"

"No, sir. I don't. If you'll leave the management of my girls to me, you just go about having a good time. Why don't we rejoin the party?" She turned toward the Girl. "Go to Bernice, I'm sure she could use your help. They're about to bring out the cake." The Girl squeezed past Bird who had appeared silently in the doorway.

"I bet you could do a lot of business with that nigra gal, Miss Gilda. You don't know what kind of opportunity you lettin' pass by."

"As I said, let me do the managing. You just enjoy yourself."

"I was kinda hopin' to enjoy myself with her," he said insistently.

"Well, that's not possible," Gilda said. The syrup froze around the sentence, and her back stiffened. Without turning she felt Bird enter the room and said, "Will you see that this gentleman gets a fresh glass of champagne? I have to go out for a while." Gilda left through the kitchen.

Bernice started to speak but stopped herself when she saw the jerky movement and aura of rage that swept along beside Gilda.

Gilda welcomed the coolness of the night air against her cheeks. They were flushed with anger. She was surprised by the rage she had felt when she sensed the Girl was in trouble.

In her lifetime, Gilda had killed reluctantly and infrequently. When she took the blood there was no need to take life. But she knew that there were those like her who gained power as much from the terror of their prey as from the life substance itself. She had learned many lessons in her time. The most important had been from Sorel and were summed up in a very few words: the source of power will tell in how long-lived that power is. He had pointed her and all of his children toward an enduring power that did not feed on death. Gilda was sustained by sharing the blood and by maintaining the vital connections to life. Her love for her family of friends had fed her for three hundred years. When Bird chose to join her in this life, Gilda was filled with both joy and dread. The weight of the years she had known subsided temporarily; at last there would be someone beside her to experience the passage of time. Bird's first years at Woodard's were remote now—Bird moving silently through their lives, subtly taking control of management, finding her place closer and closer to Gilda without having to speak of it.

Before she had even considered bringing Bird into her life she had wanted to feel her sleeping beside her. She had not been willing to risk their friendship, though, until she was certain. And Bird had opened to her, deliberately, to let her know her desires were the same as Gilda's. When they first lay together, Gilda sensed that Bird already knew what world it was Gilda would ask her to enter. She had teased Gilda later with sly smiles, about time and rushing through life, until Gilda had finally been certain Bird was asking to join her.

Despite the years of joy they had known together, tonight, walking along the dark road, Gilda felt she had lived much too long. Only now was it clear to her why. The talk of war, the anger and brutality that was revealed daily in the townspeople, was a bitter taste in her mouth. She had seen enough war and hatred in her lifetime. And although her abolitionist sentiments had never been hidden, she didn't know if she had the heart to withstand the rending effects of another war.

And as always, when Gilda reflected on these things she came back to Bird: Bird, who had chosen to be a part of this life, a choice she seemed to have made effortlessly. Gilda had never said the word *vampire*. She had only asked if Bird would join her as partner in the business and in life. In the years since she'd come to the house she always knew as much as was needed and challenged Gilda any time she tried to hide information from her. Bird listened inside of Gilda's words, hearing the years of isolation and discovery. There was in Gilda an unfathomable hunger—a dark, dry chasm that Bird thought she could help fill.

But now it was the touch of the sun and the ocean Gilda hungered for, and little else. She ached to rest, free from the intemperate demands of time. Often she'd tried to explain this burden to Bird, the need to let go. And Bird saw it only as an escape from *her*—rather than a final embrace of freedom.

Thoughts jostled inside her as she moved—so quickly she was invisible—through the night. She slowed a few miles west of the Louisiana state line, then turned back toward her township. When she came to a road leading to a familiar horse ranch within miles of her farmhouse, she slackened her pace and walked to the rear of the woodframe building.

All of the windows were black as she slipped around to the small bunkhouse at the back where hands slept. She stood in the shadows listening. Once inside she approached the nearest man, the larger of the two she could see in the darkness. She began to probe his dreams, then sensed an uncleanness in his blood and recoiled. His sleeping face did not bear the mark of the disease that coursed through his body, but it was there. She was certain. Gilda was saddened as she moved to the smaller man who slept at the other end of the room.

He had fallen asleep in his clothes on top of the blankets and smelled of whiskey and horses. She slipped inside his thoughts as he dreamed of a chestnut-colored bay. Under his excitement lay anxiety, his fear of the challenge of this horse. Gilda held him in sleep while she sliced through the flesh of his neck, the line of her nail leaving a red trail. She extended his dream, making him king of the riders as she took her share of the blood. He smiled with triumph at his horsemanship, the warmth of the whiskey in him thundering through her. She caught her breath, and the other ranch hand tossed restlessly in his sleep. Although she no longer feared death she backed away, her instincts readying her hands to quiet the restless worker if he awoke. Her touch on the other sleeper sealed his wound cleanly. Soon his pulse was steady and he continued to explore the dreams she had left with him. As their breathing settled into a calm rhythm, Gilda ran from the bunkhouse, flushed with the fullness of blood and whiskey.

The road back felt particularly dark to Gilda as she moved eastward. The clouds left little moonlight visible, but she was swift. Blood pounded in her head, and she imagined that was what she would feel once she finally lay down in the sea and gave up her life. Her heart beat with excitement, full of the need to match its rhythm with that of an ocean. There, Gilda would find her tears again and be free of the sounds of battles and the burden of days and nights piled upon each other endlessly. The dust from the road flew up around her as she made her way toward home. She remembered the dusty trek that was the one clear image of her childhood. They had been going toward water, perhaps the sea. The future had lain near that sea, somehow. It was survival for her mother, father, and the others who had moved relentlessly toward it. Now it was that again for Gilda—now and more. The sea would be the place to rest her spirit.

Once back in her room she changed her dusty jacket and breeches and sat quietly alone in the dark. As dawn appeared on the horizon behind the house, Gilda let down her dark hair and was peaceful in her earthen bed. She was relieved to finally see the end of the road.

In the soft light of a fall afternoon the Girl worked in the garden as she had done for so many years. By now she knew the small plot well, picking the legumes and uprooting the weeds without much thought, enjoying the sun and air. When she looked up at the house Bird waved to her, then pulled the curtain tight across the window of Gilda's room. The Girl's reverie was lazy and undirected. She started at Minta's shadow when it crept over her.

They both sat quietly for some time before the Girl asked Minta, "How long you been here at Woodard's?"

"I was younger than you was when you come," she answered proudly, "but I think I'm gonna move on soon, though. Been savin' my money and thinkin' about goin' west where Rachel is. Look around for a while."

"How long Bird . . . has Bird been here?" the Girl asked, picking her way through the rules of grammar.

"I don't know. Long as any of us can remember. She left once, that's what I heard Bernice say, but she come back quick. Them Indian folks she come from didn't want her back."

Both girls were quiet for a moment, each feeling younger than either had since going out into the world on her own. Minta spoke with hard resolve as if to cover her vulnerability. "When I leave, I'm gone. Gonna make me a fortune in California, get away from this war talk."

"You think Rachel let you stay with her?"

"Well, she sent me a letter with her address and everything. She went to that man Miss Gilda said would give her a hand if she need it. And he put her up in a place 'til she got her own and said he'd help her find a little shop." Minta could feel the Girl's unspoken doubt. She pushed ahead with assurance as much for herself as for the Girl. "She right there on the water and got lotsa business. And she say there not enough women for anybody." A smirk opened her mouth then, but she tried to continue in a businesslike way. "She want to move if she save the money. Get in a quiet district with the swells." Simply talking about Rachel and her new life seemed to make Minta breathless. "She said the women and men there wear the prettiest clothes she ever seen. She want to get a place nearer to the rich people and leave them sailors behind."

The Girl looked aghast, trying to picture Rachel alone in a western city, owning a shop, mixing with rich people who weren't trying to get in her bed. But the image was too distant to get it into focus.

"Say, you think you want to come too? I bet we could get us a little business goin' out there the way you can sew and all."

Leave Gilda and Bird? The thought was a shock to the Girl who had never considered such a possibility; it seemed ludicrous as she knelt under the warm sun feeling the softness of the earth's comfort beneath her. And even with the war coming and talk of emancipation and hardship, the Girl had little in mind she would run away to. "Naw, this is my home now, I guess."

"Well, you just be careful."

"What do you mean?"

"Watch yourself, is all." Minta said it softly and would speak no more. The Girl was puzzled and made anxious by the edge in Minta's voice as well as the silence that followed. Her look of frustration tugged at Minta. "There's lots of folks down this way believe in ha'nts and such like. Spirits. Creoles, like Miss Gilda, and Indians, they follow all that stuff." Minta spoke low, bending at the waist as if to make the words come out softer. "I like her fine, even though some folks don't. Just watch, is all." She skittered through the garden to the kitchen door.

The Girl finished her weeding, then went to the kitchen steps to rinse her hands at the pump and dust her clothes. Bernice watched from the back porch.

"What you say to Minta, she run upstairs?"

"I ain't certain. She's so nervous I can't get hold to what she sayin' half a while. I know she wants me to go out there with her to stay with Rachel."

"What else?"

"She afraid of something here. Sometimes I think maybe it's Miss Gilda. What you think?"

Bernice's face closed as if a door had been locked. "You ain't goin', is you?"

"I'm here for the war no matter what, if there's gonna be one."

"Listen gal, you been lucky so far. You got a life, so don't toss it in the air just to stay 'round here." Behind Bernice's voice the Girl could sense her conflict, her words both pushing the Girl away and needing her to stay.

"My life's here with you and Miss Gilda and Bird. What would I do in California—wear a hat and play lady?" she said, laughing loudly, nervously. She saw the same wary look on Bernice's face that had filtered through Minta's voice.

"What is it? Why you questioning me with that look?" the Girl asked with a tinge of anger in her voice.

"Nothin'. They just different. Not like regular people. Maybe that's good. Who gonna know 'til they know?

"You sayin' they bad or somethin'?" The challenge wavered in the Girl's throat as her own questions about Gilda and Bird slipped into her mind.

"No." The solid response reminded the Girl of how long Bernice had been at Woodard's. "I'm just saying I don't know who they are. After all the time I been here I still don't know who Miss Gilda is. Inside I don't really know what she thinkin' like you do with most white folks. I don't know who her people is. White folks is dyin' to tell each other that. Not her. Now Bird, I got more an idea what she's up to. She watch over Miss Gilda like. . .like. . ." Bernice's voice trailed off as she struggled for words that spoke to this child who was now almost a woman.

"That ain't hurt you none, now has it?" The Girl's response was hard with loyalty to the women who'd drawn her into their family.

"Not me. I'm just waitin' for the river to rise." Bernice didn't really worry about who Gilda and Bird were. Her concern was what would become of this Girl on her own.

On a day soon after Gilda took the Girl and Bird with her to the farmhouse, Minta stood by the empty horse stall nearest the road. Her face was placid, yet she was again bent at the waist as if still whispering. The Girl caught a glimpse of her when the buggy rounded the bend in the road, and she leaned over looking back. She was excited about this journey away from the house, but Minta's warnings itched her like the crinoline one of the girls had given her last Christmas.

The evening sky was rolling with clouds as they drove the buggy south to the farm, yet the Girl could feel Gilda's confidence that there would be no storm. They talked of many things but not the weather. Still, from simply looking into Gilda's eyes and touching Bird's hand she knew there was a storm somewhere. She felt a struggle brewing and longed to speak out, to warn them of how much everyone in town would need them when the war came. She knew that would not be the thing to say—Gilda liked to circle her point until she came to a place she thought would be right for speaking. It didn't come on the road to the farmhouse.

When the three arrived at the farmhouse, the Girl stored her small traveling box under the eaves in the tiny room she slept in whenever they visited here. She wondered if Minta knew Gilda spoke without speaking. That might be the reason she had cautioned her. But the Girl had no fear. Gilda, more often aloof than familiar, touched the Girl somehow. Words were only one of many ways of stepping inside of someone. The Girl smiled, recollecting her childish notion that Gilda was a man. Perhaps, she thought, living among the whites had given her a secret passage, but knowledge of Gilda came from a deeper place. It was a place kept hidden except from Bird.

The fields to the north and west of the farmhouse lay fallow, trimmed but unworked. It was land much like the rest in the Delta sphere, warm and moist, almost blue in its richness—blood soil, some said. The not-tall house over the shallow root cellar seemed odd with its distinct aura of life set in the emptiness of the field. Gilda stood at the window looking out to the evening dark as Bird moved around her placing clothes in chests. Gilda tried to pull the strands together, to make a pattern of her life that was recognizable, therefore reinforceable. The farmhouse offered her peace but no answers. It was simply privacy away from the dissembling of the city and relief from the tides, which each noon and night pulled her energy, sucking her breath and leaving her lighter than air. The quietness of the house and its eagerness to hold her safe were like a firm hand on her shoulder. Here Gilda could relax enough to think. She had hardly come through the door before she let go of the world of Woodard's. Still her thoughts always turned back toward the open sea and the burning sun.

The final tie was Bird. Bird, the gentle, stern one who rarely flinched yet held on to her as if she were drowning in life. Too few of their own kind had passed through Woodard's, and none had stayed very long. On their one trip west to visit Sorel, neither could tolerate the dust and noise of his town for more than several weeks. And until the Girl's arrival, Gilda had met no one she sensed was the right one. To leave Bird alone in this world without others like herself would be more cruel than Gilda could ever be. The Girl must stay. She pushed back all doubts: Was the Girl too young? Would she grow to hate the life she'd be given? Would she abandon Bird? The answer was there in the child's eyes. The decision loosened the tight muscles of Gilda's back as if the deed were already done.

The Girl did not know why they had included her in the trip to the farmhouse this time. They rarely brought her along at mid-season. The thought that they might want her to leave them made her more anxious than Minta's soft voice. Yet each day Bird and she sat down for their lessons, and in the evening, when Gilda and Bird talked quietly together, they sought her out to join them. She would curl up in the corner, not speaking, only listening to the words that poured from them as they talked of the women back at the house, the politics in town, the war, and told adventurous stories. The Girl thought, at first, that they were made up, but she soon heard in the passion of their voices the truth of the stories Gilda and Bird had lived.

Sometimes one of them would say, "Listen here, this is something you should know." But there was no need for that. The Girl, now tall and lean with adulthood, clung to their words. She enjoyed the contrasting rhythms of their voices and the worlds of mystery they revealed.

She sensed an urgency in Gilda—the stories had to be told, let free from her. And Bird, who also felt the urgency, did not become preoccupied with it but was happy that she and Gilda were spending time together again as it had been before. She unfolded her own history like soft deerskin. Bird gazed at the Girl, wrapped in a cotton shirt, her legs tucked under her on the floor, and felt that her presence gave them an unspoken completeness.

She spoke before she thought. "This is like many times before the fire in my village."

"Ah, and who's to play the part of your toothless elders, me or the Girl?" Gilda asked, smiling widely.

The Girl laughed softly as Bird replied, "Both."

Gilda rose from the dark velvet couch. Her face disappeared out of the low lamplight into the shadow. She stooped, lifted the Girl in her arms, and lay her on the couch. She sat down again and rested the Girl's head in her lap. She stroked the Girl's thick braids as Bird and she continued talking.

In the next silence she asked the Girl, "What do you remember of your mother and sisters?" The Girl did not think of them except at night, just before sleeping, their memory her nightly prayers. She'd never spoken of them to Gilda, only to Bird when they exchanged stories during their reading lessons. Now the litany of names served as memory: Minerva, small, full of energy and questions; Florine, two years older than the Girl, unable to ever meet anyone's eyes; and Martha, the oldest, broad-shouldered like their mother but more solemn. She described the feel of the pallet where she slept with her mother, rising early for breakfast duties—stirring porridge and setting out the rolls. She described the smell of bread, shiny with butter, and the snow-white raw cotton tinged with blood from her fingers.

Of the home their mother spoke about, the Girl was less certain. It was always a dream place—distant, unreal. Except the talk of dancing. The Girl could close her eyes and almost hear the rhythmic shuffling of feet, the bells and gourds. All kept beat inside her body, and the feel of heat from an open fire made the dream place real. Talking of it now, her body rocked slightly as if she had been rewoven into that old circle of dancers. She poured out the images and names, proud of her own ability to weave a story. Bird smiled at her pupil who claimed her past, reassuring her silently.

Each of the days at the farmhouse was much like the others. The Girl rose a bit later than when they were in the city, for there was little work to be done here. She dusted or read, walked in the field watching birds and rabbits. In the late afternoon she would hear Bird and Gilda stirring. They came out to speak to her from the shadows of the porch, but then they returned to their room, where the Girl heard the steady sound of their voices or the quiet scratching of pen on paper.

The special quality of their life did not escape the Girl; it seemed more pronounced at the farmhouse, away from the activity of Woodard's. She had found the large feed bags filled with dirt in the root cellar where she hid so long ago. She had felt the thin depth of soil beneath the carpets and weighted in their cloaks. Although they kept the dinner hour as a gathering time, they had never eaten in front of her. The Girl cooked her own meals, often eating alone, except when Bird prepared a corn pudding or a rabbit she had killed. Then they sat together as the Girl ate and Bird sipped tea. She had seen Gilda and Bird go out late in the night, both wearing breeches and woolen shirts. Sometimes they went together, other times separately. And both spoke to her without voices.

The warning from Minta and the whispers of the secret religion, vodun, still did not frighten her. She had known deep fear and knew she could protect herself when she must. But there was no cause for fear of these two who slept so soundly in each other's arms and treated her with such tenderness.

On the afternoon of the eighth day at the farmhouse the Girl returned from a walk through the fields to get a drink of water from the back pump. She was surprised to hear, through the kitchen window, Gilda's voice drawn tight in argument with Bird. There was silence from the rest of the room, then a burst of laughter from Gilda.

"Do you see that we're fighting only because we love each other? I insist we stop right this minute. I won't have it on such a glorious evening."

The Girl could hear her moving around the small wooden table, pulling back a chair. Gilda did not sit in the chair, instead lowering herself onto Bird's lap. Bird's expression of surprise turned into a laugh, but the tension beneath it was not totally dispelled.

"I'm sick of this talk. You go on about this leaving as if there is somewhere in the world you could go without me."

Her next words were cut short by Gilda's hand on her mouth. And then Gilda's soft, thin lips pressed her back in the chair.

"Please, my love, let's go to our room so I can feel the weight of your body on mine. Let's compare the tones of our skin as we did when we were young."

Bird laughed just as she was expected to do. The little joking references to time and age were their private game. Even knowing there was more to the kisses and games right now, she longed to feel Gilda's skin pressed tightly to her own. She stood up, still clasping Gilda to her breasts, and walked up the stairs with her as if she were a child.

The Girl remained on the porch looking out into the field as the sun dropped quickly behind the trees. She loved the sound of Gilda and Bird laughing, but it seemed they did so only when they thought no others were listening. When it was fully dark she went into the kitchen to make supper for herself. She put on the kettle for tea, certain that Bird and Gilda would want some when they came down. She rooted through the clay jars until she had pulled together a collection of sweet-smelling herbs she thought worthy. She was eager to hear their laughter again.

That evening Bird took the buggy out and called to the Girl to help load the laundry bags inside. The Girl was silent as she lifted the bags up to the buckboard platform to Bird, who kept glancing up at the windows.

"Tell Minta I said hello." The Girl spoke tentatively when the quiet seemed too large. "Tell her not to leave without me." She figured that was a good enough joke since Minta had been deviling everybody with her dreamtalk of going west.

Bird stood straight, dropping the final bundle on the floor of the buckboard, and looked down at the Girl. "What does that mean?"

"I'm teasin'. She keep talkin' about movin' out there with Rachel like I goin' with her."

Bird turned silent, sat, and grasped the reins of the restless horse. The Girl felt more compelled to fill the air. "I'm not goin'."

"You could, you might want to. Eventually you'll want to start your own life, your own family somewhere." Bird's voice was even, but the Girl recognized a false quiet in it from the times she had heard her arguing with Gilda or talking to drunken clients.

"Any family startin' to do will be done right here." The Girl felt safe having finally said what she wanted out loud. She looked up at Bird's face shyly and was pleased to see the flash of Bird's teeth sparking her grin.

Bird climbed up to the seat and spoke casually, the voice of the woman who always kept the house. "I'll stay in town tonight and return tomorrow evening for tea. If there is any danger, you have only to call out to me."

Bird drew the horse out onto the road, leaving the Girl on the porch wondering what danger there might be. Her warning not to have concern was more frightening to her than Minta's cautionary words.

Upstairs, Gilda was silent in her room. She did not join the Girl after Bird was gone but came down later in the evening. She moved about the parlor, making a circle before resting on the arm of the sofa across from the Girl who sat in Bird's favored chair. The Girl's dark face was smooth, her brow wide and square under the braided rows that drew her thick, springy hair to the nape of her neck. Gilda wore pants and a shirt cinched tightly at her waist by soft leather studded with small white beads. She spoke to the Girl in silence. *Do you know how many years I have lived?*

"Many more years than anyone."

Gilda rose and stood over the Girl. "I have Bird's love and yours, I think?" The end of the sentence curled upward in a question.

The Girl had not thought of love until the word was spoken. Yes, she loved them both. The remembered face of her mother was all she had loved until now. Tears slipped down her cheeks. Gilda's sadness washed over her, and she felt the loss of her mother, new and cutting.

"We can talk when I return." Gilda closed the door and was lost in the darkness.

The Girl walked through the house looking at their belongings as if it were the first time she had seen them—their dresses folded smoothly and the delicate linens, the chest that held small tailored breeches and flannel shirts that smelled of earth and lavender water.

She touched the leather spines of the books which she longed to read; some were in languages she did not recognize. Sitting on the edge of the bed that Gilda and Bird shared, she looked patiently at each item in the room, inhaling their scent. The brushes, combs, and jars sat neatly aligned on the dressing table. The coverlet, rugs, and draperies felt thick, luxurious, yet the room was plain. Without Gilda and Bird in the house the rooms seemed incomplete. The Girl walked slowly through each one as if it were new to her, crossing back and forth, searching for something to soothe the unease that crept up into her. Everything appeared just as it had during all the days she had been with Gilda and Bird, except that she felt someone had gone before her as she did now, examining objects, replacing them, pulling out memories, laying them aside.

When the house became cold, the Girl built a fire and curled up on the sofa under her cotton sheet. She fingered the small wooden frame with its rows of beads that Bird had been using to teach her accounting. The clicking of wood on wood was comforting. When Gilda returned she found the Girl asleep, clutching the abacus to her breast as she might a doll. The Girl woke up feeling Gilda's eyes on her and knew it was late by the chill of the air. The fire glowed faintly under fresh logs.

"We can talk now," Gilda said as if she'd never gone out. She sat beside the Girl and held her hand.

"There's a war coming. It's here already, truth be told. . ." She stopped. The effort of getting out those few words left her weary.

"Do you understand when I tell you I can live through no more?"

The Girl did not speak but thought of the night she decided to escape from the plantation.

Gilda continued. "I've been afraid of living too long, and now is the end of my time. The night I found you in the cellar seems only a minute ago. But you were such a child, so full of terror, your journey had been more than the miles of road. When I picked you up your body relaxed into mine, knowing part of your fight was done. I sensed in you a spirit and understanding of the world; that you were the voice lacking among us. Seeing this world with you has given me wonderful years of pleasure. Now my only fear is leaving Bird alone. It's you she needs here with her."

The Girl looked at Gilda's face, the skin drawn tightly across the tiny bones, her eyes glistening with flecks of orange. She wanted to comfort this woman who'd lifted her out of her nightmares.

"You must want to stay. You must need to live. Will you trust me?"

"I never thought to leave you or the house. My home is here as long as you'll have me," the Girl said in a clear voice.

"What I ask is not an easy thing. You may feel you have nothing to go back to, but sooner or later we all want to go back to something. Usually some inconsequential thing to which we've never given much thought before. But it will loom there in our past entreating us cruelly because there is no way to ever go back. In asking this of you, and in the future should you ask it of others, you must be certain that you—that others—are strong enough to withstand the complete loss of those intangibles that make the past so alluring."

The Girl said nothing, not really certain what Gilda meant. She felt a change in the room—the air was taut with energy.

"There are only inadequate words to speak for who we are. The language is crude, the history false. You must look to me and know who I am and if the life I offer is the life you choose. In choosing you must pledge yourself to pursue only life, never bitterness or cruelty."

The Girl peered deeply into the swirling brown and flickering orange of Gilda's eyes, feeling herself opening to ideas and sensations she had never fully admitted before. She drew back, startled at the weight of time she saw behind those eyes.

"Don't be frightened by the idea of death; it is part of life in all things. It will only become worrisome when you decide that its time has come. Power is the frightening thing, not death. And the blood, it is a shared thing. Something we must all learn to share or simply spill onto battlefields." Gilda stopped, feeling the weight of all she wanted to say, knowing it would be too much at once. She would leave the rest to Bird.

The Girl listened to the words. She tried to look again into the world behind Gilda's eyes and understand what was being asked of her. What she saw was open space, no barriers. She saw a dusty road and heard the silence of determination as she felt the tribe close around her as it had closed around Gilda, the child. She saw forests spanning a distance of green too remote for even Gilda to remember.

"My dream was to see the world, over time. The real dream is to make a world—to see the people and still want to make a world."

"I haven't seen much, but what I've seen doesn't give me much appetite," the Girl said, remembering the chill she felt from Bernice's words about the war's aftermath.

"But what of the people?" Gilda's voice rose slightly. "Put aside the faces of those who've hunted you, who've hurt you. What of the people you've loved? Those you could love tomorrow?"

The Girl drew back from the fire in Gilda's voice. Her mother's hands reaching down to pull the cloth up to her chin as she lay on the mattress filled her vision. Her mother's darkened knuckles had loomed large and solid, something she had not articulated her love for. She remembered hearing Bird's voice for the first time below her in the house announcing the entertainment. The deep resonance sent a thrill through her body. Minta's soft warning was all but forgotten, but her tender concern which showed in the bend of her body filled the Girl with joy. The wary, protective way Bernice had watched her grow, their evenings alone in the kitchen talking about the ways of the world—these were things of value. She opened her eyes and looked into Gilda's. She found love there, too. And exhaustion beyond exploration. She could see no future in them although this was what Gilda wanted to promise her.

Reading the thoughts that Gilda tried to communicate, the Girl picked her way through. "You're offerin' me time that's not really time? Time that's gonna leave me by myself?"

"I've seen this world moving on many different paths. I've walked each road with curiosity, anxious to see what we would make of our world. In Europe and to the south of us here have been much the same. When I came here the world was much larger, and the trip I had to make into the new world was as fearful as the one you've made. I was a girl, too, much too young to even be afraid.

"Each time I thought taking a stand, fighting a war would bring the solution to the demons that haunted us. Each time I thought slavery or fanaticism could be banished from the earth with a law or a battle. Each time I've been wrong. I've run out of that youthful caring, and I know we must believe in possibilities in order to go on. I no longer believe. At least for myself."

"But the war is important. People have got to be free to live."

"Yes, and that will no doubt be accomplished. But for men to need war to make freedom. . . I have never understood. Now I am tired of trying to understand. There are those of our kind who kill every time they go out into the night. They say they need this ex- hiliration in order to live this life. They are simply murderers. They have no special need; they are rabid children. In our life, we who live by sharing the life blood of others have no need to kill. It is through our connection with life, not death, that we live."

Both women were silent. The Girl was uncertain what questions she might even ask. It was like learning a new language. When she looked again into Gilda's eyes she felt the pulsing of blood beneath the skin. She also sensed a rising excitement that was unfamiliar to her.

"There is a joy to the exchange we make. We draw life into our- selves, yet we give life as well. We give what's needed—energy, dreams, ideas. It's a fair exchange in a world full of cheaters. And when we feel it is right, when the need is great on both sides, we can re-create others like ourselves to share life with us. It is not a bad life," Gilda said.

The Girl heard the edge in Gilda's voice but was fascinated by the pulsing blood and the swirling colors in Gilda's eyes.

"I am on the road I've chosen, the one that is right for me. You must choose your path again just as you did when you ran from the plantation in Mississippi. Death or worse might have met you on that road, but you knew it was the one you had to take. Will you trust me?" Gilda closed her eyes and drew back a little, freeing the Girl from her hypnotic gaze.

The Girl felt a chill, as if Gilda's lowered lids had shut off the sun, and for a moment she was afraid. The room was all shadows and unnatural silence as Gilda disappeared behind her closed eyes. Finally, confusion lifted from the Girl who was intent on listening to more than the words: the highs and lows, the pitch, the rhythm were all molded by a kind of faith the Girl hoped she would reach. It was larger than simply a long life. It was a grand adventure for which her flight into freedom had only begun to prepare her.

"Yes," the Girl whispered.

Gilda opened her eyes, and the Girl felt herself drawn into the flowing energy. Her arms and legs became weak. She heard a soft humming that sounded like her mother. She couldn't look away from Gilda's gaze which held her motionless. Yet she felt free and would have laughed if she had had the strength to open her mouth. She sensed rather than felt Gilda pull her into her arms. She closed her eyes, her muscles softened under the touch of Gilda's hand on her arm. She curled her long body in Gilda's lap like a child safe in her mother's arms.

She felt a sharpness at her neck and heard the soothing song. Gilda kissed her on the forehead and neck where the pain had been, catching her in a powerful undertow. She clung to Gilda, sinking deeper into a dream, barely hearing Gilda as she said, "Now you must drink." She held the Girl's head to her breast and in a quick gesture opened the skin of her chest. She pressed the Girl's mouth to the red life that seeped from her.

Soon the flow was a tide that left Gilda weak. She pulled the suckling girl away and closed the wound. Gilda sat with the Girl curled in her lap until the fire died. As the sun crept into the dark room she carried the Girl upstairs to the bedroom, where they slept the day through. Gilda awoke at dusk, the Girl still tight in her arms. She slipped from the bed and went downstairs to put a tub of water to boil. When she returned to finish dressing, the Girl watched her silently.

"I'm not well," the Girl said, feeling the gorge rising in her throat.

"Yes, you'll be fine soon," Gilda said, taking her into her arms and carrying her downstairs and outside. The evening air made the Girl tremble in her thin shirt. Gilda held the Girl's head down over the dirt, then left her sitting alone on the back stairs. She returned with a wet cloth and wiped her mouth and face, then led her inside again. She helped her remove her clothes and lifted her into the large tub standing beside the kitchen table. Then she soaped, rinsed, and massaged the Girl into restfulness, drawing out the fear and pain with her strong, thin hands as she hummed the tune from the Girl's childhood. She dressed her in a fresh gown, one of her own bordered with eyelet lace, smelling of lavender, then put her back to bed.

"Bird will return soon. You mustn't be afraid. You will ask her to complete the circle. It is she who will make you our daughter. Will you remember that?"

"Yes," the Girl said weakly.

"You must also remember, later, when time weighs on you like hard earthenware strapped to your back, it is for love that we do this." Gilda's eyes were fiery and unfocused. The power of them lulled the Girl into sleep, although she felt a pang of unease and hunger inside of her. Gilda's lips again brushed her forehead. Then she slept without dreaming.

She awoke abruptly to find Bird standing over her in darkness shadowed even further by a look of destructive anger, her eyes unblinking and dry.

"When did she leave you?" Bird's voice was tight with control although her hands shook as they clutched several crumpled sheets of paper.

Gilda had said don't be afraid and she wasn't, only anxious to understand what would happen now. "It seems long ago, before dark. She wore her walking clothes and said you would complete the circle. I was to be sure and tell you that."

Bird stalked from the room. Downstairs she stood on the porch, turning east and west as if listening to thoughts on the wind. She ran to the west, through the field, and disappeared for three hours. Her clothes were full of brambles when she returned. She went to the cellar and climbed part way through the door. She could see the new sacks of fresh soil stacked beside the ones she and Gilda had prepared so long ago. She stepped back outside and let the cellar door drop with a resounding thud, then came into the house where the Girl lay weak, unmoving except for her eyes, now dark brown flecked with pale yellow.

Bird looked down at her as if she were a stranger, turned away, and lit a lantern. Again she read the crumpled pages she'd dropped to the floor, then paced, trying not to listen to the Girl's shallow breathing. The darkest part of night passed. Bird stood on the porch again and peered at the stars as if one might signal her.

When the sun began its rise Bird retreated to the shadows of the house, moving anxiously from corner to corner, listening. She was uncertain what to expect, perhaps a ripping sound or scream of pain inside her head. She felt only the Girl weakening upstairs and a cloying uneasiness. In her head she replayed recent conversations with Gilda. Each one came closer and closer to the core.

Gilda had needed Bird to step away so she could end this long life with the peace she sought. And each time Bird had resisted, afraid of losing the love of a woman who was the center of her world. Upstairs was the Girl, now in her charge, the one who'd given that permission for which Gilda had yearned.

Full daylight came behind the closed drapes. Bird stood tense, her body a bronze rod, dull and aching, her full length of flesh and hair calling out for hours. The answer came like the sunlight it was. She felt Gilda lying naked in the water, marveling at its coolness and silence. Then she dove into the darkness of the tide. Without the power of her native soil woven into her breeches, she surrendered easily. The air was squeezed from her lungs and she eagerly embraced her rest. Bird felt a moment of the sun's warmth, her head filled with Gilda's scent. In her ear was the soft sigh of pleasure she recognized from many mornings of their past together, the low whisper of her name, then silence. She knew the knife-edged sun rays stripped the flesh from Gilda's bones. The heat seared through Bird, lightning on her skin and in her marrow. Then, like the gradual receding of menstrual pain, Bird's muscles slackened and her breathing slowed. The crackling was silenced. It was over. Gilda was in the air no more.

Bird went upstairs to the Girl whose face was ashen, her dark eyes now flecked with orange. A frost of perspiration covered her body, and tears ran down the sides of her face. She opened her mouth but no sounds came out. Bird sat against the pillows and pulled the Girl into her arms. She was relieved by the cool tears washing over her brown arm as if she were weeping herself. Bird pulled aside her woolen shirt and bared her breasts.

She made a small incision beneath the right one and pressed the Girl's mouth to it. The throbbing in her chest became synchronous with the Girl's breathing. Soon the strength returned to the Girl's body; she no longer looked so small.

Bird repeated the exchange, taking from her as Gilda had done and returning the blood to complete the process. She finally lay her head back on the pillows, holding the Girl in her arms, and rested.

Their breathing and heartbeats sounded as one for an hour or more before their bodies again found their own rhythms. Even then, Bird remained silent.

"She's gone then?" Bird heard her ask. She only nodded and eased her arms from around the Girl's body.

"I'll build a fire," she said and rose quickly from the bed. Alone in the room Bird found the crumpled letter and returned it to the box Gilda had left on the dressing table. She heard the sound of a robe brushing the carpet below as the Girl moved about laying wood on the fire, then settling the kettle atop the stove in the kitchen. She called to Bird to come down. Her voice, now strong and vibrant, was a shock in the late afternoon quiet without Gilda.

They sat in the twilight in front of the low flames, not speaking for some time. Then Bird said, "She wanted you to be called Gilda."

"I know."

"Will you?"

"I don't know."

"It will be dark soon—we must go out. Are you afraid?"

"She said there's little to fear and you'll teach me, as always." They were quiet again.

"She loved you very much, Bird."

"Loved me so much that she traded her life for yours?" Bird almost shouted. In all else there'd been some reasoning, but she could find none in this. Here in the place of the woman to whom she'd given her life sat a child.

"I'm not a child, Bird. If I can hear her words and understand her need, why can't you? I didn't steal her life. She took her road to freedom—just like I did, just like you did. She made a fair exchange. For your sake."

"Fair exchange?" Bird was unnerved by the words she had heard so often in the past when she had been learning the manner of taking the blood and leaving something in return—how to partake of life and be certain not to take life. She chafed under the familiar words and inflection. "You for her?" Bird spit it out. "Hundreds of years of knowledge and wit in exchange for a girl who hasn't lived one lifetime yet."

"It's not just me, it's you. Her life, her freedom for our future. You are as much a part of the bargain as I am. She brought me to this place for your need as well as for mine. It's us seeing the future together that satisfies her needs."

Bird heard the past speaking to her, words she had chosen to ignore. Tonight she stood face to face with their meaning: Gilda's power over her own death was sacred, a decision all others were honor bound to respect. Bird had denied Gilda's right to her quietus and refused to even acknowledge that decison. It was a failure she could not wear easily.

Darkness seeped through the drawn curtains of the parlor. The glow of the almost-steady flame burned orange in the room, creating movement where there was none. The two women sat together as if they were still at their reading lessons. Finally Bird spoke.

"Gilda?"

"Yes."

"It's time now."

They dressed in the warm breeches and dark shirts. Bird took Gilda's hand and looked into the face of the woman who had been her pupil and saw the childlike roundness of her had melted away. Hunger filled her eyes.

"It is done much as it was done here. Your body will speak to you. Do not return to take from anyone too soon again: it can create the hunger in them. They will recover though, if it is not fed. And as you take from them you must reach inside. Feel what they are needing, not what you are hungering for. You leave them with something new and fresh, something wanted. Let their joy fill you. This is the only way to share and not to rob. It will also keep you on your guard so you don't drain life away."

"Yes, these are things she wanted me to know."

"I will teach you how to move about in indirect sunlight, as you've seen us do, and how to take your rest. Already your body sheds its mortal softness. You'll move faster than anyone, have the strength of many. It's that strength that you must learn to control. But we will talk more of these things later. It is better to begin before there is pain."

Gilda and Bird turned west. Their path through the flat field was invisible. Bird pushed aside all thoughts for the moment, remembering only her need to instruct, to insure that the girl gained enough knowledge for her survival. Gilda allowed the feeling of loss to drift through her as they sped into the darkness. Along with it came a sense of completion, too. There was certain knowledge of the world around her, excitement about the unknown that lay ahead, and comfort with her new life. She looked back over her shoulder, but they had moved so quickly that the farmhouse was all but invisible. Inside, the fire was banked low, waiting for their return.

Chapter Two
Yerba Buena: 1890

Gilda's eyes opened abruptly in the black room. She remembered where she was—the guest room at Sorel's—but still felt disoriented and reluctant to leave her dream behind. It had been like this for many of the nights since she had left Woodard's and traveled west. She would be filled, just before she woke up, with the same dread she felt the evening she discovered Bird was gone. She would relive the certain knowledge that Bird was nowhere near, that no matter where she searched there would be no clue to use in locating her. With her eyes open in the dark, Gilda let the feelings rush over her once more and replayed the last conversation between them.

She had found Bird pacing beside her narrow bed after they were out finding their share of the blood. It was time for them to retire, but Bird seemed unable to sit, relax, or look Gilda in the eye. Gilda had moved to the small cushions on the window seat where she had spent so much time as a girl learning to read. She had tucked her long, dark legs underneath her and watched Bird as she did when she was a child, waiting for the lesson to take shape.

When Bird finally stopped her pacing and looked down at Gilda, a smile broke through her clouded face. But it didn't hold long, and Bird simply said, "I will leave here tonight."

"Where do you go?" Gilda had asked, trying not to let her voice sound tremulous.

"I think to my family."

Gilda hesitated only a moment, letting her practical nature take charge in shaping her response. "They must all be dead now, you know that." And indeed the mother and brothers that Bird had left behind were dead. Or if not, they would never accept Bird as their child—a girl who had aged little since she was cast out by her brothers thirty-five years before. But surely they must be dead, Gilda thought, remembering the terrible campaign that had been waged against the Lakota to the north of Louisiana in the years before the end of the war between the states. The news of the mass killings, the hanging of thirty warriors in Mankota by the U.S. military twenty years ago still sent a shiver through her body. Surely there'd be no one. . .but Bird broke into her thoughts.

"There are others of my people. There will always be others."

Gilda swallowed loudly, pushing down her impulse to beg Bird not to leave. This restlessness in Bird felt much like what she had witnessed in the one now dead. Bird had struggled futilely to hold on to her; Gilda was determined not to make that same mistake with Bird.

"Will you take something of mine with you when you go?"

Bird nodded. Gilda rose from the window seat and ran down the hall to her room. She returned quickly, handing Bird the wood-handled knife she had kept since she was a girl. The rust on its blade was perhaps mixed with the blood of one who had tried to return her to slavery, yet the edge was still sharp, the handle strong.

"I no longer need this. I gave myself freedom, and you've given me life. Maybe you can use it on the road."

Bird took the old weapon tenderly, staring at it as if it might shift shape or tell its story aloud. She looked at the girl who was now a woman and said, "You will want to take to the road again yourself someday. I'll make a trade." They both smiled, for it had been some years since they had first traded the blood that linked them forever.

Bird took from her cabinet a small knife set snugly in a leather casing decorated with the tight quill-and-bead work in an angular design for which Bird was known. Gilda clutched the warm leather to her breast and looked around the room in which she'd spent so much of her childhood. She didn't know how to ask the question without betraying Bird's right to live or die as she chose, so she spoke it simply, trying to hold an even tone. "Do you go to end it? To die?"

Bird turned toward Gilda, but her eyes remained blank. She held Gilda in her opaque gaze with a power she'd not used often. The dark brown flashed orange and red as the thought whirled around inside of her, then back and forth between them. Gilda could feel the tumultuous confusion that besieged Bird tumbling inside her own head. She picked through the feelings of bitter regret, sadness, loss, trying to find her answer. But the confusion was too complete. Still Bird answered her aloud, "No."

"Later," Gilda went on, "if the answer resolves itself truly as yes, will you come to me first . . . simply so that I may do my leave-taking honorably?" She didn't mean her request to sound like an accusation, but she saw Bird flinch.

"Of course I will come to you when there is some resolution. When the vision has made itself known, you will know it too."

"You've prepared your way?"

"Yes."

Gilda thought of the many nights Bird had been gone for long hours. She must have been traveling the countryside hiding her caches of home soil. She didn't know what else she might say, so Gilda only stared at Bird's back when she turned, ready to pack now that things were settled. Gilda tried to let go of her old fear of being alone, of losing her family again. She wrestled with herself to remember how long a life was now hers and how many more chances she had to be with Bird again in the future.

She let go of her anxiety and allowed the love she felt flood through her, knowing Bird could feel it too. Bird turned back to look at Gilda, her eyes glistening. But there were no tears for them.

"Yes," Bird said urgently, as if in lovemaking. Then she turned to the chest where most of her clothes lay folded neatly.

Gilda had watched Bird leave less than an hour later on horseback with a small travois strapped to her saddle to carry her traveling pallets of soil, books, and clothes. Her figure had looked small, ancient, from the window of Gilda's room. Her firm legs were wrapped tightly in rough leggings, and her straight shoulders were covered with a dark blanket tucked tautly into her belt and saddle.

The feeling of anxiety that awoke Gilda a few minutes earlier had been the same every evening since Bird's departure from Woodard's. Even here in the secured room of Sorel's home on the western coast.

After her long journey on an unfamiliar road she thought her rest would finally be quiet, deep. But her waking now was not much different from the mornings when she had remained at Woodard's managing the house alone.

She jumped up, throwing the satin coverlet to the floor, and glanced back at the silk-covered pallet, one of the many she had carried with her or left in secured hiding places. She breathed in the strong scent of Mississippi soil rising from within the pallet, then lit the oil lamp beside the porcelain bowl. She poured water and washed her face slowly, gazing at her image in the oval mirror on the wall above. There she was, her dark eyes flecked slightly with orange, signifying the hunger that was beginning to gather itself inside of her. The thick softness of her hair was pulled back into a single braid that started at the crown of her head and ended at the base of her neck. The kinkiness of it reassured her—not at all the look of a ha'nt or spook as many thought her and her kind to be.

Her face was there in the mirror, not banished to some soulless place. It was there just as it was for the others who lived here with Sorel, or for those who visited his gambling room and bar each night. Others. Gilda staggered slightly at the thought. There would be others, Bird had promised her before leaving her alone. Sorel had assured her when she arrived on his back doorstep the morning before. There would be others.

She had found the place easily. It still stood at the same crossroads that Minta had described in her letters so long ago. But even if it had been moved fifty times in the twenty years since Minta left Woodard's and made her home in California, it would have been impossible not to find it. The gambling rooms and hotel were well known by both rich and poor in this muddy, waterfront town that was straining so hard to be a city. And to those like herself it was a home of sorts. They came late in the evening to gather in the back rooms and bar, talking, laughing, mixing with the townspeople as if there were no difference between them. Bird had told her once that she had spent the evening here with five others and carried the memory as if it were a dream. Five plus Sorel and Anthony. Gilda was not certain she was prepared to meet so many at once. She also dreaded speaking with Sorel to learn what he knew of Bird and her disappearance. She left through the rear door, which opened out into a dark alley beneath bright stars.

Gilda wandered to the top of one of the many hills, walking east, and looked down on the bay and the small lights twinkling around it. It was a breathtaking view—houses and businesses all ablaze with light, some of it provided by the electricity that was changing her world. She could not imagine what a world with endless light would be. But she didn't fear it, only found it curious.

· A wave of emptiness swelled inside her as she thought of all the things she hadn't shared with Bird: somewhere Bird knew of this new light too. Ahead of her a man swung down from a horse and looked at one of its hooves. Gilda walked up behind him in silence, her movements fluid. She seemed to caress the air rather than cut through it. She had grown used to searching the sleeping night for someone with whom she might trade for life's blood. In the ten years she had traversed the countryside around New Orleans with Bird, it had become natural to her to exchange dreams or ideas for a share of life. She did not need to struggle to remember the words of caution about her power, or to remain aware of the one with whom she shared. The exchange had become an important part of her living and of her understanding of those who remained mortal. She approached the man with only the thought of natural communion in her mind, as if she were about to sit down with the women in the old kitchen at Woodard's or to speak with a merchant in town. Feeling her presence, he turned. She caught him up in her gaze, then probed his mind for what he might be seeking and was surprised.

Gilda had never encountered such a void of desire in her life of night-traveling with Bird. He seemed full of only himself. She sensed a greed for gold much like that pervading the air of the whole town, but it was bolder, sharper. Little else appeared to be of consequence to him. He was on his way to gamble and thought only of winning—even if it meant cheating. Gilda sliced the soft flesh of his neck and caught him up in her arm. She bent to him in the shadow that protected them from the endless electric night below. She sucked insistently at his life blood, almost losing herself in the need for the blood and in her disappointment in the smallness of his vision. Gilda felt him sagging in her arms, then quickly slipped in among his thoughts with the idea that cheating was merely a way of shortening the possibilities for his own life.

She urged this realization into his resisting mind as she took her share of the blood, as she held her hand over the wound, waiting for it to heal and for his heart to pump the much-needed substance back through his body. Once his heartbeat felt more regular she leaned him against the saddle of his horse. Gilda left him there— dazed and ambivalent about his dishonesty. As she turned to walk away she realized she was now very anxious to talk to Sorel, to hear whatever he had to say.

She covered the distance back to the rear door of Sorel's quickly, slipping into the room she'd been given. Using a damp towel she hurriedly wiped away some of the mud that clung to her boots and swatted at the dusty smudges on her face. The distant sound of music and voices made it impossible to be alone any longer. She had traveled by horse for many days, avoiding people except when it was time for the exchange. Suddenly she wanted the feel of people near her, the smell of them sweating and living, changing before her eyes. She needed to feed on their laughter and games in the light this city offered.

Gilda hurriedly locked the door to her room with the key Sorel had given her so ceremoniously, then slowed her steps deliberately as she descended the stairs to the public rooms. She took the seemingly endless time of the descent to listen to the sounds coming from the rooms to the right and left of the stairway and wide foyer. And to watch the people who only glanced up at her casually as they moved briskly past the stairs to their destinations: one room with a grand piano and a singer of some note who held a small audience enthralled; two other rooms with gaming tables and people, mostly men, bent over them furiously winning or losing. And the salon, its perimeter outfitted with plush settees and small tables so that anyone, even women alone, would feel comfortable being there.

The long shining wood bar with its equally polished brass foot rail was lined with men who were leaning and talking in low tones. The electric lights blazing from the wall sconces made everyone's face seem unnaturally pale. She was certain that few, if any, of those gathered here were as she was, but they looked unlike any people she had ever seen before. She didn't know how much was her own deep fatigue, the special quality of the light, or simply the gaiety of the salon in contrast with the rough roads of the past few years.

She was not in charge here as she had been during the time after Bird left. She hesitated inside the door deciding whether to sit on one of the brightly striped settees, as all of the women seemed to have done, or to follow her impulse and stand at the bar with the men. She stiffened as she heard, *Perhaps you'll allow me to show you to Monsieur Sorel's table. He asked me to inform him of your. . . return.*

Anthony had spoken without speaking, which unnerved Gilda when done among others. Yet she followed him as he turned to the left and directed her to a slightly larger table near one of the broad, draped windows looking out onto a small circular driveway.

"May I bring you something?" Anthony said in his soft, rather low-pitched voice. He felt her hesitation and gave her time to orient her thoughts.

Gilda sensed several people in the salon turning to stare at her—some discreetly, some not. Anthony seemed to notice nothing. He spoke again. "I would be impolite to boast, but Monsieur Sorel has his own vineyards in Europe, vinted by monks with impeccable taste. We have the most excellent red known to the palate. Of course, if you're fond of this champagne that seems to have taken everyone's fancy, we have that as well. But perhaps you'd prefer something to take away the chill of this damp night. I'm afraid most nights here are damp. One becomes accustomed to them, though. Even to love them—with time."

Gilda had picked up the thoughts of the patrons around her in a desultory way. They revealed disapproval of both her well-traveled clothes and her dark skin. But Anthony's words, all delivered in such a soft and soothing tone, made Gilda forget the people gawking at her. His attentions became all encompassing. She gazed into his immense deep, blue eyes and was taken by the very slight smile that lurked behind them. His hair was a forgettable brown color and his build was slight. His hands, however, were quite large, imposing and solid with stout veins running their length. Gilda let him comfort her with his mild words about the city.

Before she could speak, Sorel's voice boomed out from halfway across the room. "The champagne, of course, Anthony. What else do we serve when family returns home?"

"Of course," Anthony said with only the hint of a smile at the corners of his mouth, as if he found smiling ostentatious. He bowed almost imperceptibly in Gilda's direction and turned toward the door. As he receded from the room, the space was filled to overflowing with Sorel. He appeared even larger tonight in the salon among these genteel people than Gilda remembered from their first brief meeting in the morning when she'd arrived at his back door. He wore a finely tailored blue suit and brightly embroidered shoes made from some soft material; at his neck was a flurry of silk.

There was a light scent of Arabian musk about him that was enticing. As with Anthony, when Sorel spoke it felt as if they were absolutely alone rather than standing in the middle of the patrons of a busy salon. The people behind them shifted in their seats almost as one body, rising slightly to actually see who Gilda was and to be certain that Sorel noticed they were smiling. Gilda let her senses take in the entire room again to better understand the full influence Sorel had. He moved lightly for a large man, delicately fitting himself into the curve of the settee so that he was both beside her and also able to look her in the eye. Gilda noted that of the perhaps thirty people in the room, only about five were absolutely unable to accept her presence. And even they—each separately, with almost no real conscious knowledge of their strategy—resolved to sit for a while longer so there would be no chance that Sorel would interpret their departure as an insult to one he had named as his family.

Gilda, who'd been gazing without focus at Sorel's thick mustache, looked up into his dark eyes and heard him. *But we shall know. Will we not?*

She smiled. Sorel laughed so loudly that the drapes at the window rippled. Gilda matched his mirth with her own. He reached across the table and took her hands in his, leaning forward to kiss them, but was unable to contain his laughter. They both continued to laugh until Anthony appeared with the bottle of champagne.

"As usual, Anthony, you have quite a sobering effect on me. He serves each meal as if it were the last supper," Sorel said with a smile, barely restraining another outburst.

Anthony was unmoved as he opened the bottle with just the appropriate pop of the cork. As he was about to pour he stopped and said to Gilda, "I believe that in the homeland of your mother's people the first libation is poured into the ground in honor of the ancestors."

Sorel's gleeful smile turned to one of pride as he looked at the small, tightly muscled arm that held the large bottle effortlessly. Anthony continued holding the bottle away from the table above the shining wood floor.

"I honor your ancestors. I honor our ancestors." Anthony solemnly poured sparkling wine onto the floor. The conversation in the room around them continued, but in a distracted way, with everyone keeping one ear on the activity at Sorel's table.

"You welcome me with great humanity," she said as Anthony

poured the champagne into delicate crystal. "And with great honor," she added, raising her glass in Sorel's direction when his was filled.

"Let us just hope it is great wine," Sorel said softly. Anthony left the bottle in a bucket of ice and moved away from the table.

Sorel's salon was noted for its wine cellar, and the pride of that reputation shone on his face as they sipped in silence. He spoke in a supple voice, slightly accented by the knowledge of many languages. "I know much about you. Your face has been in my mind for some time now. It is difficult to believe that finally having you here with me would exceed the pleasure of anticipating your arrival. But it does."

"You continue to be gracious to me, Sorel, even though I arrive unannounced, muddy, and—"

Sorel cut her off. "Please, as I've said, we're family here. Your arrival could never be unannounced. Wherever we are we must expect each other. This is a family lesson we've learned well. You, too, have learned it or you would not have come to me."

"I came to. . ." Here Gilda stopped, uncertain what she thought would be the result of her coming. She could ask about Bird, but once her whereabouts were known what would Gilda do? What then did she need to know from this man who'd been like a myth to the women at Woodard's? What had she come here for?

"I need to know much. Where the questions begin though is a question itself. I would ask where Bird has gone, but I know that that is something I will learn if I wait for her to tell me herself.

"I would ask where I go now that I've given over ownership of Woodard's to Bernice's daughter and come to this hill city full of light. Or I could ask what I might need to ask."

"And to the last I would answer there is nothing to ask. You'll stay here with me to continue your lessons as it was meant to be. Bird will answer the questions you have for her in her own time."

Gilda started at the sound of Bird's name spoken aloud by another, as if she had been afraid all along that Bird was only a dream.

"She's been here and prepared us for your arrival. She needs to spend time apart. Listening to the people who gave her first life. Listening to the missteps she has taken. Reuniting with herself."

"Reuniting?"

"Yes."

Anthony returned and filled their glasses silently, then leaned down and whispered in Sorel's ear so softly that even Gilda could not hear what was said.

"I'm afraid we shall be joined shortly by another. We'll continue our talk later," Sorel said, looking directly into Gilda's eyes. She heard the deliberate use of Bird's own tone, one she had often used when they studied in the twilight of her room so long ago.

"If you were to succinctly sum up what you've learned," Sorel continued, "what few words would you employ? Now, without the benefit of philosophizing?" Sorel's deep-set dark eyes no longer twinkled as they did most of the time when he spoke. They were unwavering at this moment, much as Bird's had been when she taught history or languages to Gilda.

"Betraying our shared life, our shared humanity makes one unworthy of sharing, unworthy of life." Gilda spoke easily. She had not known how deeply she felt the lessons she had learned.

"You are a most accomplished student, my dear. We're proud of you beyond our greatest dream. The second lesson, which will become equally as important, is that there are many who do not share this belief. In fact, they thrive on commitment to the abject converse of that lesson. You will come to recognize them with ease. In the meantime there are several people I should like to introduce you to—Ina and Joseph, Juan Jose de Ayala, Esther—none of whom seem to be about this evening. But we shall see to your introduction into society posthaste."

Sorel sat back on the settee with a look of satisfaction on his face. Soon, however, a slight shadow settled on his forehead. He sipped from his wine, not glancing up at Gilda for several minutes. His gaze then began to slowly scan the room. When it stopped at the door the shadow descended over the rest of his face. His brow tightened as the woman who stood poised in the doorway made her way toward their table.

The red of her hair was a beacon superior to the electric candles lining the walls. Gilda turned away quickly to watch Sorel's reaction. She was puzzled. He was both annoyed and pleased to see this striking figure in the doorway of his salon. If this was the visitor who'd been expected, Sorel was not prepared to speak of her.

Gilda absorbed Sorel's feelings of pleasure and anxiety as fully as she could before turning her attentions to the woman herself. As did much of the clientele in the salon. Her russet curls cascaded onto her shoulders, which were draped in deep blue satin. Although her dress covered her from neck to toe, it managed to be more provocative than anything Gilda had ever seen.

She strode toward their table with a lanky walk as if she were strolling in breeches on a country road, yet the lift of her chin and the deliberateness of each step were elegant. Beneath unfashionably full brows were deep-green eyes sparkling in unnatural competition with the champagne on their table. Her full, wide mouth was painted a shade of red that perfectly matched her hair.

Sorel rose nimbly from the settee and took her hand, pressing it gently to his lips. Anthony appeared behind them both, his mouth set grimly and the knuckles of his large hands almost white as they gripped the new champagne glass. Gilda stifled the impulse to rise next to Sorel.

"Gilda, may I present Eleanor. Eleanor, I hope you'll join us?" He spoke to her almost shyly.

"Of course," Eleanor said in a deep but breathy voice as she slipped in beside Gilda. She seemed to consume Gilda in one glance, her evaluation evinced in a thin smile that was both remote and enticing. Sorel sat down at the other end of the curved settee facing them, and Anthony poured wine in each of the three glasses.

"Eleanor has the distinction of being homegrown royalty. Her family has lived here by the bay longer than perhaps any other. Since before the ships, before the gold, before the traders. Alas, they have all died out except Eleanor and her uncle, Alfred."

"And he is probably seeing his last year even as we speak," Eleanor said with no trace of sorrow. "But let's not talk of the old and dying, rather the fresh and vital. You, my dear, are new to our jeweled bay. What news do you have to bring us from the uncivilized hinterlands?" The lights sparkled off the lustrous material of her dress, making her seem synonymous with the bay.

Gilda felt an unfamiliar discomfort, her words stumbling over each other inside her. She almost shook her head in an effort to sort them out and avoid sounding like a stammering child. She was further unnerved by the certain knowledge that this woman knew exactly what was going on inside of her. Her words finally came together when she turned her gaze away from Eleanor and back toward Sorel. He was much like Bird in his capacity for clarity, and Gilda relaxed under his steadying influence.

"I'm afraid what you say about the hinterlands may be true although I'd hesitate to refer to them as uncivilized. I've spent the better part of two years journeying by horse and by foot from Louisiana to the east, then north and west, seeing the most wondrous sights. Trees and deserts of such magnitude I might never have believed they really existed, except that my eyes have always been quite healthy. And there is almost no pleasure greater than lying down in the warmth of benevolent wolves listening to their thoughts."

Eleanor hid her surprise under a question. "And do they have thoughts?"

"All living things have something we can consider thoughts."

"And did they never have thoughts of devouring you?" Eleanor asked with a wickedly brilliant smile.

"Of course. But as I've said, the trip was civilized and we know those thoughts are everywhere, not just the in the woodlands." Gilda responded, surprised that she had spoken so freely with this woman.

Eleanor's voice was low and solemn as she spoke. "Then that explains your outerwear. I was afraid for a moment some new fashion was sweeping out from the east and I was frightfully outmoded." Her eyes twinkled impishly, softening the words. She reached for Gilda's hand across the table. "You must let me dress you."

Gilda felt her face flush with the heat of embarrassment and again was plunged into speechlessness. This time she feared it was permanent. Sorel came to her rescue.

"What a splendid idea. How better for two people to come to know each other than from the outer garments in." His laughter edged out uncertainly as he looked around for Anthony, who was on hand with a second bottle of champagne before Sorel could speak. A glow of girlish innocence suffused Eleanor's face. She dimmed the dazzling light surrounding her by closing her eyes, as if turning the damper on a stove. This left her face more accessible, youthful. Gilda wanted to wander the streets with this woman, looking at fabrics, learning her city. She still felt a bit of the awe that had almost crushed her earlier, but now her body rang with a sense of adventure.

Eleanor refocused her eyes on Gilda. "Then I shall call for you here in the salon, perhaps about 3:00 P.M. We can take tea together and shop until the merchants have run out of time and cloth." The embers of her smile flared as she turned to look directly at Gilda. Faint orange flecks mixed with the malachite green of her eyes. Gilda had the surprising desire to go on the hunt with this new woman. Instead, she rose from her seat before Sorel could do so himself to let Eleanor move from behind the table.

Eleanor and her dress sparkled as she stood; Gilda lifted the woman's hand to her lips before she thought about it. She stopped midway, realizing how odd she must look to all the others in the room, then continued planting a lingering kiss on Eleanor's hand in a move more casual than she felt.

"Till then," Eleanor said, then bent to kiss Sorel lightly on the forehead. She swept from the room with a curt nod toward Anthony, who stood watching them from across the room near the end of the bar.

Gilda sat down, feeling slightly chilled by the loss of Eleanor for the rest of the evening. It took a moment to realize that she again felt in need of the blood. She was surprised that the desire rose so soon, but it was unmistakable.

Before she could speak Sorel said, "I know that Anthony would be more than pleased to accompany you this evening. To show you some of our city by night. He's a most knowledgeable guide. And he's eager to know more of you, New Orleans, and the path between there and here."

Gilda was relieved to have been handed a direction. "Yes, that would be wonderful."

Anthony appeared beside the table and said, "I will meet you outside your door in ten minutes, then."

Pride returned to Sorel's smile as Anthony made his way through the room and spoke a few instructions to the bartender. "Later, when you return, Anthony will show you to our parlor. We can talk more there. You've spent a few difficult years of adjustment and growth. It's unfortunate that Bird's departure had to come when it did. But none of us chooses our destiny or it wouldn't be called destiny, would it?" He laughed lightly before he continued.

"Now is the time for healing, for resting. Laying claim to the things you know but aren't yet certain of. Yerba Buena is just the place for this."

"I would say thank you only because that's the propriety I've been taught," Gilda responded, "but I know it is inadequate."

"On the contrary, it's ostentatious between us." Sorel rose and took Gilda's hand as she stood. She hurried from the room, a tension gripping her shoulders and stomach, one she couldn't remember ever having before.

Anthony stood on the stairs below the thick wood outer door of Gilda's room. He seemed surprised at the change in her appearance: she wore a dark, heavily knit sweater and a man's cap. Gilda was comfortable returning to the guise of boyhood that had cloaked her during her travels west, releasing her from the pretenses and constrictions of womanhood.

"Quite a transformation." Anthony said. "I wondered how you were able to travel unmolested. Let's walk toward the water."

"I realized before I left home there would be no place for me on the road, alone. Even with my advantages I'd be fair game for every male passerby. It seemed easier to simply keep to myself and let people make presumptions. A funny thing though...," Gilda began to chuckle softly, "at least four times—four times—on the road, even in a small town just east of here... four times I met others just like me. I mean women dressed like boys. Just going around from place to place trying to live free. I didn't dare say too much, but we recognized each other so easily. Four times!"

Gilda and Anthony laughed out loud together. "One 'fellow' and I had a great talk. He said he had a friend in California who married a woman and had been living with her for ten years. Said the only thing she missed was wearing perfume. Gave her wife an expensive bottle every birthday!"

Anthony laughed uproariously, grabbed Gilda's hand, and began to run. They moved quickly, leaving their laughter behind hanging in the empty air. When they stopped they stood near the dark docks of the bay. The fog rolled around them, clinging to the warmth of their clothes. They walked silently down streets and through alleys until Anthony saw one with whom he would share. Gilda was unused to searching so openly, among so many people, but followed Anthony's lead, hanging back when he indicated.

A young man stood near the entrance to a lodging house about to light a cigar. Gilda stepped into the shadows; Anthony walked up to him with a match in hand. As he struck the match his gaze caught the man and he walked him backward out of the lamplight. There was no sound, but Gilda was able to peer into the darkness and see through it, observing Anthony in the secret moment of exchange. She looked away toward the lights that sprayed up the hills behind them and waited. Quickly it was done. She heard Anthony speak softly to the man leaning weakly against the wall. Then he lit the match and held it to the dark cheroot still in the man's hand. The man said "thank you" in a rather thin voice and took a deep inhalation of the smoke. Anthony returned to Gilda's side. Together they walked in silence further along the docks.

"There are many here who enjoy the terror we can bring to others. They live as much for that as for the blood," he said abruptly.

"Yes, I've heard this but I don't understand it."

"Human nature remains with us, I'm afraid," Anthony said. "And if you've really no grounding in this world, no understanding of its wonders and that we are simply one of those mysterious wonders you...some feel they must be gods—or devils."

"Anthony, you sound so ominous. Like those who told stories of us in New Orleans. To hear some of the tradesmen talk we were ha'nts, or vodun priestesses, or ghouls."

"Ghouls, perhaps. Some here are certainly that. What else can we call one who thrives on ripping out another's throat, or on deceiving people into ruin or servitude. I would say they are ghouls."

"Among us? You mean here in this town?" As her question erupted she felt the years of sheltering at Woodard's were in glaring evidence.

"Yes. They can even be found some evenings in the salon sipping champagne with Sorel."

Gilda gave a start but held back her questions. "On the road I met many more beasts on two legs than on four. My fears were not of wolves or mountain cats. They have an understanding of the reasoning of nature. I found it comforting to share that reasoning that needs no words. But with men there is no reasoning at all sometimes."

"Then you will understand what I say about human nature being twisted to unreasoning." Anthony's voice became taut. "There are those who burn like small fires waiting to engulf, to consume whatever comes near them."

Gilda sensed an urgency in Anthony's words but was distracted by a man sitting alone atop the driver's seat of a carriage. He held the reins of the horses absently, accustomed to hours of waiting for his passengers. She laid her hand on Anthony's arm lightly, then sprinted ahead and silently ascended to the seat beside the nodding man. She listened for his thoughts a moment, catching them up in her own.

She felt reassured. Unlike the man whose blood she had taken earlier, this one was full of thoughts and dreams. The dominant one now was a hope that his master would end his evening early so he could go home to his own wife and children.

Gilda almost beamed with joy at such a simple yet wholly fulfilling desire. She held him in her thoughts and leaned forward, moving his muffler from his neck, and lanced the flesh gently. She took her share of the blood and read his thoughts of his family. She was particularly pleased at the warmth this man held in his heart after the chilling conversation with Anthony. She made the exchange, reinforcing this man's simple pleasure and using another part of her mind to reach out to his master. Gilda found him inside the crowded gambling rooms behind the carriage and implanted in him the sudden need to go home and be with his family. She sealed the opening and gazed at the dozing face. It had a mildly contented smile.

She and Anthony continued their walk, flushed with the warmth of life. They turned northward toward Sorel's and were almost mounting the final hill when Gilda asked, "How long have you known Sorel?"

Anthony was surprised at the directness of the question. Because of the nature of their history, most left the exposition of their lives to be inferred from conversations among themselves rather than inquiry. Few of them would ever ask such a direct question of another, of personal things such as one's last name or birthplace. Such questions made it feel as if one had to, suddenly, be accountable for one's past life.

"Many years." He felt the deliberately vague response surface involuntarily. He started again. "We have been together for one hundred years. We met in France. They were difficult times. Not unlike those that have just passed here. He brought me into the family, although he had to be cajoled to do so. That is a story for another time. We've lived in many homes in Europe, but it is only here that we've been happy—for fifty years. He talks of going east, but I've convinced him we've much to do here. The east seems steeped in a truly insidious atmosphere just now. To shoot a president—in the back no less!" Anthony shivered as if remembering other atrocities as well before going on. "Bankers and politicians conspire over every dinner table to mortgage farmers into submission. There is a smugness that I'm sure would do nothing but enrage him. And me. I'm afraid we much prefer the rough directness of the ambition we find here." Anthony took a deep breath, exhilarated by sharing his personal thoughts so openly.

Gilda had not heard such talk of politics since the nights around the kitchen table with the women at Woodard's. In her travels she had spent little time with others and certainly was never in one place long enough to encourage that type of discussion. She understood again how much she had missed the company of others like herself. She was eager as she asked, "Are there many others here of Sorel's family?"

"No, he has been rather cautious in that respect. Which some say is foolish. Many create new family members as if gathering an army around themselves. This is not what we mean by family."

Gilda thought again of Eleanor but was uncertain what she might ask about her. Anthony sensed her confusion and continued to speak, giving her time to make up her mind.

"Sorel is correct, I think, in believing that to choose someone for your family is a great responsibility. It must be done not simply out of your own need or desire but rather because of a mutual need. We must search ourselves and the other to know if it is really essential. To do otherwise is a grave error, the result of which can only be tragedy. You will meet those who've been brought into this life mistakenly. An impulsive moment of self-interest or vindictiveness or. . ." He trailed off for a moment. "These are not the families that bring solace or that last in harmony."

"Do you think you and Sorel will be together forever?"

"Of course. Either in each other's company, as we are now, or separate and in each other's world. One takes on others as family and continually reshapes that meaning—family—but you do not break blood ties. We may not wish to live together at all times, but we will always be with each other."

"This sounds too sweet, a false comfort to me right now. There have been too many losses, too many broken ties."

"I know," Anthony said gravely, "but it is true that the passage of time can bring clarity if we remain open to it. Think of us standing here in the fog now." He stopped and again took Gilda's hand, looking into her eyes. "If I love Sorel, that is true here standing with you, or back in the salon, or in the past, or in some future time when he and I are side by side, or in the future when we are not side by side. There is nothing to change that. If I'm not by his side and need him, I call out and he is there. If I speak to him now he comes to me. You do it."

Gilda didn't know what to say. She felt foolish but called out in her mind to Sorel, saying only, *I feel alone.*

In return she felt Sorel reach out to her, the warmth of his affection washing over her as if he stood at her side. She heard his answer. *How can this be? I've given you my best man. . . in fact my only man!* Anthony and she laughed again and turned toward home.

Gilda begged off her meeting with Sorel, feeling too full of thoughts. She decided to leave her questions until the next evening after her shopping trip with Eleanor. She lay quietly in her bed, plunged in the solid darkness that was natural to her now. She saw the green eyes with flecks of orange and realized that the hunger she had seen in Eleanor's eyes had not been for the blood. She tried to push the face away from her and think of what she wanted to ask about Bird, but could not. Instead she looked only into the blackness and let it take her in until she slept.

When she awoke the next afternoon she could feel the activity of workers around her preparing for the evening's events. It reminded her of many afternoons at Woodard's. She listened to her body for a bit to see what the hour was, then rose and lit the lamps. Outside she saw the sun stretching west, so she opened the shutters and thick dark-red curtains, letting in the soft light of afternoon. She was just beginning to move about the room and decide what to wear for this adventure when Anthony knocked at her door. "We've prepared a bath in Sorel's parlor and some fresh clothes."

Gilda luxuriated in the tub but felt uneasy. She was uncertain if it was the discomfort their kind often felt when submerged in water, or the proximity of the bay, but the bath was not as enjoyable as she'd expected. Again she heard the light tap on the door that she'd come to recognize as Anthony's. "Yes?"

"Shall I come and wash your back?" he asked timidly.

Gilda hesitated a moment, not sure what the mix of feelings was. "Yes."

He entered shyly and took the large sponge she handed him. "To be alone can be very frightening in a strange place. I didn't want you to be frightened."

"I was, Anthony. I didn't realize it until you knocked at the door. It reminded me of past times when I've been completely open and uncertain which direction was my true way. And there was no one here to say the soothing things."

"Then that is why I've come." He hummed softly as he rubbed

the soft oily soap over her back and breasts, down her dark legs and arms. He washed the thickness of her hair as if it were a task he'd done all of his life, rinsing out the soap with fresh water from a bucket more easily then she could have done herself. She stood when the bath was finished, and they laughed like children when Anthony poured another bucket of water over her head. He held open a large towel, and Gilda relaxed comfortably as his arms encircled her and his large hands rubbed the dampness from her body. He seemed to be brother and sister to her at the same time.

"Here are some light things to wear." There was some hesitation before he continued. "You plan a shopping venture today. . .with Eleanor." It stood as a statement rather than a question.

"Yes. Sorel agrees I really have nothing appropriate for these circumstances," Gilda responded with a hint of defensiveness. Something in the shape of his words made her wary.

Anthony sensed he had said more than he should have. He responded with encouragement. "You'll have quite a time of it then. Eleanor frequents the best dressmakers and has access to fabrics known only to her. And she enjoys the challenge of bending the tradespeople to her will. Please remember, though, everyone here is like two people: be certain to learn both faces. It can be dangerous if you don't."

Anthony left the room as Gilda dressed. She thought of his admonitions as she put on the silk blouse and soft, serge skirt but forgot them entirely as she descended the stairs to the salon. She stood at the bar with her foot on the rail, feeling completely refreshed by the bath and the prospects of new clothes and a new life. She had two sips from her glass of champagne and exchanged glances with two gentlemen who looked at her with puzzlement and the impersonal distance she had noticed since her arrival. The bartender made small talk knowing her to be a special guest of Sorel's. There was little need, however, to entertain her: Gilda felt strong and Eleanor arrived promptly.

Again as she entered the room the early clients of the salon all looked up. Eleanor didn't hesitate to walk directly to Gilda and take a place beside her at the bar.

"May I order some champagne for you?" Gilda asked.

"No, I'll sip from yours and then we're away on our adventure much more quickly." With those words she tilted her head back and drank down the rest of Gilda's wine. They left the room, climbed into Eleanor's carriage and set off like young girls at play.

"I hate those awful trolleys that plague our streets now." Her voice was petulant and made Gilda want to wave her hands above the streets and banish all the offenders, although she herself found them intriguing and was anticipating her first ride. During the afternoon Eleanor often expressed her dissatisfaction with the changes in the city. Gilda commiserated.

It was not until the first shop they visited that Eleanor learned exactly what a task she had at hand. "I'm afraid I will be comfortable in gowns only intermittently," Gilda said, unmoved by the dresses the dressmaker proffered. "I think we best outfit me with everyday clothes first."

"But surely you'll wear dresses," Eleanor responded incredulously.

"I don't think so," Gilda said, trying not to sound too adamant. She didn't want to offend her new and intriguing friend but recognized immediately what she would feel most comfortable in: pants—whatever effect that had on the society that Sorel proposed to introduce her into. She decided she was already outside of it. Most would only see her as a former slave, so why should she force herself to emulate them unnecessarily.

"It sounds as if I've a Bloomer Girl on my hands," Eleanor said with some humor.

Gilda looked puzzled, uncertain whether or not she was being insulted. She responded to Eleanor's smile with one of her own as she said, "If that means I'll do whatever you ask except wear skirts everyday, then that's indeed who you have."

"Umph," was the sharp retort. This made shopping more of an adventure than either had anticipated. The dressmakers were alternately dismayed, disgusted, and challenged. After three hours Gilda had been fitted for several outfits. Under Eleanor's steely influence Gilda had conceded to a design that from a distance looked like a skirt but was, in fact, split like pants and afforded Gilda the freedom of movement she would not forego. Atop the yards of cloth draping softly at her hips and down her long legs would be a tight bodice much like those worn by most women in town. Gilda insisted, however, that they all button down the front like jackets. She added soft shirts beneath them, and in some cases ordered matching ties to complement the fabric of the skirt/pants.

Gilda was languishing at the end of the day on the dressmaker's divan, ready to go home, when Eleanor insisted on at least two gowns. The fabrics were luxurious, and the dressmaker seemed inured to Eleanor's whims; she extolled the plunging neckline and exaggerated hip that was so popular in the salons and that made Gilda uncomfortable. Gilda finally took pen in hand and drew exactly what she wanted, bowing slightly to Eleanor's will. The craftswoman had obviously dealt with Eleanor for many years and felt secure in how hard she could push. She became silent, then grew attentive as Gilda sketched a bodice. It was much like the others she had ordered but cut lower so the glistening fabric would frame her breasts and shoulders in a way she was not accustomed to but willing to try. She extracted about two yards of material from the skirt design so that the cloth would fall smoothly across her hips rather than envelop her.

When she and Eleanor were satisfied that the dressmaker would follow her instructions, even if under protest, they closed the door behind them and stepped out onto the muddy wooden-slatted walk, filled with satisfaction.

"You're more willful than I'd thought," Eleanor said with a smile. "Will you fight me on where we have tea as well?"

"Not at all, I'm in your hands." Gilda felt invigorated by dealing with the merchants and dressmakers. It reminded her of the old days in New Orleans when she and Bird had gone shopping for the house. She followed Eleanor into the carriage which soon deposited them at her salon, much smaller than Sorel's and nearer the waterfront.

They took a seat in a modestly appointed room outfitted with tea tables and brightly upholstered divans. A waiter greeted Eleanor with familiarity and deposited an ice bucket at their table. He returned in a moment with a bottle which he opened and poured, never speaking.

"I've my own stock here. Not as extensive as Sorel's, of course, but . . ." Eleanor said, leaving the sentence in the air with an impish air of helplessness. A man walked up to their table and looked down with bold curiosity at Gilda. He directed his question to Eleanor.

"What have we here, my sweet?"

"We have a rude man ruining a lovely evening, my sweet." The sharpness in Eleanor's retort startled Gilda, but so, too, did the uneasy feeling she experienced under the man's fierce gaze.

"I can't have been here that long," he responded with a false languor.

Eleanor looked up at the man whose thick blond hair fell carelessly over his unfocused eyes. They were a deep blue, and just at the edge of the pupil Gilda could detect the flecks of orange. She sensed the anger rushing through Eleanor's body as she tried to will the man to go away. He simply ignored her, addressing himself to Gilda directly.

"I am Samuel. You must be the Gilda we've heard about." He extended a long, thin, unpleasantly pale hand. Gilda reached out her hand. He shook it as if she were a man before raising it tentatively to his lips. She was uncertain whether he would kiss it or take a nip to see how negroes tasted.

"I'm at a disadvantage then because I know no one as yet."

"Except Sorel, the Great, and his minion."

Gilda bristled. "If you mean Anthony, I'm sure even you can discern how inadequate a title that is for him. Perhaps you'd like to think of a more suitable one before we continue to get to know each other better." She felt Eleanor's amusement.

"I, of course, meant to say *companion*," Samuel countered with a smirk.

"I'm sure," Gilda said, then turned to Eleanor, deliberately closing Samuel out of her vision. "What were we saying?"

"I've sent my messenger to Sorel's. Anthony will know exactly what of your native earth to package and deliver to the dressmaker. There's a wonderful process that will make the soil and fabric almost as one. She has been my dressmaker for some time and will know what to do. She's satisfied herself that it has to do with herbalism and nothing more—here that's not exceptional. Many have grown accustomed to the new knowledge of the ancient Oriental sciences. But I expect the dresses will take a bit longer because she will try her best to ignore your instructions and then simply succumb and construct the best clothes of her lifetime." Eleanor reached over to lift the bottle of champagne and refill their glasses, ignoring Samuel. He turned on his heel and stalked away.

"You were wonderful. I can't believe it—he's such a pest sometimes. He just has no discretion whatsoever. You would think after all these years he'd know better."

"Why has he such a dislike of Sorel?"

"It's a long and tedious story, my dear. Like most of us, Samuel is full of jealousy and hate. He just hasn't learned how to handle them properly yet. He's not a bad fellow, actually. We've had our moments," Eleanor said, looking at Gilda with guileless eyes. "Will you stay with us long?"

"I don't have plans for the moment. I'm content here and have no home to which I can return. To settle in one place again for a while might be good for me."

"Then you're not rushing off to hunt for the Indian woman?"

"Bird? No, I think not." Again the reality of someone else's knowledge of Bird was startling.

"Good, I've need of you here. It can be so boring sometimes. Nothing but rude men tearing up the mountains looking for gold and other ways to make their fortune. I need civilized company."

That said, Eleanor settled back in her chair as if she had made the decision for Gilda. They stayed together for two more hours before Eleanor showed Gilda to the carriage and instructed the coachman to return her to Sorel's. Gilda left after they had promised to meet again in two days' time. Gilda was happy to be alone in the regenerative silence. She asked the driver to let her off as soon as she recognized the area. She slipped him a coin to quiet his misgivings, then began to walk slowly up the hill toward the house.

The lights sprang to life around her as she picked her way across the muddy planks toward the brightness that was Sorel's. She passed much smaller homes, woodframe buildings that seemed to tumble over each other down the hill. It was such an unreal landscape to Gilda; she almost giggled with fascination. She took in the damp air with deep breaths and found it energizing.

Gilda gasped in surprise when Samuel stepped out of the gathering darkness in front of her. He looked less supercilious now, but Gilda stood still, firmly and defensively planted on her feet. When he finally spoke his voice sounded nothing like the haughty, angry one he had used earlier.

"You mustn't try to take her away. If you do there'll be trouble—for us all."

Gilda said nothing, as if she were accustomed to meeting jealous rivals on foggy streets. Her silence forced Samuel onward. "She'll deceive you, as she did me, as she does everyone. She's not sweetness and light, I'll tell you that. My life was happy before I met her. Ask anyone. My wife was. . ." Samuel's voice was choked off by a dry sob.

Gilda reached out for his arm. "I don't know what you mean, or what you want. How can Eleanor have hurt you so? She couldn't have meant to—"

"She meant it. She's a deceiver, that one is. She killed my wife to have me. She bewitched me just as she bewitched her before she grew tired of her company. She'll do the same with you. It's life to her!" He looked around him, suddenly remembering he was on a public street.

"Perhaps you people from Africa know of these things. It's the devil, believe me. You must know this yourself."

Gilda tried to cut into his speech, to silence the foolish words, but he continued. "I know she was lost to it unfairly. . . she was lost unfairly. As I was. Can you understand? I was lost even more unfairly than she. I said neither yea or nay. Samuel's voice rose higher as he spoke, a discordant arpeggio. "I was asked no questions so could give no answer of consent. It's an unfair bargain she made. But she's dead now. . .don't interfere."

Gilda could make no sense of Samuel's words. He sounded like he'd lost his wits in the fog. She tried several placating gestures, but they were wasted on him.

"Stay away. Please."

The current of pleading in Samuel's voice chilled her more than if he'd been threatening her. His misery was sincere, but Gilda could not accept Eleanor as its cause.

She took a step backward to let him pass. "I'm expected at Sorel's."

Samuel turned on his heel abruptly. Gilda barely discerned his back: he moved away so quickly he almost vanished. She stepped into the space where he'd stood just seconds before and could still feel the heat of his body in the air.

She continued up the hill at a less leisurely pace, anxiety and questions making her footsteps sound more quickly as she got nearer to Sorel's. She would ask many questions when they sat down together at their appointed hour in his rooms.

When Anthony tapped softly on Gilda's door she put down her pen before finishing the last sentence she'd been writing in her journal. She opened the door eagerly.

"Shall I show you to Sorel's room?"

"Yes, thank you."

"Perhaps later in the evening you'd like to go out as we did last night?"

"Yes, Anthony, I'd like that." She walked beside him as he led her down a back stairway and into a hallway that did not appear to be accessible from the front of the house. Anthony knocked on a large, heavy door and then stepped aside as Sorel opened it widely.

"Come in, my dear. Anthony will bring us glasses while we talk."

Gilda stepped inside a spacious sitting room filled with huge chairs, thick rugs, and electric lamps burning brightly beside heavy candles in polished silver holders. A fire burned in the fireplace although the evening was not very chilly. Sorel indicated chairs near the fire and plopped down unceremoniously in one nearest it. He wore a fully cut, elegant blue suit and soft, velvet shoes in the same shade. His bulky body looked extremely tidy and mobile. His sartorial splendor made Gilda anxious for her new clothes to arrive.

Sorel's eyes betrayed a dark corner of concern before he even spoke. "I hear you've met Samuel."

"Yes, he was introduced to me in the salon where Eleanor and I took tea." Gilda felt a bit like a child explaining herself to a parent.

"I was referring to his approach to you this evening, on this street."

Gilda did not conceal her surprise. Her honest expression washed away Sorel's mood. His familiar laugh boomed and his eyes began to twinkle in the way that Gilda had, in this short time, already come to anticipate.

"You'll find this is more a village than a city, my dear. Everyone knows everything here; at least they think they do. I only wished to warn you not to let Samuel upset you. He's a very disturbed person."

"He holds a grudge against you. I found that disturbing. I've taken you at your word and begun to look upon you and Anthony as family, so I wanted to understand his ill feelings toward you...and toward Eleanor."

"It's a rather unpleasant story. And one in which he is not wholly blameless. He's weak, self-centered."

"Samuel called Eleanor a deceiver. He says that she killed his wife."

"Her life has become devoted to the thrill of entrancing others," Sorel said. "As they grow more enthralled with her, she grows stronger. On its surface a harmless addiction, I suppose, but one she's not managed well."

"It's difficult to see any of this in the charming woman I've been with all afternoon."

"I know that. It has been difficult for all of us to see what Eleanor's life has become. We are a small community. Those of us who can withstand that uneasy pulling of the sea's waters swirling about the bay feel firmly rooted here and protective of each other. That has included Eleanor. But this thing with Samuel and his wife is very upsetting for many of us."

"How could she have killed someone? I don't understand." Again Gilda felt like a child set down among her elders. The weight of Sorel's manner told her he spoke the truth, yet it was counter to everything she felt about Eleanor.

"I'm sure Bird has talked to you of those of us who live through terror, thrill-seeking. Not everyone has the instinct for love. Eleanor lives through deception, the thrill of conquest. When she is done she moves on to the next and the next. This is a seaport town. Many people visit her salon."

"This doesn't make any sense to me."

"It won't until you let yourself understand our world better. We have life, but this does not mean we are better people. In fact, we must struggle even more than mortals do to remain good. How easy it is for goodness to have no meaning when punishment, retribution—or hell—have no meaning. It makes as much sense for Eleanor to choose thrill-seeking or Samuel to choose murder as it does for you and me to choose love and family."

"But what of Samuel's wife? And why does Samuel feel as he does about you and Anthony?"

"I think we can leave the first question 'til later. I can't bear to talk of death now. Perhaps in a day or two when we've had more time together. As to the second, it is rather simple. Both Anthony and I tried to warn him. To make him let go of his obsession with Eleanor. It is difficult to face the living evidence of your own foolishness on a daily basis. And that brings us to Bird."

Sorel rose from his chair with a litheness that surprised no one who had spent any time in his company. The glide of his step was so delicate that his feet appeared to barely touch the carpet. His large hand was graceful as it plucked the champagne bottle from its bucket. He gently popped the cork and admired the bubbles as they poured into the slender glasses. Sorel returned to Gilda and handed her the glass in a light but expansive gesture.

"Although most of us have no tolerance for food or drink, all of my children enjoy champagne. It must be an inherited trait—in the blood, perhaps." His eyes sparkled like the bubbles as he resumed his seat.

"When Bird looked at you she saw how she had failed in her duties," Sorel began. "It made her bitter. She had the good sense to separate from you, to renew her acquaintance with herself and her own people rather than to stay about longer than she could bear and re-create her bitterness in you. She remained at Woodard's long enough to be certain you were trained in our ways. Eventually the people of that town would have begun to wonder at her enduring youth. You yourself must have seen some of that."

"Yes, the women sometimes commented on it just beyond my hearing, or so they thought. They attributed it to my blackness. To them the African has a magical power over the appearance of youth."

"That must explain my enduring good looks then!" Sorel said, laughing.

"Then there are strains of Africa in your blood as well?" Gilda asked, peering more closely at the pale skin and dark eyes.

"In what great, civilized nation are there not?" Sorel leaned forward and tapped the rim of her glass with his own.

"For Bird to move onto her own path was inevitable," he continued. "I'm afraid she just didn't prepare you properly for it. And that was a result of her own tumultuous feelings—sadness at not living up to her duties to aid a loved one who wished to pass on to the true death, and her need to see her own people from whom she's been separated for so many years. While she has prospered, they have not. She could not but feel these things difficult to explain."

"But we had always spoken of what was in our hearts to each other. It was to her that I first told the stories of my mother and sisters. The work on the plantation. It was to her that I first described the blood on my fingertips and on the cotton which frightened me so much as a child. And she told me of her mother and her brothers thinking she was a witch, making her leave their camp to keep from contracting the fever. She said these things to me full of pain."

"Yes, but she spoke to you as a child. Now you are an adult, and it is often impossible to see that transition in our children. Her confidences of the earlier years were ones made to help heal a child.

She could not bring herself to turn to you for advice. When she is able she will come to you. Or if you need her dearly enough. I think the most important thing for you to do in the meantime is live. It is a very involving job, which takes much concentration and practice."

Sorel looked up at the sound of the knock on the door. Anthony entered, whispered in Sorel's ear, then picked up the champagne bottle and poured more wine into their glasses.

"Anthony tells me I have some guests I must address personally. If you like, Anthony can relocate you and the grapes at our table in the salon, and we'll move on to lighter topics." He rose and hesitated barely a moment for her response and then swept out through the heavy door.

"It's a tiresome city official who likes to make much of his ability to sign—or not sign—permits. He always arrives too early or leaves too late and must have Sorel take notice personally," said Anthony.

He picked up the bucket with the wine and ice. "And you may want to stop in your room before joining us in the salon. A package was delivered for you."

"Oh, Anthony, what? What is it?" she asked breathlessly.

"How am I to know? I'm not in the habit of opening the packages of others unbidden." Gilda rushed around him and up the stairway to the foyer leading to the main stairs. She was running unceremoniously, unaware that those about to enter the gambling room stood gaping at her. She remembered the first time she exchanged gifts with the women at Woodard's. The mystery of wrapped packages still left her breathless. She felt the same as she had when she received her first crinoline or her first pen so many years before.

In her room a brown paper bundle sat securely tied with string wrapped generously around it. She pulled the string to one side like a child, struggling with the wrapping a moment before she remembered her strength. She snapped the ties, then folded the paper back to reveal a lavender wool two-piece dress with black piping. The rich color belied the severity of the cut. A note fell from the folds:

I remembered this old suit from some bygone day and rushed it back to the dressmaker. I promised her much more than she deserved if she was able to complete your personal alterations within four hours. I sent my mes-

*senger to oversee the task. Perhaps it was his stern gaze that made her nee-
dles fly. I would be most pleased to see you wearing this gift when next we
meet. Until then, an eternity, Eleanor.*

Gilda clasped the note in her hand as she held the dress in front
of her. It was like nothing she'd ever worn before, but clearly the
dressmaker had taken her instruction well. The wide skirt had been
divided to make a pantlike garment that would not be unduly noticed. She could feel her heart pounding and see by the movement
of the note in the mirror how her hand trembled. "Oh, dear
mothers, what is this?" Gilda spoke to the silent room.

She laid the dress across the armchair and went back downstairs
to the salon. Anthony poured champagne for her as soon as she
took her seat at Sorel's table. She looked casually about the room,
meeting all eyes that dared to meet hers. She enjoyed listening to
their thoughts, or screening them out while listening to her own
heartbeat. All was simply passing time until her meeting with
Eleanor in two days.

Several hours later, she and Anthony walked back toward Sorel's
together. He related some of the history of the town and pointed
out the main houses of the area—Duncan's, Ralston's, Sutro's. And
then the church, Mission Dolores, whose cool quiet reached out for
Gilda. They sat in the churchyard to listen to the fog and boats on
the distant bay below.

"Although its name means sadness, I've always enjoyed the solid
familiarity of the chapel and its grounds. And it is the sole place
where one may be assured of privacy."

Gilda turned to look at Anthony, catching a concerned tone un-
derlying his words. "What privacy must we need that can't be found
at Sorel's?"

"Maybe it's not really isolation from people themselves, but other
distractions—wine, colors, music. These often obscure the issues
that must be addressed."

"I haven't known you long, my friend, but I feel you're walking
widely around some unpleasant task. Your anxiety arouses my
own," said Gilda.

Anthony looked at her more directly now. "I speak only because
I do consider myself your friend, your family now. But I know that
you've not been with us long and don't know our ways, or at least
the ways some of us have chosen."

"It's been a mere, what, forty years since I made my way to free-dom? A rather small time, I understand, in comparison to others. But for me it's much longer than I could ever have hoped to live. See-ing those you love pass from you either under a lash or simply of old age before their time is not something that keeps you young and innocent, as I'm sure you know. When I left New Orleans I traveled for many hundreds of miles in many directions, securing places for my native soil, opening bank accounts, establishing holdings that would endure with time as I had been taught to do. It soon became clear that although the institution of enslavement was no longer sanctioned, our world had not become a more hospitable place for me or my people. Often it was only the gifts that I acquired in this new life that saved me from those we call civilized. My safest, sur-est moments were spent in the wild with those we call animals. I doubt there's much here for which I am not prepared."

"I don't think anyone can be prepared for the deliberate murder of a human being. To some here this is a sport. I speak of it now be-cause I know Sorel. We've had the pleasure of each other's company for many years. Even in the face of brutality he has a difficult time speaking of it, although he condemns it with all he knows."

Gilda felt her back stiffen. "And what murder are we speaking of, specifically?"

"The murder of Samuel's wife."

"Do you say, as he does, that this was done by Eleanor?"

"No. Although I'm certain she's capable of it." Anthony rushed on to keep Gilda from interrupting. "Her game is to instigate de-struction and watch the pieces topple rather than wield the sword. She thrives on the energy fueled by rampant jealousy and compe-tition. She is one of those who does not bother to remember the faces."

Gilda sucked in her breath sharply. She heard Bird's voice tell-ing her that death was inevitable for all life. It was the wanton de-struction of life to no purpose that was the sin.

She had spoken softly, as if respect could only be truly conveyed in whispers: "There will be a time when death comes at your hand. When this happens, when you must protect yourself or those in your care, the real sin would be in taking life easily. The only way to maintain any humanity is to remember the faces of those who've died. To carry them within ourselves so that whatever good might have remained in their spirits has someplace to dwell. You cannot kill, then forget their faces without forgetting some part of yourself."

Gilda did not believe that Eleanor was capable of such callousness. Anthony could see the disbelief entrenching itself further behind Gilda's silence. "I don't ask that you believe me. Only remember the things in which we keep faith and believe that it's possible there are others for whom the word *faith* has no meaning. When you see this in someone's face you'll know it."

"What I see is an immense hunger for companionship, for love."

"Because that is what you want to see," Anthony continued. "I say these things not to upset your new-found enjoyment nor to drive you away from us. I say them for the same reason I said them to Samuel—because they are true. His disbelief saved neither his wife nor him." Anthony stood stiffly. "I've many things to attend to in the salon. I'll tell Sorel you'll be along before he retires." Anthony disappeared past the headstones into the diffused evening light.

Gilda remained apart from Anthony and Sorel in the days following this conversation. Both men seemed to be watching for her anxiously whenever she appeared. On the afternoon Gilda expected Eleanor to come for her, she dressed in the purple outfit Eleanor had provided. It was firm across her back and fell softly over her thighs. She loved the feel of the material moving around her body, as if a breeze attended her. In spite of her confusion she couldn't resist seeking out Sorel before setting off in her new clothes. She found him in the salon at his table reading a newspaper. When she came through the doors his face lit up—first with simple pleasure that she appeared to be seeking him out and then with excitement at her new appearance. She had pulled her hair back in one braid circling the base of her head at her neck and added combs with small pearls at each side. She no longer resembled the frightened girl Bird had spoken of but was a woman of style and purpose.

"Ah, it is the west and Gilda is the moon!" Sorel said, letting his affection and admiration flood the room.

She moved quickly through the salon, aware that the late-lunchtime patrons were looking at her. She tried to slip into the seat, but Sorel held her hand to his lips and would not let her sit. "You must not hurry when you are dressed as a monarch. That is cruel to those of us who've hungered to gaze upon you."

Anthony came up behind them with the glasses that seemed to always be at hand. "Perhaps she's not as gluttonous for attention as some of us." He nudged between them with his narrow hip, making Gilda fall onto the settee unceremoniously. She laughed, relieved to be somewhat less on display. Sorel sat with an aggrieved expression. "By that I suppose you mean me?"

"Not at all. I meant myself," said Anthony coyly, "for it's I who continually stand about, with all eyes on me wondering whom I shall attend next. Creating conversation and curiosity wherever I go."

The three laughed while Anthony poured champagne into the glasses. When he had retreated, Sorel was quiet. Gilda took several moments to think of what to say. She expected Eleanor's driver at any moment, yet she wanted to begin her afternoon with good feelings.

"I feel a bit like an errant child. I've much confusion about everything that is going on around me. It is a new world for me."

"Yes, Anthony has told me many times that I'm much too self-involved to notice that others take many different paths. I fear I may not have accepted your independent judgment as honestly as I should. Perhaps learning most of what I know about you through Bird's reminiscences of you as a child has weighted my perspective too much."

As Sorel took a breath, Gilda sat forward with her question. "I must ask this—please know I feel I must or I would not. Do you believe that Eleanor killed Samuel's wife?"

"No, I don't!" Sorel's response was vehement. "But what was done was, in some ways, much worse. The death of Samuel's sadly neglected wife was a blessing; the sin was in bringing her into the family at all. She was young, gullible, quite taken with Eleanor, and after the years of ill-treatment by that fool, it was not a surprising turn of events. It was a sorry, sorry occurrence that I regret, one that I tried to but could not prevent."

"But what of her part?" Gilda asked, trying to keep her voice even.

"Many things are within our power. To draw others close, to enrapture them, is a simple one. Eleanor partakes of the joy of our existence merely through the exercise of this power."

"But I'm no plain, neglected wife searching for attention. Why do you and Anthony insist that I must be wary of her?"

"You, my dear, are even more of a challenge: an equal—a mystery. Don't underestimate the magnitude of her need."

"But you seem to care for her so."

"I do. I've known her since she was a child. It was only through an error in judgment, my own, that she is as she is today." Sorel seemed to have shrunk inside his unhappiness. "I thought she would become more mature. Learn to respect our ways. Clearly in my anxiousness to keep her with me I had not really looked at who she was or what her real relationship was to this world. She is as a daughter to me, but one who only takes. In a charming, entrancing way, but only takes—never gives."

Sorel looked up as a footman approached their table and said no more. Gilda stood and leaned down to kiss Sorel. She held one dark hand against his pale cheek and pressed her lips against his face. She was afraid of his words and saw how difficult this had been for him. She whispered, "I'm not alone. My fears were misplaced."

Gilda was surprised to see Eleanor's eager face as the coachman opened the door to the coach. "Wait," she said, making Gilda stand a moment before climbing in, much as Sorel had done. "Yes, the color and cut fit you wonderfully. I thought so." Gilda felt heat rise in her face but simply concentrated on lifting the skirt and climbed into the carriage.

"It was very kind of you to loan me this—"

"Don't be silly. It was meant for you, for you to wear it for me. Now," she tapped the side of the coach, "I've a wonderful surprise." She said no more as the carriage made its way through the late-afternoon streets. It halted at the pier, and the coachman held their hands in his leather-clad grip as they stepped down into the milling crowd. Eleanor pushed her way forward, ignoring annoyed glances. A young man who stood at the front of a line of people waiting to purchase tickets turned stiffly, but immediately smiled at Eleanor's glowing presence. He touched his hand briefly to his cap and stood aside to let them purchase tickets for the ferry across the bay.

Gilda's stomach lurched when she realized the nature of the surprise, but she remained quiet as they backed away from the others who were waiting and boarded the ferry. Her mind raced for the source of her panic. She knew the dangers of water, its ability to draw their powers from them, yet she also knew there were many of their kind who took sea journeys. Sorel and Anthony themselves were proof of the protection their home soil afforded them. Yet

Gilda felt herself shift uncomfortably inside her own skin.

She noticed that Eleanor clung tightly to her arm as she guided her inside the small, open-air enclosure, and continued to do so even when they were seated. Neither spoke as the ferry filled around them, nor during the damp, rolling journey across the bay. As soon as the boat docked, Eleanor left it with the same precipitous gait. Gilda followed close behind.

Eleanor did not slow her stride until they were somewhat away from the crowd. "That's where we go," Eleanor said, pointing at a green peak rising sharply just north of where they stood. Gilda looked puzzled but was so pleased to be on solid ground again she didn't care if it was the side of a mountain.

Around them some people were boarding a small caboose that seemed to climb by a circuitous route. More people were walking toward the ferry. Gilda and Eleanor moved away from the bay on a broad path marked by wagon ruts. Eleanor pulled her skirts tightly around her and said with an impish smile, "I suppose you feel quite superior, you with your bloomers! They're quite appropriate today, eh?"

"I don't think I could have resisted wearing this dress, no matter the journey." Gilda pulled up her hem and tucked the ends into her waistband.

"Mt. Tamalpais," Eleanor said after a few minutes at a brisk pace, and turned toward the woods. At first they strolled easily. Gilda took in the magnificent size of the trees and the musky scent of the undergrowth. It reminded her somewhat of the pine forests she slept in during her travels away from Woodard's. There didn't seem to be a trail cut into the woodland, but Eleanor proceeded with assurance. They stopped several times to admire large, low-lying foliage and once to observe a small stump covered so thickly with dotted lady bugs that they seemed to be undulating flesh. Because they were not following any of the trails others used, they passed no one, although on occasion they heard voices as visitors passed downward out of the chill of the late afternoon.

Gilda enjoyed the solitude—and the companionship. She had begun to feel the pulse of the town in which she had arrived so full of anxiety and questions. She could see its beauty, understand why Anthony and Sorel would wish to live here. The lights of the city were simple diversions; these woods and this mountain were at the real heart of what California was. They reached the top quickly, even with their minor explorations. The undergrowth was thick, but Eleanor led Gilda to the western slope to a spot she had obviously visited before.

They stepped out of the trees as if onto a balcony, and the red ball of the sun slipped gracefully downward before them as if it knew they were looking. Gilda gasped and stepped backward reflexively into the trees' shadow.

"It's alright. The hems are woven with your soil. And here, just at this juncture, with the sun so close to the horizon, the rays have little effect."

Eleanor clasped Gilda's hand and pulled her closer. They watched the sun's color shift and change in reverent silence. Eleanor slipped her arm around Gilda's shoulder protectively. The rhythm of their breathing synchronized as they let the slight warmth of the sun touch them. It soon dropped behind the horizon, and darkness gathered in the woods around them. They stood for a moment, Eleanor still holding Gilda.

When she was able to speak, Gilda said, "That was one of the most beautiful sights I've ever seen. I had no idea such a thing was possible. I mean without covering or shelter. . . so close." Her voice was filled with awe.

"I've wanted to show this to someone, someone who would see it as I do. The closeness of it." Eleanor turned back toward the now dim horizon with its spray of colors fading behind. "So close, yet far. We will never look upon the sun with the innocence and delight that others have. Here the fog that rolls in off the bay constantly makes the sun a hidden treasure."

"How long have you been coming here?"

"Since I was a little girl. My uncle first brought me after my parents died in the fire. It was Christmas many decades ago. So many people died. . . homes were destroyed. He pointed toward the setting sun and told me that I mustn't be too sad because they were there—and didn't that look like a wonderful place to be?"

Eleanor's voice sounded almost like a child's. "He took such good care of me all those years. He tried to give me the things he thought my parents would want for me. So hard he worked. When I look at him now, shrunken and weak, it's difficult to remember him with a short sword cutting his way through the undergrowth and branches until he found just the right spot so the sun would be close enough to feel. Now I wait for him to die, to join them there—to stop looking at me with fear and confusion, wondering why I remain young and he grows old."

"What then, when there's no one left to remember you as a child?" Gilda asked.

"There's always Sorel and Anthony," Eleanor said with a hard-edged laugh. "Let's get back," she added sullenly.

They made their way down the slope quickly, arriving just as the ferry was preparing to load the few remaining citizens who'd spent time on the mountain or with the giant redwood trees at its base. They sat on a bench at an angle so they were able to watch Tamalpais disappearing in the fog as the ferry returned to the city. The carriage and driver were waiting in the same spot, and in a few moments they were seated under a lap robe, being driven to Eleanor's salon.

After their arrival, Eleanor told Gilda to follow her, and walked toward the back hallway. The encountered a woman in an apron about to enter a kitchen. Eleanor ordered warm water and towels, then she and Gilda went into a small anteroom behind the main room. Within moments the maid appeared with a wash basin and steaming pitcher. Two fluffy towels hung from her arm as she strained with the heavy burden. Eleanor had collapsed on a settee beside a small table and lamp. She jumped up as soon as the girl set the water on its stand. "Go, go," she said impatiently, and the girl backed out of the room.

"This city is filled with such mud it's possible there could be more here than on all of the mountain. But still. . ." Eleanor was speaking distractedly as she wiped at the dirt on her face and hands. She then dusted the hem of her skirt. "Next time, perhaps we'll both wear breeches and caps."

They finished removing the dust and leaves that clung to their clothes and walked back out to the public room. Once again a bottle of wine was brought to their table before Eleanor spoke. Gilda looked around the room, this time more carefully than when she had visited before. The patrons of the early evening were few. Eleanor spoke just as Gilda noticed this. "We are more likely to entertain guests later in the evening, after the theater. One night we had what felt like all of the Tivoli in here at once. Clamoring for wine and the like."

Gilda could hear the hint of disdain in Eleanor's voice and wondered why she bothered with such an endeavor if she didn't enjoy it. And again Eleanor responded, "One must find ways of keeping up with people. Sorel is quite right, this is the best way of doing so—"

"Please don't do that," Gilda said.

Eleanor looked surprised. Then a subtle shift in her features conveyed hurt feelings. Gilda felt that perhaps she had done something wrong, although she was taught that to so casually take advantage of the ability to read the thoughts of others was rude as well as a poor substitute for interaction. Nonetheless, she couldn't help thinking she had been too sharp with Eleanor.

"I just feel uncomfortable when you answer my questions before I've been allowed to decide whether or not to ask them."

Eleanor didn't quite look mollified but sipped from her wine without saying anything.

Gilda continued. "On the plantation all of our activities, all of our needs were supposedly met. We were told what we could eat, what we could wear, when to waken, when to retire for the evening. My mother resented that bitterly. She did all she could to make small variations in the routine, in the proscriptions, so there was some sense that our lives were our own. She used to say, 'It's a gift. We can keep our thoughts to ourselves and out of their hands.' My thoughts have often been the only place I could live freely."

Eleanor looked contrite as she took Gilda's hand in her own. "Please forgive me. Sorel says I'm like a spoiled child sometimes. I just wanted us to be close. I'd not thought about how different your life has been from mine. Tell me about the plantation. I've wondered what it would be like." Her voice was again like a child's, thoughtlessly probing.

"There's little I can tell you, really. I remember things as if I'd seen them through a very small window. The backs of my sisters and the others dragging long bags of cotton, the sound of their breathing, much too heavy for children. My mother sweating in the cook house. I don't remember her anywhere but inside the house. Isn't that odd? Only in the kitchen or going up to take care of some illness or other. But never out back where my sisters slept. I know she went down to the cabins when the preacher came, but I don't remember her there with me. I remember how it felt when she held my hand. It was a narrow world, much of which I've gratefully forgotten."

"But tell me of your escape. Bird spoke of that to Sorel."

Gilda didn't want to reach so deeply inside. She related the bare facts of her decision to escape and the simplicity of it.

"But Bird said you had to kill a man to get away?" There was a curl of excitement to her question.

"Yes."

"How old were you then?"

"Much too young to have to kill someone. It's not something I care to dwell on, Eleanor, as I'm certain you can understand. At any rate, my life at Woodard's was much more interesting."

With that she began to talk of the women at Woodard's, and how she and Bird used to infuriate the shopkeepers with their language games. Gilda and Eleanor passed several more hours talking and laughing. The room was beginning to fill with noisy patrons and smoke.

"I think it's time I return you to Sorel before he sends out the Vigilance Society to rescue you from my clutches." Eleanor waved and caught the attention of a waiter whom she instructed to alert the coachman. "I hope we can have many other adventures together."

Gilda felt the soft fluttering of her heart as Eleanor's voice dropped to an almost imperceptible level. "Yes, I'd like that."

"I will plan an outing to the opera next time. You might as well get a whiff of California culture. We've the best houses anywhere, I'm told. The dressmaker should have completed her tasks within the month. We can test our design skills on the public."

Alone in the carriage returning to Sorel's, Gilda tried to imagine what an opera house would be like and how she would look in the gown she had ordered. When she entered the salon Anthony met her at the door. The room was considerably quieter than the room at Eleanor's and somehow did not have the overhanging cloud of smoke.

"Sorel's gone to his room to read for the evening, but he asked that you have some wine if you wish." Gilda felt let down that Sorel was not around. She turned to leave. "I think I'll go out on my own for a while. Perhaps when I come back."

Gilda left and was down the driveway before Anthony could speak. She walked aimlessly for some time before realizing she was back on the dock where she'd been earlier with Eleanor to catch the ferry. It was almost deserted, but the sound of music and voices from nearby taverns prevented it from feeling totally abandoned. Gilda looked out across the bay. She could see little past the fog-enshrouded harbor.

She turned away from the disquieting tidal waters and leaned back on the railing, listening to the darkness. A man several yards away walked toward one of the pubs. She let her mind draw him down the pier to her. When he emerged from the fog he had a look of vague surprise. She pulled him to her and held him in her mind's control, then sliced the flesh on his neck and took the blood while listening for his thoughts. She insinuated herself inside his preoccupations, seeking out one that might benefit from her aid. When she had slipped an idea of her own in among his, she felt the loosening of his unconscious, Gilda closed the wound and leaned him gently against the gate. She sped away from him, then slowed to enjoy the feeling of the damp mist on her skin. Gilda strolled casually, ignoring the fact that she was one of the few women on the street. The men who moved around her looked curious but said nothing. They were startled by her dark skin and the force of her stride.

Once back in the salon, Gilda sat at Sorel's table and waited for Anthony. The bartender smiled at her in greeting. Some of the patrons didn't give her more than a glance. Gilda was comforted by even these casual indications of her place within the household.

"Are you well?" Anthony asked as he stood beside the table.

"Yes. I was just listening to thoughts."

"Sorel was worried when you didn't return."

"I'm sorry. He needn't have worried. Eleanor and I had a wonderful evening, visiting our childhoods."

"She rarely talks about that time, of her parents, or the fire in which they died."

"I think she's changing, Anthony. She spoke of them, of her uncle, and even took me to a secret place she's known since her childhood. Whatever has haunted her seems to be surfacing, ready to be expelled."

"I wish it were true, for Sorel's sake as well as hers."

Gilda was surprised to hear the note of desperation in Anthony's voice.

"Eleanor has meant much to Sorel. It's a great sadness for him that she's turned out to be so difficult. She's not been able to be happy and has insisted on making others miserable. Sorel feels quite responsible. In some ways, he is. In any case he'll never leave California while Eleanor is so unpredictable. This thing with

Samuel and his wife has almost undone him." Anthony sat down beside Gilda, exhausted by the words.

"And what exactly is this thing with Samuel? It's a mystery no one wishes to clear, it seems. What am I supposed to believe: your innuendos or Sorel's?"

"There are facts, Gilda. Eleanor took Samuel's wife. She did this against all reason. And, in a fit of childishness, she took Samuel as well. We tried to warn each of them, but to little effect. When his wife was found, Samuel swore Eleanor had taken her life. Eleanor was not the one who took the final drop of blood from her, who hacked her head from her body. But we assume Samuel did this to be with Eleanor. She continues to taunt him as if these were children's games with no consequence. The danger I speak of is the chance that you will become tied to Eleanor before you see what else there may be for you. And with Eleanor comes Samuel. The stink of his horror and guilt is there for all of us. You've no need to take this into your life."

"But I've told you, she's grown wiser. These were horrible events, yes, but the results of her inexperience, her fears. When I made my way from the plantation, before I was found and brought to Woodard's, I had to act rashly to save my life. I killed a man. I've no regret that he is dead and that I survived. Only that the choice had to be made at all. This does not mean I have the soul of a murderer. Eleanor needs the time to learn who she is in this life just as I do."

"She has as much time as she needs. As do we all."

When the evening deepened, Gilda went to her room to take her rest. She double-bolted the inner and outer doors, checked the windows, and hung her outfit across the chair. Sitting at the desk and writing in her journal, she realized how much she missed having her trunk with her. She put it in storage when she left Woodard's but knew that now she might send for it. The metal cross her mother had given her, the frayed clothes she had worn when she was found and brought to Woodard's, the comforter from her bed there—all these were simple items she had no real need for, but which represented the family as she knew it.

Gilda finally laid down on the covered Mississippi soil, her enthusiasm for the evening muted by the solemnity of her talk with Anthony. Deep inside her, however, was the kernel of excitement and curiosity—new dresses, the opera, and Eleanor at her side. Gilda closed her eyes with some difficulty and asked the night to take her.

By the time her dresses were ready and Eleanor had announced what evening they would attend the opera, Gilda had spent additional time with Sorel in which the budding relationship between the two women was not the topic. But there remained an undercurrent of sadness in Sorel whenever Eleanor or her driver appeared at the salon to call for Gilda.

Eleanor and Gilda were both surprised when Sorel announced that he and Anthony were also attending the opera the same evening and asked that they meet beforehand in his salon. Gilda's formal gown was a stunning success, but no more so than Eleanor's red gown in a design suggesting modesty in spite of the scarlet hue.

Gilda was fascinated by the soft weight of the skirt at her own waist and the light reflecting on the fabric. For once, she had little concern for what others were thinking as they observed her. In the lobby of the theater she was much too busy looking at them. The glitter of jewelry was a sight she had never imagined. It seemed a foolish competition with the light off the bay and the electric lights that circled it.

The four of them were an elegant ensemble. Gilda was so excited by being with Sorel, Anthony, and Eleanor together that she could hardly pay attention to the singing. She tried to understand the meaning of the ear-shattering sounds and ponderous movements around the stage but realized that any appreciation she had for the opera would be achieved later, under less distracting circumstances. The music and movement stirred her, but not in the way it was intended. It brought to the surface long-buried memories of the songs the workers sang on the plantation.

She felt the monumental elegance of the rhythms and the urgency that had been missing from her life for some time. She had not heard music such as that since her escape. Sometimes the women at Woodard's would sing around the piano, country songs from their childhoods, or bawdy songs from the wharf, but nowhere did she hear sounds as compelling as those she had run away from. She added music to her growing list of reasons to remain with Sorel for a while. And for the first time she had something to look forward to.

After the program was over, the four of them hurried away from the bustling audience. They offered greetings to the many people who recognized Sorel but did not stay to talk with anyone. Eleanor was met by her driver and reluctantly left Gilda with Sorel and Anthony. Once back in Sorel's rooms the three—Sorel, Anthony, and Gilda—sat quietly in front of his fire, each listening to individual thoughts.

Sorel spoke first. "I'm pleased we were able to spend this time with you and Eleanor. You seem to have had a salutary effect on her."

"I think she's needed someone closer to her own age. . ." Gilda started.

The three of them laughed uproariously and spent another hour talking of the opera and its audience. Gilda excused herself when she began to feel the need to go out for the blood. She wanted time alone to think of the music and clothes she'd seen. She went to her room and donned the dark breeches, jacket, and cap she wore when she went out at night. In spite of her enthusiasm for the evening's gowns and jewels, returning to the clothes she had worn on the road soothed her.

As the weeks passed, Gilda most often hunted for the blood alone. Occasionally she shared the time with Anthony simply because they enjoyed walking the city together. Eleanor had asked once if she would like to join her to search for the blood, but Gilda said no. Afterward Gilda was uncertain why she responded this way. Her trips with Eleanor remained, for the most part, afternoon forays to dressmakers or other merchants where one or both of them made purchases.

Sorel promised to arrange other theater excursions in the coming weeks, but Eleanor remained noncommital. Gilda visited Eleanor's salon frequently, and they sat together talking of their pasts for hours, ignoring the patrons around them. With Eleanor, Gilda saw much of the surrounding countryside and learned about the medicinal plants, flowers, and animals that existed on the edge of the city.

Coming downstairs one evening to await Eleanor's coach, Gilda entered the salon hoping to spend some time with Sorel before she went out for the evening. Her trunk had arrived intact and sat comfortably in her room. With its arrival, Gilda felt her place here secured.

She had examined the soft leather case and its practical knife, wondering where Bird kept the old knife she had given her in exchange for this one. The rough cross from Gilda's mother had an

odd attachment for her. She knew it was a Christian symbol although her mother had not really believed in their God. She had
clung to the dim memories of the gods of her homeland. The cross
was more a signpost. It marked a time in life, like the signs erected
at crossroads. She had packed the comforter at the last moment,
not really sure why. It was a crude thing made by one of the girls,
the hem not quite finished because of the need to wrap it for some
holiday. Gilda's things now seemed natural additions to her room.

Sorel joined her in the salon as soon as he heard she was there
but waited for her to speak. Gilda wasn't certain how to express her
sense of satisfaction. She spoke anyway. "I understand more now
why Bird felt as she did. I understand it's only a turn, that our roads
can meet in the future. I don't have to run after her. My life is wherever I am."

Although his voice remained even, Sorel looked angry as he
said, "So you've given up your search?"

"No, I've just come to believe, as you said, Bird will seek me out
when she's ready. I still await word."

"And in the meantime?" Sorel asked.

"I will stay with you, if I may. Learn the lessons that remain for
me. There are still many ways that I must become accustomed to."
Gilda felt Anthony just behind her and looked up at him. He was
staring intently at Sorel, as if he wished to still his speaking. Gilda
was unnerved by what appeared to be discord between the two
men.

She went on in the hope of making Sorel understand the clarity she had recently begun to feel. "I've no doubt Bird will return
to my life, but I must not suspend my progress until that time. Perhaps I don't need her at this moment as much as I'd thought."

"Don't think that you replace one with the other: Bird with
Eleanor. Let me assure you that Eleanor is in no way suitable as a
substitute for anyone, least of all Bird." Sorel's voice was tight with
anxiety. "She will fail you in ways that Bird never could."

"She's not tried to leave me."

"In time you might wish that she did." Sorel took a deep breath
before going on. "I love her as my own, but you will see she has only
her own interests in her heart. There's no room for any other. I cannot talk of her as if she's no concern to me, but look honestly at her
as I've done. The women who brought you into this world were
honest, honorable, devoted people. The gift of life was in them be-

fore they joined this family. Eleanor is beautiful, charming, clever, but she does not have that gift. She may never have it. Becoming one of us merely bestows the power of long life. It cannot light the fire of living in one who has no spark of it."

Sorel's words sat heavily on Gilda as she rode to her meeting with Eleanor. She decided to put them aside and use only her power of observation and visceral reactions—much as she had done when among the night animals on the road. This would decide her course of action. Still, she was shaken by the obvious truth that hung in the air: in all their time together it was Eleanor who controlled every moment. Gilda began to taste her own naiveté in responding to desire, a sensation with which she had had little experience.

Once the footman had escorted her to Eleanor's table and she was seated across from Eleanor, looking into the deep green of her eyes, Gilda fought her sensation of falling.

"The outfit is perfect, you beautiful thing. And who'd believe such a devilish pantaloon contraption would be so engaging. Look how everyone gazes at you and tries to pretend they're not.

"Yes, I'm so grateful for your help these past weeks." Gilda was silent, uncertain how to continue.

"Don't be silly. It was a purely selfish act. As anyone will tell you, that's my only motivation. How could we have the delightful evenings together that we've had with you in dusty breeches? That's not the sort of company I could endure, I assure you." Eleanor's eyes flashed with mischievousness.

The room felt close to Gilda. Unlike Sorel's rooms these seemed stuffy, smoky, noisy. The men at the bar were a bit loud and drank too much. The edge in the conversations around her felt too close for her to be comfortable among these strangers. Gilda looked around the room and recognized a few faces, regulars here but ones seldom seen at Sorel's. She thought she glimpsed Samuel slipping out the door. She recognized the intensity in the bend of his body. He frequently hung around the edges of the room when she was present but had not approached her since that night on the street.

A deep exhaustion descended over Gilda that begged for quiet, a cessation of thoughts, simple enjoyments rather than the complexity of the unknown. She felt trapped here among these anxious people. Within her view were at least four others like herself and Eleanor. In their faces she could see juvenile preoccupations or convoluted machinations, the need to be entertained at any expense.

"Might we walk outside for a while? I'd like some air," Gilda said. Eleanor looked puzzled for a moment but signaled over her shoulder. A waiter appeared, and she told him to bring her a cape. They stepped out into a cool fog. She dismissed her driver, and the two of them walked downhill toward the bay. Eleanor linked her arm through Gilda's and then spoke. "What is it, my little one? You seem distracted. I've been waiting for so many days to be with you again, and you seem to be somewhere else."

"Yes, I think that's true. There's so much for me to learn while I'm here—"

"And I intend to teach you—"

"Sorel and Anthony have done quite well, thus far."

"What is it? Do you worry about your Bird? I think you must learn that we all make our own lives. That's just the way of it."

"No, Bird is not a concern for the moment." She was silent as they continued their walk down the shadowy street. Eleanor pulled her suddenly toward the darkness beside an unlit house.

"Why are you hiding from me?" She held Gilda's gaze in a grip of fire. Gilda felt her body yielding, sinking into the soft, satin-covered breasts. She tried to break the gaze but could not. Eleanor's mouth was on hers, and Gilda pressed harder into its fierce strength reaching out for her.

The kiss bruised her mouth. Yet Gilda matched its power, feeding a need inside her like no other she had experienced before. Her hand became entangled in the mass of red curls, and she pulled at it while pressing Eleanor's mouth tighter to her own. She heard only her own breath and Eleanor's. The woodframe building behind them seemed to creak with the energy of their bodies against it. The dry, old wood sounded as if it would ignite with the desire that passed between them.

Gilda felt the sharpness of Eleanor's teeth as she bit her lip and continued to press her mouth onto Gilda's, taking in her blood. Gilda became confused, unsure how to protect herself. She did not want to be bound to this woman by blood, but her desire was a tide she feared she could not resist.

She heard nothing in the world except the beating of their hearts and their breath rushing between them. She felt only the silkiness of Eleanor's hair in her hand and Eleanor's iron grip at her back until the sound of a crash echoed somewhere, perhaps inside her own head.

She staggered backward, unable to imagine what had fallen from the building's upper stories to daze her. She looked upward at the blank eyes of the building as her knees buckled and she toppled over. She closed her eyes for a second, then panicked.

"Eleanor," she screamed, and tried to focus the blur. Eleanor was there, against the wall, with a look of horror spreading across her face. And there, too, was Samuel.

"I warned you to leave us, you black demon. I warned you." Samuel's face was engorged with hatred. He turned to Eleanor as if to hit her, but her look of horror quickly became one of derision. He turned back to continue directing his anger at Gilda.

She recovered herself and sprang to her feet. "Samuel, you're a foolish man. You've nothing to gain by this."

Gilda felt blood slipping down through her hair, staining the collar of her new outfit. She was stunned but no longer disoriented. She could see from his eyes, almost before he was sure of it himself, that Samuel would attack again. As he came at her with the iron pipe she grabbed it in midair. He would not release his grip so Gilda swung it around in front of her, taking Samuel with it. He hit the wall beside Eleanor with a force that shook the woodframe. The pipe dropped to the ground, and he leapt at Gilda without missing a breath.

The force of his assault knocked Gilda back to the ground. He was atop her with his hands at her throat. She had never struggled with one of her own, only those who did not understand her strength. It was a moment before she realized Samuel was not trying to strangle her but to rip open her throat. Over his shoulder she saw Eleanor standing quietly. Gilda saw her look once up and down the street to see if anyone approached, but she maintained a gellid calm that unnerved Gilda more than Samuel's attack.

Gilda used her own head to butt Samuel's face, stunning him. She forced him aside and raised herself high enough to deliver a punch to his jaw. He fell backward. The surprise seemed to have robbed him of all his strength.

"Kill him, it must be done. We must be rid of him." Eleanor's words, softly spoken, were full of desire and promise. Gilda looked down at the blond hair now laced with blood. Samuel began to gather his strength for another attack.

"You kill him, Eleanor. It's your wish that he die, not mine. He's a fool of your making."

"Kill him! He'll haunt our every step if you don't." Her urgency made her voice become more shrill. "How can we live if we don't rid ourselves of him right now?"

The face of the one man she had killed on the road north from Louisiana floated up from the quiet place in the back of her mind. And with it the revulsion she had felt at the deed. He had meant to kill her on the dark road but had died himself, never knowing why.

"How?" Gilda screamed at Eleanor. "I don't think we can live at all if we do this." Gilda invoked reason, still unable to recognize the eerie lust in Eleanor's face. Samuel looked at Eleanor with disbelief and rage. He leapt up, no longer afraid of her power over him, and sprung forward to finally vent his anger at Eleanor. She swatted outward and sent him sprawling.

"You must be done with it, I beg you." Gilda heard the forced guilelessness in Eleanor's voice that she had sensed before, but this time its falseness rang more clearly.

"No, Eleanor, I can't kill him for you." Samuel tried to stand again, his face swollen, the fire in his eyes undampened. "You best keep up your guard, Samuel. I will not kill you for her, but surely, sooner or later, someone will."

"My dearest, please understand, he's plagued me ever since the unfortunate death of his wife. A death he caused. Can't you see how he blames me? But it was he who took her final blood, not me. I couldn't stop him. He took her final blood." Eleanor's voice rose in anguish and desperation. "You have to help me be free of him. You must." This last was icily imperious.

Gilda stepped back. "I'm no longer a servant, Miss Eleanor. We been freed."

Gilda turned on her heel as she had seen Samuel do. The force of her movement and intent propelled her forward into the dark, obscuring fog.

Away from the fire of their hatred, Gilda felt uncertain what direction to take. She soon found her way toward Mission Dolores. On unsteady legs she approached the bench where she sat before with Anthony and sank down gratefully.

She began to moan. There were no tears to come to her eyes now—something she had become accustomed to once she was taken into the life. But she moaned as its equivalent, a high, keening sound of anguish as she once heard Bird do. She moaned for the loss of the one who had made her, for the loss of Bird, and for the loss of Eleanor. She moaned for the desperation of her need and desire, for the magnitude of her ignorance of the world.

"Will I ever know?" she asked aloud of the tombstones and stars. The wind around her was silent, and the fog was like a blanket. Looking at the graves of the churchyard, she was suddenly curious about what was beneath them. What would it be to lie still beneath these carved stones, to finally have peace?

"I hardly think you're ready to find out, do you?" Anthony spoke in a soft voice above her. He dropped to his knees in front of her and reached up to wipe the almost-dried blood from her brow. "Have you any wounds?"

"Not that bleed now. He was, as Sorel said, a weak man." Anthony drew a handkerchief from his coat and wiped at her face as she released a stream of words in lieu of tears. "I couldn't kill him. Even seeing how he wished to kill me, to kill her. I couldn't do it."

"There was no need. That is an important lesson," said Anthony.

"Lesson! Aren't you listening?" Gilda almost shouted. "I could have destroyed him, happily. What does that make me? I've never, in all the time that's been given me, never wanted to kill as much as I wanted it tonight. I think it was only her entreaties that saved him. Saved me. The mesmerizing innocence of her voice was betrayed by her words."

"What saved him was you. You are not as she and he are. Come home now. Sorel is waiting to spend time with you."

Gilda walked in silence back to the house. She sensed Anthony standing in the hall as she washed her face and hands in her room and changed into clean clothes. Anthony said nothing when she emerged from the room, her hair rebraided, a dark shirt hanging loosely from her shoulders. Neither spoke as they descended the back stairs to Sorel's rooms. Inside, the fire burned low; Sorel sat before it with a book open on his lap. Gilda sat opposite him. Anthony stood across the room behind her.

"There has been some trouble, then?"

"Yes. It was as you said. Eleanor. . ." Gilda stopped.

"Yes, she's not learned the true ways. She will continue to be a most unhappy child."

"If Samuel doesn't destroy her on the street where I left them."

"He won't. He's a fool but also a coward. To take the life of the one who brought him into this life is certain destruction. It would remain to me—to us—," he looked toward Anthony, "to then destroy him. You understand this? You've been taught this?"

"Yes, but it's never had much meaning. There were only the three of us. . ."

"Every lesson has meaning, Gilda. I think you must see now that it is a long life ahead. Each day will be a day to live out these lessons."

Gilda heard the sound of Bird's voice. The room seemed filled with her presence. "I hold a grief inside of me that will not give way. Each one I've loved has been lost to me."

"Not each one. Anthony and I are not lost. And Bird is only on a journey. Forget the simple concept of time that you've lived by these past few years. You have much time now to love again. To learn when it is safe to love. We may learn this lesson together."

Gilda examined Sorel's room, then peered over her shoulder at Anthony standing in the shadow. She had expected to only pass a night or two and then be on the road again. The darkness of night's roads no longer seemed as inviting. The prospect of resting, healing, learning, drew her.

Later, when she looked back at the time spent with Sorel and Anthony in the town by the bay, she was always startled at how quickly the years flew by.

Chapter Three
Rosebud, Missouri: 1921

Aurelia surveyed the room, looking for the exact element that made her parlor so different tonight. Of course, hosting the Church Circle with Alice Dunbar there to address them was one of the most exciting things to occur in Aurelia's young life. Her year of widowhood had made some days unrelievedly bleak, and tonight's event was a great departure from the routine to which she had become accustomed. But she had always thought of her life as satisfying, perhaps even more so in widowhood which had bestowed an unfamiliar independence. Tonight there was something more.

She turned to Edna Bright who was about to shepherd Alice Dunbar back to her train. Edna's husband waited outside, and Aurelia could feel the nervous connection between them. His impatience with female social niceties, "talk and twitter" as Aurelia had heard it called, was a cloud over Edna's head. Inside, Edna warred against herself—her desire to stay and hear more, to say more, battled with the knowledge that he waited. The longer she lingered, the more the women's efforts would be belittled. Aurelia moved to Edna's side and gave Alice Dunbar one last good-bye. Aurelia was taken again by the unwavering gaze of her piercing eyes, a look that felt both challenging and seductive. A moment later Dunbar was out the door and waving backward on the lamplit street.

As the remaining wives of the Church Circle departed, Aurelia sensed the difference she had been trying to identify. The room really was no longer her dead husband's sitting room: it had become hers now. The friends who'd been here were here to be with her, not just with their minister's widow. The four-poster bed in the narrow room across the foyer was now her bed; he no longer was part of its definition. And the attic full of bric-a-brac accumulated before their marriage was hers, too.

And there was Gilda. She wasn't in the room at the moment, yet she was everywhere. Her favorite chair was angled in the corner next to its ornate reading lamp where she sat many evenings, first as Aurelia's comforting neighbor, later as a special friend. Books she had given as gifts filled a shelf in the parlor, and the garish windchimes from St. Louis tinkled in the air that rushed in through the open door. Aurelia was suddenly anxious that the women leave so she could have her home and friend to herself again.

When the door finally closed on the last guest, Aurelia looked at her reflection in the mirror above the sideboard. She admired her plumpness and the glow in her eyes. "Not a bad-looking woman," she'd heard from neighbors, quick in their attempts to coax her back into community social life.

Aurelia stacked the napkins for the laundry, remembering how surprised she'd been when Dunbar accepted the invitation to visit the Church Circle and speak on working for the race. It was fitting that Dunbar should come now when Aurelia's home was full of energy. Aurelia hadn't felt this independent since she was a girl playing in her parents' yard.

Gilda worked alone in the kitchen washing the fragile china cups, saucers, and small dishes as Aurelia brought them in from the dining room. The task was comforting in its normality and reminded Gilda of Bernice, the cook who used to drift into her own world back at Woodard's, her heavy brown arms glistening with soapsuds while she hummed to herself.

Although Aurelia continued to wear the dark cloth of widowhood, she felt light and careless tonight, savoring the high-pitched laughter still ringing inside her head.

"I don't think I'm going to stop smiling for at least a month," Aurelia said, carrying the folded tablecloth into the pantry. Her voice had the edge of Missouri yet was still round with the music of the Delta. "She was so inspiring. We think of these things ourselves, of course, but it often takes someone from outside to show you how to do something."

"The ladies of the Church Circle will never be the same," Gilda said sardonically. She didn't mean to make light of it all but she had found Alice Dunbar a tiny bit pompous.

"Oh dear, you didn't enjoy the talk, did you?" Aurelia asked.

"No, I did," Gilda protested. "It was a fine evening, and I'm pleased the group was inspired. Work with the poor is crucial..." She didn't want to criticize when Aurelia was so clearly ablaze with enthusiasm. Aurelia was Gilda's first friend since she'd left Sorel's, and it was difficult to navigate her way. She longed to share much with her but wasn't certain she'd be able to hold back anything once she began. Most of her feelings stayed buried within deep folds of protection, finding their way out only through the pages of her journal or letters to Anthony.

Both women were silent for a while. Gilda dried the silverware while Aurelia returned to the parlor, plumping the pillows and finishing putting the room in order. She came back to the kitchen with a purposeful step and announced, "I know she's a snob. She was taking inventory of everything in sight before she determined if I was a worthy hostess or not. But what she said was important. That's all!"

Gilda's laughter rang out fully. This was one of the qualities that made Aurelia so appealing: she was both naive and wise. The Alice Dunbars of the world had much to offer Aurelia, but intimidation was not part of it.

"I couldn't have put it better myself," Gilda said, and they laughed together, pleased they'd averted their first disagreement so easily.

Aurelia's dark, shining face was made more alluring by her broad smile. Her softly pressed hair was pulled back in thick girl-like braids. She was heavier than Gilda. Her breasts strained at the wool of her bodice, and a wealth of gabardine swung loosely around her full hips. Gilda was sure that even the most recalcitrant of Aurelia's Sunday school students must eventually come to adore her face.

Once the dishes and linen were tended to, Gilda prepared to leave. The hour was still early, but the full moon already hung lazily above the western hills. It was several miles east to her small farmhouse, and the practical necessity of restricting her public travel to a motor car made the trip from the town limits of Rosebud to her farm longer than it would be if she simply traveled by foot.

She marveled at the automobile's popularity and had come to enjoy the calming influence driving sometimes had on her. It took several years for the townspeople to become accustomed to seeing a black woman driving. And after all, Gilda—"the widow who bought the Wirth farm"—was always a bit of an oddity to the communities, both black and white. She attended the most important weekly event in the black community, church service, dressed in the staid colors of widowhood, but kept herself apart from most social activity. She made frequent forays into St. Louis and did a minimal amount of shopping in town, contributing to the aura of mystery that surrounded her. It was known she maintained a full garden and gave away a good portion of its yield; that she had an independent income; that she kept to herself except for time spent with Aurelia and her nearest neighbor, John Freeman, also considered somewhat of an outsider. When Negro factory workers were fired to make way for returning white soldiers after the end of the war, he had drifted west from St. Louis and used his earnings to buy farmland.

To blacks she was an eccentric who was, they conjectured, overly affected by the death of her husband. Whites thought her much too bold. The officers of Rosebud's one bank had been cautious when Gilda purchased the farm on the edge of town. They were accustomed to a more supplicating attitude from their colored citizens. Running a bank in a fast-growing town gave them a somewhat broader view than most, but they were ill at ease with any woman who did not negotiate haltingly for a mortgage. Instead she outlined instructions for a transferal of her funds with the assurance of a white man. Yet none of the citizens of Rosebud, black or white, could find any specific act that would lead to opposing her presence in town. Her obviously secure financial status and clearly superior education gave her a curious place among them.

Gilda took much pleasure in the occasional encounters she had with the townspeople. The modest shape of their aspirations, their solid sense of endurance, the complexity of their social interactions were life energy for her.

In the three years since she moved onto her land, rumors had circled around her based purely on the imagination of others. For in spite of her unconventional attitudes and independence, Gilda behaved as any upstanding woman alone in a new town would.

With the death of Aurelia's husband, a minister much her senior, it seemed natural that the two widows console each other. Aurelia turned to Gilda because she was solicitous without exuding the condescension customary from those who had known her since childhood. Gilda talked easily of places and customs Aurelia had never heard of before, speaking as if they were just around the bend in the road. Tonight was the first social event she organized on her own, and it was Gilda who made her think she could manage it.

Gilda's lean, self-possessed carriage and soft humor cut through the edgy chill of death that left Aurelia feeling helpless. She gravitated eagerly toward Gilda's aura of self-reliance and adventure. It contrasted brightly with her own practical competence in everything from mending linen to repairing hinges.

Aurelia had escaped much of the hardship that was everyday life for many blacks in their area. Her parents' position as educators had kept poverty from dominating her small, comfortable world. The nightriders who regularly terrorized blacks in the towns to the south and west of Rosebud had never taken hold in her county, leaving the small enclave of freedmen to build solid lives.

As her parents' only child, Aurelia had enjoyed unbound days of sunlit adoration. Daily married life remained unchanged: her husband replaced her father as patriarch, guiding her along a preordained social path. The death of her parents and then her husband left Aurelia financially comfortable but with little direction. She began to see the poverty and fear in the newly arriving blacks who lived on marginal farms with insufficient yields or labored in St. Louis factories for the lowest wages. Gilda's steely calm made these new shadows less frightening. While she looked not much older than Aurelia's twenty-five years, the way she moved, the seriousness in her eyes, spoke of great wisdom. Their mutual enjoyment of small pleasures rekindled Aurelia's hope.

When Gilda took Aurelia on drives through the countryside they sometimes wandered at a leisurely pace. But often she drove wildly, spraying clouds of dust in the air and grime on their coats. After taking the wheel the first time Aurelia never felt helpless again.

"Come, please have some sherry with me before you go home."

"Not tonight. I've a few letters to write and send off tomorrow first thing. Besides, you look a little tired," Gilda said, trailing her finger across Aurelia's cheek.

"I do not! I look like I won't sleep for a week I'm so excited."

"You'll be sorry in the the morning when there's the laundry to be done," Gilda said.

"Maybe I'll just leave it 'til the end of the week. Or let it pile up in the pantry and grow grey."

"Wouldn't Maerose Spenser love to gossip about that," Gilda said, laughing. "If you'd like, on Saturday I can help with the canning you've been delaying so shamelessly."

"Alright then." Aurelia tried to assemble her Sunday School teacher's look. "Canning on Saturday it is." She took Gilda's hand in her own. "I can't tell you how grateful I am for your help today. I'd never have had the courage to even suggest inviting Alice Dunbar, much less have her here in my house, if you weren't by my side."

"Not true. You'll surprise yourself yet. Anyway, it was great fun for me, too. We make an excellent team. Perhaps we should become impressarios."

"We'll see what kind of impressario you are on Saturday, madam!"

Gilda took her light cloak and descended the front steps. She waved a final time before driving away from Aurelia's woodframe cottage, which sat at the end of the tiny spur that served as the main street for the black population. The town's two thoroughfares—one white, one black—came together at an oblique angle around a tiny town square. People met at the dry goods store, apothecary, feed store, and bandshell often enough to think of each other as neighbors. But their lives ran off in separate directions like their two main streets, like the Missouri and Mississippi rivers straddling St. Louis.

After passing through so many towns that had been devastated then revitalized by war, Gilda was used to the multiple ways in which blacks and whites accommodated to each other. In Rosebud, the interconnection of their worlds seemed perfectly balanced. She wondered how this small town had escaped the bitterness and rivalry she had found in other places.

The orderliness of its outlying farms and the small houses of the main streets were comfortable to her. They evoked the future that she had been promised. The two streets mirrored each other's ambitions and contentment. Every house was like Aurelia's: inside, the lampglow implied infinite possibilities. On each street she found the same pattern of lamplight and the same sound of evening. But now her attention to these details was drawn away by her body's need.

Gilda drove back through the town onto the road leading south-west to her farmhouse. Tonight the car made her impatient. She longed to be free of the dress and stockings, to wear her dark, men's trousers and woolen shirt. She always looked forward to night when she'd race through the wooded area between Rosebud and St. Louis hunting for the blood. The feel of wind whipping around her swept away the long past and with it her loneliness for the company of Sorel and Anthony. When she moved through the night with the wind she forgot she was still awaiting some message from Bird.

The light from the full moon and her acute vision made a lamp unnecessary inside her house. Gilda walked slowly through the sitting room and narrow hallway to her sleeping room with its double-locked door. Entering its draped darkness, she slipped into her more familiar clothes. She went through the hall again, back to her desk, and sat down before her open journal. It had been some time since her last entry. She passed her hands over the dried ink and looked out the window to the empty road winding away from her front porch to the east and west. Three years here, she thought. What a ridiculously short time. What a horribly long time. It had been fifty years since she last saw Bird and almost as long since she left Woodard's. Yet the loss of them lay heavily on her, a weight that would not relent until she finally spoke with Bird and peace was made.

Gilda flipped the journal pages backward to a passage near the book's beginning. When Gilda and Bird were alone, running Wood-ard's together, Bird had passed on the wisdom and cunning of the woman who had given both of them life. Looking down at the flat words, she found that despite their spareness, they evoked a memory as sharply defined as a daguerreotype. She could see the full brow and stern mouth as Bird taught her the ways of the hunt. Her low and level voice hummed in Gilda's head with instructions about survival in the sun's rays, about avoiding suspicion and keeping the secret of their lives.

Bird had given her the first journal, a fine-lined green ledger. "You may want to save your thoughts here. To remember the feelings, the turn of events. It's best to write in one of the other languages in the event someone should stumble upon the book. I sometimes even wrote as though it were a fiction," Bird had said, smiling at the memory.

Gilda began by writing questions she had about their life, the many answers Bird gave her, and the many she did not.

"Why do you say others may kill and we must not?"

"Some are said to live through the energy of fear. That is their sustenance more than the sharing. The truth is we hunger for connection to life, but it needn't be through horror or destruction. Those are just the easiest links to evoke. Once learned, this lesson mustn't be forgotten. To ignore it, to wallow in death as the white man has done, can only bring bitterness."

"And what of our bodies? Do they really never grow old?"

"Only the mind grows old. You are already tighter, more solid than you were as a child. There will be no grey hair, no aching limbs, no wound that does not heal."

"And the sun?"

"A danger. It can weaken you, even take you to the true death. But it needn't do that unless you give yourself up to it or are already ill. The soil of your birthplace will protect you. All new garments can be constructed to discreetly contain pockets of it. Other things —your cloak, your shoes, all laced with your earth—will serve you. You needn't fear small doses of sun unless you're unprotected. It may even become your ally when you wish to let go of life."

As always, when Bird spoke of something that reminded her of the past she ended the discussion and turned abruptly to some other task. Gilda longed to ask Bird why the other had left them, but anytime she started to voice the question, Bird withdrew. So Gilda contented herself with lessons in the new ways of life and new languages. She had just begun to grow used to the altered rhythm of her life, to the speed and strength of her limbs, to her vision which pierced mortal duplicity, and to the reality of their isolation, when Bird announced her departure.

Gilda bitterly regretted never having confronted Bird, never demanding to know why Bird blamed her for the other's death. Instead she'd waved good-bye stolidly from her upstairs window as Bird rode away. When Gilda still found herself, after some time, listening for Bird's voice among those of the others, when she could no longer endure the earth and lavender scent of Bird's room without collapsing in dry sobs, she deeded Woodard's to Bernice's youngest daughter and started northward.

On her third night of leisurely travel Gilda built a fire in a dark clearing beside the road. She took in the warmth as she gazed at the flames but was more absorbed by the portentous shapes and shadows. In that circle of heat and light the dark, chilling shape of her life found Gilda. Panic settled on her shoulders, obliterating the past and the future. Without Bird she was floating out of control on a dangerous sea. Once again she needed to give shape to a world that was beyond her comprehension, much as she had been forced to do when her mother died. She sat before the roadside fire trying to gain a focus, some sense of anticipation, but she found no grounding for them. The wind and flame were too free. It was then she pulled out a map and began to plot her journey—marking places where she should hide caches of her soil, choosing things she wanted to see. The plains of Texas; the towering trees of California, the many communities of freed blacks. Including her stay with Sorel and Anthony, she had spent almost half a century on the road before arriving in Rosebud.

Gilda closed her journal and looked around the room, her eyes picking out the few things she'd saved from Woodard's: a colorful quilt, the small desk at which she now sat, the rows of books that lined the wall. Her trunk still held the metal cross her mother had given her and the leather-encased knife from Bird. These possessions were the legacy of a few short years and more lifetimes than most others would ever know. She shut the door of her sleeping room and the front door of the house, then walked east, slowly trying to reconstruct the time that had passed.

The years with Sorel—learning as much as there was time to absorb, from financial investing to Eastern philosophy—were as pristinely clear as her language lessons with Bird. She could feel the damp air on her skin from the evening walks with Anthony on fog-enshrouded piers. The vision of Eleanor, her scarlet hair dimming the lamplight, still took away her breath.

But many of the years were simply a broad strip of darkness into which she peered, out of which she could draw little. Whenever she wanted to remember them she read through her journal as she had just done, but still they held little meaning for her. Most decades were dazed watercolor views sketched from a distance. They provided a precise narrative of journeys but few sensations.

Tonight the full moon illuminated the road, making it feel like dusk, so Gilda moved cautiously off to the side into the thickets. On the road, or in the anonymity of St. Louis, she would take her share of the blood and then return to her books and papers to examine her memories. Her dark skin remained unlined, just as Bird had said it would. Her thick black hair, which she now wore pulled tightly back and tied in a bun at the nape of her neck, was still as dark as brushed velvet.

She moved speedily through the night, unafraid of animals or the nightriders who prowled looking for blacks whose lives were their sport. She slowed and lifted her face toward the moon. Her eyes closed. She was an eerie worshipper, part of the secret lore of ha'nts and spirits that lived with African people, even in Missouri. In the half-light Gilda felt the moon's warmth as she had once felt the scorch of the sun on her back in the fields. But here the warmth was a fascination. Once taken for granted, the moon was now the center of her orbit.

She resisted the impulse to reach out for Bird, to try to touch her consciousness wherever she might be. Too often since their separation Gilda had come to a dead-end road trying to scan the miles.

She had almost agreed with Sorel when she left California that her task now was simply to live. As she did so, among the free blacks on farms and in small towns, she came closer to knowing, through them, who she was. Her preternatural life made her an outsider, but still she enjoyed their evocation of the secrets of the past and their unequivocal faith in the future. Gilda was chagrined by her concept of *they* and how her life separated her from them. Still she took comfort in the familiar smells and sounds and the rare sense of unity that sometimes crept into her.

Gilda moved away from these thoughts by opening her eyes and beginning her sprint toward the city. Before she could quite pull away, another sensation washed over her. A restlessness, much like the angry flower that had grown inside of Bird. Gilda didn't know its root, but the need to move on, to look elsewhere for something still undefined, was like a hard wind at her back. The faint stirrings of the anxious hunger inside her turned her mind toward the blood that would replenish her life. Unconsciously, however, she planned what direction she'd follow next, not considering how she would force herself to part from Aurelia.

She had already stepped back onto the road intent on fulfilling the stirring inside her when she saw two men on horseback approaching from the west. They were moving at a good pace, as if racing, but they slowed when they noticed her and pulled up short a few feet away. One swung down from the saddle immediately. He stood before her with an angry glare that quickly turned into a leer when he realized she was not a man.

"This here's a niggah gal, we got here. What you doin' out on the road this hour?"

Gilda didn't respond but let herself breathe in the smell of the horses and sense their anxiety and dissatisfaction with their masters. There was an idle communication between them and her that went unnoticed by the riders. Gilda felt reassured by the horses' solid presence, their lack of malevolence, and their easy response to comforting messages she sent them. The other horseman dismounted holding a glistening whip coiled at his hip.

"Maybe we teach one more niggah a lesson tonight, hey Cook?" Gilda peered at the braided leather, dark with blood she could smell. She wondered who had been their most recent pupil.

"Yeah, Zach, I think there's a lesson here for sure."

Gilda still didn't move or speak. She stood as if frozen, but her mind flooded with the words Bird had given her. She was not afraid as she had been that night long ago in the root cellar. She tasted the acid of hatred inside her mouth and wanted to be full of it, to teach the lesson these two needed to learn.

"She must be mute, Zach. Don't seem to talk, do she?"

The taller man moved close to Gilda and yanked her hair, pulling her face up toward his. The moonlight glistened on her dark skin. Before he could press his advantage, Gilda grabbed his wrist, the crack of bone audible in the night. She pulled his hand from her head and twisted it behind his back, raising it so high the pain cut his voice before he could scream. She gave a sharp twist and let go only when she felt his muscles quaking with pain. He whipped around toward her again, and she smashed the side of his face with her fist. The snap of his neck broke through the night as his body crumpled into the ditch beside the road.

His fellow rider backed away, reaching behind him for the reins of his horse, but his mount deliberately twisted out of his reach and Gilda was upon him before he realized his position. She caught his whip in her left hand and pulled him backward. He fell to the ground, then scurried back off the road to the brush with Gilda bounding behind him. She cracked the whip once over his head, then lay a stroke across his back. That she hit him with his own whip seemed to startle him more than the pain. At the second lash he turned to face Gilda, his eyes filled with rage. He gasped when he saw the swirling amber of her eyes and the sinewy strength of her body, thinking that they'd been wrong, that it was a man. An Indian he thought, confused by the moonlight and his own fear. She cracked the whip this time across his chest, then his cheek, opening the flesh almost to the bone.

Gilda threw the whip down and leapt upon him, twisting his head to expose the pulsing vein in his neck. He was already faint with shock, yet Gilda sensed his disbelieving terror build. She scraped his flesh roughly with her nails and watched the blood pulse from his neck, searching for what he felt when he lay open the flesh of men. Her chest swelled with anticipation as she understood the terrible joy he experienced at demanding terror and death. She drew his blood into her quickly and then let him slip to the ground. She watched the blood continue to stream from his neck, soaking into the muddy ditch. She could feel life ebbing from him and was shocked at the excitement it aroused. One death was enough. It had been so long since she'd been caught unawares like this. She knelt beside him, holding her hands to the wounds on his neck and cheek until the bleeding stopped.

She left him nothing in exchange except a simple recollection of falling instead of the horror of the real memory. His breath was shallow, but he was no longer in danger.

Gilda was sickened by her anger and the thrill the confrontation had given her. It was the nightmarish pleasure she had seen in Eleanor's eyes and the one she feared could become hers. She climbed back up to the road and stared down at the face of the one who was dead, frozen in the moonlight. She took in his features as she'd been taught and tried to absorb some sense of his true spirit. This was only the second one. His image now took its place beside the other in a corner inside herself that Gilda seldom visited. The first one had been taken on a road not unlike this one, in the dark when mortals seemed to feel that what was done was not seen. She had not talked with anyone about that time, not even Sorel or Anthony. Just as she wouldn't speak of this death until she could talk of it with Bird.

She turned back toward her farm. Instead of her usual swift pace, Gilda took each step with deliberation. She was leaden with exhaustion. Anger had flared and burned out leaving the taste of ashes. One death. She was grateful it had not been two. When she finally arrived home she eagerly sponged the blood from her hands and face. The memory of her rage and the death made her tremble, so she avoided her desk and its temptation to record her anguish. Instead she sank into the earth-filled comforter, flying into the arms of dreamless sleep.

On Saturday Gilda paced impatiently about her house looking at maps and rereading her journals. She missed Anthony and the stern talks he'd had with her to save Sorel the pain of them. She even missed Eleanor and the coolly seductive attitude she had taken toward her after the fight with Samuel. It had helped Gilda maintain an alertness as she learned the ways of the city and the others who were like them.

Gilda waited until late in the afternoon before pulling out the purple outfit Eleanor had given her, spun from fine wool and the Mississippi soil protecting her from the fading sunlight. She went out to her garden to harvest the last of the beans that neighbors had encouraged her not to grow in this soil, then loaded her car with the bushel basket of corn, strawberries, and cucumbers to take to Aurelia. She knew most of the canning would be completed at this hour. Still, she'd made that her reason for this visit, and both Aurelia and Gilda found the pursuit of propriety a pleasant game to play.

The broad-brimmed felt hat she wore flopped down over her face leaving only her lips exposed in the amber light. She slapped the dust from her hem and decided she was presentable enough even though a fine grey film from her final sweep through the garden rimmed the soles of her boots. The cloak would hide it, she thought, if she should encounter anyone on the street, and Aurelia cared little for appearance. Or more precisely, her outlandish outfits seemed to appeal to Aurelia. Gilda decided to rinse her hands before leaving and was startled to hear a knock at her door just as she returned a towel to its rack.

There was a moment of terror when time eclipsed itself and it was again 1850. Gilda fought the panic barreling through her and searched her mind for who it might be. So rarely did she have visitors, and people did not ride this far out to visit unexpectedly at this hour, that Gilda was certain it must be Aurelia. She hurried to the front of the house trying to suppress a gnawing guilt at what Aurelia must have perceived as neglect.

She was surprised to see not Aurelia but her neighbor, John Freeman, whose farm lay further west. He was a tall, narrow man who filled the doorframe with his stiff coveralls and straw hat. Gilda was rankled by his presence but unsure why. He lived alone and worked his farm steadily and was the only person, other than Aurelia, to have ever been inside Gilda's home. Sometimes he stopped by to stand at the porch railing exchanging the small talk that was part of the ritual of farm life. Occasionally she'd discover a peck of beans on her porch or a bottle of the homemade wine for which Freeman was famous. She smiled at the memory of the rough wine that had made her feel so warm and opened the door wider.

"Well, Brother Freeman, this is a pure surprise. Have you come to continue in your efforts to persuade me with your wine to the ways of the devil?" She said this laughing as she stepped out onto the porch.

He was a reed-thin man with—at first glance—a stern demeanor, the effect of working in the sun all day. At the slightest encouragement his eyes opened wide, and his smile rose shyly from deep within brown furrows. Although he knew little about Gilda he'd taken to her from the time he first saw her squinting into the sunset three years earlier.

"No ma'am," he said in a deep voice echoing miraculously from his long neck. "That's not 'til next harvest. I expect the berries to be sweeter than ever too." Gilda sat in one of the porch's ladder-back chairs and indicated the other for Freeman.

"You know, Miss Gilda, I need to ask your thought on something," he said, ignoring the chair, "but I'ma hope you ain't peeved 'cause these ideas come up."

"I can think of few ideas you might have, Mr. Freeman, that would make me angry."

He began slowly, phrasing his words carefully for this peculiar woman who appeared to live outside of their world and to hide her own universe beneath her hat brims. "Well, you probably know that Miss Aurelia got this notion in her head to minister to the poor. Not that I'm against it, but she's took into her mind to maybe start a class or a school for them that's just up from down south and them Indians that live north of town and God knows what all! She's even talking about. . ." He broke off there, embarrassed, then went on. "Well, you probably know something 'bout all this. You two is big talkers, I know."

"I thought it a fine project, myself," Gilda asserted, then held her silence.

"I agree, Miss Gilda, you ain't gonna get no arguin' outta me on that account—"

"So what is it exactly, Mr. Freeman, we're concerned about?" As Gilda spoke she gazed out from under her hat, casually catching John Freeman's eyes. Exerting her will she corralled his thoughts, making it easier for him to be direct so they did not dance around his meaning for the next twenty minutes.

"Well, I just wondered if you thought it un...uh...unseemly for Miss Aurelia to have those people troupin' through her house, probably at night, and she'd be there alone and all. It just looks like the people in town might talk in some kinda way. You know they got nothin' better to do but think on colored folks' business. And you know white people think we're all trash no matter who's husband was a minister or a farmer or such like!"

Gilda laughed out loud at that. It became clear what caught her up short about this man: his carefully contained yet certainly passionate interest in Aurelia.

"In some ways you are right, of course, Mr. Freeman. Aurelia should not be left to bear the burden of this all on her own. Surely she should have someone to stand by her. We've discussed perhaps having the lessons out here at my farm sometimes, or even moving the lessons around to give others a chance to host—implicate everyone, in a manner of speaking," Gilda said with a glistening smile. "But those are barely plans right now. And, Mr. Freeman, we can't always be so concerned with the talk of our neighbors. Talk is mostly useless chatter that feeds no cows and brings no rain."

"You got it right there!" John Freeman said, relieved that Gilda appeared to agree with him. He was unsure if Gilda's participation made the idea more or less savory though. Everyone said two women were bound to get into even more trouble than one.

"I'm on my way to see Aurelia right now, so maybe she and I can discuss some of your suggestions."

With that, Gilda pulled her front door tight and left her porch in long strides. John Freeman tumbled quickly behind and opened the car door while Gilda put on her goggles. She climbed in and moved the car onto the road as Freeman mounted his horse. He turned back toward his farm, frowning. Gilda's words had been comforting, nonetheless, and odd as it seemed even to him, he had a lot of confidence in her.

Sitting in Aurelia's kitchen, listening to her excited talk of the new venture, Gilda felt less certain about her ability to manage the situation.

"You remember that first time you come by here to pay your respects? Why, I was so shy I was hardly able to open the door, much less look you in the eye. I remember how that sunset made your hat look like a halo, and I was so flustered I didn't know what you'd think of me." Aurelia laughed with embarrassment.

"I thought only that I'd caught you by surprise."

"I do say, you caught me by surprise. I can't remember any time I've been more surprised. Except when the Reverend asked for my hand. Even then I could tell my folks expected it, so it wasn't much of one." She laughed nervously, remembering how narrow her choices had seemed then, how broad they were now that she knew Gilda. "You looked so overpowering I wasn't certain if I should be afraid or relieved."

"You hid your indecision well," Gilda said. "I thought you were simply measuring me to decide if I were suitable enough to use the good china." They laughed together as they had done on many occasions since that first time.

"It doesn't feel like almost three years have passed. If you had seen me in the Reverend Hayne's office yesterday, you wouldn't have recognized me. I just kind of made my back go stiff like I was pushing a stuck drawer and kept talking, no matter what he said. When I asked about using the church at night for class, he just sputtered around his desk. Then when I said I wanted another night for offering social services, you know, giving out food and all, he stoppered up like a bottle. Just a year ago, even a month ago, I don't know if I'd ever have been able to be so bold. And I can tell you that if we'd had to depend on some of the other ladies, we'd be meeting in your barn."

They both laughed loudly since Gilda's unused barn was the least amenable facility in the vicinity.

"I know he kept thinking to himself: *Mercy be, this could have been my wife!* So, between guilt and relief he said yes—maybe!"

A glow of pride spread across Aurelia's face. And, indeed, she had grown a great deal in the years since they became friends. The evenings they spent together had changed: Gilda was no longer there simply to provide entertainment, to draw her out. They were accustomed to each other's tastes in discussion. Gilda came to know this new Aurelia quite well and was not surprised at her success. Still, the afternoon's discussion with John Freeman stayed with her. Beside it was the gnawing restlessness she continued to push into the back of her thoughts.

"And just what are you going to do now that he's said yes— maybe?" Gilda asked.

She didn't touch the teacup Aurelia placed before her. Instead she watched Aurelia put away the knives, bowls, and jars from her afternoon of canning. Once the vegetables Gilda had brought were stored in the back pantry, Aurelia tossed her apron onto a pile of stained towels.

"What is it, Gilda? You're not saying something," Aurelia accused with an easy familiarity. Then added, "Let's sit in the parlor. I, un- like some of us, have had enough of the kitchen today."

She gave Gilda a tart smile and did not wait for her to follow into the next room. She removed a bottle of sherry along with two glass- es from the sideboard.

"Is this going to be unpleasant?" she asked as she poured from the crystal decanter.

"I think you have to make careful plans, Aurelia, that's all. This isn't something you should take on alone."

"I'm not alone. Edna Bright is planning to help with the lessons, and if her sister is willing to work on dispensing food and you're going to give us a share of your yield, I'd say that's a fairly strong beginning." Aurelia did not look in Gilda's direction but sipped from the tiny glass and paced before the low settee.

"Of course I'm going to contribute. I've always got much more than I can ever use, and that's true for some others as well, like John Freeman. I know he wants to make donations. You'd do well to in- volve him; he'd be quite a help." Gilda listened to the voice as if it were not her own.

"Why? I've got you."

Gilda's heart pounded loudly in her chest as the room fell silent around them. She was now certain she must make plans to leave Missouri but had not expected the decision to be presented to her so soon. Despite the passing years she still felt unsure of how to know when one she cared for might be suited to this life, or when she might simply be thinking of her own desire and not the needs of others. The misery she'd seen in Samuel's eyes traveled with her.

"But I might not always be here, Aurelia." The words did not fill the silence, only deepened it. "I've told you, sometime in the future I may need to go back east. My family could call for me at any time."

Gilda's lie hung low in the air. Inside she cringed at the word *family*. The thought of leaving Aurelia for family when she still had not found Bird made her tremble. She stared in Aurelia's direction avoiding her eyes; how easily she could make her one of them. The knowledge landed heavily on Gilda's chest, almost cutting her breath from her. Aurelia would be acquiescent, eager, letting Gilda draw the blood and return it in the ritual of sharing that would bind them together forever. The pulsing of Aurelia's blood at her temple mesmerized Gilda. Here could begin a new family, she thought. Hunger and desire almost pulled Gilda across the parlor. Instead she stood and excused herself, then snatched her cloak from its hook by the door. Aurelia followed her, a look of alarm spreading across her face. Gilda stilled her before she could speak.

"I have to go. We'll talk more tomorrow."

"You'll come for church?"

"No. I must be in St. Louis in the morning."

"St. Louis!" Aurelia was appalled to hear herself almost shouting. "You can't start out at this hour. It's too dangerous!" She clutched Gilda's sleeve. "This is foolish—" She tried to continue but couldn't.

Gilda held her gaze, calming her, suggesting she read then go to sleep early.

"I'll be here before evening supper. We'll have our ride then," Gilda said without speaking. She loosed Aurelia's hand from her arm and latched the door behind her as she left.

Gilda had reached her farm and changed her clothes before Aurelia realized she was sitting in the armchair she thought of as Gilda's. The amber glow of the reading lamp was comforting, and soon Aurelia was ready to retire.

Once back on the road Gilda felt her trembling begin to lessen. She looked for the key to her hesitation as her feet carried her east. She'd never changed anyone but was certain she knew the process: exchange of blood, two times taken, at least once given. She knew the method and the timing but she drew back from the idea. Why? The restlessness Gilda felt would surely be quieted if Aurelia joined with her. But Aurelia's life was now full of many new plans and people. She had begun to make a real place for herself among people she cared for. To claim this life now would be thievery. To pull Aurelia away from the ties she'd made, the commitment she felt, and to ask her to live apart from these things would be cheating her. The idea that Aurelia might one day look at her with the same misery she had seen in Samuel's eyes wrenched her heart.

A cracking sound behind her brought Gilda's attention back to the road. She stood frozen for a moment, listening warily, not anxious to repeat the events of the recent past. She recognized the sound as a skittering rabbit and began to move briskly again. By the time she was outside of St. Louis she no longer thought of Aurelia but only of the hunger she had aroused, and of escape. She skirted the city, then pulled her hat down further as she started for its center. She was inconspicuous in the Saturday evening crowds.

Gilda walked among the people, listening to their heartbeats, letting the scent of their blood and perfumes drift past her. She turned into an alley behind a house she recognized. In the shadows of a doorway she listened to the sound of voices wafting down from the windows above. High-pitched laughter mixed with clinking glassware and soft entreaties. They made her ache for Woodard's, a place that no longer existed. She longed for the girls who years since had become old women, who most probably lay at their final rest by now. The music floated eagerly through the back door of the building which was ajar only wide enough to let one man pass through: an ejected customer stumbling homeward. Gilda stared at the building, absorbing the familiar sounds and smells, and recognized her restlessness. It was unfinished. She'd left Woodard's without knowing what her life with Bird might be, just as Bird had left her unable to say what they were to each other. Gilda wanted to reach out to Bird, but even more she needed to settle inside herself. Aurelia could not help her do that. Aurelia would be fulfilled in Rosebud, not on unknown roads delving into a past she did not understand. It was not a journey she needed, but one that Gilda did.

The sounds unfurled like a tapestry above her head; her ears picked through the colors and pitch. The sound of the stride piano was a velvet background around which scampered the unmistakable squeal of a cornet. Gilda turned sharply toward the glorious sound, one she had not heard for over a decade. In New Orleans this cornet had entranced her. She wondered if this was a record-ing, but it was not. She remembered the player who refused to be-come immortalized by the recording process, choosing instead to carry his own legend.

Gilda's hunger abated as the piercing notes wrapped themselves around her body. It was in moments like these that oneness with the others returned. The web of music bound them through the ages, through the dark, until there was but a single future for them.

Gilda leaned into the music, letting it wash over her like a spray of water. Her hunger was not forgotten. For that moment, however, it was simply fed by the sound of the horn. The thinning blood in-side her moved languidly, seduced by the tide of sound. Its abrupt ending left a piano tinkling randomly in the silence, then applause. They cheered in rhythm with the music, setting up a ritualistic pulse. Beneath it all Gilda heard a quiet sob so close that, for a mo-ment, she thought she had made the sound herself. Above her, to the left at the corner of the building, a slightly open window was dark with a sadness that seeped out from under the curtains.

Gilda felt disoriented. Then her body was released from its stu-por and spoke to her of its need. Her moment of euphoria was gone, and the fire of hunger ran through her veins. The muffled sobs reached not just her ears now, but all of her senses. A woman lay immobile, sunk deeply into her pillow. The smell of men's sex clung to her linen.

In the girl's head was a jumble of thoughts awash in resignation. Gilda rummaged through them, picking at each: the lost child, the need for companionship, shame, uncertainty about her status in this house. She felt young to Gilda, or at least young in knowledge. There was little protection around her, simply guileless perse-verance. But most amazing was that the woman was devoid of dreams. She had no fantasy or embellished aspirations on which to affix her daily life: today barely existed. She was lost in isolation. Gilda pushed into the room with her own thoughts infinitely more directed than those of the young woman. She massaged her spirit, loosened the bonds that wound tightly around the woman's chest to help her breathe easier, then dropped a veil of sleep over her.

Gilda entered the back door of the establishment and heard the patrons and business girls in the front parlor still praising the pi-ano player and cornetist. She slipped stealthily into the deserted kitchen and up the back stairway. She followed her line of control,

holding the young woman in sleep, and passed the closed doors
of the corridor. Behind some of them she heard the grunts of im-
pending and expended passion. Behind one she heard silence—
no thoughts or dreams. She entered the darkened room and was
stunned by the close air of defeat. The mirror was smudged, clothes
were strewn carelessly, and the coverlet betrayed days of filth. It was
a room in which no one really lived, not even the one who slept
here.

The girl lay on her back, a mass of auburn curls plastered to her
damp head. Her face was set in grimness, her fists clenched by her
side as if prepared to do battle with a world she cared little for. Gilda
peered into the creamy white features, wondering where along the
short path this one had traveled she'd lost her ability to dream.

Even in the fearful hours of dawn, before Gilda could be certain
there would be another night of life, dreams crept into her rest to
stimulate her mind and heart. Gilda felt such sorrow at this
diminished capacity for life, she had to restrain the impulse to shake
her awake and preach to her of the need for dreams. Instead she
held her in the sleep and pulled her into her arms. A small incision
at the side of the neck. Blood seeping out slowly. It reminded her
of the wounds she and her sisters suffered on their tiny hands as
they'd wrenched the cotton from its stiff branches. Lines of blood
covered them until the flesh was hardened by experience.

Gilda put her lips to the trickle of blood and turned it into a tide
washing through her, making her heart pump faster. Her insistent
suckling created a new pulse and filled her with new life. In return
she offered dreams. She held the girl's body and mind tightly, letting the desire for future life flow through them both, a promising
reverie of freedom and challenge. The woman absorbed Gilda's desire for family, for union with others like herself, for new experience.
Through these she perceived a capacity for endless life and an open
door of possibility.

As the blood left her body the woman's psyche responded with
a moment of terror, which Gilda used to further suffuse her dreams
with urgency. She wrapped the fear around the edge of the dream,
making it all the more compelling. Gilda did not stop taking the
blood until she felt parts of her dream become the girl's own. The
young woman began to cling to life and experience the urge to project into a future. Her mind filled with thoughts of the other women
who lived and worked in the house—the smiles she had not ac-

knowledged, the endearments and angry words yet to be shared.

Gilda pulled back, comfortable with rooting a dream inside this girl. She loosened her hold so that the young woman's breathing returned to normal, then backed away from the bed, looking down at the face full of expectation. The woman's fists were relaxed; she'd reached one hand up to cover her own small breast, where it rested as if giving assurance to a lover. The woman sighed, and Gilda slid the window open wider, slipped through, and silently dropped the two stories to the back alley. The sounds of Saturday nightlife continued to reverberate as she walked out to the street. She maintained a slow pace moving south then west to the edge of the city, enjoying the evening air and the memory of the girl's soft, pale skin. Her resurgent dreams cast a new glow on Gilda's life: in giving dreams she had recaptured her own.

Gilda gazed up at the bright, thinning moon and sniffed the clear air. The smell of open land was inviting as she left the confines of the city. It was the dreams Aurelia possessed that Gilda could not bare to disturb—her hopes for a life in the town she'd known since childhood, of the work she would do for others. These were the ties that held Aurelia to the earth, not the release from widowhood or open-ended adventure that Gilda represented. As much as she longed to have Aurelia at her side, she could never draw her away from her dreams.

Gilda thought about one of the evenings she sat with Sorel at his fireside. In talking of Eleanor and the mistaken decision he'd made, Sorel quoted Lao-Tsu: *The bright path seems dim; going forward seems like retreat; the easy way seems hard.* . . . It was Sorel's self-interested fear of going on without Eleanor that obscured what a bad choice it would be to bring her into their life. To live without Aurelia was the best that Gilda could do for both of them.

The next evening, standing on Aurelia's porch, she briefly remembered the woman with whom she'd exchanged in St. Louis the night before. The encounter had opened up new roads for her. She was anxious to move forward, certain she would find Bird soon and be able to share with her this fresh understanding of their life. When Aurelia answered her knock, Gilda tried to apologize with her eyes for leaving the night before, but Aurelia was wary.

"Let's go for our ride before the evening cools," Gilda said. She took Aurelia's hand and smiled into her clouded face. Once they were in the car Aurelia was almost smiling too. The day before felt

remote. Gilda drove slowly back through town and out onto the
road leading west. When they reached the town limit she increased
the car's speed. Soon they were both laughing out loud into the dust
that rose from the grit of the road. Gilda turned off the engine at
the edge of a rise overhanging a narrow valley, and they left the car
to gaze at the green sloping down under the red roof of the setting
sun. Gilda held Aurelia's hand again, sensing a need in both of them
to quiet the uncertainty.

"What is it that makes you different from the others?" Aurelia
asked in a fervid, youthful voice. Her dark face was placid, but her
eyes looked pained and tentative. Gilda drew back from the shadow
and turned Aurelia to face her.

Gilda's touch lightened on Aurelia's shoulders, but she did not
want to take her hands away. Instead she smoothed the woolen coat
where it fell over Aurelia's full breasts. She then traced the thick
braid arcing Aurelia's face.

"Perhaps it's that I love no other. . . no other mortal in this world
but you. That gives me a strength and clarity no one else can know."

"Then you won't leave me?"

Gilda pulled Aurelia into her arms. She felt the tremble of tears
in the young woman's lips pressed tight against her own cloak. It
had been so many years since she had simply held anyone. Aurelia fit into the bend of her arm, under the curve of her breast, as if
their bodies were cut from a pattern. Gilda's embrace tightened as
she fought to find the clarity she'd just spoken of, the clarity she
knew earlier.

"I'll go away as I said I must, but I'll never truly leave you. Your
life is here, mine is not."

"How can you be so certain of that? We've been happy!" Aurelia stumbled at the sound of the words she'd said to herself so often, hating the reality of them in the air.

"You've needed me and I've needed to be with you, but our
needs are changing. You have a world of things to do now. You won't
be bound by widow's weeds much longer. There are others here
waiting for you to emerge from mourning."

"I haven't been in mourning. I've been with you!"

"There are still those waiting for me to find my way to them."

"Who might they be?"

Gilda smiled at the edge of jealousy in Aurelia's voice.

"Someone with whom I've shared much history. We've needed

time to pick our way through brambles and cities until we knew ourselves better." Gilda stopped, uncertain what else she might say that
would make sense.

"But why must you go?"

"The past does not lie down and decay like a dead animal, Aurelia. It waits for you to find it again and again." She could not take
this woman into her life. There would be others, more in need or
with more knowledge, who would be her family. As much as she
longed to end the loneliness, to find a partner as Sorel had done,
this was not the time, nor was it best for Aurelia.

She held Aurelia as she looked out into the darkness spreading
around them, hunting for Bird in the absence of light, seeking the
strength to pull away from Aurelia. Gilda's body strained against
Aurelia's, her head pounded. She pressed her lips gently to Aurelia's temple and the side of her face just at her ear. Gilda felt the
woman's body yielding to her and forced herself away. Her gaze
pierced the darkness, and her jaw clamped shut in concentration.

Aurelia looked up at Gilda, revealing a thrill of fear and excitement at the tiny orange flecks that glowed in her eyes. With each
breath Gilda drew in the musky scent of wool and blood. Instead
of returning her stare, Gilda closed her eyes tightly.

"What is it? What have I done? Please come back!" Aurelia
pleaded as Gilda stepped away, holding Aurelia at arm's length. The
wind rose up from the valley, riffling through their coats, cooling
the air around them. Gilda heard the air moving in the grass and
the rustling of animals in the brush as she searched for the strength
to pull back from her desire. Then she heard Bird.

I am here, Bird said through the rustle of the trees.

Gilda released Aurelia's shoulders and finally looked at her. "I
can't stay with you," she said. "There are others to whom I belong.
Others who will belong to me."

"Why are you afraid?" Aurelia asked, certain that she recognized
the feeling that had been with her too much in her past. Gilda could
find no real answer. She said, "We cannot stay together, but neither
of us is as alone as she thinks."

She stopped speaking as she saw Aurelia draw inside herself.
Gilda reached in, listening to Aurelia's thoughts, letting her sense
hers—both her sadness and her newfound joy. When she looked
into Aurelia's eyes she saw her confusion at the abundance of things
running through her mind. Gilda willed her only to remember

them for the future. Neither spoke during the ride back to Aurelia's house. The decision was made, and each of them sifted through its meaning for the years ahead.

The following weeks were spent packing and shipping boxes, making arrangements for the disposition of the farm through a St. Louis law firm. The new deed for Aurelia was notarized before the full moon rose again. John Freeman looked stunned when Gilda told him she was closing her house and going east, but beneath his surprise there lay a small sense of relief.

When Gilda could delay no longer, she sat down in her nearly empty farmhouse to make the final journal entry for this life. She then started a letter to Aurelia. Their last several meetings had been difficult. The strain of not talking about the change in their lives left both exhausted each time they were together, as if they lived through the final parting inside themselves repeatedly.

Tonight had been no different. All of the questions, save one, had been asked. The *why* had not been answered. But Aurelia had steeled herself against loss, curiosity, or failure.

As they stood before the door Aurelia spoke in a small voice. "You've said that if I should ever need you, you'll come for me, come to help me. Is this something you say simply to placate, to keep me from weeping and clutching at your cloak when you leave?"

Gilda was not certain how to respond, how to be reassuring without revealing the whole of her life.

"Because if it is, I'd rather know that now. I don't want to hold on to a dream of your devotion only to find myself a fool, abandoned."

"Aurelia, I have great faith in your capability, your courage. I want your faith in me. I would not lie to you simply for my own comfort. You have dreams of things other than me. That's where I put my faith; that's where you'll put yours."

Aurelia looked puzzled but relieved to hear Gilda's strange reassurances.

Sitting before the clean sheets of writing paper, Gilda still found no words that would contain everything neatly. She held deep sorrow and fierce optimism together in her heart. Their combination with love and desire refused to be defined by the words Gilda knew. But she wanted to leave something for Aurelia to hold on to, something that made Aurelia as certain as she was of her need to move on. She wanted to leave Aurelia an understanding that stood larger than their immediate sadness and Aurelia's sense of rejection. Only the truth could do that. Gilda decided to do something she'd been warned against by both Sorel and Bird—to break silence with someone outside the family. She did this for Aurelia's sake and for her own. Trust had to follow the path cut by love.

Gilda grasped her pen tightly, spilling the legends that become reality across the page. She opened up her past as far as she could remember it, back to the dark comfort of her mother's Fulani face. She had never spoken or written these words for any but herself— words that said she was different from them all, a part of them yet apart from them. She wanted to leave Aurelia with hope, an honest hope, born of who they really were.

Gilda laid the secret open with great detail. She described her first bath, the scent of her mother's sweat, the feel of Bird's arm around her waist, the sound of laughter from the women at Wood- ard's, the thrill of moving beside the wind and how the smell of wind had changed in the years since she'd taken to the road. She even described the rush of life she felt as she shared the blood, leav- ing dreams in exchange. She told of mourning friends and family long dead. And of her fear of not dying, of not being one with the universe again.

Her secret had been kept as a protection against others' fear. The telling left Gilda lighter, ready to meet Bird again. The familiar stir inside her was not simply restlessness but anticipation. She needed no map now. Gilda folded Aurelia's letter into its envelope and looked to the east.

Chapter Four
South End: 1955

Gilda sat turning idly in her beautician's chair, listening to the news on the radio, waiting for her last customer. She watched the lights through the venetian blinds as cars sped frantically up and down Massachusetts Avenue and listened to the voices of women and men shouting to each other over the noise of car radios. Her shop sat at the edge of a row of stoops and row houses that tumbled up Mass. Ave.—as it was usually called—to where it arced over the B & M Railroad tracks. On this side of the tracks black barbers, morticians, factory workers, housekeepers, musicians, and prostitutes worked and lived. The South End of Boston gave way, at the railroad overpass, to the Back Bay—quieter, whiter, asleep by this time except for the university professor or doctor who slipped from his brownstone home to prowl the South End for drugs, music, or women. In the past ten years this transitional neighborhood had become her home.

Savannah rapped on the locked door, the clanging of her bangled bracelets overwhelming the simple tap of her fingers on the glass. Gilda rose and recoiled the lock, genuinely pleased to see one of her favorite people. The shiny copper color of Savannah's round face was topped by her crowning glory: a thick head of hair that she kept bleached white. She'd seen a picture of an aboriginal tribesman in a *National Geographic* and was seduced by the dark skin in contrast to the stark plainness of sun-bleached hair. Seven years ago, when she'd pulled the photograph from her handbag, Gilda peered first at the bronze-and-white figure, then at Savannah. She smiled like an artist embarking on a masterpiece.

Savannah's impulse had been correct. The look was striking and elegant, both qualities necessary to her business. Gilda stood watch over Savannah's emerging roots like an obsessive gardener, keeping the hair white from root to tip. Even now between touch-ups it gleamed around her smooth brown face like a medieval halo. Gilda wasn't sure of Savannah's age—her use of language and the memories she shared with Gilda indicated she'd been in Boston for at least fifteen years. But her skin was that of a twenty-year-old, soft, moist, shining from an innocence that was only betrayed by the skepticism in her eyes. It was in this odd blend of youth and age that Gilda and Savannah found an immediate commonality.

"You mind if I turn this shit off? I can't stand listening to that Eisenhower. Everything he say sound like a golf score: dull!"

With that Savannah snapped the radio off, not waiting for Gilda's reply, tossed her mink jacket onto the chair in the beautician's booth across from Gilda's, and plopped her full body down as if she were coming home from work rather than just beginning her evening.

"I'ma tell you, girl, don't listen to a thing they got to say. It's all lies. I know, 'cause I see 'em up close, if you can understand me. Close up and they be lyin' and don't even know it. Politicians read it off a piece of paper like the gospel and they don't even know who wrote it. Watch what they be doin', fuck what they be sayin'! Just like Moms Mabley say: 'Watch the cars, damn the lights. The lights ain't never hit nobody!' "

That began an unstoppable stream of conversation as Gilda washed and massaged Savannah's head. She worked casually, shampooing and conditioning while Savannah rambled on. She never forgot any incident in her life, leaping back and forth between the latest schemes of Skip, her youthful pimp, and memories of her mother's cooking years ago in Gulfport, Mississippi.

It was another bond Gilda felt with Savannah but had never acknowledged. Although she had not been back to Mississippi since the day she'd made her escape from the plantation, she carried the soil with her, and its scent made it real to her still. Her friendship with Savannah rested on the earth from which they'd come, the place where their many mothers had first been bent beneath the yoke.

Gilda closed her eyes and felt her mother's hands combing and braiding her hair. She remembered the sharp tugs and the pull of her scalp as the hair was caught back in the thick braids running like rows of corn across her scalp. Then the touch was Bird's, who had unbraided the rows and brushed the thick dark mass into one long, tight braid ending at the back of her neck. Their hands had been hard, worker hands; self-sufficient hands that still knew how to be tender. Gilda used gentle strokes to untangle the glistening white of Savannah's hair. Its color was a profound contrast to the luminescent red that had framed Eleanor's face. Although she was sad to know she'd never see the light entangled in those curls again, Gilda found that her fondness for Savannah and others in her present began to outshine that past.

Savannah's ability to carry on conversation under any circumstance amazed Gilda. She talked while Gilda dried, straightened, and curled, rarely asking questions. A brief moment of silence was broken by a loud knock on the glass door. Gilda set the curling iron back in its cradle and turned down the flame impatiently. She hated to have her rhythm interrupted, as well as her own reverie. The knock came again, louder this time. She opened the door to a man whose face was familiar. His eyes darted around the shop with an intensity that could have penetrated the partitions separating the booths.

Although she couldn't remember his name, Gilda said, in the easy voice used in the shops and bars along Massachusetts Avenue, "So what can I do for you, my good man?"

She saw that this was not a casual visit. Gilda maintained a steady gaze and a slight smile.

"Lookin' for Toya," the tall man said, pushing past Gilda into the shop. Savannah sat forward, her head poking out of the booth. Her hair was curled neatly in rows on one side and standing erect and straight on the other. The flash in her eyes made her resemble a rare bird in captivity as she snapped, "Why don't you leave that gal alone?"

"Why don't you mind your business, bitch!" His voice was flat, and he didn't look directly at her but around at the empty booths. "She said she was coming here to have her hair done." The lie was clear in the air.

Gilda remembered the girl who always wore her shiny long curls tied back in a ponytail or covered incongruously with a thick blonde or red wig. Under the mass of hair there were always the wary eyes.

"Well, you can see she's not here," Gilda said.

"If she shows up you tell her she's better off just getting her ass back up to Dale Street. Fox ain't as mad as he's gonna be. He ain't talking about breakin' nothin' yet." He grinned with a slyness that made his face resemble a rodent's.

The chilling look made Gilda want to smash him. Instead she widened her smile and stepped closer.

Savannah drawled, "Aw, leave him alone, Gilda, he ain't nobody. Just one of Fox's punks."

"How'd you like to end up in a hospital room? We could even make it a double for you and that junky faggot who rides you," he sneered.

"If that happened," Gilda said in a low, even tone, "I'm afraid your fate would not even be quite as pleasant."

The man heard the tightness in Gilda's voice and felt an unnerving coolness in the air around her body. He retreated toward the door, the itch to strike her with the back of his hand flaring in his eyes. He settled for a glass-rattling slam of the front door as he left.

Gilda took several deep breaths before she turned back to Savannah.

"Girl, you got to be more careful with those fools," Savannah said. "That nigger is as crazy as a jackrabbit, and that Fox, he's just plain evil. I seen him break a girl's arm out on Columbus Avenue just for meanness. If Toya's smart, she's got her skinny butt back to New Orleans by now."

Gilda wondered what New Orleans would be like after so many years. She could imagine Toya there, the autumnal glow of her skin gleaming in the Delta sun. Hearing *New Orleans* said aloud crystalized a picture of Bird in her mind, too, sitting attentively in the room where they studied. Gilda held the red-hot curling iron in the air to cool it down.

"What does this Fox look like?"

"Real smooth skin, light eyes. Drives a dark-green Caddy with tinted glass. He don't hang out much, except at the after-hours joints. You know him if you see him. Cool as a coolin' board, I'll tell you."

Over the years Gilda had enjoyed her relationships with the women on the avenue. In many ways they were like the women at Woodard's, but so often this world was harder, more dangerous. Their comradeship and energy always strengthened her. Savannah picked up her narrative.

It was a few moments before they realized there was a slight tapping at the window in the back alley. She put the curling iron down again and went to the door that opened into the small storeroom and the alley exit.

"Aw, shit," Savannah muttered as she realized what was happening. She went to the front of the shop to make certain the blinds were fully closed and the door locked. Gilda unbolted the door in the back room which was crowded with boxes and supplies wedged in around a small couch, where the beauticians sometimes rested between customers. Toya was tiny in the doorway. Her dark, curly hair hung in a tight braid, making her look, for once, like the teenager she was. Her dark eyes were shadowed with fear, and she stood as if frozen by the light.

"I'm sorry, Gilda. I'm sorry. I didn't know where else to go. He been following me everywhere." Gilda pulled her inside and rebolted the door. Once seated on the couch Toya trembled violently, as if the night air blew through her. Savannah came to the back room, her broad shoulders filling the doorframe.

"Give her some of that bottle they keep back here."

Gilda stared, fascinated by the delicacy of the girl's quivering shoulders. Somewhere inside she remembered her last tears, the last time she had been this vulnerable: the night at the farmhouse waiting for Bird to decide whether or not she would complete the change. She had been afraid Bird would walk away, leaving her with only the mortal years ahead. Gilda pulled a bottle of gin from behind one of the cartons and poured some in a Dixie cup.

"Toya, what the hell you doing 'round here? If you mean to get out, you better get clear out!"

Although the words were harsh Savannah betrayed her tenderness as she brushed at the girl's hair. Toya sipped the gin and looked up at the two women who stood between her and Fox's rage. Gilda turned on a small lamp set atop a carton of Posner's bergamot and sat down beside Toya. When she did she saw the dark lacerations that lined the girl's cheeks.

"What's this?" she asked.

"Fox hit me."

"With what?"

"A coat hanger. He didn't want me to leave." She took another swallow from the Dixie cup and blinked back tears rapidly. "Then he locked me in a room. I climbed out the window and down the porch into the alley. I guess he thought I'd never leave without my stuff so he didn't worry about the window."

Then Toya laughed a little, the scars on her face wrinkling into a tiny map. "He's so stupid, God! I been slipping things out for the last few months. Clothes and other stuff is already in a locker at the bus station. My money, too. He musta thought I was as stupid as him!" Then she started crying again.

"Yeah, you ain't no dummy. That's why you can't go to Greyhound!"

"When did you leave?" Gilda asked.

"Two days ago. He had me followed ever since. I been just barely keepin' out his way. I think he just wanna see how long I can hang on before I crawl back to him."

"Do you want to go back?" Gilda asked.

"The only way he'll get me is in a box. I just wanna go home."

A rage swirled inside of Gilda, flushing her skin with heat. The scars across the girl's face made Gilda hunger to feel Fox's throat between her fingers. But first she would help get Toya quietly out of Boston. Gilda didn't want a public confrontation with this Fox—the power of her anger frightened her.

The faces of the men she'd killed many years ago floated through her years of memories and surfaced. Gilda now remembered little about the circumstances except the preying eyes and the surprise when she struck, expecting only unconsciousness. She would always be angry with herself for letting her fear and rage run free. There was little comfort in knowing she had survived.

Their faces resided inside her, emptied of the ignorance and anger that had delivered them to their fate. Gilda had no desire to add another to that gallery. Somehow they seemed to merge, become one, like twin brothers. There was a sameness in death, the way that all masks resembled each other. Now, when she felt so reconnected to life, when she often sensed Bird near her, she did not want to reaffirm her partnership with death. She wanted only to be able to enjoy the laughter of the women in her shop and the sense of family she experienced with people like Savannah.

She would handle Fox simply, secretly, if possible. She felt joy at her ability to give Toya the opportunity to start life anew, just as it had been offered to her at Woodard's.

Gilda gazed into Toya's eyes and said, "You need rest now more than anything. Let go of the fear. Rest and dream of tomorrow, nothing else. I'll come in the evening."

Toya set down her drink and curled up on the couch. Gilda covered her with a thin blanket. Then she and Savannah quietly left the room. Gilda locked the door and Savannah returned to the chair, quelling her fear and anger. She had not missed the mesmerizing effect of Gilda's look and words but could not forget the times she had seen Fox on a rampage.

"That son of a bitch, that motherfucking bastard!" she said out loud, as if the hard words would release her terror. Then she fell silent while Gilda started on her hair again.

"I'll come back in the evening, slip her out the back, and get her on a train."

"I'm goin' with you. Just tell me what time," Savannah asserted.

Gilda almost said *no* but realized that any woman who'd carried a picture of an aborigine around to beauty parlors and insisted on being transformed into one in Boston in 1955 would not be dissuaded.

"I'll put together a few extra bucks. Ain't no point goin' home broke. Shit, that's all those yokels down home have to talk about!" Savannah continued.

They were both silent after the meeting time was arranged. Gilda finished the neat rows of white curls, then combed out Savannah's hair peremptorily. Savannah didn't glance in the mirror twice. She glanced at the locked storeroom door and gathered herself to hit the streets. The strain of fear made her look a bit older now, yet her smile was still brilliant.

"I better get in the wind. A few extra johns and Toya will go home in style. Let me out of this joint, Miss Square." It was an affectionate term between them. Savannah knew that Gilda had worked in a whorehouse in the past. She didn't know it had been one hundred years ago.

When Savannah was gone, Gilda mechanically swept the hair from the floor and put away her combs, irons, and brushes. She looked around the strangely appointed room, relaxing easily among thick, cold chairs with alien dryers mounted on their backs, the linoleum worn thin by mary janes and stiletto heels. On the chrome coatrack hung sweaters and extra uniforms the other women left behind, just as they did their slippers beside their beds at home. The curled edges of the *Saturday Evening Post, Bronze Thrills,* and *Photoplay* were as much a fixture as the glaring lights and polished mirrors. A woman's place, open and intimate, utilitarian like a kitchen but so easily transformed by heat and laughter. Women came here to be massaged by other women, made beautiful by other women.

Gilda checked the back door, listening for noise from Toya but hearing nothing. As she started to leave there was a firm knock at the other door. Gilda walked angrily to the front of the shop. She jerked the door open, unsure that she could keep her resolve to act calmly and naturally. Her impulse was to leave Fox with wounds as deep as those on Toya's face. But in the doorway stood a woman with brown skin. She was the same height as Gilda, and her dark eyes peered unblinking into Gilda's own. Her hair was in two braids pulled up and pinned across the top of her head. A leather band circled her throat, and earrings made from slender quills and tiny beads hung from her ears.

She stood still, taking Gilda in. There was no evidence of change in either of them, yet the time that had passed begged for some sign of difference, some outward indication they had been separated for so long. Gilda felt her breath leave her as if she'd been hit. Her mouth moved silently as she tried to speak the name, *Bird.*

Gilda backed up as Bird stepped into the room and closed the door behind her. Gilda was the child she had been years ago, like Toya hiding in the storeroom. She had thought of Bird every day, never certain when she would see her again but sure she was ready for this moment. Now that it was here she realized how unprepared she was. She found it difficult to accept the ancient reality of Bird here in this place. In her imaginings, Anthony and Sorel might easily have walked through the door of her shop, as they frequently threatened to do in their letters to her. But Bird always returned to her—in her mind—in a place untouched by the new, the transient commodities called modern.

She gasped for air and sobbed dryly. They breathed together until the air moved in unison between them. Gilda pressed her dark cheek against Bird's bronze face. She forgot about Toya sleeping in the tiny room and forgot her anger at Fox. She only wanted Bird to hold her.

"It's to a timeless place I wish to return, to the place in your heart where I hope always to belong," Bird said, hearing Gilda's thoughts. The ancient rhythms of the Lakota and Fulani peoples vibrated in the air around them as they rocked together in each other's arms, making quiet sounds that were without tears. Through each ran the questions about the past, but there was no room for the answers yet.

The deepening night reminded them that it was time to hunt for the blood. Without speaking, they turned out the lights and left the shop. Specifics of the past or their plans for the future were unimportant as Gilda and Bird hunted together for the first time in many years.

They returned to Gilda's apartment, not far from the shop, languorous with the blood but not yet at peace. Bird deposited a small sachel and pallet as Gilda pointed out the comforts of her three, small basement rooms, but she sensed Bird had already been here and examined them closely. As Gilda moved about the living room and bedroom she could feel the imperceptible shift in her belongings—the brush, the soap, the linen, the books all had been moved and returned to their places. No dust was disturbed, no order rearranged, yet Gilda could feel the difference. As a child she had examined the farmhouse rooms in much the same way, lifting and looking at everything, afraid to disturb, driven to know. She was not sure what she had been seeking but was desperate to look for an answer.

Now Bird circled the rooms anxiously, letting silence envelop her thoughts. Gilda sat on the couch resting her head on its back, surprised at her calm as she watched Bird move around the room. She had unpinned the black braids so they hung to her shoulders. Her slender body looked even smaller inside the loose-fitting coveralls she wore. The tight skin across her broad forehead was marred only by the tiny scar above her left eyebrow that Gilda remembered so well. Gilda closed her eyes, not thinking of Bird's rejection years before but of the woman who had loved them both, who'd brought them together, then taken the true death.

The rich colors of Woodard's and the muted light of Bird's sitting room where they'd shared each other's stories every afternoon were still alive for her. She smiled, recalling how one of the girls in the brothel had warned Gilda to be careful around Bird, and at how easy it had been to give herself over to Bird's loving care. She almost laughed out loud at the pinpricks she had suffered when Bird taught her to sew, and the saddle sores from her riding lessons. These were mild, childhood wounds that reminded her of the grief she'd known since they'd separated.

They faced each other, unable to move apart as night closed around them. Bird finally went to the unlocked sleeping room. There she threw her pallet atop Gilda's.

"We should lie together now," she said softly.

Gilda dropped her white uniform at the foot of the bed, and stepped out of the soft leather shoes that made her appear slightly taller than she really was. Bird stood before her naked, in the total darkness, watching as if she saw the small, frightened girl of long ago. She was so shaken by her own need to hold Gilda, she barely remembered why she'd needed to run away. The isolation had helped give her a clearer vision of what her future might be, but it also left her tight with anxiety. There had been no one with whom to share her past except Gilda. She locked the thick bedroom door and threw the bolt at its base. Gilda lay on her back opening herself. She closed her eyes with the understanding that this left her vulnerable to whatever Bird might wish. She wasn't certain yet whether Bird still held her responsible for the other's death, or if she had returned to offer her love. She knew the question was soon to be answered.

Gilda folded her hands across her breasts, making her appear much as she would have if she were really dead. She thought of her mother and the other woman who'd rescued her, both of whom had given her life, and of Bird who had completed the final change, making her live as she did now. Sorel and Anthony floated through her mind. She had hoped to see them again, to share with them all the things she'd learned since living with them. She thought of Toya, so small and young, locked inside the back room of her shop. She felt Bird probing her mind, knowing everything she knew, even the plan to take Toya to safety.

She let her mind rest as she waited for Bird to decide on life or destruction. She owed her more than her life, yet she knew she need not search for words to tell Bird how much she had meant to her when she was young. She merely waited, her eyes closed, leaving herself vulnerable to Bird's powers. The soft touch of Bird's hand on her brow felt, for a moment, as if it were her mother's. Bird then stroked her neck, slipping softly to her back and rubbing the tender spot just below the hairline where the nerves came together, sparking a tingle inside her thighs. There was no sound in the room except their breathing: Gilda's was slow, almost imperceptible; Bird's deeper, as if she were preparing to run. When Bird kissed her forehead Gilda was startled by the shock of closeness. Until now she hadn't thought about how much time had passed since she'd slept next to anyone. Bird kissed her cheek softly, then moved to her ear.

She began to whisper in a low tone that held Gilda like the mesmerizing gaze they both had in their power. Her words were soft and even. She spoke of her life and aloneness, her fear of being without anyone, always pushing away those she loved. She moved from Gilda's ear down to her breast, knowing words meant little. Gilda's was a full body, and Bird was enthralled by the reality of it. She sliced beneath the right breast and watched, through the thick darkness, the blood which stood even thicker against Gilda's dark skin. She hungrily drew the life through her parted lips into her body.

This was a desire not unlike their need for the blood, but she had already had her share. It was not unlike lust but less single-minded. She felt the love almost as motherly affection, yet there was more. As the blood flowed from Gilda's body into Bird's they both understood the need—it was for completion. They had come together but never taken each other in as fully as they could, cementing their family bond. Gilda felt the life flowing from her.

A peculiar serenity settled on the room, pressing itself firmly against Gilda's body. She had lived as it was meant she should, surviving evil of different sorts, beginning to understand the frailty of mortal life and the responsibility of her own. Her muscles relaxed, her bones sinking toward the mattress. Whether Bird would let her live was no longer a concern. Her body felt warm and light in spite of Bird's weight on her chest. She barely perceived Bird's touch.

Her head was filled with a kaleidoscope of images pulled forward from more than one hundred years of memories. The present no longer existed: her life was a line stretched through time—humming with the wind, taut and delicate, strong and wiry. The faces that sang on the line were clear and immediate, no longer fuzzy images from her childhood. Her mother sang the same song she used to sing when she rocked the Girl to sleep on their hard pallet beside the stove. Her sisters, all there with the same smiles, perspiration gathering around their upper lips, moved down the end-less open rows under the unrelenting sun. They smiled, too young to know they were held captive. She returned to the night in the farmhouse when Bird had completed Gilda's transformation word-lessly, then taken her out for her first hunt.

Bird drew blood from Gilda, much as she had done then. Gilda felt life slipping away from her. The faces of Anthony, Sorel, and Aurelia flared before her, then faded. Her body became a vessel, emptying itself, purging, turning inside out. The smell of blood op-pressively filled the room like flowers too sweet with dying. Bird lifted her weight from Gilda, who lay, waiting for death to finish its claim. She thought she understood why Bird might want her to die: it would give the past a final end. Now it did not matter. Nothing held any consequence as the muscle in her body slipped away from the bone.

Then she felt herself being lifted gently. She wondered if it could be done so quickly, if she was dead and Bird was removing her body. Bird pulled Gilda across her chest and sliced the skin beneath her own breast.

She pressed Gilda's mouth to the red slash, letting the blood wash across Gilda's face. Soon Gilda drank eagerly, filling herself, and as she did her hand massaged Bird's breast, first touching the nipple gently with curiosity, then roughly. She wanted to know this body that gave her life. Her heart swelled with their blood, a tide between two shores. To an outsider the sight may have been one of horror: their faces red and shining, their eyes unfocused and black, the sound of their bodies slick with wetness, tight with life. Yet it was a birth. The mother finally able to bring her child into the world, to look at her. It was not death that claimed Gilda. It was Bird.

She wiped Gilda's body with a sponge, washing away the blood and sweat. She lingered over her as she would a child. She whispered sweet words to her as she might a lover. They lay on their backs, their eyes staring into the darkness around them.

"You've forgiven me the other's death?"

"No," Bird responded. "I learned there was no need for forgive-ness. She had always spoken of death and its part in our lives. I chose not to hear her. Even when I felt her embracing her death with joy that midday, I refused to hear her. I stood in the farmhouse par-lor listening for her until she opened herself. Now I know it was for me to hear her become one with the waves and the sunlight. She was greedy for their touch, to feel her flesh dissolve and her consciousness slip away. She was happy, but I was too selfish to hear. All along I had been refusing her the final right that was hers, to die when and where she wished. It's the most elemental power." Bird stopped, ashamed.

"Where have you been?" Gilda had begun to understand Bird's grief.

"I've always been behind you. I returned to those of my people who survived the terrible years. Offering my knowledge and strength where it might help, relearning how to be with my own people. How to be alone. Even there on the plains I listened for you."

"She wanted me to be your family. Unless you could forgive me I would have failed her." Gilda's voice was again that of the girl learning her lessons back at Woodard's.

"You're not one to fail, my girl."

"I realized that soon after you left and I learned to live alone. It was when I tried to live again with others that I doubted myself. I didn't think I could without knowing for certain what you felt, but it has become easier. My time with Sorel and Anthony helped to heal the past."

"On the day of our first lesson I knew that you would learn well, with or without me."

"And now?"

"Now I'm here for a family visit."

Dawn was still on the far side of the sky, but they had energy only to be near each other. Their hands touched and the night passed at its normal pace, moon and stars swirling above, the sun chasing to catch up.

Before pinkness reached the sky Gilda awoke with a start. She sat up in the darkness feeling for the source of her panic. Bird's low voice beside her asked what was wrong.

"The shop. . .it's the shop!"

They quickly jumped into their clothes and ran out to the street, down the few, long blocks of the avenue to the beauty parlor. They were standing in front of the blazing flames before the fire engines left the firehouse. Gilda felt a scream rising in her throat as she stood watching the bulging glass window.

"The back!" Bird shouted, and they ran around the block to the alley. Unlike the twenty-four-hour incandescence of Mass. Ave., the alley was pitch black. Still Gilda had no difficulty making her way to the small yard that backed her shop. She bolted over the fence and Bird followed as the sound of the approaching fire engines reached them. Smoke seeped through the pores of the building; the heat was a wavy aura around it. Gilda raised her fist and struck out against the back door, creating a hole just the size of her hand. She reached inside and unbolted the door. Bird yanked it back, almost removing it from the hinges. Toya lay still as death, her breathing shallow, the spell Gilda had used to calm her into sleep still holding. Bird pulled Toya into her arms and screamed "Out!" as Gilda stood hypnotized by the sound of the flames on the other side of the locked storeroom door and by the acrid smell of gasoline.

By the time the fire engines arrived, Bird, Gilda, and Toya were blocks away. Once inside Gilda's flat they looked at the still figure. The fire had not gotten through, but the smoke had been thick. Bird listened to Toya's breathing, felt her pulse, and made reassuring gestures as Gilda watched, questioning. Bird leaned over the girl and breathed into her lungs, swelling her chest to bursting. She then drew the breath back, much as she had done with blood so many times. She breathed the rancid air out and breathed into the girl's mouth again.

"Wake her," she said.

Gilda knelt beside the couch, stroking the girl's forehead and whispering into her ear until the girl opened her eyes. She smiled at Gilda as if none of the events of the past few days had happened. Then her eyes clouded over with anxiety. She looked around, confused by the change.

"We brought you here—there was a fire at the shop."

"A fire! I was dreaming about fire but I couldn't wake up. I wasn't afraid but I couldn't wake up."

"Don't worry, no one knows where you are."

"You mean he thinks I'm in that fire, don't you?"

"Would he do that?"

"That ain't nothin' to what Fox would do."

Gilda was silent as she looked at Bird. She turned away, the ripple in the muscles across her back moving from liquid into stone. Bird turned to Toya and smiled with the sweetness of a maiden aunt.

"You mustn't worry about this for another minute. Gilda and I will take care of Fox."

"No, please don't try to face him. You don't know him. He'll kill you both and laugh. Just let me get out now. Maybe if he thinks I was in the fire—"

"No, Toya. Remain here and don't open the door for any reason."

The girl looked uncertain. After the last three days nothing seemed real to her, and she laughed nervously.

She pulled her legs up beneath her on Gilda's sofa, her eyes staring blankly into the darkness. They had said wait, so she would wait. There was nowhere else to go.

Gilda and Bird went back up to Mass. Ave. to see the small crowd gathered in front of the smoking ruin that had been Gilda's shop. They stood at a distance from the cluster of black faces whose eyes watched the white firemen with a wild array of emotions. Their anger at the white men who always seemed to arrive too late in their neighborhood was as pungent as the smoke. Still, they stood as supplicants in their nightclothes, desperate for something to survive the blaze, knowing that their appointed saviors had little personal concern one way or the other.

The flames cast an orange light onto the faces that watched with horror and fascination. Gilda caught the gaze of a man who was smiling. The flame made his light eyes look amber and red like some shining jewel. He stared straight into Gilda's eyes, unflinching. She knew it was Fox. His smile was without humor, his eyes flat and compelling. As he peered at her, Gilda saw his hatred and the joy the hatred brought him. Her body stiffened with recognition. Bird felt it too and held onto Gilda's arm as Fox pulled away from the crowd and walked swiftly up Massachusetts Avenue. Gilda recognized the fluid movement, the opaque eyes. He was one too—one of them.

In the time she had lived here she'd searched the air looking for others, and there had been none. Or so she thought. He had kept his thoughts shielded deliberately and perhaps felt safe enough simply ignoring Gilda's presence. That would no longer be possible.

Once separated from the crowd Fox turned hard on his heel and disappeared as if he had never been there. The heat of the fire filled the cool, empty space he left behind. Gilda strained against Bird's grip, anxious to follow, to find him. Bird said, "We can wait until tomorrow. He will be somewhat difficult to kill."

Gilda and Bird walked away from the blaze and the crowded sidewalk. They didn't speak until they had almost reached the door leading down to Gilda's basement flat. Bird spoke first. "I feel a bit foolish—waiting so long to come to you. No moment seemed right. I knew you were waiting for me but I was still unable to believe we could feel comfortable in each other's company. Now here we are. It's not exactly what I'd planned."

"My time with Sorel helped me to understand," Gilda responded. "After that, waiting for you to return was not such a bad thing. I've lived a good life. I've brought no one into the family, but perhaps that time is near. I couldn't take that chance until we repaired the breach between us."

At the doorstep Bird said, "I've seen much of the precious blood of my people spilled into the earth over the years. I had hoped this would be a time of renewal before I returned to them, but I can see the battle is joined on more fronts than I had realized. This Fox is like others I've observed; he will be unrelenting."

When Gilda said nothing Bird added, "We will have to destroy him to free her. You understand?"

"Yes," Gilda said, not truly understanding how this would be done.

"There may be little time for discussion in the coming hours. But I would say we need only go forward from here." The sheen of her brown face in the evening light delighted Gilda and almost dispelled her anxieties.

Toya was sitting in the same position on the sofa, staring at the door when they went inside. Her eyes showed terror as Gilda appeared in the doorway, then relief.

"The shop is probably a complete loss but I don't think anyone upstairs was hurt." Gilda put her arms around Toya who remained impassive.

"Don't think about what you're going to do," Gilda continued, "we'll take care of it. Believe me, please." As Toya began her protest Gilda just went on talking as if she had already solved the problem, as if she had no indication of the horror that awaited them.

"I've forgotten my manners. This is Bird, my oldest friend in the world." Bird laughed at the simple statement and reached down to hold Toya's hand.

"Gilda's right, let us take care of this. By tomorrow night you'll be back home with little to worry about but your mother fussing at you for being gone so long."

Toya didn't have the energy to respond. She raced through all of the questions she had and the one answer that told her that by this time tomorrow they would all be dead.

"All you have to do is remember when you face your mother and the rest of the people at home is that you managed to make it back to them. There's no shame in what you've done up here, in this life. I've done it. It was long ago, but you see no mark on me. Please just leave this time behind you, think only of home and the future," Bird said in a soft and rhythmic voice.

She massaged Toya's hand, looking into her eyes. Soon Toya was asleep, held by Bird's will. They lay her down on the couch, covered her with a blanket, then went into the bedroom.

After Gilda bolted the bedroom door they lay together in their clothes on the rumpled comforter, ill at ease with another—not one of them—sleeping so nearby. Their breathing was even and shallow, their pulses almost imperceptible. If this were really sleep it might be said that they rested well.

On Sunday evening the door of the 411 Lounge opened into another world—not separate from the rest of the neighborhood, but more of a fantasy. At seven o'clock there were few people at the bar: two black men sat perched on stools watching television. The bartender stared out the window through the venetian blinds, only glancing up briefly when the three women walked in. Bird's long cloak fluttered, filling the doorframe. He looked more closely when he recognized Toya. The avenue was buzzing with gossip.

They walked past the bar to the back and sat at one of the dining tables. Here the women and men of the street could retreat and be themselves. Pimps and business girls flirted with each other outrageously, playing out dramas constructed to make life interesting. While sometimes the games were dangerous on the street, the 411 Lounge was like the family living room. People rarely raised their voices here. Hank, the owner, wouldn't allow it. But they did, as Gilda had assured Bird, observe and gossip. If they separated from Savannah at the 411, Fox would know about it.

The chef saw the three come in and took a few last puffs on her Tareyton before going out to take their order. When she recognized Toya she regretted not having a waitress on Sundays so she could stay in the kitchen and avoid what was sure to be an explosion.

She was relieved her children had made other plans tonight and would not be slipping in through the back door to have dinner.

When Henrietta reached Gilda's table no one was ready to order. Toya kept shaking her head, saying, "I'll wait. . ."

"I got no waitress today so if you want something from the bar, you mind getting it yourself?"

Gilda remembered why this place remained calm. Henrietta was a towering column of authority. It was clear that everyone here knew what was going on, yet Henrietta's cocoa-brown face was impassive. Her large, dark eyes betrayed her anxiety for only a second. The curls that sat tightly on her forehead were flecked with grey, an impressive crowning of her six-foot-tall, two-hundred-pound body. The line from the slightly padded shoulders of her dress fell softly around her full breasts, inward at her waist, and out again around her firm hips. The large white apron she had doubled over and tied tightly at her waist gave her a no-nonsense look, a titillating contrast to the bright red slash of her lipstick.

She took in the situation and proceeded in the only way she knew how—as if these were her children, too. "You gonna be able to save anything outta that mess?" she asked Gilda. Everyone knew everything on the avenue.

"I haven't looked closely but I don't think so."

"You got insurance, ain't ya?"

"Yes, I guess that'll cover most of it. I'm just glad no one was hurt. Has Savannah been here tonight?" Gilda asked, eager to avoid the connection between the fire and Toya.

"Naw, she hardly comes out on Sundays, you know. She don't even want to talk to nobody on Sunday 'cept her kids. She calls 'em two, three times on Sunday like long distance ain't nothing." As Henrietta talked she glanced quickly at Bird, whom she'd never seen before. She seemed puzzled by the plain face and nervous energy.

"You know that boy probably comin' in here after nine o'clock," she said, turning to Toya.

Toya nodded and looked at Gilda who said, "We're waiting for Savannah, then we'll be gone. But Toya needs a good meal."

Before Toya could speak, Henrietta had settled the question. "I know what the girl likes. Let me bring you a little plate of something. I got some of those yams left over from last night. I'm gonna heat 'em up for ya. She likes that sweet stuff, you know. You girls want something? My chicken's real good tonight."

Both Gilda and Bird shook their heads no. Henrietta did not push it, although it usually made her angry when three of the girls would order one plate for all of them.

When she left the table, Bird rose to go to the bar. "I know Sorel has tried to make champagne your drink of choice," Bird said with a smile, "but I think today we should make it neat." When she returned, she and Gilda sipped from the weighty rock glasses, letting the heat of the liquor burn through them. Their blood raced like jet streams once the alcohol entered the flow. Both felt flushed, enjoying the rare taste. Toya ate in silence. Henrietta returned with an extra spoonful of yams which she plopped unceremoniously on Toya's plate before walking away.

Gilda and Bird waited. Sarah Vaughn's voice from the jukebox competed with a ball game on television. Several people at the bar turned in surprise when Savannah walked through the door and headed directly to the back booth where the three women sat.

She dropped a short rabbit jacket over the back of the seat and squeezed in beside Toya. She was wearing a silk man-tailored striped shirt which hung loosely, almost to her knees, over wool slacks. Her white hair shone brilliantly, while her face was a mask of tight lines drawn into a smile.

"So what you broads doing out in the street on Sunday? Ain't you never heard of a day of rest?" She looked at Gilda as she spoke and held onto the thin flesh of Toya's leg with her hand. Small diamonds twinkled on two of her fingers, a sapphire on a third. It matched the star sapphire in a thin silver chain around her neck. She always wore her real jewelry on her day off.

Gilda introduced Bird casually, as if they regularly met at the 411 on Sunday evenings, then asked, "How're the kids?"

"Girl, how the hell can they be? Darlene got all A's in school, so she don't want to do no homework. Daryl got all D's in school, so he don' wanna do none either!" With that she laughed loudly and several people at the bar turned. Gilda excused herself from the table and had Savannah follow her to the tiny bathroom at the back of the bar. Toya stopped eating and finally began to drink her glass of gin.

Inside the bathroom Savannah was tense. "I knew you be here today, but don' ask me how. Matter of fact, don' ask me nothin', beginnin' with who that dry one is you got with you or what the hell the fire was about. All I know is we got to get that child out of here and right now!"

"Listen, Savannah, you're out of it. Fox is more than you or I can deal with alone, so I want you to forget everything. Stay here and meet some friends for a drink or dinner."

"Are you crazy? That nigger ain't shit. He's been waiting to get his for the past five years, and if it's us that got to give it to him, then that's it, ya dig?"

"Savannah, let it go. We saw him last night. He's a real killer—"

"Girl, I coulda told you that before the shit hit. He's more'n that. The girls that leave him can be counted on one finger, so I know what the word is, O.K.? Let's just get the hell out of this joint. I ain't even sure the .45 I got in my jacket will take care of him!"

"You're right, Savannah, it won't. That's why you've got to stay out of it."

"You ever kill anybody?" Savannah asked it with a coolness that did not match the agitated movement of her hands. She didn't wait for Gilda to respond. "It ain't an easy thing, but I think that's the only way Toya gonna leave this town. And I'ma tell you at this point, after that fire, that motherfucker is tryin' to kill her and droppin' him is the only way to get her free."

"I know," Gilda said.

"Well, have you?"

"Yes," she answered impatiently. The cloying smell of the air freshener and the closeness of the walls made Gilda even more anxious. The faces floated up in her mind again, and the bitterness of those moments singed the back of her throat. Savannah was surprised by the response and by its tone.

The bathroom door swung open abruptly. Henrietta burst in, closing it tightly behind her.

"That other one says y'all get out now. She say he's coming!"

"We'll take the alley!" said Savannah.

"She done paid me," Henrietta said as Gilda pressed some bills into her hand. But Gilda did not hear. She had Savannah by the hand as they tumbled out the fire exit.

The narrow stairs went down one dark flight into the alley. A row of full trash cans stood against one wall. Bird picked her way around debris, holding Toya by the wrist with one hand and Savannah's fur in the other. Gilda and Savannah came up close behind.

"Turn right up the alley, hurry," Savannah whispered loudly. Bird peered into the darkness at her right, trusting Savannah's words and her own instinct. Their footsteps were almost silent as they ran. Both Gilda and Bird concentrated not on the running, but on the next step after the alley; there would be few safe places now.

The street light at the end of the alley was out. It was dark, and the opening onto the street was blocked by a large car. Bird stopped short. The three women almost piled into her like cartoon figures. The door of the car sprung open wide, but the interior remained murky. Gilda was angry she had no weapon. She might have taken a knife from the table or a glass. How would she cut into the man's heart, stop it from beating, with her bare hands? Bird stood motionless, searching her memory of the surrounding territory. She had not been prepared to face this one yet. More time was needed, but there was no more time.

"Back to the bar," she whispered and let go of Toya.

"No," Savannah said, "it's Skip." She ran toward the car. Gilda followed her and recognized the thin, brown-skinned young man sliding over from the driver's to the passenger's seat. His boyish face was split by a genuine smile.

"Get in, hurry up. Damn!" Savannah said as she got behind the wheel. Gilda climbed into the backseat, Toya and Bird followed. Savannah pulled the car away from the curb silently, slowly, without turning on the lights, driving as if she'd trained all her life for the getaway. "We got a house on the Cape we share with Maurice. It's closed down now, so we can hide out there for a while."

Gilda and Bird looked at each other, knowing there would be little hiding time. Fox would find them easily and follow. He only had to listen to the thoughts, sniff out the fear of the others in the car. But he had to be faced somewhere, and away from the eyes of the city was better. Neither wanted to risk a confrontation with him among the crowds of the train station. Gilda was sorry that Savannah, and now Skip, were involved, yet their choice felt natural. Bird picked up these thoughts as she sifted through her own. She held the girl close, trying to calm her with her touch. She was silent, staring ahead as if her will, not Savannah, drove the car through the evening streets.

Then Toya spoke. "I don't know what he want with me. Shit, I ain't even the big money-maker."

"Girl, you know it ain't about money with most of 'em," Savannah said over her shoulder.

"Maybe you all better just drop me off at the bus, I mean I could get on and be away before he knows. You all could just hold him back, or something. I don't even have to take it home directly. I mean, I could go a roundabout way, you know, so he won't be able to follow me."

Gilda answered. "He'd know, Toya. There's no way we can hold him or keep him from knowing. He'd be there when you got there, wherever it was. Savannah's right, we'll just stay put, stay out of town, until he comes to us."

As the car sped through the night Gilda and Bird watched the fog gathering around the road and the dim lights from the houses growing further apart. Skip was quiet during most of the ride, only speaking to answer the few questions that Savannah threw at him.

"Yes," he'd remembered the milk for the tea and the brandy and the extra clothes. He'd mailed her letters. Each response came officiously with an edge of pride. Savannah just nodded or said "uh-huh," like she was grading him.

Everyone was silent for ten miles or so when Skip said unexpectedly, "I brought your pillow, the soft one."

Gilda saw one of Savannah's hands leave the steering wheel to rest on Skip's leg. She said thanks in a clipped voice, her throat tight. They were silent again. Savannah wanted to ask questions of the dark one, Bird, but could see there would be no answers. Her glance into the rearview mirror confirmed it. The two women sat stonily with Toya wedged between them.

Savannah broke the silence with a sudden loud laugh. Everyone looked at her, startled by the sound.

"Goddamn! Me and Skip got this, what you call, contingency plan together to avoid a funeral, not lead the procession. Skip, I think your girls here need a drink!"

Toya was the first to laugh. It was as if Savannah had pricked her with a pin, releasing the tension that held her tight. Skip passed a flask to the backseat, and it circled the group several times before the tension left the air.

They finally exited off the main road and turned into a small lane. The house was tiny. It was set back and surrounded by a high hedge, its rear toward the bay. They entered the bungalow hurriedly, escaping the damp air. Gilda cautioned Savannah to leave the wooden shutters closed on all the windows as they searched with flashlights for lanterns. Once the amber glow was cast over the room, Skip and Toya exhaled forcefully. It sounded like they had been holding their breath for the entire ride. Gilda walked to the rear of the room where the kitchen remained in shadow. She looked through the back door which opened out onto a small yard overrun with weeds and dead grass leading down to the beach. Bird stood in the center of the room while Savannah unpacked a bag of groceries in the kitchen.

"What's up there?" Bird asked, staring at a trapdoor in the ceiling. A chain hung from it, a tiny brass ring at the end swaying in the air.

"The attic. It's got another small bed and a lot of junk stored for the summer," Skip answered.

Bird stood on a chair and pulled at the chain until the stairs dislodged and she could lower them into the living room. An even stronger musty smell filled the room as Bird climbed up to the attic with a flashlight in hand. She moved above them, feeling the room rather than looking at it. The single bed in its brass frame was next to a shuttered window. There was barely room to stand at full height, and the boxes left little space to walk about.

She came down and said, "We'll take that room."

"Sure. We've got sleeping bags and everything up there you want," Skip said, eager to be helpful. Bird watched him as she pushed the stairs back up into the ceiling. He was slightly built and his mocha-colored skin was almost as dark as her own. His closely cut hair seemed conservative compared to the blue sharkskin suit and dark blue shoes he wore. He looked to be about twenty to Bird. She could smell the fear in him, a boy among old women, but she also sensed his fierce loyalty to Savannah. She wondered about him for only a second, then turned to Gilda who was about to open the front door.

"Maybe Skip can do that for you?" Bird said.

"Yes, Skip, how about driving the car around back, into the yard. No point in drawing attention to the house," Gilda said.

"Sure thing." He grabbed the car keys from the table, full with his mission. Savannah chuckled and rushed over to kiss the back of his neck as he went out, looking, at that moment, as young as he did.

"O.K., I'm ready for a drink," Savannah said. "That seems to be the theme of our little get-together tonight." She unlocked a cabinet beneath the sink and lined up bottles on the small counter that stood between the main room and the kitchen area. Gilda sat on the couch, Toya on the hooked rug at her feet. Bird sat across from them in the one armchair.

Savannah glanced at each of them and asked, "Brandy all

around?" Everyone looked up when the door opened. Skip came back in as she poured. Toya trembled, and Savannah gave her the first drink.

"That's my baby, and I use that word advisedly," she said, handing Skip the next one.

The room was old. The walls and floor met at odd angles; the floorboards were worn in the way that says many people have enjoyed the house. A thin layer of dust covered the framed photographs on the sideboard: several vintage pictures of men and women, someone's parents in their youth, and snapshots of Savannah and Skip, their arms linked with two slender men in bathing suits.

Gilda recognized Maurice from Mass. Ave., but not the pale man with his hand draped intimately over Maurice's shoulder. Bird could almost hear the laughter of these carefree friends as they ran up from the beach and collapsed in this weary room. When Savannah sat next to Gilda on the couch, the cushions sank under her weight. Skip took the ottoman that matched the faded cover of Bird's chair. He stretched his legs in front of him and leaned back on his elbows. Everyone was quiet, not sure how to pass the evening.

Bird shifted in her chair after a moment, then said, "Gilda?"

"Well, I don't think anything will happen tonight," she responded, as if they'd already started the conversation in their heads. "He'll search the city 'til dawn. Go to his regular hangouts. My house probably, maybe to yours, Savannah, if the people in the bar say you left with us."

"I don't think so. Not one of them barflies likes the dude. I mean this is a guy any of them would walk backwards away from in the desert if they thought they could get away with it."

"He has persuasive ways, so we can figure he'll check everywhere in town before he comes out here tomorrow night."

"What if he comes in the morning?" Skip asked. "I mean, why should he wait? He might think we'll just try to skip town, head west..."

"He won't come in the morning. He'll be here tomorrow evening. We'll have a plan by then, but you all must do exactly as we say. No questions, no hesitations. It'll be hard to surprise Fox. But I think we have one for him. Maybe even a couple of them. The main thing is that we don't panic."

Gilda's last words were aimed almost directly at Toya. Bird

peered at her, looking for signs of hysteria.

"Fox broke my jaw once," Toya said in a softly accented voice, "just backhanded me across the room. But I never hollered, never cried. All the way to the hospital they kept looking at me, waiting. But I couldn't. Later he did things, mean things like threw out my letters from mama, then he ripped up my favorite dress 'cause he didn't like the color. I couldn't cry when he did that stuff. I knew he was waitin' for me to fall apart. He was doin' 'em to make me cry. So I couldn't, and I ain't gonna now. I'll cry when I know he's gonna leave me alone. And if that means he got to be dead to do that, then like the preacher say: may God have mercy on his soul."

"Amen!" Skip said.

The assent of the others came in silence.

Gilda rose and said, "I'm going out to scout around the house, just a bit. I'll be back in an hour."

The silence remained unbroken until Savannah spoke. "Hell, I ain't had to hide out from no nigger since 1940. You heard tell of Franklin, ain't you?" She directed her question to Toya, who nodded. "Well, he took it into his head he wasn't gonna let me leave him. Which was something else since I ain't never gone with him in the first place. He just started following me around, hanging over me like a fool. Got so I couldn't leave the bar but he'd be right there. Scared off half my customers. I was so mad I thought I'd croak the guy."

"What'd you do?" Skip asked like a child hearing a bedtime story.

"I got pretty sick of it after a while. But I ain't had no one to hang with me yet and I wasn't ready to fight no man in the street, so I took off up to Roxbury to this woman who had a rep as big as Franklin's. She call herself Danny. Fancy Danny they called her on the avenue. She wore a tiny diamond on three fingers of each hand and one in her ear. Wore the sharpest threads in town. I just went up to Danny's and asked her if I can stay at her place. She laughed and said sure. Then she asked if I want to be one of her girls. And I said yeah, for a little while, kinda nervous you know. And she said, 'I ain't never had to chain nobody yet.'

"One night he comes to the bar, the 411 matter of fact, and me and Danny and one of the other girls was sittin' having dinner. He ask me to come outside and talk to him. Danny says, 'We're all family round this table, why don't you just sit down and talk right here?' I was sure he'd jump bad with a load of bullshit, but he just glared at Danny and walked away.

"Well, Miss Danny pulled off each of them rings, wrapped them in the long silk scarf she had round her neck, and gave it to the bartender on her way out."

"Gus," Skip volunteered, pleased to take part in the story.

"Ah, what you know about it boy, you wasn't even left home from your mama yet," Savannah said, laughing.

"Yeah, it was that big, light Gus. She just tossed them rings over the bar at him and followed Franklin out the bar. She wasn't so tall, not even real big, but solid. The only way you could tell she was mad was that sweat was on her chocolate skin, making her forehead shine. Shiny like that black hair she kept pulled back in a bun. Danny come back in the bar ten minutes later, put her rings back on, and ordered a martini. I never forgot it. Cool as a cuke. And that was that."

Skip was laughing. "Yeah, didn't even get her threads dirty, I bet!"

"Naw, not a speck of dirt. She coulda even left them rings on! Franklin never bothered me again. Even after I moved out of Danny's a year later."

"A year! What took you so long?" Skip asked.

Savannah laughed, "Well, she was right. She never had to chain nobody."

Bird laughed out loud for the first time since they arrived. Skip looked puzzled but laughed too.

The night got darker. Bird refused to watch the door or wonder about Gilda. She felt the slight opening of pain in her chest. The uneasiness of it was not difficult for her now, but soon she would have to go out.

Gilda's entrance startled them out of their thoughts. To Bird she said, "I've scouted south on the bay side. Maybe you should look around as well."

Bird rose silently and left the bungalow. She, too, would return with the flush of new blood on her face. The look would be mistaken for the effects of the sharp salt air and a brisk walk. Bird hurried into the darkness. She wanted to return to the company of these people. It had been some time since she'd spent this type of sociable evening.

Not since Woodard's. The white-haired woman, Savannah, and Gilda had linked in a way that Bird envied. There was an empty space after years of separation where she and Gilda had once been united. She remembered her first sight of Gilda as a girl—she had looked so African with her dark brow and deep eyes. It was warming to see the look echoed here in the varying colors of the others. The same penetrating gaze filled their eyes almost as if the years away from their home soil had not damaged them. She had found this kind of tribal unity with her people, too.

Bird sped into the shadows until she came upon a small house that held more than one person. She slipped inside and found the bedroom of a teenaged boy, sleeping deeply as they do. She held him with the hypnotic quality of her voice while she took the blood from his arm. His desires were simple: good grades on a science test and a date for an approaching dance. Bird felt a rush of tenderness as she slipped inside his secrets, gently prodding open his sense of mathematic and scientific principles so he'd grasp ideas a bit more easily. And she left the idea that it might not matter if he had a companion or not. The evening would be a success if he simply enjoyed everyone as a friend. He did not stir when she sealed the wound and listened to his slowed pulse. As she moved away from him he turned on his side and mumbled out loud, returning to his own dreams.

As Bird ran back toward the bungalow she tried to think of ways to approach the problem, then realized there was no need for that. They were the problem—Fox would approach them. They only had to make sure they were prepared. She had, in fact, discovered something in the attic that might give them a slight advantage.

By the time she returned to the house everyone except Gilda looked like they were ready for sleep. Savannah pulled out the sofa while Gilda handed down linen from the attic. The ottoman would open up into a single bed for Toya after Gilda and Bird went up to the attic. Bird secured the doors and checked the windows, then took Savannah aside in the kitchen.

"We'll stay upstairs until late afternoon. Please, don't let any of them come up or disturb us unless there's some emergency. I'm sure nothing will happen until the evening, but keep your eyes on the road."

Savannah nodded with the crispness of a soldier.

"I saw a small boat out back with an outboard motor. Can you get that in operating order?" Bird continued without waiting for Savannah's response. "Whatever you have to do—get gas, plug holes—by this evening." Savannah nodded again, a bronze-and-platinum statue come to life in the misty lamplight.

Bird and Gilda went up the angled stairs, and Savannah closed them from behind until they fit snugly in the ceiling. Bird took a length of bed sheet and secured the stairs shut by tying one end to the step and the other to a pipe in a corner of the room. They both smiled at the primitive precaution. Bird spread her dark cloak out on the bed, its thick hem filled with the soil of Mississippi and the Dakotas. The two women lay down and drew it tightly around their bodies. The soft lapping of the water so close behind the house kept them alert, even in sleep.

Slivers of light slipped into the attic room at dawn, but neither of them stirred until the afternoon. Bird first heard the soft thud of a mallet on wood. She continued to lay still with Gilda in her arms as she listened to the repeated attempts to get an engine going. The muffled cheers of Skip and Toya reached up to the attic when it turned over.

Bird stretched, then spoke to Gilda. "Fox won't be certain that there are two of us. That is one advantage. He will also not think much of our crew: two women and a boy won't seem impressive to him. That's another advantage."

Without moving from Bird's breast Gilda said, "And there's the bay."

"And something else," Bird said sitting up. She crossed the cool, wood floor to a low chest and returned holding out a small leather pouch. She undid the leather tie that held it closed and spilled the contents onto the bed. Gilda stared down at the syringe and a clear envelope of white powder, then looked at Bird, startled.

"Skip, I think. At least it used to be Skip. That's why it was locked away up here. At dusk I'll cook it down and fill the needle. There should be enough heroin here to slow him down, if we can get close enough to him."

"You can't!" Gilda almost shouted. "Skip's worked too hard to kick. Savannah has complete confidence in him now. If she knows about this—"

Bird cut in impatiently. "Fox will kill Toya, Savannah, Skip, you, and me if he can! Haven't you understood yet? He is not a misguided youth. He possesses all the powers that you and I do. He's possibly older, certainly more merciless." Bird stopped. She could see that Gilda understood how irrelevant her human concerns were right now.

Bird brushed her hand across Gilda's forehead, down the side of her face and her jawline as she spoke. "Dear girl, the mortal ones will settle their own worries. To connect with them, yes, but you must live as what you are. Listen to the world from your own powers." Gilda pulled away and sat up on their cot.

Bird continued. "Is this why you've taken no one into this life? Is the mortal world too sacred?"

Gilda didn't speak, but her eyes were open in the shock of realization. Bird reached out to rub Gilda's cheek again, as if soothing a child, and continued talking more softly. "It is a good thing to love and care for others. That's why I travel, to learn from the people and study what they search for. But we are as we are. Our world is separate from theirs. To ignore our possibilities is to nurture only disappointment."

"It's been my one-hundred-year journey—away from my people into the world," Gilda said. "Only now have I felt like I could retrieve them, touch and be touched by them as I was before. In the shop I've grown to understand the rhythm of their lives, their desires. It's not so easy to step back and say cavalierly, 'Too bad, Savannah, we've discovered Skip's a failure, a junky liar just like you feared!' "

"There's consideration in everything. I make no suggestion callously, but their questions must be answered later, and not by us."

Gilda's assent was implicit in the quiet that surrounded her.

The other question still hung in the air. Neither wanted to speak about it, but each knew it weighed heavily. Once subdued, how to kill another like themselves? It would be far from easy. His powers, at least equal to theirs, were fueled by anger and hatred.

"I have killed," Gilda said in a tremulous voice. "I hold the faces as I should, but it was not intentional. And not one of us."

"It will have to be done. He'll accept nothing less. You've seen them, I know. Their hunger for destruction and death is insatiable. He would torment her for his own enjoyment for as long as he's amused. If we're to give her this second chance, we have to make her free of him."

"I don't know that I can do it. . .deliberately. . .to one of our own."

"Don't be sentimental here; he is not among the living. We are. He seeks only to drag others into death and thrives on watching their descent. Don't forget what you've learned about people, about us."

Gilda remembered Eleanor's frigid smile as she'd ordered her to kill Samuel, and nodded.

They pushed the stairway down, rejoining the group and leaving the answer to prove itself in the action. Skip announced that he and Savannah had gotten the engine going and that he was off to wash and then start dinner. Savannah rinsed the oil and dirt off her hands in the kitchen sink, then plopped down on the sofa with a bottle nearby.

"You think he'll come tonight?"

"Yes, just after dark." Toya's body tensed as Gilda spoke.

"You'll all go down to the edge of the water with the boat. Keep it ready to take off. I don't want anyone coming back to the house unless Bird or I bring you back. No matter what you see or think you hear, stay at the water unless you're looking right at me or Bird."

"You can't believe I'm goin' swimmin' while you two take that bastard. Besides that dinky boat can't hold but two people. Skip can watch the girl; I'll stay up here with you." Skip started to protest but, like Gilda, he felt Savannah's resolve.

Gilda stepped forward, peering into Savannah's eyes and was about to speak when Bird said, "Maybe she's right. Even if Fox doesn't think much of what we're likely to do, why don't we just give him a little surprise?"

"O.K., ladies, you're about to have the meal of your life. Skip's old-fashion-down-home recipe spaghetti with fried chicken tomato sauce." While he worked cutting meat from leftover chicken into a steamy tomato sauce, Toya stood by the back door looking out over the grey yard toward the bay.

"I guess if we got any family heirlooms that's breakable I better put them away, huh?" Savannah said, looking around at the makeshift furnishings and giving a loud snort. She slipped the photos into the drawer tenderly. The smell of garlic and tomatoes filled the room as Skip stirred the sauce which threatened to bubble over the top of a deep iron frying pan.

"I forgot to pick up Italian bread. I make a pretty mean garlic bread."

Bird and Gilda looked at each other and then laughed out loud.

"What's so funny, I ain't supposed to like to cook?" Skip asked puzzled.

"Hell," Savannah said, "Skip's a better cook than most people

I know, except my mama."

Bird said, "No, just a private joke from the old days," as she pulled the brass ring, lowering the stairs into the living room. She went up, still chuckling to herself. Savannah pulled dishes from the cabinet.

In a few moments Bird came down again, the leather pouch strapped to her belt. Skip saw it first; his shiny tan skin blanched. He stared at the bag as if it were a snake that would uncoil and spring at him.

Savannah felt his reaction and looked at Bird. "Where'd that come from?" Her voice was hard-edged. Although she spoke to Bird the accusation flew through the air toward Skip.

"I always kept that bag, just for sentimental reasons, mama. You knew that."

"Ain't no sentiment tied up with that bag, fool. Ain't nothing mixed up with that bag but death!"

"In that case it will come in handy tonight, don't you think, Savannah?"

Savannah's eyes blazed at Skip. At first he looked away, his eyes darting around the room searching for a clue to his response and escape. Then he met Savannah's stare full on and said simply, "I'm clean, Savannah. Been clean since we got together, and I expect to stay clean a long time more."

"Yeah, if we live through tonight," Savannah said, turning her back on Bird, wanting the bag to disappear not only from the house but from the past as well.

"He's coming," Gilda said sharply.

"Let's go," Skip said, as he pulled Toya by the arm, shoving sweaters into her hand.

Gilda opened the back door, letting light pour out to the yard.

"Hurry, and stay there. Don't come back up. Just stay," she said as if speaking to young puppies. Skip and Toya made their way with a small flashlight down to the boat. They climbed in and turned the flashlight off.

"Unlock the front door, Savannah."

She did as she was told and took another large drink. Bird swung the trapdoor down, sprinted up the stairs, and closed the door behind her.

"What now?"

"We'll just sit; he's not far. Bird will watch from above to make sure he comes to the house first."

"I can try to talk some sense into him, but I don't think he's the type to listen to sense."

"You're right, Savannah. All we want to do is maneuver him into position."

Gilda moved around the room inspecting objects, moving them from table to bookcase, clearing a path.

"You mustn't let him touch you, Savannah. He has the strength of ten men and not the soul of one. I'm not exaggerating, so follow my lead and stay out of his hands."

Savannah took her gun from the fur jacket, checked the clip, then slipped it between the cushions on the sofa.

"That's not going to do you much good."

"I ain't never seen a nigger could resist the persuasion of a .45."

"This is the one, Savannah. Even if you get him dead in the heart that will only slow him down."

"You talk like he's some kind of spook or something. This is 1955, girl, and I been up off the farm for quite some time." Gilda didn't answer, so Savannah drained her glass. Both women remained still when they heard the screen door open. Fox pushed the front door gently and stepped inside knowing he was expected.

He smiled callowly at Savannah. "Well, Miss Savannah, it's a little early for the summer cabin, don't you think?"

Savannah said nothing. When his gaze settled on Gilda his light eyes closed like a cat's, seeming to look at her through the lids rather than under them. "What a surprise," he continued. "I don't think we've met. Gilda, isn't it?"

She didn't respond but watched his body, narrow and thin under the soft silk trousers and cashmere sweater. His small frame rippled with energy; his long, thin fingers twitched impatiently. Dark hair cut close to his head ended in a sharp widow's peak on his forehead.

"This is going to be a real pleasure." He did not move from the door, only looked around the room. "Where is she?"

"On a trip," Savannah said before Gilda could speak.

"Really? I don't think so." He stared at Gilda, curiosity flickering across his face. "Shall I start with her or you?"

"You can start anywhere you like. I'm only interested in your ending."

"Ending? I don't expect that for some time," Fox said through a thin smile.

"Funny, I thought tonight would be a good time for it."

"Come on now, you can't be serious about this. For the sake of that simple little girl you want the true death? We two have many more things we might discuss than this little life."

"No, we have nothing to discuss at all except the value of her life, the necessity of your death."

Fox gave a short bellow, then lunged across the room with his fingers stretched out for Gilda's throat. She rolled from the couch, her motion almost too swift for Savannah to see. Fox maintained his balance against the back of the sofa while he reached out, grabbing Gilda's arm. He yanked backward, but she countered with a side kick that sent him tumbling over the couch. She watched him from a crouch, sure she heard the sound of bone.

Savannah moved to the counter, her breath coming quick, her mind racing. She could see no way of getting to the gun hidden in the sofa cushions. Fox sprung up from the floor, his mouth stretched into a snarl.

He jumped over the back of the couch toward Gilda, then shot for her throat like a dart. She deflected his hand with her own and twisted it, sending his body past her into the ancient sideboard. But he'd barely touched and cracked its wood when he swung his foot upward, catching Gilda in the jaw and knocking her off balance. He moved in quickly, punching her full in the face. She fell backward to the couch, and he dropped down, landing on her chest, closing his hands around her neck.

Savannah ran forward and leapt onto his back, her forearm clenched around his neck while she dug with her other hand between the pillows for the gun. Fox loosened his grip on Gilda long enough to fling Savannah across the room. She landed against the base of the counter and felt the snap of bone in the arm twisted under her. The pain kept her from passing out and brought her to her feet again. She could not hear her own voice howling with pain, only the silence of the struggle between the other two.

Fox, who had less height than Gilda, picked her up and grinned as he hurled her against the front door. The frame shook, her body splintering the seamed wood. She held onto the wall and steadied herself.

Fox turned to Savannah smiling, "Aren't you dead yet?"

She backed up involuntarily into the kitchen. The hot handle from the frying pan dug into her back. Although his movement toward her was swift, it felt like slow motion to Savannah. She turned completely around, grabbed the pan with the dishtowel, and flung the scalding tomato sauce into Fox's face. His scream was long and piercing as bits of his flesh fell away with the dripping sauce. He clawed at his face for a moment with bloodied fingers, his body shuddering. He kept coming at Savannah who stared in fascination at the glimpses of bone at his cheek and forehead.

She hardly heard Gilda scream "Now!" and did not see Bird drop down into the living room, cracking the stairs with the force of her landing. Bird was atop Fox before he understood that the person he had sensed hiding above was not Toya but another like himself, shielding her true nature with the force of her thoughts. She plunged the syringe into his back; the heroin sought out his blood like a lover looking for a haven. Savannah finally heard the screaming. It was a moment before she realized it was her own.

Pinned against the stove with this thing at her throat, Savannah felt frantically behind her with her good hand for something else to use. The empty frying pan lay at her feet. The leaking sauce and blood made the gorge rise in her mouth. But she choked it down as she felt his grip loosen. Bird and Gilda pulled Fox's leaden body away from hers, lying him face down on the hook rug. The floor was slick with sauce and blood. Savannah pushed her fist into her own mouth to stop the scream.

"Quick, we don't know how long this will last," Bird said, as she hoisted him up by his feet.

"Savannah, bring the butcher knife!" Gilda grasped the rug around Fox's shoulders and pushed through the back door.

Savannah moved as best she could with the pain shooting through her arm. She grabbed the thick, wooden-handled carving knife she favored for barbecues, which Skip had left on the counter. The three hurried down to the shore with their burdens.

They found Skip holding tightly to Toya in a silent struggle. "It's them, it's them, O.K., O.K.," he said, trying to keep her from breaking free and running toward the house.

Bird shouted at them in the dark. "You two get back up to the house. Skip, you're going to have to take Savannah to the hospital." He let Toya go and rushed toward Savannah, who moved carefully. Gilda and Bird deposited Fox in the boat.

"Here," Savannah said, her body trembling with the pain as she handed them a knife and the gun she'd retrieved from the sofa.

"Is he dead?" Toya said in a small voice. "What do we do now?"

"He's been dead for a long time, Toya," Gilda said before turning to Skip. "Get Savannah to a doctor, to look at her arm. Take Toya with you. Don't come back before dawn."

They heard a slight stir in the boat as Skip, Toya, and Savannah made their way unsteadily through the sand back up to the car.

Bird turned him over and pulled the shirt from his chest. His eyes were open and glazed. They knew he saw them.

"Can we do it," Gilda stated rather than asked.

"We have to. He'll never stop until he's killed us all," Bird said, taking the wooden handle in her hand and raising it above his chest.

Fox's hand shot upward, grabbed her thin wrist, and began to bend it backward. He did not move his body, only his forearm, as he worked to shatter the bone. Gilda took the knife from Bird's imprisoned hand and plunged it quickly into his chest. She pulled downward making the flesh open like done sausage. Still he stared blankly and held Bird's wrist as if they were bonded together. Gilda could see the pulsing heart, the organ that pushed this body forward in time. It had somehow been given the power to survive, yet had been turned to stone. Such a thing of mystery: a heart open to the air, beating like a child's, innocent and free.

Gilda looked into Fox's eyes. They were empty, like black stones.

"I'm sorry," she said.

"Do it!" Bird screamed, still struggling, breaking each of his fingers away from her wrist with a raw snap.

Gilda reached inside his chest—the warmth startled her. When her fingers brushed the delicate sides of his heart, his eyes softened. Orange swirled through them for a moment before they settled into a moist brown. He looked at the women for the first time as a human, then closed his eyes. Gilda pulled the heart from his body and threw it onto the sand, glad to be rid of its disturbing rhythm.

His grip finally loosened. Bird slid his shoes off and looked again at his dark face. He didn't appear at all as he had in life.

"So here it is at last . . . ," Gilda said as she gazed down at the boyish quiet that had transformed his face.

". . .the distinguished thing," Bird said, finishing the quote they'd heard from Sorel.

"I'll take the boat out a bit." She waded into the salty water. Its insistent tide made her uncomfortable but was unable to draw her strength from her. Her native soil rested snugly in her shoes and the hem of her pants. She used the knife to cut Fox's protective clothing from his body, leaving it in a bloody heap in the boat. She pressed the small anchor into the sandy bottom and stood for a moment feeling the bump of the boat against her body.

She waded back in and found Gilda in the backyard trying to start a fire in the brick barbeque. The paper and twigs finally caught and the fire burned low under the dark, fleshy thing. They continued to feed twigs and paper into the flames until the red turned to ash.

They were sitting side by side on the sofa when both realized they needed to go out for their share of the blood, or daylight would find them too weak. Neither relished a hunt now, nor the blood, wanting only to rest and forget. Instead they left together, winding their way toward a clump of houses to the south and entered two separate places. They were relieved to find what they needed, eager to return to the bungalow. They both washed the blood and sand from their bodies in the narrow shower when they got back. They sat on the sofa watching the first pink light push its way into the sky; then they heard the others at the door. Savannah's eyes were dulled by painkillers the doctors had given her, but she looked around the room in panic. She held onto the huge cast with her good hand.

"Is it done?"

"We think so," Bird answered. Skip led Savannah to the chair and gently put her feet up on the ottoman.

"I guess I better clean up some of this mess." He scrubbed away the red stains, trying to pretend it was all tomato sauce.

"When the sun is up full, I want one of you to go out to the boat and pull it in. Come back and tell me what you see."

Savannah rested her head on the back of the chair. Toya paced around the shuttered room until Skip told her to sit down. Bird pulled the girl's head into her lap and rubbed her forehead. Gilda sat on the floor beside the couch, her head back against the cushions. Skip mopped the floor. Although their eyes were closed, no one slept. All seemed afraid to disturb the silence.

Finally Gilda opened her eyes and said, "It's time. Someone check the boat."

"I'll go," Toya said.

"No! Let Skip go," Savannah said, shuddering at the memory

of the bleeding face.

"I can do it," Toya said sharply. "If it's really over I want to be the first to know. If it's not over now, then it don't matter who goes out, does it?" She went out the back door, her long, thin braid hanging down her back. Savannah and Skip watched from the step as she waded into the water, unhooked the anchor, and pulled the row-boat in without looking inside. She hauled it up on the shore, then turned to look down, unsure what she expected to see. There were fragments of the sweater and pants, stained and crusty with blood and salt water.

She ran back to the house, her laughter and words floating be-hind her. "There's nothing there! Only clothes," she screeched.

The band of tension across Savannah's face refused to be bro-ken by relief until she saw for herself. She rushed down to the boat. Toya stopped and waited, her laughter suspended until Savannah turned back toward them and screamed, "Clothes!"

Gilda and Bird retreated to the attic while the others packed. When the afternoon sun began to fade, Skip pulled the car around to the front of the house. He had burned the clothes and thrown the tarp back over the boat. They piled into the car, silent, un-believing.

"I still want to leave," Toya said.

"Me and Skip will get you to the train," Savannah told her. "I think you need a little rest first, and we'll fix you up with some clothes. Can't have you goin' home from Boston lookin' like some-thing the cat drug in."

Gilda and Bird listened to the plans. When the car turned off of Route 3 into the South End they were unsure where they should go next.

"Drop us on the corner of Mass. Ave.," Gilda said. "I think we'll stop in at the 411."

"Why break up the party now?" Savannah challenged, her laughter booming as Skip swerved the car smoothly around the cor-ner. "I haven't had so much fun since I totaled my powder-blue Cadillac."

Skip laughed loudly.

"Aw, boy, what you laughing at, you was still pickin' cotton be-hind your mammy when that happened. 1945, I think. I didn't even see the goddamned truck. I'ma tell you it was more than just my life flashing before me. Broke both my arms that time."

Her laughter was infectious. By the time they entered the darkened room they were all laughing. Several people sitting at the bar looked up at their arrival, noted Toya's presence, and the bedraggled appearance of them all. They, too, were soon laughing as the five passed them heading toward the back tables. It was easier than asking questions.

Chapter Five
Off-Broadway: 1971

Gilda hooked the weighty ring of keys back onto her belt loop and hung the padlocks from her pocket. Their metallic jangle reminded her of the sound of Savannah's West Indian bangle bracelets as she tapped on the beauty shop door. But that was many years ago. Savannah had opened her own beauty shop in Mississippi, and when Gilda last heard from her, Savannah's hair no longer needed to be bleached white. Gilda reached up, pulling down the ponderous metal gate that protected the theater in a fluid motion.

"Let me help with that."

Only mildly surprised to hear Julius' voice, Gilda did not turn.

"Thanks," she said softly, and continued tugging the rusted metal grill. He smiled when it clanged to the ground. Gilda tossed him one of the padlocks, and they knelt to secure the gate. His back was schoolmaster straight as he struggled with the stiff, old locks. She liked him: he was an efficient company manager who had a feel for what would and would not work for a small group with little money. He didn't treat the actors like self-indulgent children nor the technicians like a nuisance.

"All set. Now how about a drink?" Julius said, breaking into Gilda's thoughts.

"Why didn't you go along with the others?"

"It didn't seem right, leaving the stage manager here alone to lock up while we were celebrating a snap first run-through that couldn't have happened without you."

Amusement sparkled in her face as she looked up into his dark brown eyes. He was fairer skinned than she, a slight sprinkling of freckles crossing his nose that matched the brownish-red color of his close-cut nappy hair. The streetlight glinted on the small sapphire shining in his left ear. His shoulders were broad, his waist slim. With his full lips and polished smile he looked more like an actor than an administrator. They walked across 23rd Street to Sixth Avenue and stood on the corner while Julius waited for Gilda to answer his invitation.

"Let's walk a bit," she said. Then, after a block, "There's a cafe just opened on Cornelia Street."

They were silent most of the way. The waning moon cast a soft yellow light over midnight. Gilda was grateful to be moving after sitting in the tiny lighting booth for three hours during the rehearsal. She savored the feel of the night air on her face and smiled at being alive—still. The shine in Julius' eyes rivaled the other light as he took her arm.

Once they were seated in the restaurant he felt familiar, as Aurelia had, and Gilda relaxed into the comfort. He ordered a cappuccino before saying, "Tell me something."

"Yes, what?"

"Anything. Like where you're from. What you want to do. How'd we end up working our asses off for this little white theater company when we're supposed to be about nation-building?" He laughed wryly at the wilted sound of the rhetoric.

"In my father's house there are many mansions."

"Oh god, a Baptist!"

The young, white waiter didn't bother to look at them as he delivered their order. He sniffed sharply at the sound of their laughter, then turned on his heel, looking like an eager actor. It was amazing to Gilda how they all seemed to struggle to achieve the same trim body, coiffured hair, and characterless movement, yet still hoped to be different from each other. Since her arrival in the City she had watched them auditioning for each of the three shows she'd worked on—young, stunning, transitory good looks full of edgy ambition. They, more than anyone else, reminded her of the difference between herself and mortals.

She almost laughed when she thought of that word—*mortals*. It had taken many years before she was able to make the distinction in her thoughts, and the demarcation still felt fussy at times, not quite uncrossable.

"I was hoping for something a little more specific."

"What's to know?" came her sharp response. "I come from a small town in Mississippi no one has ever heard of and doesn't even exist anymore. Not even as a bus stop. I love the theater. I write songs. The world is the world. That's why we're here. When we get tired of it, we'll do something else."

"That cuts the conversation, doesn't it."

Gilda immediately regretted being so abrupt. But looking across the table she found it hard to really see him. His separateness as mortal felt like an impenetrable curtain between them, one she wished didn't exist.

"Not really, it's only the variations that make the human story interesting, right?" She strained across the table trying to reignite his enthusiasm. "I mean, it's the same ones over and over again. But the specifics are what make Baldwin different from Hemingway or Shakespeare or Hansberry. Why do you feel uncomfortable being with a white company?" she asked with genuine curiosity.

"I made all the sit-ins for the movement. While I was in college, protest was practically a credit course! Suddenly I look up and find all my dashikis folded at the bottom of a trunk and I'm helping to manage money for a group of middle-class white kids who want to play theater."

Gilda sensed there was more, so she let the rattling noises of other customers fill the air as Julius shifted in his seat, uncomfortable with the casual way white patrons coming in tried to size them up. Dangerous? Noisy? Exotic?

"I decided to leave off reading the papers 'til the end of the day. I get so P.O.'d I can't get my feet under me, you know? And then I go there and I like it—the work, most of the folks. But shit, man. . .'"

Gilda understood: Attica filled the headlines. She, too, tried to push the news of death out of her mind. She'd seen the pictures of inmates killing and being killed, lined up in the prison yard, and the image was always the same as her memories of the slave quarters: dark men with eyes full of submission and rage. Their bodies plumped with bullets were the same ashen color as those fallen beside the trees to which they had been tied as punishment. She understood his restless anxiety.

"I know people from other companies, black companies. The New Lafayette folks are still around."

"Whoa! You know the New Lafayette?" he asked incredulously.

"Of course. They were the reason I first came to the City. I thought those guys were going to change the world. The rituals, the spirit. They held black life in their hands; they reached inside me in a way. . ."

Julius was eager to pursue. "Did you see *To Raise the Dead and*—"

"*Foretell the Future!*" Gilda broke in and they finished in unison, excited by their memories.

"So what happened to those guys?" Julius continued. "I mean, not all of them could be dying to go to Hollywood. It's like they just evaporated."

"They wanted to work like everybody else, I suppose. And white people stopped feeling guilty and donating money. Most of the men we marched with ran out of liberation ideas. They had a big dream about black men being free, but that's as far as it went. They really didn't have a full vision—you know, women being free, Puerto Ricans being free, homosexuals being free. So things kind of folded in on top of themselves."

"Shit, who the hell's got time for all that. . ."

"Ask the folks you don't hang out with after run-throughs who's got time for all that. You think these companies breeze through life on righteousness? I had a friend, a brilliant woman who devoted her life to a little black company, doing the scut work, the kind that's just got to get done and nobody's willing to pay for it. She figured the brothers would be ready when nation time came. She worked like crazy: grant applications, giving advice backstage when directors got stuck, and housecleaning when they said they were too busy to get to the theater on time. But when nation time came she might as well have been wearing a sheet! Grant money went to every brother in the place but not to her. A row of cotton is a row of cotton, so if you think she felt any different from how you feel, you haven't really been thinking." Gilda was surprised at the depth of her own feelings, about the disappointment she had seen on the faces of black women over the years.

"Damn, hold up. I get it. I ain't hardly trying to say that."

Gilda didn't really hear Julius. She struggled to keep herself from slipping backward into the past. The hot rows, their leafy stalks licking at her legs, the heavy sun overhead. Her sisters moved quickly down the rows, making it into a game. She tried to keep up but never could. And the first time she fell into the dirt, face down, almost smothering, she waited for the lash she was accustomed to hearing around her. But her sister's hand had lifted her effortlessly and dragged her along as if she were just another burden like the sack of white cotton.

Looking into Julius' eyes Gilda remembered he could not see these things, and her words felt too sharp. She didn't want to go back into the past; it was too far away, and they were all dead now.

"As long as you, me, and Irene stick wih this company it won't just be a group of white kids playing games. Irene is supposed to direct a play next season," Gilda added.

"Yeah, I know. I guess I wasn't prepared. Fisk is a far throw from Manhattan and I miss it. You know how it is, you fall into a groove and the roll is long."

"You better catch a new groove!" She thought for a moment she had been too sharp again.

But then he laughed and said, "Power to the people!" and the past was in its proper place.

"I suppose you want to go somewhere they can pay you a living wage. A bourgeois wage. What do you want to do with all this experience?"

"Right now I want to just hang with you." Gilda looked at Julius, taking in all that made him who he was. There was a calm assurance in his manner. Also a tentative nature about him that could be read as aloofness. His eyes told her he was lonely in the City. Being with her now was something he had wanted for a long while. And something else she couldn't yet decipher.

"Julius, I don't think it would work. I like you, but let's not ruin a good friendship."

She saw pain flicker across his face for an instant before evaporating. Gilda hated the way men shifted gears to protect themselves from humiliation.

"Hey, it was just an idea," he said as if she'd just turned down tickets to a basketball game. He started to pick up his cup, but Gilda held his eyes, probing to see exactly what he felt. The camouflage and subterfuge were sometimes too exhausting for her.

Her gaze caught him up short and revealed his sadness. She saw how alone he really was. His parents were dead; he had no close relatives. Having nothing to keep him in the South, he had come to New York City. Gilda was the first person he'd reached out to in the two years since his arrival. In spite of his cynicism about working with a white theater company, Julius was eager, just as Aurelia had been. He sustained a vision of the world made better in part by his efforts and those of people he respected. Gilda shuffled back through her memories of his interactions with the company, the director and actors. She recalled his swift expertise and grace. He was young yet not easily intimidated. His sense of self was strong, but for the moment he was adrift, needing a friend more than a lover.

She slipped back, releasing the gentle hold she'd had on him and letting him regather his thoughts, then said, "I've got a great and longtime friend who owns a bar in Soho. Will you go with me sometime? We can collect old actor stories and drink fine wine. You tell me your problems, I'll tell you mine."

"Did you know it, you're a poet?" Julius responded with a wide smile, as eager as Gilda not to lose the friendship they were building.

She said good night to him on the corner of Seventh Avenue and Christopher Street. Gilda walked north to her small garden apartment in Chelsea, wondering how Julius had survived the harshness of the city. The relationship he fantasized between them could never be, yet his loneliness drew her. It mirrored Aurelia's melancholy in some ways, but was more profound; somehow it suited him in spite of his struggle against it.

As she got to her door she put Julius out of her thoughts. She resisted the confusion he stirred in her, deciding he was best considered when she was among friends. Once out of her workshirt and square-cut painter's pants, she curled up in the large overstuffed armchair that sat in her small living room. Heavy velvet curtains shut out the drafts and what light there was outside. She pulled out her old copy of the *Tao Te Ching.* Lao-Tsu's laconic writings lay gracefully before her. She took comfort in knowing that she could read the calligraphy characters as easily now as did contemporaries of Confucius in the sixth century B.C. The pen strokes were warm and familiar: *The nameless is the beginning of heaven and earth. The named is the mother of ten thousand things.*

The delicate figures did not soothe her restlessness. She looked at the clock: it was only 2:00 A.M. Gilda did not have to be at the theater again until six in the evening; the hours yawned before her. So much time. She considered dressing once more and going over to Sorel's club. There were sure to be a couple of her friends there about this time, others like herself who slept through the day and lived at night. The disparate, tiny group who formed a makeshift family were always there.

But she had little patience for idle conversation and was uncertain whether she was ready to discuss her feelings with Anthony and Sorel. The urge to simply escape, to leave and forget the world here for a while, hovered over her. But the play was opening in a couple of weeks. She couldn't go away for at least two months.

She expelled a sharp breath of frustration. How good it would feel to go to San Francisco, she thought. She missed walking the streets of the city, feeling its age and newness, the history curled around her there. It was as far into the past as she ever ventured. And there was an ease among the people. One that Sorel, during his decade here, had not yet been successful in transplanting to the east.

Here she felt smothered by ambition. Recognizing the absence of that in Julius made Gilda smile. She closed the book and went out into the postage-stamp garden. Because most of the businesses closed up shop at dinnertime, and there were few habitable apartment buildings, the area was quiet at night. Gilda's tenement, owned by her holding company, in turn owned by her investment company, was similiar to those around it, except the heat and hot water always worked and the sidewalk was clean. It contained a mix of Americana: Francisco, a Dominican cab driver; Danny, an Irish man who had been the building's superintendent for fifteen years, his wife Tillie, and their stream of grandchildren; Rodney, the black actor who went off to his job at the Transit Authority every morning and returned in the evening with his dance bag over his shoulder; and Marcie, a young Puerto Rican who lived just above Gilda. He was the only actual friend she had in the building. Marcie had invited her up a couple of times and she'd accepted without thinking twice. When she sat on his studio couch, enveloped in the Indian bedspread and fluffy pillows, she realized how difficult his charade was. During the day he was Marc at his job at the telephone company. He had been one of the first male operators and wore it like a badge of honor. But what he wore best were sable eyelashes and capri pants.

"I'm a free man. What I wear is my business!" she heard him shout after slamming his door behind a quickly departing relative. He and Gilda had been on good terms ever since then.

Except for his younger sister who slipped downtown to visit him on holidays, his family had generally stopped speaking to him years before. Gilda knew he welcomed neighborly intimacy as much as she did.

Gilda gazed up at the stars and then turned to look at Marcie's window. The shades were drawn, but she could see a glimmer of red light underneath. He must have company, she thought, and dropped the idea of visiting him. He always went out by himself at the beginning of the evening but inevitably had someone with him when he returned home. In the morning, by choice, he was usually alone again. They had spent many mornings together over the coffee whose aroma enticed Gilda even though she never drank it.

She considered Marcie for a long time when thinking who might want to join her in her life. He was strong, directed, devoted. But Gilda saw him, like Aurelia, too tied to the life of the present. His world was now, not the expanse of time between now and the future. She tried to envision Julius against such a horizon.

Gilda felt impatient with her self-indulgence. Either use the time or leave it alone, she demanded of herself. She couldn't understand why Julius upset her so much. It was certainly not the first time a man had propositioned her. She passed off their suggestions so easily, though, that they usually never remembered they had made them. What was upsetting her then? Gilda found her comfort with women. That was just the way it was. Julius was full of the manufactured responses that men somehow inherit from their dead mothers and fathers. Damn! He still reached out to her through the night air.

Gilda went back inside and slipped into her jeans and T-shirt. She pulled a sweater over her head, relocked her front door, and started walking south. She was seated in Sorel's rear booth before she realized she was going there. Anthony stood formally beside the table looking much as he had when they first met—somewhat pale, wiry, his large hands preternaturally still at his sides. He looked like a student, yet Gilda felt as if she had returned home to her teacher.

"I'm afraid you've arrived much before Sorel. He will not be back with us for a week, perhaps two."

"I know, Anthony. I just wanted to be here. To see you."

"Splendid. May I bring you a bottle then? Sorel has been hoarding things for you to try since you've not been to visit us in so long."

"Only if you'll sit with me for a while."

Anthony nodded, then turned to the tall door at the back of the pub where Sorel kept his personal favorites stored. As often happened Gilda was comforted by the ease with which Anthony, Sorel, and she had become accustomed to the new manners the world had to offer.

In many ways the mores of this time were much more complex, obscure—there was a great deal of room for surprise. She looked around her. Here she was not an object of curiosity as she had been long ago. Some of those present she knew and nodded to; but they, sensing her desire to be alone with Anthony, remained at their own tables. The sound of the room was much softer than the one in which she first sat with Sorel. Few mortals came here, and there was no gambling room—only a long bar, a few booths, and a billiard table. The bartender raised his glass in her direction, and she smiled in easy camaraderie. Anthony returned and opened a bottle of wine, a burgundy, and described how Sorel had expanded his wine holdings in that region.

"What, no champagne tonight?"

"I've tried to make Sorel understand it's an overrated drink. For years he's humored me, but still he loves those bubbles. I, myself, prefer a hearty drink that stays with you through the chill of night." With that Anthony poured the dark red wine into wide-mouthed glasses, then sat across from Gilda in the high-backed booth.

They sipped silently, with Anthony only muttering a small sound of appreciation. Gilda spoke before she knew exactly what was going to be said, in much the same way as she had unwittingly discovered herself in front of the club. "I have a friend, a young man, I think I'd like to bring with me to Sorel's homecoming gathering."

Anthony did not rush in with words but waited for Gilda to continue. She reached across the table and poured more wine for them both.

"I really look forward to Sorel's report from New Zealand. I expect he and Bird have caused quite a stir among the landowners there. I wish Bird were returning with him. Anyway, my friend is a young man a bit at odds with himself right now, but I would really like you to meet him." Her voice trailed off to a whisper. Then she said, "And I'm afraid. I can't have another loss like Aurelia or Eleanor."

Anthony reached across the polished wood of the table and rubbed one finger across Gilda's hand, whose fingers were wound tightly around the bowl of her glass.

"And this friend has a name?"

"Julius."

"He takes a place in your heart?"

"As a friend, yes. I feel none of the overwhelming rush of desire that blurred my vision with Eleanor. Nor much of the foreboding that stifled me with Aurelia. But I'm still uncertain. It would be so easy to make a mistake, to cause such horror. I won't do that." She could feel the fear rise in her throat and knew that Anthony sensed it.

"Did you know that before the end, Eleanor came to see Sorel almost every evening? It was quite sweet, actually. She would sit at his table after you moved east and simply look out with him at the many people who visited the salon. They spoke often of her childhood when they first met. And he talked with her of Europe. She developed a consuming desire to visit just from those conversations. It seemed a refreshing change had set in, for a few years at least. Sorel thought she was trying to find peace. Your stay with us forced her to face something none of us had been able to. Her creation was a mistake, and she continued to contribute to the bitterness that surrounded her. She took no responsibility for her life. I think Eleanor came to see what a waste that was. Sorel was really very happy to spend that time with her."

"Yet she took the true death."

"Yes, but not, I think, because of any mistake in judgment on Sorel's part. But rather on her own. She knew she had done a foolish thing with Samuel and his wife. She had set something in motion that would haunt her always, and Samuel would never relent as long as he lived. Her decision to take the true death was a decision not to destroy him. She said as much before it was done. She asked of you on occasion," Anthony finished in a soft voice.

Gilda felt a nervous chill slip down her back. She took a large sip from the glass of wine. "But Sorel has been devastated by her death. How can you speak of it so simply? I'm sure he's not feeling the easy relief you seem to think."

"I don't presume any easy relief. Sorel has his grief, as do we all.

But he'll not be ended by it. He can live with his mistakes in judgment. If you're not willing to take that chance, then you must reconsider how you will spend the coming years."

After a while he spoke again. "I imagine you feel some degree of disloyalty to Bird in your desire to bring one among us. This is unnecessary. I'm sure Bird would say the same thing to you if you gave her a chance."

"You may be right. I still feel stuck, as if I were part of a wheel spinning in place. Knowing the right thing to do. . ."

"Stop trying to make the perfect move; trust your instincts more. You've been through quite a bit in the past years. I'm sure you're as good a student as you've always been."

"I can't be a student for all my time!"

"We are students for all our time if we're lucky enough to know it. But that doesn't mean you wait for Bird to grant you some dispensation before you really live. She can be mother, father, sister, lover—but she cannot create the family for you. You are part of our family and you will create others to be a part of it. This is no one's mission but your own."

"When she came to me in Boston I believed she would stay."

"Even when she said she would not?"

"Yes."

"You think of it as running away from you. For her it may simply have been running to other things that are most important. You were on your own, your world set. For Bird the world is travel, pulling together the strands of knowledge about her nation, other people from whom she's been separated. You are a part of her life, but Woodard's is gone; it will never be again."

"That day in the farmhouse, when I lay in the bed waiting for Bird to come back from Woodard's, my greatest fear was that she would decide not to complete the process, that she'd leave me to the mortal life. I was certain I'd never learn to live in the world I'd come to know. It was the most fear I had ever experienced, apart from the constancy of terror that was plantation life."

"But she didn't. She knew this life was one in which you would excel, she knew you'd learn to be. . .as we are, a living history. You don't need Bird at your side to be this. You need only look forward, just as you did the day you decided to escape the plantation."

Gilda didn't respond. Anthony went on as if she had.

"Since there's no overwhelming reason not to, why not bring this

Julius to Sorel's welcome-home party. You're bound to see more clearly after drinking that silly champagne all evening." The smile gleaming on Anthony's face made Gilda laugh. They didn't speak of Julius anymore as they sipped the wine. Gilda left through the heavy oak door.

She walked east enjoying the coolness of the night air as it invited the morning. When she stood in front of Julius' apartment she looked up at the ancient building adorned with peeling fire escapes. East First Street was almost deserted, and the streetlamps glared and sparkled on the broken glass in the gutters. A *walk-up, no doubt*, she thought.

Gilda easily coaxed the ineffectual lock open and entered his apartment. It was clean and orderly despite the crumbling state of the building. His desk was covered with neat stacks of papers, and books stood lined up in rows. Julius, lying naked under a blanket on a mattress on the floor, shifted uneasily in his sleep. Looking down at him it was easy to see what a child he was. The beard that grew in during the night was soft on his chin, and the whiteness of his teeth was inviting under his partially opened lips. His reverie was of her as she entered the dream.

She glanced at a family snapshot that sat framed beside the bed and at the large posters of Angela Davis, Ché Guevera, and Malcolm X that hung on the walls. She pulled the covers from Julius' body. He stirred, opened his eyes, and she caught him in a gaze he couldn't break.

"The dream doesn't have to end," she said softly, then lay down beside him, touching her fingers to his skin as lightly as the years touched her unlined face. She held him in her arms and kissed his full lips, listening to his satisfied murmurs. His eyes closed again, convinced this was a dream. She ran her hands across his body making his flesh tingle. Julius held her tightly, his lips seeking hers. His body responded as a man's, and she lay across his lean thighs and chest providing a comforting sensation. Her hands were as hypnotic as her eyes. As the moment approached when his mind provided the gratification his body hungered for, she sliced across the flesh of his neck with her fingernail and watched the blood ease slowly to the surface.

She pressed her lips eagerly to the wound and drew the life from him as his body exploded with the joy of his imagination. She listened inside of him and was surprised to see the image of the snapshot that sat atop the stack of books beside his bed. She stopped as she felt his pulse weaken, held her hand on his chest, and lifted herself away from his body to ease his breathing. He relaxed into satisfaction. She spoke soft, hypnotic words in his ear until his breathing became regular.

"Good-bye, sweet baby," she whispered.

Gilda was back on the street in only a few moments and inside her apartment so quickly it felt as if she had never left. She slipped out of her clothes and took a quick shower. The running water made her slightly uncomfortable even though she'd lined the walls with the Mississippi earth she carried everywhere with her. The towel felt good against her skin, and she had no regrets. He would wake in the morning satisfied, as would she, and both could still be separate.

She pulled the silk comforter over her naked body; the earth lining the bed frame beneath her felt cool and familiar. Gilda tried to remember what her family had been like. She was Tack's child. She knew that wasn't her father's real name but one they called him because he was so good with horses. He worked in the tack house and had been sold away before she was born. Her mother's face was the only one she remembered clearly. Everyone said that, unlike her nine sisters, Gilda resembled her mother. She had been rather tall, her smooth dark-brown skin topped by a full head of thick hair she was endlessly trying to manage so it would not be an embarrassment to the mistress. She worked inside the house, unusual for a woman of her deep color. Her skills with herbs, in addition to her cooking, made them reluctant to lose her to the fields and the sun.

Instead she died from the influenza she caught taking care of one of the endless white women who got sick. Knowing she was now just another slave, likely to be sold away, Gilda had run. She wasn't sure what *sold away* meant except that she would disappear like her father had. She regretted leaving her sisters but knew it would only be a matter of time before they'd be sold away too. That had been so long ago.

Gilda remained as determined to survive now as she had then. She knew about the empires of black people in Mali and Ghana, and although there didn't seem to be much hope at the moment, she would wait and work and move around the world toward the future. As she looked in the mirror, seeing her mother's eyes staring back out at her was comforting. Bird's presence in her walk, the sound of Bernice's laughter in her own, all made the connection to life less tenuous. Finding those she loved within herself eased the passage of time.

Life was indeed interminable. The inattention of her contemporaries to some mortal questions, like race, didn't suit her. She didn't believe a past could, or should, be so easily discarded. Her connection to the daylight world came from her blackness. The memories of her master's lash as well as her mother's face, legends of the Middle Passage, lynchings she had not been able to prevent, images of black women bent over scouring brushes—all fueled her ambition. She had been attacked more than once by men determined that she die, but of course she had not. She felt their hatred as personally as any mortal. The energy of the struggles of those times sustained her, somehow.

Gilda tried to rest now. This was not really sleep, not until that final time when the earth or sea would close around her and the fragments of her body.

She wondered why Julius had no brothers or sisters. Why he'd been left so unequivocally alone in the world. The movements of the sixties had fueled Julius' vision of the future, too, but to Gilda, George Jackson's death this past September signaled the end of that era. Angela was somewhere out there alone now with a cause but no community. The horror of slavery appeared to reap endless returns.

Gilda recognized her repeated attempts to grasp what the right step might be. Her need to shrug off human entrapments was strong, but her bond with the past life was deeper. She shoved the thoughts out of her mind, burying the turmoil they caused by promising herself a trip to the West Coast no matter how she managed it.

The darkness of her room was complete. No shadows played behind the locked door. Everything was still above her as she lay in her restless tomb. *To die but not to perish is to be eternally present.* The words of the *Tao* played in her mind, lulling her into sleep. She succumbed to the silence of dawn while the world around her prepared to awaken.

During a break in rehearsal, one week before the play's opening night, Gilda ran through the words to a song she was writing at the same time as she scanned the production book checking the light and sound cues. She glanced down at the cast milling around restlessly as the director worked to reblock an actor's movement. The route from one chair to another became everyone's focus as they weighed what effect the minute changes would have on their positions. The play was a political polemic full of naive hope and loud music, not unlike many others that were playing the off-Broadway boards at the time.

Denise, the dance captain, was a brilliant dancer and charismatic singer. David, the second male lead, was a born comedian. But the play itself was just a sketch.

The director had been invited by the company partly because of the name he had made directing a popular antiwar musical, and also because word was out that he was in emotional trouble. He had been replaced on a Broadway-bound production the year before. Those were just the qualities that made him irresistible to this anarchistic little group. Gilda sensed him flounder for a second under the pressure to make a quick, clean decision about the moves.

She called out from the booth, "Excuse me, Charles, but Equity rules say they have a break about now."

There was laughter in her voice. They all knew times when they'd worked hours on end, eating hurriedly only when their characters were not required on stage.

Charles was grateful for the interruption and replied, "Well, if we must bow to the tyranny of the masses, I'll spring for coffee." Someone took orders for the run to the deli, Gilda untangled her legs from the wires, and Sonia, who worked the sound, climbed down from the booth. Julius stood at the bottom of the ladder, a tentative smile on his face.

"You going out for something to eat?"

"No, I want to talk to Charles about the blocking problem."

"How about later after the rehearsal?"

"Not tonight, Julius, rain check." Gilda walked away, cautiously ignoring the look of disappointment on his face.

That night, after the gate had been drawn, Gilda headed downtown, enjoying the brisk air and trying to wipe the memory of Julius' face from her mind. She crossed 14th and walked until coming to West Street. Men's bars studded the neighborhood, sleazy landmarks in the crumbling dock area. Gilda rarely ventured to this part of the City. Its aura of danger—the excitement and pain—was not usually appealing to her. She crossed under the West Side Highway to the piers where young men, most trimly bearded, paraded to entice other men. There was danger in taking blood here: the men's bodies were frequently saturated with drugs and alchohol, and Gilda didn't know with what or how much. But tonight, danger was all that would satisfy her.

She walked stiff and wide-legged with her hands in her pockets so that no one would notice her womanhood. She passed a middle-aged white man who hurried toward the street, tucking in his blue button-down shirt and closing a vest over his slightly bulging belly. He looked backward over his shoulder quickly, as if the man who had just given him pleasure would leap on his back to destroy him at any moment. Gilda saw the young man with curly hair leaning against the pilings, rinsing his mouth with beer from a bottle, then spitting into the Hudson. He poured some beer on his hands, wiped them on his denims, and started toward the street. Almost without hesitation he popped a pill into his mouth, washing it down with the last of the beer. The bottle crashed into the abandoned warehouse building behind him.

As the glass tinkled among the other broken bottles, he noticed Gilda coming toward him. He walked a little taller, eager to check out the new figure. Just as he realized she was a woman, Gilda caught him with her eyes. No, tonight was not a night of love. It was a night of feeding.

Gilda held him in her gaze and wiped his mind clear. His eyes opened wide, unseeing, as she pushed him backward into the shadows of the shell-shocked warehouse. She turned his face to the wall, pulling the jacket away from his back and neck with an easy rip. She pressed his body hard against the rough building and sliced open the skin on his neck. He moaned slightly as he felt the pressure against his body. Gilda took his blood easily, barely thinking of what might be in his mind. A small thing, actually. He wanted to visit a friend who was sick but somehow never found the motivation. He felt guilty. Gilda took her share of the blood, and by the time she released him, his resolve to make the visit was firm. The drug that diluted his blood pulsed through Gilda's veins, light exploded in her head, and her breathing raced dangerously. She didn't care. She just wanted to forget her own indecision and the boy who sold his body on a crumbling dock.

She pulled back and held her hand over the wound. Her eyes were out of focus and her hand leaden with what she was sure were depressants. Reaching into the front pocket of his jeans she found a slender ampule. His breathing was shallow and didn't improve, so she flipped off its cap and passed the popper quickly beneath his nose. His heart rate quickened, and soon his pulse rose. His body stiffened in its struggle to consciousness. She threw the container over her shoulder into the river and left him there, against the building, clinging to life with tenacity. Gilda ran quickly, even though the drug made her feel stiff and uncertain.

Once free of the area she walked more slowly, looking at the people on the street and enjoying the movement of the lights. She could hear sounds coming from the buildings around her as if they were programmed through a stereo in her ear. The music from a penthouse above was as clear as the clink of dishes in the storefront diner. She arrived home, took a shower, and tried to wash away the smell of the city.

Gilda sat outside in the back, watching the stars and listening to the music from Marcie's place, where tonight a blue light glowed. That meant he had more than one guest with him. She heard the laughter and salsa floating down. Gilda wondered if the boy on the dock came home to friends such as these—unexpected and challenging. She watched the stars until they faded and dawn started to take over the sky.

The show opened a week later. So few things went wrong that Charles was triumphant and the cast confident they would run forever. At the cast party they milled around Charles' West 97th Street apartment, reliving special moments, releasing the tension that had been stored for weeks. Gilda sat at a narrow counter watching the young faces. She was pleased with the show—it made a statement and showed off good talent. The group sat stroking each other's egos for getting this far. Critics would be coming in three days, so the edge was not completely off, but they were good and they knew it. Julius came around to the back of the counter and offered to pour her a drink. Gilda declined and turned back to the rest of the group. Night sparkled outside the large uncurtained windows as Julius stood sipping from a large glass of scotch.

"Drinking alcohol is not good for you," Gilda teased with a little smile. He ignored the remark, and they were silent again. Then Julius said, "I had a dream about you the other night. You came to my pad and woke me up to make love to me. I was. . .well. . .happy.

But then you left and I couldn't breathe. I thought I was dying. I couldn't wake myself up and kept calling you, begging you not to leave me there, dying, but I couldn't get the words out."

Gilda sat very still staring past Julius at the photograph of Greta Garbo on the wall behind him. When she caught his eyes they were pinpoints of curiosity. She looked around the room feeling him holding on to her.

"I know you're trying to keep from getting into something with me. I'm not a complete fool, sisterlove. You made yourself pretty clear. But I've got to let you know how it is for me. I can't imagine life without you somewhere near me. If it's as a friend and not a lover, then let it be that. Just don't ice me out."

Gilda watched him sip from his glass. "Are you so alone in the world that you need to settle?"

"I'm not settling. My mother used to say that one good friend is worth a thousand...well you know. I don't want to lose our friendship when the show's over or the company's gone or I find another job."

"You don't understand what it means to be my friend."

"Maybe not, but give me a chance to deal with it. Nothing I do in this business or my career means anything if I spend my life alone. You don't understand that, do you?"

For a moment Gilda heard Skip's voice that evening in the Cape Cod cottage when he assured them he wasn't using drugs, that he had nothing to apologize for. His voice and Julius' became one in their urgency.

"I understand being alone better than you can ever imagine. I've learned to appreciate being alone and how to choose one's companions carefully." Her words made Julius' brown skin flush pink, showing up the dark freckles.

The life I offer is not for you. I feel for you as I would if I had a brother I loved. Trust that no matter where you are in this world if you ever need my help, it is only for you to ask and I will be at your side. In that we will never be separate.

With these words, Gilda remembered the last time she made this promise. The forlorn acceptance that had shone in Aurelia's eyes was all Gilda had asked for. Julius couldn't offer such acquiescence, but surprised at the outpouring, tears welled in his eyes. He blinked to hold them back, then looked quickly about the room.

No one hears. The words are for you alone, Gilda said.

It was then Julius realized that her lips had not moved. He had heard her clearly nonetheless. She slid from the bar stool and walked toward Charles, standing alone near the table laden with bread and cheese. She made her good-byes quickly, then left, eager to be rid of the brightly lit room and Julius' need.

As Gilda walked toward Broadway she knew that if it were possible for her to cry, she would be doing so now. She turned downtown looking forward to the distracting sights between the Upper West Side and Chelsea. At 96th Street she was fascinated by the glare of the Red Apple supermarket and the newsstand bursting with publications. Couples speaking in the frenzied Spanish of the City congregated in front of the dance hall located above the heavily shuttered jewelry store. The Riviera and Riverside movie theaters were the only things that stood silent at this intersection.

She didn't stop at 95th Street, only glanced up at the dark marquee of the Thalia. The ubiquitous *Jules et Jim* was playing. Gilda wondered idly how many times she'd seen it. It was on the bill with *Ship of Fools*. It must be Oskar Werner week, she thought, just as Julius stopped beside her, short of breath. He stood in her path, blocking light from the corner liquor store.

"You understand me so well . . . feel so much for me, but you walk away. I can't accept it," Julius said, not entirely certain now that he'd heard her earlier words.

"You have no choice," Gilda said, her anxiety making her impatient. He grabbed her arm. "Please." The word was simple and plaintive. His hand on her arm was strong and urgent, but she broke his grip with little effort.

"Why can't it be different? How do you know?" His voice was childlike as he faced this complete unknown. The strength in it demanded that she answer honestly.

"Don't interfere with me. It's my decision. That's all I have to say to you!" Her eyes and her voice were mesmerizing. She left him standing puzzled and hurt on the corner as she made her way to Riverside Drive. She walked hurriedly downtown, her pace so quick that those nearby never saw her.

She rushed into her apartment, locked the door, and went out to the backyard, turning for solace to the endless, familiar stars. They were friends that had lasted through time with her. The window opened behind her, and Marcie called down from his apartment.

"Hey girl, what the hell you doin' out there? Come on up and get a drink."

"No, thanks. I've had enough for tonight. You having a party?"

"Naw, those punks left already. I'm just watching the late movie. You wanna watch some TV?"

Gilda walked over to the second floor window so she wouldn't have to shout. "No, I'm going to relax for a while. Opening nights are always like the end of a race."

"Was it good?"

"Yes," Gilda responded, letting her pleasure surface. "When you want to see it I'll reserve a couple of comps for you."

Marcie's brown eyes sparkled.

"Hey, hey yeah, how about Saturday? Can we come on Saturday?"

"Sure, I'll leave two tickets for you at the box."

"Yeah, girl, I'll dress up real sharp, you know! Let it all hang out!"

"You'll like the show, too. Just don't bring any stuffy types, you know...politics..."

"Honey, I got principles. I got to know how you vote before you take off your coat!"

As Marcie closed his window and went back to the television Gilda marveled at the clarity of his world. She had never met anyone quite as satisfied as Marcie was with the decisions he made in life. Gilda went back inside and settled down with a book, certain that rest would completely elude her.

On the night of Sorel's welcome-home party, Gilda took a change of clothes to the theater. She was getting rid of her sweaty jeans and T-shirt in the women's room after the show when she heard Julius call her name outside the door.

"Well, I've got you cornered in there. Everyone's just about gone so no one can rescue you. I'm here to invite you out to a night of frantic disco and assorted other depravities, sisterlove."

His youthful fear was barely concealed behind his bravado. Gilda said nothing and continued to change her clothes, packing her work outfit in a plastic bag to be stowed in the lighting booth.

She opened the bathroom door wearing a mauve jersey blouse and matching pants, soft leather boots, and a hint of lipstick.

"Aw, shit!" was all Julius could manage to say.

"Is that a critical opinion or are you waiting to get in here?" Gilda said with a smile.

"I guess you've already got a date," Julius said, realizing that he'd never seen Gilda wearing anything other than her work clothes.

"In fact I'm going to a party for a dear and old friend of mine," Gilda responded. Having made and remade her mind over the past week a number of times, she finally decided to simply wait and see what the evening brought. There had been no time to speak with Julius during the show, and so she left herself open to whatever happened. She was happy he had sought her out.

"I was going to ask if you'd like to come along. Hang out for a while. It's a rather old crowd, a kind of a white crowd, so there won't be much discoing. But I would love you to meet Sorel and Anthony."

The confusion was swept from Julius' face by a smile. "Right on! I'm down. But do I need to change? I probably should."

"You look fine. You always dress like you're ready to meet somebody's parents anyway."

She let Julius climb up the ladder and toss her bag of clothes into the lighting booth before they pulled down the heavy gate and put on the padlocks. They flagged a taxi and were climbing out in front of Sorel's pub before Gilda really had a chance to think about her decision—or if she had made one. It had been over a year since she last saw Sorel. He'd spent most of the time in New Zealand and she'd been working with the theater. She had avoided talking to him, afraid to hear anything more about Eleanor's death, afraid she would feel, in some part, to blame. Julius grasped her arm gently.

"Are you O.K.?"

"I'm fine. I just realized what a long day this has been. But everything is everything," she said laughing, using a phrase tossed around at the theater. A few minutes later Gilda pushed the heavy oak door open. People looked up as they entered. She heard Sorel's exclamation above everyone's and saw him pull away from his circle of friends. He looked the same, his large body dressed in impeccably tailored clothes, soft, colorful shoes, his eyes sparkling like the champagne he liked so much.

"Ah, my child, we've been waiting."

"Some of us work, you know, at jobs, not globe-hopping." She fell into his arms laughing as he encircled her.

"You call that a job, scampering around on ladders all day and singing all night? You just neglect me because I'm old!"

"Careful how you abuse me; I've brought my boss along to set you straight." Julius grinned and tried not to look embarrassed.

He experienced the slight discomfort he felt when in a room filled almost entirely with white people. Without looking around he could feel their appraisal. He held onto Gilda's hand even as Sorel began pulling her into the room. Julius felt a moment of sharp panic as her hand left his and he stood alone. The others continued to look him over, and some were smiling. He still couldn't quell the cold chill that flooded him. He felt a little dizzy, overwhelmed, but by what he could not tell. Julius jumped at the hand on his arm.

"Come, sit at Sorel's table. Gilda will want to make a proper introduction." He looked down to see a large, pale hand guiding him effortlessly into the room. Anthony tried to soothe Julius' thoughts with his own when he sensed the boy's discomfort.

Once seated beside Gilda he felt less unnerved, especially when she turned her smile on him and introduced him to Sorel and Anthony.

"I'm pleased to meet you. Until today I haven't met any of Gilda's friends, so this is a real treat."

"We're more like family after all this time," Sorel said before turning to Anthony. "Will you bring up that bottle I put to chill earlier?"

Anthony turned away from the table, and Sorel laughed raucously. "He thought my trip might quench my thirst for champagne —he knows nothing of obsession!"

Those around him laughed and turned to their own conversations. When Anthony reappeared Sorel continued. "We, too, have met few of Gilda's recent friends. Let's have a toast. To the family of friends we gather about us. May we live and love eternally!"

He raised his fresh glass toward Julius who took a tall, fluted glass offered by Anthony. The entire room joined in the toast, and the din of conversation rose and fell casually.

"Sorel and Anthony have been my teachers in many things," Gilda said, looking at Julius with an impish glance. Here among these people he thought she seemed younger, almost like a student. The space between them appeared to lessen.

"And you've been ours. Have you ever been to San Francisco, Julius?" Sorel asked.

"No, I just about made it up here to New York. I'm still a country boy."

"Let me tell you of a country!" Sorel responded.

With that began a round of stories about his trip to New Zealand that lasted into the early morning hours. Julius was amazed at the capacity Sorel and Gilda showed for champagne. He stopped drinking sometime after 2:00 A.M. They had both continued and were somehow still coherent. Just before dawn Julius noticed that most of the patrons had departed and the bartender and Anthony had cleaned away the glasses.

"We better be off, my sweet," Gilda said to Julius. He warmed at her affectionate touch and rose from the booth.

"Maybe we could get you to come uptown and see our show," Julius proffered shyly. "It's just an off-Broadway showcase, but we worked pretty hard."

"Do you hear that, Anthony? Shall we get out our theater capes and venture north?" Anthony gave only a brief smile.

"Of course we shall! The cauldron of experimentation, doing away with musty conventions—you name the night and we'll be front row center to shout bravo."

"Please come next weekend, then," Julius responded.

Gilda felt awkward at never having invited Sorel and Anthony herself. It seemed so natural when Julius did it, yet she had never considered letting these worlds intersect, until tonight.

They said their good-byes and stepped out into the deserted street. Julius was about to suggest that they walk west to a street where a cab was more likely to be cruising when one pulled up in front of them, as if summoned. Gilda slipped inside and was quiet on their short ride uptown. She kissed Julius lightly on the cheek when they arrived at his building. He got out and leaned down into the window before the cab could move.

"Thanks for letting me meet your friends. It means a lot to me that you did that. They've got a real family feel, you know?"

"Yes, I guess Anthony and Sorel have been family for me here."

"And this Bird he was talking about. She sounds like a real deal. Like landowners down under may never recover!" Julius laughed with a purity of spirit that thrilled Gilda. "When she lands on these shores again the U.S. government is in deep stew."

Gilda laughed loudly. Through his eyes Gilda saw Bird as the hero her own curiosity made her.

"Catch you later, sisterlove." He tapped the cab, signaling it to pull off, and turned back toward his door.

The next day at the theater a box was delivered for Gilda. When she opened it she found a note from Sorel apologizing for not giving it to her at the party. Nestled in soft tissue paper was a large, flat rock. And in a separately wrapped package there was a note from Bird and an ancient, carved arrowhead. Gilda ran her hands over the cool stone in the privacy of the bathroom and put the letter from Bird in her pocket to be read later at home.

Gilda opened Bird's letter while sitting in the armchair that night. It was a single page crammed with tight script that described where Bird had been living.

The final paragraph turned abruptly:

I suppose you've considered bringing someone into our life. I, too, have thought of this but don't think I'll ever learn to settle down long enough to teach someone in the same way as you've been taught. Sorel and Anthony have been good and constant, but I do worry about you. You must make roots for yourself, for you are my roots. I will be listening for your thoughts and planning to see you before too much time has passed.

Gilda wondered how much of her thinking had aleady found its way to Bird over the past months. She walked outside to the backyard and paced for a minute or two. Marcie's windows were completely dark, and the alley surrounding the yard seemed quiet for a change. She looked up again at the stars, remembering Bird telling her that the stars would be their link. Wherever they were in the world they would look up at the same stars.

Gilda went back inside the apartment, then left through the front door, moving quickly to the Lower East Side. When she let herself into Julius' apartment she discovered he was not there. She sat quietly on the bed and waited. It was almost 1:00 A.M. when he came home. His eyes were gleaming as if he'd had a bit to drink, but he did not move like he was drunk. Gilda remained silent as he took off his leather jacket and laid his briefcase on the desk. Gilda was sitting on the mattress, her eyes closed as if in meditation when he entered the bedroom. Julius wasn't sure he really saw her.

He noted that the curtains were all drawn in the room and that a curious quiet hovered over everything. His confusion kept him from speaking. He stood numbly at the foot of the bed, looking down as she opened her eyes and spoke.

"I don't want to trick you, Julius. Or seduce you. I want you to see the family I bring you into. It's a family that I've belonged to for more than one hundred years, yet I've been alone, too." He felt the gentle pressure of her mind. His guard relaxed, and what she said felt both alien and natural.

"I need an ally, a brother. If you want it, life can be yours, and we will be sister and brother throughout time. Our love will outlast the tears, the plays, the lights, these old buildings. What you must sacrifice may be too much, but once done it is final."

"You're talking some other language."

"Yes, I am," she peered into his eyes, making his mind let go of the world around them. He became open to the words and could understand without her speaking aloud.

He said, "I want to be with you. That's all that's important to me."

"That will not be enough. I'm not offering some melodramatic romance where the audience sighs sweetly at the final curtain."

"I know that."

"But you can't really know, no one can, until it's done. Until it's too late. It is commitment as you've always fantasized it—in college dormitories when you talked of revolution, in the theater when they speak of changing the world. The reality of it can never be as one imagines."

Julius looked both excited and afraid, but the solemnity of Gilda's words were ameliorated by the kind love he saw in her eyes. She both warned and entreated him at the same time. "I offer you the capacity to live on until you decide it is over. There are many who would love you in those years. I am only one," she said in the kindest of voices as she closed her eyes.

Julius knelt on the bed and looked around at the faces on the walls. He took in the books and other little things that identified this as his room. The picture of his mother and father as they had been when first married stood beside his bed as it had all of his life. He had tried to project himself into that photograph so many times since their deaths to recapture the comfort of their love.

Gilda listened patiently to his thoughts and let them evoke the sadness that still rushed in when she thought of those she had once loved who were now dead. She opened her eyes and her arms; Julius lay in them like a child. She ran her fingers gently over his face and neck, enjoying the softness of his skin, smiling at the freckles that marked his nose and cheeks. He raised his hand to her head and thrust his fingers into the short, nappy hair that framed her face, pulling her face down to his. She encircled him with her arms, kissing his eyes and nose. She felt his pulse begin to race as she passed her hand over his chest.

She pressed her lips to his in a gesture that was full of the ex-

citement she'd held inside herself for so long. It was a kiss both passionate and chaste, leaving Julius feeling like a child in her arms,
yet still a man. When she sliced the flesh on his neck, he opened
his eyes in shock but did not try to pull away. His body trembled,
then lay still, as the life drained from him into her. Gilda stopped,
bit her own tongue, and kissed him hard, breaking the skin inside
his lip. She thrust her tongue into his mouth.

He took back his blood, now mixed with hers, gagging on its
sweet texture. Gilda pulled back again—two times more—to draw
the blood from the wound in his neck. Each time she took him closer
to the edge of life, letting Julius feel that perimeter and the abyss
beyond it. She drew out his life and waited for him to make a sign
of protest. If he did she would leave him to his life and wipe these
moments from his mind. But he only opened wider for her. His eyes
lost their focus, and his body was limp. Gilda pulled her shirt from
her chest and sliced an opening below her breast. She pressed Julius
to her, waiting to feel the power of his mouth taking in the life she
offered.

He began to suck at the blood insistently, finally understanding
the power that moved between them. Electricity surged through
him. His head pounded, blocking out all thought until he heard
Gilda speaking inside of him.

*And what do you leave in exchange? This is your first lesson. You must
never take your share of the blood without leaving something of use behind.*

Gilda felt his moment of confusion. He'd been lost in the blood
and didn't yet understand their way. She repeated her question and
was immediately flooded with the sense of well-being only a child
can feel when lying in the arms of its parent. She opened her eyes
and looked up at the snapshot of Julius' mother, feeling the complete joy he had felt as a child. He left this most exquisite feeling with
her, his gift as he pulled back from Gilda's breast. She closed her
eyes in joy and held his hand to his wound, letting him help heal it.

She touched her reddened lips to the bridge of his nose and his
forehead as she murmured words too soft for anyone in the world
to hear. Her thoughts silenced him when he started to speak. *Sleep,
there is much to be done tomorrow.*

With her back against a thin pillow she held him until he slept
comfortably. Inside his dreams she planted calming thoughts that
would hold him in peaceful sleep until she returned. She let herself out, looking up only briefly at his shrouded windows before

making her way back to her own apartment. Her mind raced trying to organize the things that had to be done.

She removed two large duffels from her closet. She changed into
her boots lined with her native soil and the cloak Sorel had had
woven for her by the seamstress who created her new wardrobe
years before. It was rare for her to actually spend so much full daylight time out-of-doors. Regular errands that required little effort
weren't uncommon, but this trip would use all of Gilda's resources.
Deciding not to wait for a taxi, Gilda started for the airport on foot.
She could be in Virginia by noon, fill the bags with his Virginia
earth, and be back in time for the half-hour call at the theater. As
she moved quickly through the City, past the tunnel, the factories,
the cemeteries, and shipping firms, she tried to keep her mind only
on her destination, but a myriad of thoughts rumbled around inside her with the noise and disturbance of the planes roaring
overhead.

She tried to remember her own response to the truth of the
choice she had made and to imagine how Julius would react. No
matter what he'd said about friendship there might be little solace
once he really understood what world he now belonged to. She was
taking him away from the life he knew, and she could not provide
solid answers to what this life would be.

Words from the *Tao* came to her: *Give up sainthood, renounce wisdom . . .* The airline terminals were just ahead. The simple truth was
that it was done.

They would be each other's family now. It's more important to
see the simplicity. She could only hope her judgment had been
correct—that it was a good choice for Julius as well. She closed the
door to doubt and began to anticipate the night when she would
have Julius to show the world to. They would care for each other
until they returned to the source, the stillness and the movement
that is the way of nature. There would be no sad past between them
as there still remained with Bird. When they were ready to travel
separately they would be certain it was the natural time for that to
happen and not filled with shadowy anger or fear.

Her Mississippi soil lay comfortably inside her shoes, protecting her from the weakening properties of daylight. She hummed
a soft tune to herself, one her mother had sung while preparing
poultices and compounds for the mistress' perpetual headaches.
Gilda smiled remembering her mother's dark face and began to

laugh to herself as she settled in the plane. She imagined what kind of companion Julius would be—his enthusiasm and idealism just the thing she needed to face eternity. She looked below at the thousands of tiny lights that sparkled in the receding city and remembered the first time she had seen a city shine with electricity. The lights were such a gaudy imitation of the stars. Gilda strained her neck to see out the window through the clouds. But dawn was upon the City, and the stars had moved on. She wondered if Bird was also looking up at them now. She pulled down the window shade and put her head back, listening.

After a moment she heard Bird whispering in her ear. It was a soft murmur of comfort, not words, but sounds meant to elicit ease. Gilda relaxed and sent out her message: *We've finally delivered a brother for me.*

Chapter Six

Down by the Riverside: 1981

Gilda left the party sure that the young girl, Effie, had been flirting with her. Although Gilda often went to parties that Ayeesha gave, she accepted the separation that stood between herself and the others. She had sought them out, eager to understand the excitement of their lives. The energy around them reminded her of times past when the smell of both the old world and the new was in the air. Ayeesha, Cynthia, Kaaren, and the others were much like those at Woodard's in their edgy wit, yet they also had the innocent spirit and toughness of the women dressed in men's breeches Gilda had met on the road when she first traveled to Sorel's.

As she sat at the piano in Ayeesha's large, spare living room, Effie stood across the room, motionless; her gaze never wavered from Gilda. It was entrancing and unnerving—much like those that passed between many of the women—and its raw enticement left Gilda wary. Still she cherished singing for those enchanting women who were so full of ideas and plans. It fulfilled her in a way that was different from the nights of singing on a bandstand amidst clouds of smoke and noisy ice cubes. The checks from the clubs in the Village or across the river in New Jersey never enriched her as much as the women's tender hands on her back or the dazzling smiles they showered on her as they had done tonight. Ayeesha, a librarian at the Schomburg Center in Harlem, lived for these weekends when she would invite groups of friends, mostly women, to her large Morningside Heights apartment to listen to music or poetry, or simply to eat together.

The rhapsodic declarations of the Black Power Movement of twenty years ago gave way to exciting variations in this setting. It was here that Gilda found the substance behind the rhetoric for which Julius had longed. Ayeesha herself wrote plays and collected musicians, poets, and painters around her like the colorful beaded bracelets from West Africa that climbed halfway up her arm. Gilda looked into Ayeesha's face and those of her friends and saw Aurelia, Bernice, her mother and sisters. It was a link she searched for in each new place she lived, one she regretted breaking when she moved on.

It was actually Savannah's look that Gilda saw in Effie's eyes—knowledge that was beyond simple experience. Effie always came to the Saturday night or Sunday afternoon gatherings. She stood apart, youthful and eager, yet somehow demanding. Her clothes were plainly designed, usually in a single color. She favored deep earth tones such as rust and maroon, accented with a piece of bright cloth or large jewelry. Her outfits seemed understated and sophisticated in contrast to her youthful appearance. Gilda glanced her way periodically but spent almost no time talking with her.

Once outside, the sound of Gilda's boot heels was muted, her movement swift as she descended the marble steps of the large, old apartment building. She started down Riverside Drive toward her apartment in Chelsea. The October air was brisk and fresh on her face. She glanced at the New Jersey skyline and sidestepped Effie's memory.

Gilda felt an almost imperceptible change in the air as the sun's rays began to push dawn into the sky. The rush of the river was unlike the placid surface of the Charles in Boston. Its roiling motion reminded her of the Gulf and how it must look and sound to one submerged in its waters. Yet its persistent rush forward deceptively implied deliverance rather than death. Walking alongside it she blocked the din of traffic and let the water's sound fill her head.

Inside her apartment she bolted the doors and undressed for a shower. She looked around the small space, so peculiarly her own. The piano she had bought once she stopped working in theaters stood in one corner, its niche barely carved out of the mountain of

books surrounding it. Bright cloth draped the ceiling and walls, hiding the fake wood paneling. Heavy blue-velvet curtains covered the
windows, whose panes Julius had painted over with city scenes.

The Eiffel Tower adorned the top half of one; the marketplace
in Accra enlivened another. Boston's Beacon Hill wound its way up
the glass door leading to the back garden. This was only one of the
changes Julius had brought into her life. Just as the brilliance of the
colored glass was a delightful surprise each time she drew back her
curtains, his presence provided unexpected pleasures. To arrive
home just before dawn and find him perched on her steps waiting
to talk with her about a show he was working on, or about his newly
acquired passion, painting, made Gilda understand what had been
missing in her life—the demands of intimacy.

Julius had blossomed in his new life: seeing the city with Gilda
or joining Sorel or Bird on jaunts around the world. She wondered
where he was just now as she pulled the drapes closed and dropped
her clothes on the armchair. She stood, not so tall without her boots,
before the full-length mirror, while the steam from the shower filled
the bathroom.

She marveled at her body's fineness. Her brown skin shone like
a polished stone; the rounded stomach and full legs were unchanged from those of her ancestors. Her teeth gleamed against soft
lips, and through the fog her dark eyes looked back at her as alive
and sparkling as they had been when Gilda first saw herself in a
looking glass 150 years before.

Gilda washed these thoughts away as she lathered the rose-
scented soap over her body, rinsed clean, and turned her mind to
sleep. She unlocked the sleeping room and lay down, naked except
for the beaded juju bracelet, a gift from Ayeesha, that adorned her
arm. She was still, looking at the shadowless ceiling for a few
minutes, then closed her eyes, resolved not to think of Effie.

Instead she once again brought Julius to her mind. He had been
out of the City for several weeks, and she was beginning to miss
him. He had so easily become a part of her existence, always full
of jokes and tricks, ready to explore. Julius traveled, learning new
cultures from the people themselves, while Gilda preferred the
world as it passed her by on the streets of the States. No matter how
often Bird, Anthony, or Sorel extolled the virtues of travel, Gilda
was never as swept up in its appeal as they were. She had ventured
north through Canada and south through the Americas but real-

ized that while an expanse of ocean was only somewhat daunting to the others, to her it was paralyzing. It was as if she were being asked to make the Middle Passage as her ancestors had done.

Julius would return soon with slides and stories; she was content with that. The languor brought on by dawn began to seep into her bones, draining away her anticipation of his return and her curiosity about Effie. She closed her eyes—locked in and safe—to sleep the sleep of the dead.

When she awoke it was Saturday. The evening would not be just another late night singing in New Jersey, but an event. Ayeesha and some of the women who spent their weekends with her were borrowing a car and coming to see her perform. She made one phone call, to ask Anthony when he expected Sorel to return, then spent the afternoon reading.

She'd finished *The Foxes of Harrow* and was anxious to discuss it with Julius. They would spend hours trying to figure out where in the canon of black literature someone like Frank Yerby fit. Gilda felt exhausted by the layers of reality that weighed down his words. She gazed at his gentle brown features on the old book jacket, hoping to glean what he might have thought of himself—a black man writing almost exclusively about white, southern society. Who was he inside those carefully constructed yet superfluous manners?

Who were the characters, really? Where could she fit him within her life, her experience of the past century? How was he of value to her, to Ayeesha and the others? She tossed the book back atop the pile beside her easy chair, then dug down toward the bottom to locate the tattered copy of the *Tao* which was never far from her.

She leafed through its pages not seeking, simply stopping at words as her eye caught them: *Precious things lead one astray.* She tossed that book aside, too. Sometimes she wanted meaning. She hungered for puzzle pieces that fit snugly with each other and pointed the way toward past or future. At such moments Lao-Tsu simply infuriated her, leaving her with expanses much too great for comfort. And even then she remembered something of it: *Empty yourself of everything. Let the mind rest at peace.*

She stretched out her legs and listened to the sounds of the building for a while. When the sun dropped down to the west Gilda went out into the tiny garden and looked up at Marcie's windows. He soon appeared from behind a curtain, throwing the window up exultantly.

"What you doing down there, girl? Why you rooting around in that garden at this hour?"

Gilda smiled up at his brown face enhanced by slight traces of makeup. "I'm killing time, till I go to work. What an awful phrase—*killing time!* Ugh!"

"Here, I got something for you. I bought this thing last week but honey, it's not for me."

Marcie disappeared back into his apartment, and the brightly colored cloth at his windows fluttered. Gilda felt excitement and curiosity. He wore flashy clothes yet had a style Gilda admired. She couldn't imagine anything he'd buy that he "couldn't" wear. Except the pair of five-inch silver heels he'd pronounced deadly and tossed in the garbage two days after paying seventy-five dollars for them.

He reappeared in the window with a gossamer-thin scarf in varied shades of green. Marcie dropped it down gracefully so that it looked like a mythic bird lighting on Gilda's shoulders. She reached up and caught it, enjoying its near invisibility.

"It's exquisite, Marcie. I have to pay you—"

"Don't be a toad, girl. The thing is you. I got to run. I was just going to leave it on your doorknob on my way out. I got a date. . .details to follow." He made a large kissing sound with his lips, shut the window, snapped the sash locks, and was gone.

Gilda held the scarf up to her face, sniffing the faint scent of his perfume, and listened to her own breathing. Yes, this was a closeness whose value she had relearned in the ten years they'd been neighbors. There was an easy way people could be with each other once they became accustomed to habits, likes, dislikes. It was comforting to be tossed a scarf by someone whose footsteps are part of your life. She felt even more anxious for Julius' return so they could argue over Frank Yerby.

Later, in the tiny dressing room wedged behind the club's stage, Gilda tried on her new scarf in several different ways. The shades of green came alive beside the tan silk pants and shirt she wore. The sharp and sweet sounds of the jazz trio on the bandstand invaded the room. She smiled at her recognition of their riffs, another intimacy she enjoyed. Working with musicians had become an excellent replacement for the theater, which was too demanding, requiring her to be attentive to too many people. Singing, writing words, and making them melody were central to the life she had made for herself.

Not only was it less personally consuming than doing theater work, but there were so many small nightclubs and cabarets along the East Coast that Gilda could perform regularly without having too much attention focused on her. And unlike working in the beauty parlor, moving around from club to club assured her the distance she reluctantly understood she needed between herself and others. She enjoyed shaping her own life, even though it rarely meshed with others.

Bird continued to see each continent as a challenge, although she did maintain communication much better now than she had in the past. Sorel, Anthony, and Julius were never away from the City for long, nor were they long in it. Sorel spoke often of closing his place and moving north to Canada. He had yet to make any real plans though. Each year Gilda noticed how much more difficult it was to keep the world away from her door. The small amenities that communities historically observed had fallen away; electronics made communication so swift that intimacy was expected at every turn. With increasing frequency Gilda considered living away from people. For the moment, however, the clubs suited her.

She walked to the side of the bandstand for the group's last number and saw the women sitting out in the audience, attentive but impatient for her to appear. In her head she heard Bird's voice, just as she had the first night at Woodard's. It was low and inviting yet full of the precision wrought by respect for the performance—Minta singing in her high, clear voice, or Fanny and Sarah's duets. The sound of voices and music from Bernice's kitchen had captured Gilda's imagination forever.

There was Kaaren the sleek, with her red nail polish and high-heeled shoes, sitting next to her lover, Chris, whose stern face was softened by the curls falling over her forehead. Ayeesha sat slightly apart, her thick dreadlocks tied up in a richly colored strip of Ghanaian Kente cloth. When she opened her mouth in a smile the light played off the tantalizing gap in her teeth. Cynthia, next to her, was tiny and brown, like an exquisite museum miniature of a Nigerian work of art. Laverne sat tall, looking slightly apologetic as her long legs sprawled into the narrow aisle between the tiny tables pushed together for them. Gilda was pleased to see the shy Alberta out with the group.

"Good for her," Gilda thought as she listened to the applause for

the musicians. Her friends were a responsive audience: most of
them were clapping and stomping their feet. Only Marianne applauded with reserve, reluctant to give a man anything. Her eyes
darted around the room, looking for danger or an exit. But the
others reveled in their anticipation of Gilda and let their excitement
spill over onto the trio. Leading the applause was Effie, leaning forward at the edge of her chair.

Gilda heard the pianist introduce her before he left the bandstand. She blinked several times, drawing her face into the open-
eyed smile her fans expected from her. She climbed to the stage,
stood looking down into the audience, and sang a cappella, "I love
you for sentimental reasons. I hope you do believe me. I've given
you my heart."

For a moment they were hushed by the ringing quality of her
solo voice, then they applauded wildly. When she sat down at the
piano it was only she and the women—as it had so often been
before.

Gilda looked out into the room, unable to see them clearly over
the lights shining into her eyes. "I want to sing a song I wrote that
I haven't sung for anyone before tonight. It's dedicated to someone,
of course, but I'm not sure who yet," she announced wryly.

Her long fingers danced over the keys, gathering the rhythms
and melodies of many ancient worlds. The notes cut through the
smoky air, silencing the random conversation. Her voice came out
softly when she sang, caressing the air before slipping into the
microphone.

"My love is the blood that enriches this ground.
The sun is a star denied you and me.
But you are the life I've searched for and found
And the moon is our half of the dream.
No day is too long nor night too free.
Just come, be here with me."

The applause engulfed her. Each song brought her closer to the
audience. It was in these moments that she felt most at peace with
the mortal world at whose edge she lived. She kissed the air around
her before stepping down from the bandstand. Even as she eagerly
absorbed her success, she calculated how she could weaken the tide
of their adoration. It was the only way she'd be able to go on lux-
uriating in the pleasure the singing gave her and still avoid the fo-

cused attention that could bring her life under suspicion. She must soon again become one of those many singers who blazed brilliantly then disappeared—Shirley Austin, Margo Sylvia, Ronnie Dyson— names most never quite remembered.

Now she joined her friends at their table, signaling the bartender to send over the bottles of champagne she had ordered. The waiter poured freely as the women congratulated Gilda.

"Your new song is too good, girl. Why've you been keeping it to yourself?" Ayeesha said, barely concealing her penchant for organizing and promoting.

The women basked in Gilda's success and the adoration of the strangers who approached to greet her. Gilda wondered at the wealth of stories the women told as they filled the room with their voices. Effie sat opposite Gilda, adding occasional comments but not initiating any story herself and never speaking directly to Gilda. As the conversation moved around the tables, Gilda tried to remember everything she knew about Effie. She used to live in a cabin in New Hampshire. She wrote for a magazine. She had no relatives on the East Coast. She was expecting to take a new job, according to Ayeesha, and move south within the year.

Effie gave little away about herself, and Gilda had consciously avoided probing. Small-boned but tall, her hair was cut close to her head, making her resemble a gangly bird about to leave its adolescence. She was the youngest of the group around the table, yet smiled sagely at each tale. She watched Gilda's movements and listened to the sound of her voice. When their eyes met, the exchange was a spark as sharp as flint on steel.

As the evening lengthened, Ayeesha began to encourage them to gather their things and start back to the City. For Gilda, the moment of leaving was unrehearsed but as sure in its script as any closing curtain: the amplifiers and microphones were unplugged and the tips collected. They invited. Gilda demurred. The usual engagement she relied upon as a proper excuse to disappear sprung to her lips and hung its shadow over the crowd.

She felt resistance from someone who strained her energy. Gilda turned it back on her, breathing outward in a long sigh that was imperceptible outside the circle of the women's table. Her breath was sweet, like rosewater. The scent of it wiped their minds clear for less than a second. None of the women resisted. They accepted her need to pass the night alone. Only Effie dug her hands into her jacket pockets and moved away stiffly. Her hard gait as she walked out to the parking lot was a startling contrast to her usual girlishness. Gilda watched in puzzlement as they departed.

She left soon after, driving the small car she used simply for crossing the Hudson River through the tunnels. She drove to the top tier of the long-term parking lot located on the Manhattan pier and locked the doors. She listened for a moment to the purity of the sound of the wind blowing off the river. Her head snapped around as she thought she felt someone in the shadows. A subtle aura surrounding her usually kept troublemakers at a distance so she rarely experienced the harassment that befell most women on city streets. It was one level of anxiety Gilda was grateful to avoid. Still, she peered into the late-night darkness with a sharp eye—all was quiet. Gilda descended quickly to the ground level and waved to the watchman as she left. He tweaked his bristly mustache as he waved back, just as he always did. Even this simple exchange had meaning for her now: he knew her, accepted her in this world.

Gilda sat in her backyard garden and looked up at the tenements rising around her, listening to the noises that lay in the air above: babies sleeping in their cribs, Ismael Miranda singing through the speakers of budget stereo components, the low sounds of lovers.

She reached out into the night expecting to feel Effie somewhere, but instead there was nothing. Stretching her senses in all directions, the city night swept over her, but Effie was not to be found. Gilda felt the hairs raise on her arms. She pushed her puzzlement away, retreating from the desire she felt gnawing at her, and withdrew from the night, returning to her rooms. She sat before her mirror bathed in candlelight, watching her own eyes for some resolution to her confusion. The evening hung in the air around her, but Gilda pushed further into her past.

There had certainly been other friends, friends whose love she had shared, whose graves she'd adorned with flowers. She thought of the bouquet she sent to Sorel when she learned of Eleanor's death. There was no funeral, no grave, yet she'd sent the flowers so Sorel would know she still thought of Eleanor. The electricity of her red hair, the urgency of her kiss burned inside Gilda even now, making thoughts of Effie more unsettling. She pinched out the candle and crawled beneath the silken comforter, finding no comfort there. The ceiling remained a blank space above her. Gilda was unable to project any images except the face of the girl who hummed the tunes as if she knew them all.

She turned over onto her side, unused to having rest elude her. Gilda drew her knees up close to her chest and curled her toes, vaguely recalling what it had been like to be a child. Shortly before the first rays of morning sun began to touch her painted windows, she slept.

She dreamed she was back at Woodard's where there were many rooms. Sorel, Anthony, Bird, Julius each had their own and moved about the house as if it were a hotel, locking the doors and unlocking them frequently. She felt at ease because Woodard's seemed to be much further from the city than it had actually been. Gilda walked from room to room checking, she thought, to be certain all her guests were accommodated. She soon realized she was searching for someone. She opened doors endlessly through the day, until late afternoon when she awakened from the dream that had held her.

Before she dressed that evening, Gilda sat at her piano in the corner nearest the window playing the shadow game. The sun stole through the sky falling past the Hudson into the west. As it passed across an open alley opposite her rooms the fading yellow rays reflected through the opaque gold on her windowpane. The painted Eiffel Tower turned into a beacon, and the refracted light cast shadows on the floor. She watched from the piano bench, poised like a cat, taut and confident, unseen by its prey. She tried to spin a world from that drop of light. She imagined it bathing a park, children sweating as they played beneath it. She listened for the sound of their high-pitched voices and sniffed at the air for the scent of their childish perspiration. She imagined the light's glare dancing on the river, making thousands of tiny mirrors. Before she could fix the pictures in her mind the light was gone and evening had begun.

That night she sang in a Queens nightclub, a place that welcomed local homeowners and winners from the racetrack at Belmont. The songs came easily but did not wipe the horrible memory from her mind: the blood she took this evening had almost cost a life.

As she had walked downtown earlier, through the streets teeming with trucks during the day, she'd come upon a man, black and sure, smoking in a car parked on the now-empty street. Through the window she could see that he was strong, so she had no fear he would miss the few ounces of life she would drain from him.

She slipped into his mind, holding him immobile as she eased his car door open and put her arm around him. The terror in his eyes was quelled by her tranquilizing stare. She sliced a small opening behind his ear and drank slowly. Unable to focus on his thoughts, she held him to her breast as if they were lovers. His blood, warm and soothing, flowed into her; the spark that is all life rekindled in her veins. She closed her eyes for a moment and was distracted. All her thoughts closed in upon themselves. Where ordinarily there was a spectacle of color and sound for Gilda during the exchange, now there was nothing except the sensation of drowning in a vacuum. She felt the man's flesh at her mouth, heard the sound made as she took the blood, but it was all beyond her conscious reach.

Panic rose inside her as she forced herself to return, to search his mind to make the exchange. She found only quiet. His consciousness was too still. She had taken too much.

His lids fluttered over unseeing eyes, shocking her. Anger at her indulgence and carelessness flooded through her, then mystification. In the many years of making the exchange, she had never committed such an error. Others enjoyed the moment of their victim's death, reveling in satiation, but Gilda didn't need to kill, nor did she want to enjoy it. She held him close and felt desperately for his pulse.

Gilda resisted the impulse to give him her own blood, to make a quick exchange that would assure his life. Bringing a stranger into their life with no preparation was a more grave offense than letting him die. She sealed the wound and waited. When his pulse steadied she raised his lids to see if the focus had returned to his pupils. She sat him up, resting his head on the car seat. His face was smooth and dark, the nose classically African. She had not left him with anything in exchange and felt like a thief. But she experienced relief at not having to add his face to that sad, private place where the dead resided. When his breathing was closer to normal she stepped out of the car quickly and ran her tongue over her unpainted mouth, clearing the last vestige of red, searching for her performance smile. Her skin felt flushed and cool, not warm as it should. She had a prickling sensation at the base of her spine that unsettled her. Looking down the dark street she saw nothing unusual, no one watching, so she continued on her way.

Her songs that night were sung savagely, filled with the anger she felt at her carelessness. She spit them out at the smiling faces, and somehow they took her pain as excitement and applauded her anguish. Through her second set she still could not clear the incident from her mind, could not find a reason for such a thing to have happened.

The unmistakable weight of death had made his body sag in her arms, and the memory of it filled her with a revulsion she could not dispel. She assured herself of his survival, although the contours of his face in her mind seemed set in death rather than sleep. When the evening was over she hurried from the club, leaving through the back door. The rancid odor of garbage and decay filled the alley, as did the sound of scurrying animals. Her footsteps were silent among them. She returned to the street and walked past the place where his car had been. He was gone. There were no police barricades or other lingering signs of anything particularly eventful.

The City was alive with people who, during the day, were locked into their own coffins—offices, shops, factories—each one waiting for release into the freedom of night. Gilda walked briskly toward Houston Street and Sorel's, anxious to talk to someone who might understand what had happened. Anthony was not in sight when she stepped inside the dimly lit room, but the bartender waved to her with familiarity. She nodded in his direction as she sat in Sorel's rear booth. Within moments Anthony appeared beside the table. Gilda wasn't certain what she wanted, but as always, Anthony was prepared when he sensed her confusion.

"I'm pleased you've come tonight. I had planned to send a message later this evening. Sorel and Julius will return soon."

"And Bird? Has she said if she'll come back with them?"

"Bird? No, she says nothing. Although Sorel indicates she has made somewhat of a home for herself. If she were to come, you would know before any of us, I'm sure."

Anthony turned back toward the door that led to the rooms holding Sorel's private stock and his office. Gilda relaxed against the leather-covered cushions and resisted the desire to rest her head on her arms. She looked about the room instead. Three others sat at the bar. One clearly had stopped in, unaware what establishment it was. The bartender was carrying on an animated conversation with him, carefully learning if the visit was indeed happenstance, planting the seed of forgetfulness so the patron would not be able to deliberately find Sorel's again. The other two were familiar customers she knew to be as she was, as they all were, sharers of the blood.

Anthony reappeared with a teapot and cups. He looked much the same as he had when Gilda first met him in the West almost one hundred years before. Instead of tying his plain brown hair back in a ponytail, he now wore it loose so that it fell forward, making him seem somewhat younger.

The aromatic blend was soothing. Gilda sipped at her cup appreciatively. She was quiet for a moment, thinking how to describe what had happened, but Anthony began to speak before she could formulate her questions.

"I'm afraid I must tell you some news that is not altogether joyous. As you know, the grief of Eleanor's leaving us still sits heavily on Sorel. He understands Eleanor's need to take the true death, nevertheless her loss affects him deeply. You're a great solace for him since you, too, understand the depth of feelings one might have as far as Eleanor was concerned."

The neutrality of Anthony's voice was carefully modulated. But as he continued, Gilda sensed the tension behind his words. "It was some time after her loss that I was able to persuade Sorel that coming East was our best course. And I believe this has been a good choice. We don't encounter many from those days. And everything about this city is so different from the cities of our past that Sorel is totally absorbed in learning of this new life."

"He hardly seems able to learn of this city with the world traveling he's done in the past years!" Gilda said, laughter in her voice. She repressed the giggles that the image of Sorel and Julius globe trotting stirred in her.

"Well, that's as it will be. Although he speaks of moving back to the West or exploring the north country, he truly loves it here. But I'm afraid that joy may not last long."

Gilda heard the uncertainty in Anthony's voice and felt the anxiety gather around them.

"Samuel is here."

The statement was made simply, with little inflection, yet its weight was unmistakable. The chill at the base of Gilda's spine returned.

"We've not seen him in quite some time. He was desperate after Eleanor's loss. No one, Samuel least of all, expected her to embrace the true death, ever."

Gilda heard in his voice Anthony's effort to speak charitably of Eleanor. He went on with little indication of this difficulty. "She was linked to this world in many ways. Her appreciation of its beauties made her cherish her life in spite of the difficult attitude she frequently exhibited. She did what she could to explain to Samuel what direction would be best for him, but his own weaknesses took the upper hand; the behavior you witnessed was minor in light of his later excesses. Finally, he left the area."

Gilda read into Anthony's words that Samuel had been forced to leave the city because his imprudent actions threatened the safety of the community. Remembering the childish cruelty she had seen in him, it was easy to imagine how difficult he had become.

"He's not presented himself here, as one should," Anthony continued, "but he's been seen by others."

"Yes," Gilda said, understanding taking shape inside her head, "he's been following me." She saw the alarm in Anthony's face as she continued. "Every time I went into the night I felt something just beyond my reach. And tonight, I was taking the blood...somehow...my mind was wiped blank. I was scarcely able to control the exchange. I didn't understand—it must have been Samuel. I recovered myself, but the danger of it left me shaking."

Anthony gripped his cup with tense fingers. Gilda reached over to touch his hand. As always she marveled at the darkness of her flesh next to the whiteness of others. It seemed an extraordinary gift—this variety of textures and hues. She failed to understand how it instilled such fear and horror in others. Anthony's grip loosened, saving the life of the china.

But his eyes were dark with anxiety as he tried to control his voice. "I've asked Sorel not to delay their return any longer. But I implore you, please remain out of harm's way until then.

"Samuel has no real understanding of our world. That was the curse that Eleanor visited upon him—taking him without considering his suitability. Yet she spared his life by taking her own and still he doesn't understand. It was her one true act of unselfishness, though I wonder if it was not the wrong choice."

"What can Samuel want with me? I parted company with Eleanor so long ago."

"In his head it's all the same. Time has little meaning to us...to him. You were a turning point in her existence. Even Samuel recognized that. Before you left us you saw the subtle change in her."

"But he meant nothing to her. I saw that in her eyes whenever he tried to approach her," Gilda said, shuddering at the memory of the coldness in Eleanor's voice as she demanded that Gilda kill for her.

"The passion between you, even when you wouldn't be trapped by it, allowed her to take her own life instead of his," Anthony added. "He can do nothing but blame you; that's no surprise."

All was said in such even, low tones that Gilda felt mesmerized. The truth was there inside the sound rather than in the words themselves—things she'd already known. She shivered at the knowledge that she might again be held responsible for someone's death.

Gilda searched for images of Samuel. They emerged from the unfading incandescent memory of Eleanor, dim outlines of a stunted man, confused to the point of incoherency. These impressions of him were more vivid than his physical appearance.

"What is it he wants of me?"

"He's probably not certain himself. To torment you with doubts as he's tormented, perhaps. You must be more selective when you share the blood, focus on very specific images, never let your mind stray. Clearly he's not ready for any type of confrontation or he would not be playing these childish games."

Anthony's words were reassuring, but Gilda was still full of questions. He seemed to sense that and continued. "I believe it may even be Sorel, not you, Samuel truly seeks. Sorel is the progenitor, the father. He may need Sorel to force him into balance. It might even be a good thing that he's abandoned his self-exile and come to us. I suggest you simply be cautious. By using you now he's playing out his anger until he can do what he's come to do."

Gilda felt her anxiety return. "But what can he want from Sorel?"

"Punishment, forgiveness, the true death? We can't know until he appears on our doorstep to tell us. And I'm certain this is exactly what he'll do once Sorel has returned."

With Sorel would come Julius and news of Bird. Gilda relaxed into her seat and took a sip from her cup. The question of Effie seemed less urgent, less frightening now. She couldn't imagine how she would stay out of Samuel's way. The City was, in spite of its magnitude, a small one.

"Gilda, I speak as I believe Sorel would if he were here." Anthony looked deeply into Gilda's eyes and continued to let her hold his hand. "You're trying to see Samuel's behavior through the light of reason, through mortal experience. Well, Samuel is neither a man of reason nor a man. You resist this understanding of him, and of all of us."

He watched Gilda's features become set, almost frozen, as if to disguise her rejection of all he said. He continued talking but looked away into the shadows of the dimly lit room. "You've searched admirably for your humanity. Indeed, this is the key to the joy found in our lives, maintaining our link in the chain of living things. But we are no longer the same as they. We are no longer the same as we once were ourselves. You know this when you are with your friends. Don't ignore it. It's not wrong to look to them for their humanity, but your life is with us. We'll go through the ages with you, and you cannot take them all with you. A corner must be turned here, or you will remained as unfulfilled as Samuel."

Anthony stopped, aware that the urgency of his words was gathering energy around them. Others were beginning to notice the intensity and making an effort not to take in what he said.

"I'm more aware of this separation than you can know," Gilda responded. "When I look into the faces of women I trust, like Ayeesha or Savannah, I still see the gulf between us. I'm adrift without moorings in this world."

"Then you must take hold, or you will always be as rootless as you fear you are."

Gilda sat for a few moments, knowing there was little else to be said. "You'll be here for the welcome-home party?" Anthony asked as he saw Gilda preparing herself to leave.

"Of course."

"Sometimes I think he goes away simply to give us a reason to hold celebrations!" Anthony said with a smile. Behind it Gilda could see his anxiousness.

"Not a bad reason, I'd say." Gilda realized she'd been holding onto Anthony's hand during a good part of their conversation. She gripped it tightly for a moment before getting up from the booth.

Gilda listened all around her on the street while looking directly ahead as she walked toward home. She sensed nothing but knew that Samuel could be shielding his thoughts to prevent her from locating him. She didn't pick up any particular presence, however, and proceeded north quickly, sidestepping the pedestrians who crowded the West Village. As she crossed 14th Street the freneticism diminished sharply—fewer people on the street, less garish store windows.

She walked past the turn she would take to her own home and went to the river. The crumbling docks stood—just barely—a hollow testament to the city's decay. Men still moved along the river's edge, seeking out pleasure or simply enjoying the open air, but most of the warehouses were collapsed in upon themselves or barricaded. The men were less curious about her presence. Women seemed to have taken to the streets almost as much as men in the last decade. Gilda walked out to the end of the one pier that remained open and stood enveloped in darkness and the sound of the river. She let the uneasy pull of the water take hold and tried to imagine its cold fingers gripping her body. It had been salvation for some, a passage to freedom from the burden of life. Was she responsible for their deaths? Looking into the water she understood why this way might be chosen. And in seeing this she remembered more clearly those who had made this choice. They were not women to be led or misled. Their choices had been theirs alone.

Gilda turned back toward her own street leaving the uneasy attraction of the river behind her. As she came to the corner of her empty block she was relieved to be at home again. She strode over the two steps leading down to her door. Opening it, she heard a noise behind her and turned sharply.

"Gilda?" Effie stood above her on the step. Gilda was startled by her abrupt appearance. Her mind ran in confusion through the excuses she could use to send her away.

"I've been waiting for you to return. I hope you don't mind."

"No, I'm happy to see you." Gilda's words rang with honesty.

"May I come in for a moment?"

Gilda noticed the slight trace of an accent she could not identify that somehow had escaped her attention. Effie looked tall standing on the steps, with the shadows hiding her youthful face. Gilda thought of the possible reasons she might say no before opening the door and standing aside to let Effie enter first. She turned on the lamp which glowed a dull red beside the overstuffed armchair. She felt awkward. No one outside the family had ever been inside before.

"May I offer you something to drink, a cup of tea?"

"No, thank you. I just wanted to talk with you for a moment."

Effie removed her short jacket and sat in the chair. Gilda paced the room uncomfortably. She wanted to ask how Effie knew where she lived even more than she wanted to know why she wanted to talk to her.

Gilda excused herself to wash her hands in the bathroom, taking time to try and frame her questions. When Gilda finally sat down on the small trunk in front of the chair in which Effie sat, Effie spoke immediately.

"I know that you consider me a child."

She spoke with a bit of a smile. "I think you know that. . . ," the girl faltered a moment, her words trailing off into the thick quiet. She glanced around the room before going on. "You know what I feel for you, I can tell this, but I had to speak directly. You must say that you do not care for me, then I will leave."

Gilda sat stiffly on the trunk watching the dark skin of Effie's face shining under the glow of the lamp. Her lips were pressed firmly together holding back—what? Gilda met a blankness when she tried to probe. She played mindlessly with the studs that lined the edge of the trunk. Under its lid lay a few of the treasures that made up her inheritance: the clothes she'd worn when she ran away from the plantation, the knife in its leather casing that Bird had given her in exchange for her own wood-handled one; the tea cup and saucer Aurelia had so carefully wrapped for Gilda to take when she left Missouri; and from Savannah and Skip, a charm bracelet with its single tiny silver brush and comb. Beside them lay the rusted metal cross her mother had made for her and a brown-edged journal that had belonged to the woman in Louisiana who had found her. Spread across these treasures lay the dark cape woven for her by Bird. Its thickness was weighted by the protective earth lining the hem.

"Old memories are so empty when they cannot be shared," Effie said softly, watching Gilda's surprise.

"What do you mean?" Gilda asked as she rose from the trunk and walked over to the piano as if seeking its protection.

Your coolness is a device to push me away. I know it's not what you want. You're scampering around inside of your own thoughts when you should be joining with mine.

Gilda remembered the first time she had heard the words that came without talking. It had been long ago, yet her sense of alarm returned quickly. Gilda turned to face Effie, looking directly into her eyes for the first time. The lamplight swirled hypnotically, drawing her inside. This girl, Effie, was a woman centuries older than she! In a brief moment Effie's history unfolded behind her eyes and Gilda saw a woman both young and old, who'd lived longer than any other Gilda had ever met. There was no reason for Gilda to run from her. That this woman was as she was, had lived the same way for so many more years, was miraculous and familiar. Gilda was stunned that she had not been able to see it; had not discerned the subtle shield Effie employed to protect her thoughts as those of their kind often did.

Effie took Gilda into her arms too quickly for her movement to be seen. They walked together from the living room to the small, dark sleeping room. Gilda locked the door behind them and watched as Effie ripped at the lining of her jacket. She removed a handful of rich, moist soil. She pulled back the comforter and pallet, sprinkling the earth into that already lining the platform. Together they slipped under the comforter. Gilda luxuriated in the weight of Effie's lean body on her own fuller one. The questions of only an hour before fled as she pulled Effie's mouth down hard upon her own. She left behind the shadowy dreams of desire and embraced the solid flesh that made dreams real.

Effie's mouth and hands were tender, insistent—demanding Gilda's pleasure be allowed its own way. Gilda enjoyed the sensation of yielding. She let go of worry about Samuel, of thoughts about Bird, and of desire she carried from the past. When she felt the welling of heat inside her she knew the release would be greater than any she had known before and she opened her eyes to catch Effie's gaze. The intent blazed inside the darkness of Effie's face. Her gentle rocking escalated, enveloping them both in a web of sensation. At the final moment Gilda closed her eyes, drawing inside herself as the power of her desire erupted around them. The air seemed to fill with the weight of them, humid movement on their skin. Gilda squeezed her eyes shut, listening to their breathing until it slowed and became almost imperceptible. She looked again at Effie and marveled at the flecks of orange swirling in her eyes.

They watched each other until the orange faded to brown. Effie let her head rest on Gilda's shoulder as she said, "We'll talk of Samuel tomorrow."

Gilda wasn't surprised or upset to hear her thoughts verbalized by Effie; the fact of their union rested on her as easily as Effie's slim body. She closed her eyes and listened outward beyond the locked door of her room, past the apartment walls. The building, the street, seemed as they should—quiet sounds of night. Gilda let her arms enfold Effie, comfortable in the complete blackness of her locked room, the morning light kept safely at bay.

The following afternoon Gilda showed Effie the trick of light that Julius had created by painting her windows. Effie watched distractedly, then said, "I think you should leave here for a while. What you've told me of Anthony's assessment seems logical. And what I've sensed of Samuel himself, following you, listening to you as he's been doing these past weeks, fits. But I believe he's more unpredictable than any of us can trust."

Gilda felt anxiety rise within her again, but part of it was anger at Samuel for his intrusion into her life here, for his part in Eleanor's death.

"If Eleanor was willing to give Samuel the opportunity to learn to live our life, perhaps you will too." Effie's voice deepened with the years of living. Gilda heard the age in her gentle firmness as she continued, "It's Sorel who can help him, Sorel whom he must see. You are only a convenient obstacle. I suggest you remove yourself."

Gilda felt an unfocused panic rise inside of her—she had finally made a home here with those she loved around her. "In spite of all I've learned I'm not much of a traveler. . . ."

"Then you needn't travel. Simply move your residence. Come north with me to my home in New Hampshire," Effie said. "It's quiet, the land is lovely, there are many things to learn there."

"Why should I run away from my home, my family, for Samuel's sake?" Gilda said, thinking of how much she'd been anticipating Julius' and Sorel's return.

"I'd not thought of it as running away. Movement is life for us. You've been trying to make a life for yourself. I've felt it in everything you ever said. But this can't happen with Ayeesha and the others, unless it is one of them you wish to bring into your life?"

Gilda barely shook her head. Her brow furrowed as she spoke. "One would think that our life would make such decisions easy. But I look into their faces, and no answer comes to me. Or the answer is no. I can never be certain so I back away, come close again, then retreat. I keep hoping to see the need for this life in their eyes as I did with Julius. But it seems their needs are bigger than the simplicity of longevity."

"It's that simplicity that seems to make you stumble. You are looking too hard." Effie continued in a strong voice. "You insist upon seeking guidance. Let me be a guide for a while. Follow me."

Gilda was silent, thinking of the reasons this might be impossible—Bird, Julius. Effie continued as if the sound of her words themselves would be convincing. "Long ago I searched for others, terrified I would find them, terrified I would not. I had been brought to Greece and sold as a trinket, given as a gift. The woman who was my mistress barely saw me except when showing me off to her friends."

A thread of bitterness ran through the words in spite of the placid expression on Effie's face. "I'm sure she grieved—as if she'd lost her favorite piece of jewelry—when I was stolen away by the one who gave me this life. But I was not as fortunate as some: he was neither kind nor intelligent. He used me simply to slake his own thirst, possibly not even realizing that the hunger began to grow in me. When he feared that my color made him too conspicuous, he abandoned me with little thought, on an island in the Aegean. But I was befriended there and taught to moderate my hunger, to live among people until I had the courage to move about the world. I've been among many of our people in all the places we can be found. Encountering Ayeesha and her friends when I first came to this country was a great joy to me. They reconnected me to a part of myself I'd never fully known. Learning of Sorel and you gave me even greater pleasure."

Effie smiled at Gilda's look of surprise. "Of course I know of Sorel, as I am certain he must know of me. Not my name, but that I've been living within the City. I've found that information travels very quickly among us. Although he's been away from his establishment he must certainly be aware of my presence, just as he is of Samuel's."

Effie could feel the resistance begin to melt away from Gilda, but she also sensed the deeper concerns that must be addressed. She spoke only after giving Gilda time to let the concerns take shape.

"It's not an unkind thing to make a new home. And it will be one where all whom you love are welcomed. When you sing, I listen to your thoughts. The words and music are an engaging tide, but beneath them always are the people I could know only through you— Bird, Julius, Anthony.

"The first time we met I knew you were not a simple mortal as you pretended." Effie's face looked briefly like a girl's. "In the lands and times in which I've lived, searching the minds of others has not been as remote a possibility as it seems today, particularly in this country. That's why my thoughts are shielded as a matter of course. I let down my own guard only when you sing for us, or on the nights I've stood hidden in the backs of clubs where you performed so I might learn more of you."

"But why didn't you make yourself known to me or Anthony? Why were you hiding?"

"I need only make my presence known directly to Sorel. He is the only elder here." Again the years of experience rang in her voice. Gilda sensed an understanding of the traditions of their life deeper than she herself had known.

Effie continued. "I've traveled to many countries and not remained for any length of time. The home I've prepared to the north, in New Hampshire, is private, safe, yet not very far from the cities. And surely Sorel and the others might come to you there."

Effie was surprised at the continued resistance. "You don't see it, do you?"

She sat back and looked around the room, then again at Gilda before going on. "Our lives must change with the change in mortals. That's the nature of our lives. We move among them, but we can never be of them. The cities and the principles on which most societies are built have been poisoned. While this is of great concern to us, we have to remain apart to protect ourselves, to protect them. We must all make safe places. I'm not suggesting we abandon them—our lives are inextricably bound together. But a broader view of what our place in this world will be is sorely needed."

Gilda felt uncertain. The world was just coming into focus for her; she couldn't visualize change in the future as Effie did. Each new era had somehow slipped in around her and she'd adapted to it rather than thinking of herself as separate from it, part of another line of history.

"I would like to see this land, your home there," Gilda said, almost surprising herself. "But Sorel's homecoming, we'd have to return for that. . ." Gilda stopped before adding that she needed to hear from Bird before making such a move. She realized that she needn't consult with anyone. Bird would know of this move as she knew of everything. Looking at the rich color of Effie's dark skin and the complex texture of her hair pulled tightly into a braid at the back of her head, Gilda sensed the familiarity that had made her so attractive from the beginning. She was both plain and luminous, young and old, contrasts that embodied all of what their world was supposed to mean. The contradiction of who she was—both living and not living—shone through in her.

"And Samuel, what of him?" Gilda asked.

"That's a matter for him and Sorel to sort through. Its outcome has been settled already, at least existentially. It only remains for Sorel to return and put it into motion."

Gilda tried to puzzle out the ripple of feelings that moved through her like a shifting tide. Clearly Julius had found his place in this world much more easily than she. His eye was ever on the horizon although he was as loyal to Gilda as anyone could hope for. He, like Bird, had easily altered the rhythm of life to fit himself, not the limitations of mortal time.

Gilda sang her new song at the going-away party that Ayeesha held for Effie.

"My love is the blood that enriches this ground.
The sun is a star denied you and me.
You are the life I've searched for and found.
And the moon is our half of the dream.
No day is too long nor night too free.
Just come, be here with me."

The words grew big in her heart and spilled out onto the bright faces of Kaaren, Marianne, Cynthia, Laverne, others. She let her mind open with the song, and Effie listened to her thoughts. The regret they both felt in separating from the women who hovered around them now blended. But rather than being multiplied, it was countered by their anticipation. Gilda remembered other times she had taken leave of newly made friends and for once felt no sadness. Their lives went on within the cycle that was their nature. As Julius had become her brother, Effie would be her sister. For the first time the years ahead seemed rightfully hers.

Chapter Seven

Hampton Falls, New Hampshire: 2020

Gilda dropped the receiver into its cradle. The crash was impersonal, final. She turned the power of the video monitor back and pressed replay in order to see the tape she had made of the national magazine show. Gilda stabbed at the pause button. There she was in full color. Although she was shrouded in a straw hat and glasses, it was all too clearly her image. For the past two days her literary agent had left word that he was in a meeting, and she'd had nowhere to vent her anger at this voyeuristic intrusion into her privacy.

She punched out again, this time releasing the pause button. There was another photograph of her, annoyingly recognizable, obviously taken when she was unaware of it. The room was filled with the silky voice of the announcer who seemed to relish describing Abby Bird, Gilda's literary alter ego, as "mysterious" and "reclusive." These were not, after all, capital crimes. And then that phrase again—"fetishistic flight from publicity."

He called her the nation's most popular author of romance novels. She could hear him thinking both *how quaint* and *how lurid* although he said neither. Gilda had chosen that particular genre because it was one of the few forms of written literature the populace still followed. Newspapers and magazines had been relegated to the nostalgia bins since the *New York Times* folded in 2010. And few people could remember when they had actually held one of the literary classics in their hands. She'd also chosen the field because of its anonymity and the not uncommon practice of using pen names. This magazine show with its spotlight on Abby Bird was only the first, she was certain, in a relentless series of assaults on her life.

Writing romances was, for Gilda, a way of sharing some of the many stories she had gathered through her long life, much as songwriting had been. The journals she'd treasured for years and the lessons they held had become a fine field to harvest for characters and ideas. To many, the stories she wrote seemed curious, archaic, even though the periods in which they were set were rarely more than 150 years old. Having conspired to forget their past, the generations plowed ahead at top speed to some mythical future as if the wild west existed in the stars. Gilda had written the stories of their history, cloaking it in adventure and mysticism, and they sold.

Until this moment it had been simple. Ten years ago she had easily used her silent powers to convince an agent to represent her and a publisher to buy her series of adventures. They never saw her face to face, and as social systems slowly unraveled, her reclusiveness was not worthy of particular note. Abby Bird's books made money, encouraging the publisher to accept her insistence on complete privacy.

Effie had first become addicted to the stories and persuaded Gilda to market them. Even when she was there, listening to the click of keys from Gilda's workroom, Effie had to keep reminding herself that it was *her* Gilda writing them, not some other person named Abby Bird. Their success had eased Effie's mind. Gilda showed no signs of dissatisfaction with her life in the small town. For her, the stories were an urgent message—a way of speaking with thousands of people in distant places, places she had been to or hoped to visit in the future. She insinuated herself into their homes and their thoughts, and they welcomed her. It was also a way of keeping contact with the changing world outside Hampton Falls.

When Gilda began writing she settled in for a long stay. It was from her electronic enclave that she communicated, writing books and letters on paper, and communiqués on video, to almost as many people as read her books.

Hampton Falls was perched precariously over the ocean between Massachusetts and Maine. Most of the population of about a thousand citizens traced their lineage in the town back two hundred years. Much of the yearly tourism had declined to almost nothing because the coastline was so polluted. The people who remembered the fishing industry sat around talking about it to each other. Those too young to remember left town as soon as they could. The village had shifted slightly with Gilda's arrival, making a small place for her in their social lives, but they still considered her and Effie strangers.

To the fans with whom Abby Bird communicated, however, she was no stranger. Many read every book she wrote; others simply sent her letters.

Gilda kept up with her family. Bird, whose name she had taken for part of her pseudonym, still wrote in a distinctive script on paper mailed in vellum envelopes covered with foreign stamps. Bird's letters were often brief. Perhaps the elusiveness of such contact was painful. She reported things: the status of the current Native leadership, the secrets of Belgian lacemakers, archaeological finds in Peru. Each item of information held an urgency that implied all things were connected. Often she wrote announcing a visit in a letter that would arrive by post, weeks after she had already come and gone on her way again.

Effie was fond of sending clippings, song lyrics, leaves, shells when she was traveling, any artifacts she found on hand, sometimes even interesting labels from new clothing. She habitually sent a separate package for herself so that when she returned home she, too, had a gift to open.

Sorel and Anthony were unpredictable. Sometimes huge scrolls would arrive, filled with flowery script—formal epistles recounting their adventures, inquiring about hers, discussing philosophical questions. At other times tapes would be broadcast on their mail channel, frequently staged like a video program: Sorel interviewing Anthony or vice versa, or the two of them engaged in debate. They almost never presented themselves live on video. Sorel felt that it was ill-mannered and crude.

Julius was a communiqué buff. Each fortnight, without fail, his signal would ring like a secret knock. Gilda would tune into the video, and there would be his shining face on tape, or sometimes live from a place she would never have predicted.

But the novels were the real joy. They helped her find new people with whom to communicate. One young black woman in particular, Nadine, a nascent fiction writer in St. Louis, wrote by post regularly. When Gilda received the first letter her hand trembled with recognition of the penmanship. The sense of the envelope itself told her who it was from: Aurelia's great-granddaughter. Although she had known of her, had followed her with her thoughts, she had not expected to really communicate with her. She'd been aware of all of Aurelia's progeny yet had studiously avoided any direct contact. Aurelia's daughter had continued to live in Missouri, near her mother, until marrying late in life. In turn, her daughter and granddaughter were raised in Arkansas.

Aurelia's great-granddaughter, Nadine, had been deaf since birth and had an uncanny sense of language—how words felt inside rather than how they sounded. Her handwriting and her sense of humor were much like Aurelia's had been. She sent Gilda embroidered tales full of the news of her city and her rich yet isolated life. Although she had not yet had the courage to show them to anyone else, she sometimes included one of her stories. She wrote of a future she would never know. An idealistic world of utopian equality and mystical adventure.

Through Nadine's letters Gilda had enjoyed tales of Aurelia's successes. She spoke with passionate admiration for her great-grandmother's activism, a tradition she was trying to carry on in her own town. Municipal resources seemed to have been depleted to a level not much higher than that of Aurelia's community when Gilda lived there.

Gilda always wrote back to Nadine, spending hours over the letters, afraid to reveal too much of herself but cherishing each word. Nadine's was a name Gilda remembered as she lay down to rest in the pink morning hours.

Because Nadine communicated on paper only, never using the videophone, Gilda remained satisfied trying to picture Nadine in her house or walking about her neighborhood. It was difficult because much had changed in the world since Gilda moved to Effie's New Hampshire retreat. The economy had taken a sharp downturn. The health of the cities had failed. Many people had abandoned the sterile concrete canyons for hills and valleys they thought would provide fresh air and water. Many had starved there, unable to read the weather or rotate crops. Some died at the hands of those trying to drive them away from their already overburdened land. Much had changed.

Still Gilda's hair was not really grey nor her face lined. When she looked into the mirror her familiar image formed easily, reminding her of what the Fulani people had always known: the spirit was just that—an intangible thing that did not die with the body. Her essence as an African still shone through her soft, wide features.

She saw not just herself but a long line of others who had become part of her as time passed. The family she had hungered for as a child was hers now. It was spread across the globe but was closer to her than she had ever imagined possible. She felt comfortable with most of her life on the New Hampshire coast: some of the few remaining forested areas were not too far to the north, and the movement of the ocean, with all its discomforts, still intrigued her. With so many people retreating from the fouled coasts, Gilda's taking up residence in the woodlands of New Hampshire assured her privacy. And when those in her family wanted to rest from their travels, she had the accommodations to welcome everyone.

She smiled at the old memory of Effie using that possibility as an enticement to move north. The first years there had been tentative, each of them spending as much time elsewhere as in the rambling cottage set into a secluded hillside. Little by little Gilda had moved things from her apartment in the City to the house. It was almost two years before she brought her trunk. The carefully tended quilt now lay across the back of a chair that sat facing the fireplace. She stopped wondering if she would ever bring a partner into this life herself, as Bird had been brought in. Instead she focused on all that Effie wanted to learn about blacks in America, about Gilda's past, and on her writing.

Effie had outfitted Gilda with a full wardrobe for the outdoors woman: flannel shirts, hiking boots, rain gear. Together they'd observed the subtle yet sinister changes in the world around them. The frequent coastal storms were not the least of them, and Gilda's bright yellow slicker and gum boots were put to use more often than she would have expected. Still the home they had made remained quiet, and the town in which they lived was primarily unchanged. Again Gilda played the eccentric for the townspeople as she had in Rosebud. But she did not regret her move. Although she returned to the City frequently she was always eager to sink into the chair before the fire.

That was all now at risk. Gilda started at the tinkling sound of the videophone. Could the press be after her so soon? But then she recognized Julius' coded rings. She turned from her desk to the console and pressed the buttons, cautiously leaving the shadow screen on from her side.

"Well, sisterlove. Are you practicing your autograph?" Julius' freckled brown face was split by a glowing smile, then uproarious laughter.

"You saw the show?" Gilda said, flipping the view button.

"Sister, everybody in the Americas saw the show. You still don't have any idea how much your fans dig you. Girl, you're like a celeb —get it?"

Gilda couldn't suppress her own smile. Julius had managed to hold on to his natural flair for using black slang in spite of now speaking at least twenty languages and having lived in almost as many different countries. His short Afro haircut, fierce devotion, and colorful vocabulary had remained unchanged for over fifty years.

The first time Julius had come to visit her at the cottage he'd teased her relentlessly. The idea of Gilda living in the woods and wearing hiking boots seemed too anachronistic even for him. Gilda had let him tease, releasing all his anxiety about the change, making him understand he still had a place where she was. In creating that understanding with Julius, she had come to accept the manner in which Bird led *her* life.

"Listen, Julius, I know you find this amusing, but this is dangerous for us. I've been safe here. We've all been able to be safe at the cottage. What happens when the paparazzi start trying to track me down for exclusive interviews and all that madness? I don't think we can risk a TV documentary!"

"Hey, how's this?—'Lifestyles of the Undead!' " Julius kept laughing but tried to continue. "You in a Borsalino hat and dark glasses, interviewer trailing behind nervously, conduct a tour of the house . . .and grounds." This last bent him over with mirth, and his face disappeared from the screen.

"Julius, please listen. You don't seem to hear the seriousness of this. If they find me they won't stop until they know everything. Muckraking is like a disease. Anything to keep from paying attention to real problems. We are slowly poisoning ourselves to death, and I bet this story about me could beat that one into the top of the show on any of the networks."

When Gilda left the City she had removed herself from Samuel's potential violence, but that was only escape from an individual. She stopped collecting newspaper articles about the bombings, rapes, and starvation, and the ease of her disconnection now weighed upon her like the rocks on which the cottage stood. For decades she had watched history on the video—marches, movements, more bombings, rapes, killings, more movements. This place had always seemed safe. She couldn't believe that Julius was taking it so lightly.

His face reappeared, and he tried to calm down. "Listen, Gilda, I get your drift. But you been holding down the fort so long, sister-love, you forgot about the outer limits. I mean the world does exist beyond your property line, ya dig? I mean, like right now I'm in Iowa. You think you got problems? Citizens here are still trying to decide if brown people and white people should eat sitting at the same table. Which is pretty funny since there ain't that much food to speak of. The GrassRoots Coalition is having trouble organizing the people into any type of protests. You and me—we're lucky. We can't ever forget our dependence on this earth. They don't have that insight. It's a serious joint, and they're just starting to cop to it. We been practicing for—shall we say—a while. It's a hard row to hoe, all the way around, doll."

"So what are you suggesting?" Gilda said, forgetting all the words it had taken for Effie to convince her to come north.

"All is relative, ain't that what Sorel says? Long is only long if you think it's long. I say fold your tent. Get in the wind. Forward all your calls."

Gilda remained silent.

"Listen, you're the one who taught me that safety, stasis, ain't the natural way of living things. You could do anything. How about joining Bird? She's working in Central America on land reclamation. Or how about Iowa?" Julius continued. "Who was that old dude you used to quote, about the tightrope?"

"Papa Wallenda. 'Life exists only on the high wire. Everything else is just waiting.' "

"Right on!"

Gilda almost spoke, then stopped. Julius was silent for a while and simply watched the thoughts shifting like shadows across her dark face. Gilda tried to grab hold of the images in her mind. Bird, who had traveled relentlessly for decades, was rarely happy until the next journey was on the horizon. And she herself had loved learning each new town, seeing how black people were manifest around the world. Why was it here, in this small enclave, that they found themselves rooted? Potbound, Julius might say.

Gilda rang off and retreated to the small sitting room to build a fire. She laid each log carefully, letting her mind be absorbed by the task. Absently she held a match to the twigs at the bottom and sat back to enjoy the flames as they blossomed and began to consume. Sitting in the old chair she was comforted by the feel of the knots in the quilt at her back. The heat and light of the fire were so much like the rays of the sun that she closed her eyes and thought of the wondrous visit with Eleanor to Mt. Tamalpais. Part of her regretted not ever returning to that spot and looking out at the setting sun. She wondered if such a spot still existed, or if it was all impossibly overgrown, or worse—paved over, rat infested. She had heard on several news shows that California had suffered very badly in the past decade. Overpopulation had created economic collapse. She had not been back there since leaving Sorel's salon, and it was difficult to imagine it any way other than what she'd known. Gilda had drifted deeply into the snapshots of the past when the ringing of the videophone startled her.

She bolted from the chair but stood paralyzed by the phone unable to pick it up, fearing it might be a reporter. Gilda waited, and the ringing stopped as the recorder started. As soon as she heard Effie's voice she pressed the interrupt and full-view buttons. Effie stood before her in a phone facility with a look of concern on her face.

"Ah, wonderful, you're there," Effie said, relieved that Gilda was still at the house. "I hate leaving messages on these things. I can see that you've heard about the show."

"I've heard, I've seen."

"And?" Effie asked, expecting Gilda to have distilled some plan by now.

"Julius suggests I disappear for a while. But there's so much I care about here. I'm afraid that if Abby Bird begins running she'll never be able to stop. And I've been happy here."

"If you've been happy in Hampton Falls you can be happy somewhere else."

"But this is the home you've made—"

"Made and can remake. Remember when you first came to the cottage? You looked at the hillside and the building and the trees and said, 'How perfectly ordinary!' You had the delight of a child, for something there represented the life you wanted. Well, Hampton Falls can't do that anymore. And it is, after all, only a representation of the life. The nation around it is dissolving. I think you should see it through your own eyes, not just others'."

"But I haven't had the chance to really know this place, the ocean, the trees, you."

"You, Bird, all of us are part of a network that is naturally outside the daily workings of this universe. Finding the balance between participation and withdrawal—how to sing and not be a superstar, how to write and not become a public figure—is difficult. You've understood that balance for some time. Don't forget what you already know. Sorel and Anthony have made many homes. This was my first on this continent; I've certainly always expected to have others."

They were both quiet, trying to really see each other past the electronic gadgetry that linked them.

Gilda knew how much Effie disliked speaking on video so felt uncomfortable with her own indecision and stubbornness. "Perhaps I might visit. . . Missouri, or Julius is in Iowa—"

"Those are fine ideas." Effie stopped as she saw the clouds clear from Gilda's face, replaced by a broad smile. Her dark skin was glowing again.

"Listen, Effie, I have to go. There are a million things to do now. There'll be a message."

She faded the screen out and set about getting organized. It all seemed so simple suddenly.

She worked furiously for two days, preparing her papers and shipping away things for storage she might want in the future. Once again she opened the old trunk she'd had since Woodard's and let her gaze caress some of the objects. Folded inside was a newspaper clipping that barely held together. Gilda didn't unfold it. She simply looked at it, knowing the words inside. It was an obituary for Aurelia Freeman of Rosebud, Missouri, who had warranted a lengthy encomium because of her respected position in the black communities of many surrounding towns.

Her work with the poor and the uneducated had been noted and rewarded by numerous citizens and civil rights organizations before her death in 1966. Gilda sat down for a moment to feel the hard beating of her heart at these memories. Over the years she had listened for Aurelia many times, enjoying her successes vicariously. By slipping into her thoughts she was able to sense Aurelia's inner peace and the small part of herself she maintained should Gilda ever return. Only once did Gilda make contact. Through a dream she had tried to communicate the joy she felt at the goodness that filled both of their lives. She had also listened for the lives of Aurelia's daughter and granddaughter, from wherever her travels had taken her. It was not until she received the first letter from Nadine that Gilda actually communicated. It was as if she had willed the girl to write to her.

Gilda folded her colorful quilt on top of her things and closed the trunk with a new leather strap in preparation for shipping. She pulled a file from the back of her desk drawer that held a short letter to her agent and publisher and a large check for the foundling home in town. She made quick adjustments on her will and had it authorized by video after looking up the address for the main offices of the GrassRoots Coalition. She made certain that Abby Bird's other legal papers were in a prominent place in the house. She finally sifted through the few letters she kept, reading many of Nadine's to herself before feeding them into the woodburning stove. She opened one of the last envelopes to glance briefly at the pages before tossing it, when a paragraph Nadine had written about a year before caught her eye:

They think because I'm deaf, I'm stupid. They think they love me because they don't make fun of my deafness. They don't see that this is not enough to be called love. Doing nothing can never be called love. My mother said her gran'ma taught her that. Did I ever tell you every one of us got Nadine in our name somewhere? She said gran'ma named her for a special gift someone had given her years ago. . . .

The letter went on with other stories. Gilda folded the pages and slipped them into the small pack she would take with her.

Carrying a few items, she went outside. She deposited the letters in the postbox at the end of her lane and walked down the road against a brisk wind toward the cliffs that dropped down behind their land into the Atlantic. She folded a shirt, a pair of slacks, and socks into a neat pile on a precipice overlooking the tumultuous water below. Its constant motion tugged at her, as the many rivers she'd known had done, yet the sound of surf against rocks was a comforting roar. It seemed a fitting demise for the legendary Abby Bird. Gilda's pulse quickened at the idea of moving about the world again. She took an easy stroll in the deepening dusk through the woods near her house. She tried not to go over her lists of things to do, wanting simply to listen to the sound of the ocean and the trees. She enjoyed the leaves crunching under her boots and the feel of branches slapping her back as she made her way toward what was no longer her home.

Once inside the dark cottage, Gilda sensed danger. She walked steadily to her bedroom without turning on the living room light and unlocked one of the two bolts that held her sleeping room safe. Then she moved toward the kitchen, measuring her casual stride with deliberation.

As soon as she turned her back, the man who was hidden in the shadows tried to slip into her bedroom. Gilda leapt silently for him, seizing his collar and lifting him from the floor. She held him pinned against the door and looked over her shoulder toward the light switch. The lamp lit itself, revealing a young man dangling like a marionette from her left hand, a camera at his feet. Her voice spit words that burned. "Who are you? What do you want?"

"I want the story on Abby Bird. They're paying me for the story!" The young man realized he had risked his life for an obscure byline, but it was too late. The cynical young reporter believed in a cliché for the first time: his life, in fact, did pass before his eyes.

"There is no story to be told," Gilda hissed.

The young man struggled not to kick his heels against the wall. He felt foolish enough already. He'd always thought it a stupid idea—skulking around some pop writer's house looking for love letters or whatever else editors thought bought viewers. Especially silly as other real news darkened around them. He tried to maintain a look of staunch professionalism from his precarious position while he estimated his chances of survival and breathed at the same time.

"But then, again, perhaps there is a story," Gilda said, loosening her grip so that his feet reached the floor. She smiled pleasantly, as if Abby Bird had just offered him tea, then hummed a soft, lulling tune. Her eyes held his while she moved into his mind, edging it into unconsciousness. She sliced neatly into his vein with a much-practiced gesture and drank the blood quickly. Gilda drew from him only enough to sustain herself, and in exchange for the life he shared with her she left him his story.

Abby Bird, noted novelist and respected naturalist, died today by her own hand in protest against the destruction of the environment by ordinary people. She left her entire estate, including projected royalties and her extensive mailing list, to GrassRoots, an internationally known activist organization.

Gilda smiled at the epitaph she had composed for the illustrious Abby Bird. She felt as proud of that as she did of the books the author had penned. She sealed the wound gently and held his pulse until it returned to a more normal rate. She easily carried the man outside. Moving through the woods, she found his car parked two miles from the house. He would awaken shortly with the satisfaction of having scooped a top-of-the-show story for his network. She hurried back to her house and pushed the shutters closed, securing them from inside. She turned on the video monitor one last time and switched to the general message board. *Welcome Home,* she typed, and it appeared in big letters on the screen. Gilda locked the message in, then coded outgoing messages to family members to be stored until they tried to contact her.

She walked around the house as she had done with every home she'd abandoned over the years. She looked at things being left behind, touched surfaces as if memories might be absorbed through her fingertips. She would miss the wonderfully huge wood stove and the sound of Sorel's laughter when they sat around it sipping champagne. Something about the way the snow lay in winter on the hill sloping down from the house reminded her of the old farm on the road out of New Orleans past Woodard's. Bird had noticed that, too. When she came to visit she spent much time seated atop the hill simply staring out as if she could see Louisiana.

And there was a pristine, purposeful quality about the whole place that made her think of Bernice. She let all the memories find their way to the top of her thoughts. Although the loss made her wistful, there was little sadness this time—having made one home she could make another.

Once more she left her house, this time carrying a pallet filled with Mississippi soil, a backpack, and a small ribbon-tied bundle of letters. She looked down the road remembering what it had been like to travel alone from place to place, listening to people in person rather than electronically. In the back of her mind the dangers of that first journey sat in hulking shadows. She had to peer at them closely to make herself remember that each journey was different; the fears she'd had so long ago needn't beset her now.

Gilda hesitated a moment to decide on her direction—north toward what had once been called Canada, or south? She turned southward thinking Arkansas might be nice this time of year. She moved slowly, afraid of her destination. What would such a meeting hold? She would not be able to explain who she was to Nadine. Yet seeing Aurelia's great-granddaughter filled Gilda with excitement and impatience. Touching this part of her past, even briefly, would help her go forward. She was eager to hear more of the GrassRoots Movement, to know what she and the others might do. Feeling discontent but doing nothing was no longer enough.

She began to pick up her speed, passing from the highway into the wooded margins that surrounded the many towns now close to collapse or abandoned entirely. Gilda was eager to meet the girl whose name meant Hope. Her tent was folded, the wind was high, and all calls had been forwarded.

Chapter Eight
Land of Enchantment: 2050

Gilda stood barely breathing, her gaze resting on the green-and-purple glow of the grotto that opened beyond the entrance to her cavern. Its warming phosphorescence reminded her of the blinking lights circling the sign that marked the town limits of the sad little place where she had found Nadine. By the time Gilda arrived, those lights were all that was left working, and Nadine faithfully replaced bulbs and checked the electrical line. The pulsing, theatrical bulbs were Nadine's joy, the symbol she had taken as a reason for pushing the town to hang on. Gilda saw, during her stay with Nadine, that almost everyone else had given up, abandoning hope of food, work, relief of any kind. Townspeople scoffed at Nadine and other members of GrassRoots who persisted in their demands that people turn around the way they lived. Nadine signed furiously to everyone and laughed in her muffled chortle when they refused to understand her. Then she began again, certain that they would catch up. As Nadine toiled over handbills instructing people how to live without comforts but not feel degraded, Gilda saw the bend of Aurelia's head and the strength of Aurelia's resolve in every motion. The lights were the one luxury Nadine felt they all needed.

Gilda took the same route out of town when she left for the last time just so she could see Nadine's sign once more. Each time she returned to this cavern, the memory of Nadine and Aurelia returned with her.

Soon the guards would be in place and she could retreat behind the bolted door of her chamber far from the light of day and from the Hunters. She would be able to lay down to rest. Gilda had little faith in her highly paid guards, not at the prices the Hunters were offering, so once behind that door she would let herself out of a hidden panel and into the maze of rock-strewn corridors that surrounded her underground adytum. She would then wander randomly until she found a niche that felt safe, undo her canvas bedroll soft with Mississippi soil, lay her lean body down, and wait for night. The caverns and mine shafts of the Southwest were numerous, convoluted, and still intriguing to her, but their air was oppressive and made her feel as much a prisoner as any cell. The grotto's dampness caused all of her clothes to mildew; everything had to be scrubbed daily to make existence bearable. She yearned for the peace and comforts of her coastal cottage, now gone.

If she stayed much longer she was certain the Hunters would find her and bribe one of the guards. Sometimes, wandering the dank, rough corridors, she thought it might be worth it to give herself up to them. There were many rumors: the life being offered was service, not servitude or destruction. It was said that only those who resisted sharing their blood were dealt with harshly. Gilda knew better. In light of the ruthless way the decline of the planet had been shepherded, she listened to no rumors—only the bits of information that Julius passed on to her and the others.

Thoughts of the Hunters, armed with drugs and other weapons to ensnare her and her family, caused Gilda to shiver with the memory of her escape from the plantation. In unsuspecting moments she felt the bounty hunter's hand on her childishly thin ankle as he dragged her from beneath the hay. Those who came now were more silent, more expert, but essentially the same. Their approach filled her with a familiar terror.

Living along the tree-thick coast of the Atlantic, it had been easy to miss the air of disposability that threatened all living things—trees, oceans, people. It was on her journey to visit Nadine that Gilda saw the wasteland the country had become and understood how far back it had been thrown by the fever of desperation and solipsism infecting so many. There was little pleasure in remembering.

The things she held sacred became fewer: her mother's broad Fulani face; the sound of Anthony's and Sorel's voices as they argued over wine; Bird's voice inside her head; the ease with which she had learned to live with Effie; and sharing the blood with Julius. It had been life freely given, not the travesty being demanded of them now. This horror was slavery come again.

The psychological impact of having no distant future to contemplate was staggering. People had grown restless and impatient with themselves, then surly and ruthless. Finally, they had discovered the existence of the Vampire. They began to believe in the myths they had heard with chilled pleasure as children and to put their faith in the creatures with infinite regenerative powers.

Gilda and her family had retreated from society, taking less blood than they needed, creating fewer like themselves. Even the most flagrant terrorists among them, those who thrived on the fear of their victims, ceased their killing in the attempt to escape discovery. The full transfusion of their blood gave eternal life to the hungry rich, who now sent out the Hunters to capture them. Once transformed, however, the wealthy broke the one commandment held by her kind: never kill one's creator. In her lifetime she had seen that recklessness in only one other—Samuel.

Gilda finally settled into a rocky alcove on her cool pallet, hoping that Julius or Effie would answer the call she sent out before she slept. She closed her eyes and felt no one but knew they would answer. Soon she'd be assured of their safety and able to make her way to them.

When Gilda awoke her body told her it was dusk in the world above. She started sharply when she saw Houston, one of her guards, standing in front of the entrance to the place where she hid. His broad back and narrow hips were unmistakable, as was the blond hair he wore tied with a scarf as long and bright as the hair itself. She did not move but watched as he shifted uneasily under her gaze on his back.

"Why are you here?" she asked.

He didn't turn but spoke looking straight ahead. "I came upon you as I made my rounds. I know that you sometimes slip away from us but this place is too exposed."

"You understand that to know my sleeping place means death?"

"Yes."

"Then why have you stayed?"

"I've watched you sleep before. I couldn't leave you here for someone else to discover."

Houston's back gave no clue to his thoughts. Gilda was sure she could take him easily; she need only hold him with her gaze and he would fall before her. Then she would not have to go out to gather life from anyone tonight. Perhaps that is why he is keeping his back turned, Gilda thought.

"Face me."

Houston turned to her, his large body a contrast to the simple lines of his face, smooth brow, hairless skin, and full lips held firm across his teeth. He looked Gilda in the eye, something none of the other guards did.

"Have you become a Hunter? Do you hunt me?"

"No."

"Then you seek my life for yourself?" Gilda asked, knowing as she spoke it was not true. There was no callousness about him. Unlike the wealthy who had inherited the earth he was curious, uncertain. It was this that made him a good guard, a strong ally.

"Answer, please."

"No."

"What then? I have little patience at this moment!"

"Your guard, as always."

Gilda stared steadily into his eyes searching for the edge that was sure to appear if he was lying. She looked behind his thoughts and found the curiosity that had become familiar to her, blended with the gut animal smell many men carried when around a woman. She laughed thinly and saw the puzzlement on his face.

"I'll have the nightly reports in my chamber," Gilda said. She walked away brusquely, taking care not to touch him as she passed.

She entered her room and lit the candles that she preferred to the omnipresent fluorescents. She pulled a stiff brush through her bristly, close-cut hair. The past attempted to flood in on her. It pushed at the wall curtains and against her breasts, trying to sweep her before it, to engulf her in weariness and fear, but Gilda snapped her eyes open and forced her concentration onto something in the present: the half-full decanter of red wine glistening in the light. She wound herself around the facets of the bottle and slipped inside the smoothness of the vintage wine, feeling its soothing coolness. She wanted to remember which one of the wines this was so she could let Sorel know how pleasing it had been. The light playing on the glass brought his booming laughter to her. She stood entranced until the sound of movement forced her back.

Houston entered with the two others she employed to watch her cavern compound. One was a thin, older man, not yet fifty, whose eyes and body appeared to be perpetually on the edge of starvation. But he was alert and fast; perhaps knowing he was in the final stages of his life made him so. The second was a young woman of about seventeen, plump and clever. She seemed to never sleep and was always everywhere with a smile. Gilda knew she snuck off some afternoons to see someone, a lover or her family, but she never shirked her duty. Gilda paid them fairly, was even generous when she could be, but kept herself at a distance except during these accounts on the security of the cave and the surrounding landscape.

They reported what went on above in the half-abandoned cities several kilometers to the north and east, trying to speak casually, as if they were not sitting in a cave beneath the earth with a woman who could live for eternity, or might just as easily kill them. She had offered the one thing she knew would bind them to her: sharing of her blood, which she promised to do just as she left them for the last time. The old man had refused. His lungs were already gone, as well as all of his friends. The young woman said yes, maybe. As yet she had not declared herself. She worked tirelessly to help her family but said she feared the hunted life. She seemed content with the money to be made as a bodyguard. Houston had said nothing, only took his pay and hovered nearby at all times.

Gilda listened impatiently, hungry to be outside in the freedom of darkness walking the dry bed of the Rio Bravo. She tried to remember what night had felt like long ago—full of promise, the shadows inviting. Evenings arm in arm with Effie, walking until they were both full from the sights they'd seen. Discovering new cities and people, then hiding themselves away from the sun until night came again for them. They had not done so in almost a decade.

She had seen Julius more recently. The challenge of eluding the Hunters ignited a sense of adventure that sporadically led him to her side. He spent their reunions telling tales of the others and playing recordings of newly created folk music he had collected from around the country as proof that the human spirit was still thriving. Then night concealed his departure.

Sitting here with her guards, the only personal contact she dared to make, the night no longer held the meaning it had in the past. There was no freedom above. The Hunters were everywhere, using telepathy, sonar body tracers, and decoy tricks to find the sleeping places. Unable to wait any longer Gilda abruptly dismissed the group in the middle of Houston's report. She changed quickly into the dark green one-piece she favored and a short jacket. Her boots were silent on the rocks as she climbed the gradual incline to the mouth of the cave.

There were no city lights in either direction. The desert was silent except for the slight rustling of the camouflage tarp that hid a small hovercraft. There was no moon. The contaminated atmosphere rarely allowed it to break through the earth's grey blanket.

Gilda turned eastward in the darkness and began to run at a speed that soon made her invisible, covering the distance of a hundred kilometers in a quarter of the time it took the hovercraft. She felt conspicuous as she came into town. Almost everyone on the street was in pairs or groups of three and four. Few ventured out unaccompanied.

She wandered, watching and listening before she went to take her share of the blood. She slid easily into an apartment window and took from a sleeping man, who experienced a slight disturbance of his dream. When she heard a key at the front door Gilda slipped a pleasing idea into the greyness of his dreams and fled.

The night had cooled, and there were few people on the street when she emerged. Many of the apartment buildings were abandoned, making the city's darkness almost complete. Two high-rise luxury towers at the northern edge stood empty in blackness, solemn obelisks serving as tombstones for the entire city.

Before she turned down the boulevard that led to the edge of town she felt a presence behind her. She slowed her pace and listened. Light, reflected from a shop window, cast a dull glow, but most of the street was dark. It was the unmistakable stealth of a Hunter. The reflex stimulants they used, making them faster and stronger than the weakened population, was evidenced in the very silence of his steps.

He kept pace with Gilda but held his distance, hoping, she assumed, to track her to her sleeping place and then overcome her. Gilda turned into a narrow alley of smaller buildings and low stoops, ran for a few steps, then backed into a doorway and threw an empty ash can down the alley. It clanged in echoes through the street for just long enough; the Hunter came around the corner, running. Gilda reached out and grabbed him by the throat, cutting off his wind and voice. He made a small choking sound but couldn't move or Gilda's fingers would have ripped out his vocal chords. He swung his hand up in a swift chop to dislodge her grip. His strength was considerable, but Gilda's was greater.

She pushed him away before he could strike her again. He hit the opposite wall and bounced forward like a toy. In the darkness it was impossible to tell anything about the Hunter except that he was of narrow build, wiry, and vicious.

As he crouched low to use the ancient martial arts, Gilda spoke in a soft voice. "Leave me. I have no wish to kill you."

There was no visible reaction to her words as he continued toward her. Gilda turned to run, certain she could disappear before he had a hint of her direction. He grabbed her arm as swiftly as one of her own kind. His grip and the counterforce stretched her arm away from its socket. The pain shot from her shoulder to the back of Gilda's head. Her mouth opened, but only breath escaped.

Her foot rose smoothly, the toe of her boot catching the edge of his chin in a ballet movement marred only by the blood that arced from his nose as his head snapped backward. For a moment there was a look of terror in his eyes. The mythology of the Vampire still had power even for the Hunters. This one already regretted not waiting until she slept before he attacked. Even with biphetamines he was not fast or strong enough for her, and the smell of blood was in the air.

Gilda hit him full in the face with her left fist, feeling the slippery wound of his flesh. He lurched backward but didn't fall. He struggled forward again, and Gilda peered through the sheet of blood over his broken face into his clouded eyes. She could see the haze of drugs that held him upright, conscious and able to resist her will. But in this, too, she was stronger. She held his gaze long enough to rip away his memory, then knocked him unconscious with a brisk crack of her palm on his forehead.

He sat on the coldness of the pavement like a child oblivious to the pain that tore through his body. Gilda left him there and sped away.

Once back at the entrance to the cavern she stood for a moment and sniffed the dry night air. It was clearer than usual. Such a close call with a Hunter was unnerving. She ignored the pain in her shoulder, certain that it would dissipate by tomorrow's nightfall, and tried to focus on the nighttime sky and her next move.

Bird had made her way south early and settled in the less industrial lands where it was somewhat easier to remain undiscovered. It was said that some of their kind had escaped Off-world, but there were few facts to put faith in. To Gilda, crossing that great expanse of sky was as frightening as crossing the boundless sea.

The Off-worlders had rebelled, refusing to take any immigrants who could not prove need. They monitored all applications as if their lives depended on it. And they did, Gilda thought. Still the Government refused any attempt to reverse the train of destruction they had put into motion.

Gilda's gaze held on a small patch of grey sky that slowly brightened to reveal the luminance of a waxing moon. As the night breeze blew the heavy chemical clouds away, her heart raced at the sight of her beloved moon.

Then her body became rigid as the message entered her thoughts: *Effie and Julius are safe. They will be joining Bird before the next full moon. They are enroute to South America. Sorel and Anthony have preceded them. There is safety there. . . Love! Faith! Love!*

The contact was broken, and Gilda's body slumped. Houston rushed forward, catching her arms from behind. She broke free instantly and spun around ready to kill. When she saw Houston looking down at the empty air between his arms, she laughed. His shock increased at the sight of the filth and blood on her clothes, but he said nothing as he recovered himself. The night shook with Gilda's laughter for the first time in years. Houston joined in because it felt good to laugh freely in the night.

"I'm sorry Houston, you startled me."

"I thought you were fainting."

"We don't faint, Houston."

"All women faint," he said, chuckling.

"No, Houston, all women do not faint. They haven't in some time!"

Houston looked chagrined until he saw that Gilda still smiled as she gazed at the faint glow of moon.

"Houston, soon I'll give you everyone's wages for next month."

"Yes." Houston was invaluable because he didn't ask questions.

"In the event that I have to be away for a while, you may pay the others until I return or send you a message."

"Yes."

"Perhaps you can take some time away if I am not here. Visit your family or friends?"

"There are none anymore," he said with almost no inflection.

"Is that why you remain unresolved about the blood?"

"Yes."

"What do you want out of this world, Houston? It's dying. Perhaps you should be contemplating how to live instead of dying with it."

"If it dies there is little I can do but die," he said. "What's a world without people?"

"What about Off-world?"

"The money for such a trip, not only the fare, but the bribes, the health tests. . . I'd have to work several lifetimes for that. The Government has us trapped here. The charity ship sent by Off-worlders stands waiting, almost empty, while the healthy make themselves ill working to accumulate enough money to bribe their way to life."

"There must be some answer to this disruption of immunity, the diseases, the meteorological tilt," Gilda said without much conviction.

"The answer is greed. We are dying of greed. I don't know the cure for that."

They were both silent, looking out into the surrounding desert, searching for hope, while behind them the female guard slipped away from the entrance to the cave and crept downward to her post. Her hands trembled as she searched the lining of her jacket for the microcommunicator. The decision had been made; she would radio the Hunters. When they arrived she'd collect her reward: passage Off-world for her and her family. The guard was happy she'd been so clever. As soon as Gilda slept it would be over.

Gilda worked at her desk under the lamp's glow for an hour, putting together the payments for the guards and packing the few things she would carry. She was careful to leave her chamber with the appearance that she would return. She took only a pallet of earth, her mothers's rough metal cross, Bird's leather-encased knife, a heavy cloak especially woven and lined with soil, and her copy of the *Tao*. She decided to fold the ancient quilt that had been with her for so many years inside the pallet. Gilda was saddened to leave the desk she had sat at through the generations. It alone had been witness to the years of recording her life. Early in the decline, when travel was not restricted, she had allowed Bird to transport most of her journals south with her. That was a time when Gilda still believed there would be many more years of writing at her desk.

She removed three sets of forged health certificates from the familiar drawers. One set she put in a brown envelope with a large stack of currency and marked it for Houston. The other two she slipped inside her body belt. Smaller envelopes addressed to the other guards and the larger one she left in the center of her desk. Gilda blew out the lamp.

At the opening she looked out onto the glowing rock at the shadow of the girl guard, who stepped forward, smiling. Gilda glanced around as she did before each dawn, then nodded. She realized she had never liked that smile, and her attempts to probe the young woman's thoughts inevitably yielded simple yet pervasive preoccupations with her family. Gilda preferred the taciturn face of Houston or the sprightly resignation of the other guard.

Gilda rustled around in the room for some time before slipping out through the silent panel and making her way about the winding passages. She easily removed a boulder that should have required a dislaser blast and disappeared into the darkness.

Houston watched silently, a little sad that she was gone but also relieved. He didn't think she would have been safe here much longer. Entering her chamber through the hidden panel he took the papers from the desk. He sat down before it, listening for the stillness of the guard outside. Houston opened the envelope addressed to him and tried not to gasp aloud at the sight of the health papers and money. He stuffed them in his pack and went back out through the panel. He found a distant spot where Gilda might have chosen to sleep and stood guard over the emptiness.

Outside, the desert was silent. Gilda embraced the wind and the darkness as she sped eastward toward the city. She would hide for a time in the tombstone high-rises before beginning her journey south. She knew she should feel anxiety or fear, but she was filled with anticipation instead. She wanted this journey. She expected to look at things along the way, not just look for something. Once all of them were together, they would plan a future much different from the one envisioned by the Government.

In the years since leaving the home she had shared contentedly with Effie, Gilda had come to enjoy making the leap into the unknown that was at the heart of traveling. But in her journeys she had learned to let go of searching. She brought no one else into the family, and no longer questioned herself relentlessly. Her time was spent learning to be more than human. She saw more deeply into life, further into the past and through lies. But the future was as much a mystery to her as to anyone—a delicious reason for being, she thought.

She slowed her pace so she could enjoy the desert air, hoping to spot a few city lights as she approached. It was much like the evening she arrived in the Arkansas town where Nadine lived. She'd come south and west from New Hampshire, avoiding Mississippi almost unconsciously as if bounty hunters might still be searching for the girl she had been. The darkness of the road was finally broken by the invitation of those circling lights, the township sign that Nadine had described so vividly in her stories and had struggled to keep going. They'd spent weeks together, their thoughts flying back and forth with an intensity that was almost audible. Nadine shared what she remembered of her great-grandmother. It was in these memories of Aurelia, and Nadine's determination, that Gilda found understanding. Leaving Aurelia behind hadn't been a missed opportunity; it had been opportunity fulfilled. Nadine was proof that Gilda's decision had been a good one. Gilda glimpsed dim lights ahead as she neared the city and picked a high-rise in which she could rest and listen for further word.

She breeched the security system with ease. The entire building had been emptied. She chose to hide where it would be least expected: in full view of the city, in a sealed penthouse apartment. The rooms were heavily curtained, but the air was fresh. Gilda crept around the blackness, comfortable in its warmth. As soon as she opened the bedroom door she knew someone was there, very still, barely alive. She was uncertain what to do, when she saw the vague outline of a figure on the bed. As she moved closer, the person did not stir but breathed in shallow gasps. Gilda tried the bedside lamp. Of course it didn't work; all the power was disconnected. She felt the waxy end of a candle melted down onto a small table.

Gilda pulled a drape away from the window. It let in little light for there were no stars, but she could now see that the figure was a woman, tall and brown-skinned. Gilda felt her pulse and knew the woman was dying. Her cheeks still had color, but the weight of death was upon her. Gilda was shocked. The woman did not look as if she had begun the deterioration yet. Her body was full and healthy, not wasted by the failure of her lungs or muscles. When she knelt beside the bed she saw the half-empty pill bottle sitting neatly beside the glass that smelled of distilled palm wine. The answer was clear: the woman had chosen death rather than wait for death to choose her.

Gilda looked at the sleeping/dying face, curious about what had led her to this moment. There was no clue in the velvet skin, as dark as Gilda's. She appeared to be in her mid-thirties but was without any of the pain lines that marred most faces now. Her brow was peaceful, her hair cut in a loose, curly, old-fashioned Afro. It was deep brown, with a streak of pure white above the temple that was shocking against the dark furrows of the soft, nappy hair. Gilda could not stop herself from stroking it. Her fingers slipped through the softness, and Gilda felt her own heartbeat increase. The woman stirred slightly, moving her head toward the touch.

Gilda put her hand on the woman's slack jaw and breathed into her lungs, realizing even as their lips met that it would do no good. She was appalled by the thrill of pleasure that shot through her at the warmth of the woman's mouth, and a small cry of sadness escaped her. Gilda waited no longer. She pulled back the light quilt tucked around the woman's chest, and her own breasts pulsed with excitement, desire, and shame.

Once Gilda had unbuttoned the rough cotton blouse she slashed with the firm fingernail of her baby finger and put her mouth to the woman's skin. She glanced only briefly at the round breasts. The intoxicating odor of perspiration and sleep filled her senses as she drew the blood quickly. The woman's pulse became more faint, and the languor of the sedative began to wash over Gilda as she dragged herself up to the woman's mouth. She moved slowly, the drug which had been meant to kill the other now racing through Gilda. She bit her own tongue, then the soft membrane of the woman's mouth. She thrust her tongue inside and held the woman's head tightly against the pillow. The blood flowed between them. Their pulses dropped, then rose again, in harmony.

The throbbing in Gilda's head was echoed in the woman. Both became flushed and damp as Gilda collapsed beside the quiet body, her hand held tightly over the wound in the woman's chest. Gilda had little strength left, but again she moved down to the woman's breast. Her lips tingled at the touch of skin, and hungrily she pulled the life from her again. Then, just as eagerly, she gave it back. This sharing of the blood was a desperate act as Gilda willed her to live.

Gilda drew back to look at the brown face now drawn into a mask of pain—the eyes open, unseeing. There were deep textures in their enveloping brown color. She closed the lids gently and said silently, *Sleep. Love. Love.* As the tendrils of unconsciousness wound around her Gilda sensed the message: the route Effie and Julius would be taking to reach Bird. She sunk onto the pillow beside the dark woman.

Their rest was drugged and held them for too many hours. When Gilda awoke it was dusk. She was in need of the blood but afraid to leave the woman before she awoke. Walking around the apartment she found stacks of books, some old food and bottled water, packets of letters. Most of the personal furnishings had been stripped away leaving only the large pieces of furniture and the woman's belongings. Gilda wondered how long it had taken her to climb the thirty-six floors with her heavy boxes. And why had she chosen the top floor? Perhaps, Gilda thought, because she never planned to come down again.

Gilda went to the bed when she heard the woman stir, sitting silently until she opened her eyes.

"My name is Gilda. You are. . .?"

"Ermis." She closed her eyes and appeared to sleep.

When she opened them again she said, "I'm going to be sick."

Gilda took the wastebasket from beside the bed and held it for her. Ermis gagged, spewing out the contents of her stomach until she heaved drily. Gilda then laid her back on the pillow and bathed her face with a wet cloth, much as had been done for her many years before. She offered her a glass of water. Ermis rinsed her mouth and fell back again, exhausted.

"I had planned to be dead now," Ermis said in a whisper.

"Why?"

"There was no reason to live on. My family, the moon. . .everything's gone."

"Your plan has been half-fulfilled," Gilda said with a cool edge in her voice, masking the anxiety she felt.

"Half?" Then Ermis looked more closely at Gilda. She saw a brown woman of immense strength. That could not be hidden beneath her loose-fitting tunic. Gilda was shorter than Ermis and leaner. Her gaze was unwavering, and the dark-brown color of her eyes was flecked with orange.

"Vampyre?" Ermis said the word calmly with the ancient pronunciation, but her face filled with terror.

Gilda closed her eyes tightly, making herself completely vulnerable to this woman who feared her and to show her abdication of power. At the same time she looked inside to reassure herself she had not done an evil thing. When she heard the ringing laughter she looked sharply, afraid the woman had gone mad.

"Vampyre!" Ermis said again, laying back on the pillow, then slept.

When Ermis was finally awake she and Gilda stood at the window looking down on the city which was settling into evening. Gilda explained that she must go out.

"I'll return shortly to share the blood with you. Or, if you prefer," she handed Ermis a small packet of herbs, "I will see to a proper completion and interment." Ermis remained silent as the door closed.

When Gilda returned, Ermis was seated by the window, the curtains tied back. The packet lay unopened on the floor beside her. She turned expectantly and saw the change in Gilda. Her eyes were bright and her body even more fluid and powerful. Ermis felt a hunger she'd never had before. She did not wait but pulled Gilda to her on the wide living room floor beneath the starless sky. This time Gilda's lips explored the whole of Ermis' body shamelessly before sharing the blood that gave them both life. They slept on the pallet where Gilda had mixed the home soil of Ermis with her own.

On the next night they went out together, Ermis moving cautiously, still unused to the strength of her body and the quickness of her reflexes. They walked around the city watching the wary faces that did not meet their eyes. Gilda showed her how to move silently and stun, so there was no resistance, struggle, or death. She explained how best to come into someone's dream and take the blood while they slept, arousing no suspicions. And how to leave something behind in exchange—life for life. Ermis became swift and unafraid.

Gilda talked of their escape once they were back in the high-rise, explaining the things they would need to take with them, but not revealing their destination. Ermis did not inquire, only nodded and said she would be ready.

Then Gilda said, "You are not bound to me. Don't feel obligated to take this journey if that's not what you want. You can still end your life if you wish, or go on alone."

Ermis met Gilda's gaze, a look she still didn't fully know although she recognized a multitude of emotions hidden behind its opaque veil. She said, "I wanted to die because there was no one left to wish that I lived. That's no longer the case, is it?" The sparkle in her eyes warmed Gilda.

"Why did you laugh that first night, when you knew?"

"It was the perfect twist to my story: I, alone in a penthouse at the bottom of despair because I was unloved in a dying and unloving world, awake to find myself in the possession of the most valuable commodity on the planet—long life. And it's a life freely given by a stranger."

"I feel I must explain more of my world to you than simply the exchange and secrecy. There are many questions to this life, many of which I've not answered for myself. Many of which may *never* be answered."

"I believe I'll run on. . ." Ermis said, the lilt of her voice providing the music to the old gospel song.

"When I came upon you, I knew you had planned your own death, still I sensed your wanting me to stop it. There was hope inside you even as you stood with death. I needed that in you."

Ermis continued to hum the song as she listened to Gilda.

"It was knowing and not knowing that made me do it. I wanted the chance to be with you."

They lay down together beside their few possessions, ready to rise and depart quickly. At first dusk they left to gather other pallets Gilda had hidden along the southern route. They quickly transferred the hard-packed New Mexico soil Ermis carried into half of the indestructible sleeping pallets. They traveled by hovercraft, then by foot, packhorse, and then on foot again, doubling back on their own path but always moving southward.

Intermittently along the way Gilda told Ermis of the others, but they didn't speak during most of the journey. Nor did they pause to enjoy the few remaining aboriginal villages of Mexico. They moved quickly, only delaying when they felt they were being observed. They stayed hidden until the last moments before dawn, finally taking their share of the blood, retracing their steps to sleep in caves or ruins.

Early evening shadow found them, several days later, filled with anxiety. They were in the area that had once been called Panama but was now part of Mexico. Crossing the Canal would be a particularly dangerous part of the journey. The rushing waters below the narrow footbridge had the ability to drain them of their strength, but Gilda felt confident she could guide Ermis through this difficult passage.

Their boots and the hems of their clothes were lined with soil as partial protection. In addition, they would cross the Canal as soon as they awakened—before they took their share of the blood— in hope that the edge of hunger would push them onward.

Their anxiety caused them to awaken early. It was then that Ermis heard breathing and whispered voices outside the entrance to the cave.

The two women did not move. They waited for the Hunters, who sounded uncertain whether they should leave and return earlier on the following day or try to make the catch now in the gathering dusk. They finally drew deeper into the cave toward the two who lay as still as death, listening to one another's beating hearts and the metallic scraping of narco darts hooked onto the belts of the approaching Hunters. The women waited until the Hunters were within their reach. Each Hunter carried a paralyzing dart in his hand as well as the smell of sweat and greed.

When he saw the women the larger of the Hunters drew his breath in sharply, and the other motioned him to silence. They stood, one on either side of the pallet, then crouched down over the immobile women. As they bent, one of their canteens fell forward grazing Ermis' head. She emitted a low hiss, and in a second she and Gilda leapt up, pinning the men quickly. They knocked the darts to the ground. One Hunter tried to run back toward the cave's opening, but Ermis picked up a dart and tossed it swiftly. It caught him just above his left elbow. He took a half step, then fell as if the ground had disappeared beneath his feet.

The other Hunter swung forward behind her, evading Gilda and bringing his fist down, dart in hand. His aim was sure: the center of Ermis' back. Gilda moved to deflect it, and the tip pierced her hand before she swung it around and buried it in the Hunter's chest. The blood that bubbled up around the wound sickened Gilda. She watched death collect him, memorizing his face just before she felt a blazing light blind her.

Until now, all had been muffled silence. As she held out her arms to catch Gilda's falling body, Ermis screamed aloud, her bellow shaking rocks from the wall of the shelter and echoing down the stony corridors.

Ermis clutched Gilda to her breast under the sifting dust and clay as anguish and fear swelled inside, choking off her piercing screams. She was relieved to feel Gilda's heart beating weakly. She carried Gilda and their burdens out to the road, then walked a few miles with the several hundred pounds balanced precariously, just to get away from the cave. She left Gilda hidden in a thicket and went off to get their share of the blood. The cave had been chosen because of its isolation, so her journey was a long one. She returned to share the fresh blood which would hold Gilda's pulse steady. Ermis probed the muscles of Gilda's legs and arms. The drug did not seem to have damaged them; they were weak but still had resilience.

Knowing so little of this life, Ermis was sure of nothing. They had to cross the Canal, but what then? Others would be waiting for them somewhere, others who knew what to do. But where were they waiting?

Ermis watched Gilda for signs of movement, the question screaming inside her head. Then the answer came. Ermis sat transfixed, her eyes almost as still as Gilda's. Inside her head she heard the voices as if a breeze had entered and blew gently across her mind. *South to Peru*. They would be waiting at the *old ruins of Machu Picchu*. The sound of the place was so ancient to her, she was uncertain she had ever heard it said aloud. But she pictured the place clearly and almost saw the two who would be waiting.

Ermis rested until darkness was total. The sky was almost clear of clouds, and a few stars hung in the emptiness as if it were an ordinary night. She took little time to appreciate the special quality of the evening. She gazed into Gilda's face looking for signs of improvement and for answers about how they would continue this journey. Then the picture came to her of a travois. She used the belt from her tunic and other bits of leather strapping from their pallets to tie together their packs and lash them to an awkward litter made from green tree limbs. She tied Gilda to it, molding her limp body around their possesions. Ermis then attached it all to her waist and walked swiftly southward. The pull of the water very soon made her muscles feel thick and arthritic. By the time she was in sight of the footbridge and the rushing water below, her teeth had begun to ache with tension as she held her jaw clamped shut.

If the litter hadn't been tied to her, Ermis would not have had the strength in her arms to hold it. Each foot moved leadenly in front of the other, keeping rhythm with the halting beat of her heart. She fixed her eyes on the other side of the Canal although her vision was blurred. The steady movement of Ermis walking rocked Gilda's paralyzed body.

Inside her head Gilda began to hear one voice, Bird's, saying her name repeatedly, as if Gilda were a child outside at play, unable to heed the call of a parent. She settled her mind on the voice and let the rocking motion take her back to it. She heard the sweet intake of breath.

Ah, so finally you come to me in a place I've made home, Bird said.

And we can leave this world together. Gilda heard her response as if she'd spoken aloud.

No, my girl. I think not. I have flown from nest to nest since Woodard's. And we've not had time enough to know this world together.

Gilda felt protest welling inside of her. The Hunters would be relentless; there was little chance the atmosphere could be saved. She knew no reason to remain.

We remain because this our home. We both have lost land here. Should we leave it all to them? I will not.

Gilda was able to open her eyes. She watched the determined back pulling her and the weight of many things behind.

Yes, we'll stay.

Gilda focused her will outward, alongside the others she knew drew them forward.

Ermis blinked to clear her sight and peered into the darkness. She felt the presence of others but saw nothing. She propelled each foot mindlessly, no longer feeling them. There had been a cool spray of water, but the air was dry again and all she knew was the weight of the travois dragging at her body, the bridge turning to stone, then to road dirt. Still she walked on afraid to stop. The dust of the road finally became real to her as the water's hold on her senses was loosened. They had made it across.

There were only a few hours left in the night. Ermis needed to seek cover before dawn. She bent down and wiped the dust from Gilda's face, whispering in her ear. Gilda's eyes opened slowly, no longer opaque. Ermis felt for Gilda's pulse and was relieved. Checking the bindings, she took up the litter again.

She found shelter among what she originally thought was simply a rock fall but then realized was an edifice collapsed in upon itself. She lifted the slabs of rock and burrowed beneath the rubble until she had made a place large enough for them both and their bundle of things. She held Gilda in her arms and listened to their breathing until sleep took them. When the day blossomed they both shifted uneasily but were unharmed by the small rays of sun that filtered through the rocks.

Ermis awoke with a start as evening's coolness seeped through and realized that Gilda's breathing was almost normal. Indeed, when she lifted Gilda's head, her eyes were open and clear. Ermis decided not to move further until there was some other sign of recovery.

And soon Gilda raised her hand to Ermis' face. "Your courage is great," Gilda said in a hoarse voice.

"I couldn't leave you any more than you would leave me."

They had not spoken of that night in the penthouse or the bag of herbs that had been left behind.

"I have heard," Ermis said with a sound of hesitation, "many voices in my thoughts."

"Yes," Gilda said, "it's been difficult for me to understand, but Bird has been with me."

"Those who come to meet us are closer each hour. There were others, urging me on," Ermis continued.

"Effie and Julius, Anthony, Sorel. I don't imagine they wish to give up on me just yet." Gilda smiled at Ermis fully for the first time since they came together.

They crossed the mountains side by side. A few more stars showed themselves, giving them assurance. Gilda stopped short and looked up at them with admiration, as if they could look down and see her. She felt her lungs expand with the air scented by the thick foliage. The night itself seemed green as the rustle of leaves grew louder. She closed her eyes, remembering those first glimpses of the road she had seen inside the woman who rescued her so long ago. It had been much like this one—narrow, winding, almost enveloped in the abundance surrounding it. She looked more closely at an enormous leaf, reaching forward from the darkness. The light veins and soft curves of its outline offered a universe unto itself, a wonder as yet unexplored.

She turned to Ermis. "We will build large campfires, then you must tell me your story. Who you've been and what life has been like for you. There will be stories and dancing again."

They walked, and Ermis hummed in a low voice. She said, "My mother loved hymns, gospel music. She wasn't a religious sort at all, just loved the music. She said it was so pure, it made her think of the history. It was a funny sight, my mother and father crooning "Steal Away to Jesus," snuggled together on the porch swing as if it was a romantic ballad." They both laughed out loud.

"I think you'll enjoy our family. Julius knows every gospel song ever sung and every bit of slang since 1968. And Bird will have much history to give you about your home territory."

Gilda stopped short. On a ridge to the south in the quickening sky she saw two figures in silhouette against a silver moonbow. Julius and Effie were parallel with them, moving eastward toward Machu Picchu. Gilda pointed, and Ermis' smile broadened. They turned southward to meet them. Gilda was no longer fleeing for her life.

AFTERWORD

The author's great aunt, Effie Johnson. This picture appeared on the original cover of *The Gilda Stories*.

"WE TAKE BLOOD, NOT LIFE LEAVE SOMETHING IN EXCHANGE"

A T 15 I HUDDLED IN THE DARK every Saturday night with my best friends from the neighborhood to watch old scary movies on *Thriller Theatre*. We giggled and gasped with the same hormonal abandon that we cheered a high school basketball team or pursued a forbidden kiss under the shadows of the huge chestnut tree on our block. I always favored Dracula because (I thought) of the clothes. The elegance of dressing for dinner in silk and suits, even when dinner was just downstairs, appealed to the romanticism that pushed its way up to me through cracked cement and tenement life. The drama of Dracula's opera cape was the embodiment of power in a world in which nothing was certain. It wasn't until later that I understood Dracula's appeal was more than the allure of fashion. His lone figure in endless and doomed pursuit of a companion who would live with him forever was a tailor-made hero for a melodramatic little girl who felt abandoned by divorced parents.

When I wrote the line: "We take blood, not life. Leave something in exchange" for the 1996 stage adaptation of *The Gilda Stories* I'd all but forgotten those childhood years when I was sure I was the only one who could understand Dracula's suffering. I'd been studying vampyre mythology and writing vampyre fiction for over a decade. That compact political statement, which doesn't appear in the original novel, evolved during the collaborative process it was my privilege to participate in over a three year period with the Urban Bush Women Company. The words are a distillation of my own re-imagining of an ancient myth that has become imbedded in western culture. It's a compelling mythology, but one which I, as a lesbian feminist, needed to excavate and reshape before I could claim vampyres as my own. Even as a child I never was quite comfortable with the dead bodies that littered Dracula's path to fulfillment.

In writing those words I discovered what is most important about the epic tale that is Gilda's story. The words postulate that we are interconnected, that our survival is dependent on our exchanges with each other, and that our balance is kept only when we give and take as needed. Not new sentiments, but certainly they represent principles which are at the core of a fuller, more balanced experience in the world.

Yet it's not the philosophy or principles that have made Gilda so popular over the years. I think the endurance of the story has its root in the tension of two elements whose interaction confirm the feminist principle that "the personal is political." The first is the emergence of the story from a highly active political period. I first imagined Gilda in the 1970s and 80s, which were every bit as socially active as the 1960s. The U.S. government was systematically decimating the Black Panther Party; adults in Boston and other northern cities were physically attacking young people being bused to integrated schools; Laos was invaded and Viet Nam was still being laid waste; women were finally forcing the police to take rape charges seriously.

The difference in the 70s and 80s was perspective. My "baby boomer" generation of activists—civil rights, anti-war, feminist, ecologist—was now tumbling out of the arms of college and onto the mean streets of the professional world. Evaporating was the coziness of single issue politics—the deceptive place where even if you were being slaughtered at least the appearance was that we were all in it together and we were all—in our separate groups (Black, female, pacifist, etc.)—like each other. In the 80s I was learning, as a lesbian feminist of mixed race, the more complex world that is identity. Class was no longer something related only to merry old England and Tsarist Russia. Sexism was a disease as wide spread in communities of color as everywhere else, proving that even the powerless will finds ways to wield power if only against their own. The cauldron of social activism didn't stop bubbling when the 60s were over, the flame was just on low, more diffuse and all but ignored by mass media.

My impulse to shape Gilda into the heroic figure she became grew out of that sense of connection between art, politics and everyday life instilled by the activism of those periods. The Black Arts Movement's inflammatory poetry readings, the songs which opened doors of consciousness for women, the literary journals of lesbian activists were calls to action that rose from deep in the heart, transmuting the pain of oppression into art. The urgency of those times informs Gilda's every act and observation as well as her personal development.

Also contributing to the eternal life of the book are the emotional experiences that drive the story of one woman's coming of age. That her process spans two centuries is almost incidental. It is the ground from which that process springs that makes Gilda familiar to the reader as well as larger than life. Gilda is an ordinary girl facing the daily developmental issues imposed on girls by western society—surviving abuse, discovering her self-worth, shedding the social construct of girls as victims. At the same time she's an extraordinary figure forged from deprivation and insights that can only be hers. But the relationship between those very different aspects of Gilda makes space for readers to see themselves—engaged in ordinary struggle and simultaneously able to affect significant change.

The novel itself emerged from highly personal events, giving further credence to the feminist precept "the personal is political." After college I left home and moved to New York City, leaving behind in Boston my great grandmother, Grace. We'd been very close during the years she raised me so her passing soon after I ventured away from the proverbial nest was a great blow for a girl who takes her melodrama seriously. It was stunning because I couldn't even imagine that someone I loved would die. She was just there and always would be. For someone who thought of herself as reflective it was a great slam for me to realize how little thought I'd given to leaving home and leaving her.

For years I would often forget she wasn't at the other end of the phone. I imagined every significant event in my life as I retold it to her. That led me to think about the possibility of her living forever. Then, of course, the philosophical questions—if I could make her and my fabulous grandmother live forever, did relatives I didn't care for have to be immortal too?! I slipped into the vampyre mythology through this familial back door while I was comforting myself with the idea of eternal life for those I loved and meandering through all the theoretical possibilities of creating such a population. I started by writing a vampyre story that centered around a heartbreaking loss and the efforts of several characters to keep close those they loved, even after death. It was a romantic effort that fortunately has yet to see the light of night. Gilda grew out of those exercises in which I tried on vampyre mythology to get a sense of what that one change—eternal life—would have on the fabric of existence.

The next defining event in Gilda's birth was a sadly typical one. I was standing in a phone booth on a Manhattan street corner. Two young men of color walked by and felt entitled to harass me. Of course, they didn't consider making comments about my body or telling me what they could do with it harassment. They didn't see that their idea of fun was humiliating and dehumanizing to women in general and to me in particular. And they certainly had no idea that centuries of such casual objectification had a debilitating affect on human relations.

What they did see was a colored woman go berserk, pick up a bottle off the curb and threaten their lives. The rage that hurtled toward them was so shocking they scurried away to leave the "crazy lady" alone. It was my craziness, my breaking with the traditional response, that frightened them and made me feel safe.

My sense of outrage at being denied the dignity of making a public phone call pounded against me like the waves of a turbulent ocean hitting a sea wall. The crash was hard and it sprayed in all directions. The most fruitful result was my understanding that this same rage was felt by millions of women daily and that most often men are oblivious to the damage it causes. I could tell this was true because when I told the story on college campuses and in bookstores I was always met with knowing and sympathetic nods from women who were relieved to hear out loud that such a "little" thing could tear at the fabric of our lives. Sexism could be like a pebble that needs to be removed from a shoe; a tiny thing that throws off a woman's gait, causing her to limp, sometimes unconscious-ly, to avoid pain every day.

The subsequent result of that street corner encounter was the first Gilda story called "Joe Louis Was a Heck of a Fighter." It recounts Gilda's encounter with a young thug who has no idea who he's messing with. I thought it would help me work out some of my anger as well as give me practice reshaping vampyre mythol-ogy (Where would she sleep? How does she make money?). I wrote the story of Gilda's revenge on the erstwhile mugger/rapist and there encountered my first serious philosophical questions: How did I feel about Gilda killing? Because she'd been abused should she abuse her power over mortals as traditional vampyres did? What did it mean that she had to live on the blood of others? What was her rela-tionship to the mortal community?

I pondered these questions as they related to vampyres each time I sat down to write and soon realized that they, of course, had more significant ramifications than the events unfolding in my gothic adventure. These were versions of the questions I'd been taught to ask when, as a young girl in Sunday school, I was studying the Baltimore Catechism. They were the questions posed by my great grandmother's spiritual beliefs that grew out of the soil of the Ioway tribe. They were the issues raised by my belief in feminism and my need for a viable approach to re-envisioning the world.

The questions helped me develop a distinct vampyre philosophy that is grounded in my family's code and feminist thought. Contemporary Christians developed the coda: "What would Jesus do?" Bringing it closer to home, Xander, the one stalwart boy/friend in the TV show, *Buffy the Vampire Slayer* asks: "What would Buffy do?" As I worked on the segments over the years, I often asked myself "What would Gilda do?" More often than not the response was a combination of elements from the women in my family. What started as my own angry out-burst at a personal affront on the street evolved into a set of responses to injus-tice that suggest that girls are not as powerless as they're taught they are and that individuals and society have the ability to change. Ironically, as I examined the moral questions that were inherent in the unfolding story I learned more about what I believed as a feminist activist. Through the writing I embraced more fully the philosophy that was giving shape to the writing.

That first Gilda story didn't end up being included in the novel but appears in a Firebrand anthology entitled *To Be Continued*. It was there in the rewrites, though, that I came to my first, and most significant realization. For Gilda to work for me and my audience, the vampyres had to break the traditional mold. When Gilda wreaks vengeance on the man who attacks her, she could easily kill him and remain undiscovered. But how would that be different from anything that has gone before? How would it be different from men who kill their rivals, or men who start wars over territory? It wasn't. Simply because the hero was a woman didn't make murder palatable.

From that came the idea that the family of vampyres to which Gilda belongs would not kill unnecessarily. They could take blood without killing! It seemed such a simple concept I couldn't believe it took so long for it to emerge. But then what happens if the vampyre participation is so easily accommodated? Where is the tension of the story?

And what did I think about taking? When the book first appeared one critic felt that taking blood from an unknowing participant was as much an exploitation as taking the blood and leaving a dead body. I think the potential dead body would disagree! I also think that symbiotic relationships aren't always immediately and mutually agreed upon. A mother nurses a child because of the social imperative as much her own desire. When a mother refuses that nurturing one of the covenants around which society is built is broken. If I could move the one who provides the blood from "victim" to "sharer" (knowing or unknowing), the nature of the power in the relationship would be different.

Then isn't the sharing, even with an unknowing sharer, ameliorated by Gilda leaving something in exchange? In my imperfect world it is. I make the assumption that we all, given the information and free will, would choose to sustain those around us. For me, the interesting aspect to helping mend a problem is understanding it and helping others comprehend the small and larger aspects of it. So, rather than leaving behind a complete solution to the problems of others as if she's Robin Hood taking from the rich and giving to the poor, Gilda's gift is to point toward what's needed. A little wind at one's back, so to speak, rather than the keys to a car. And Gilda knowing she must leave something in exchange—rather than killing—is part of the tension of the story.

Ultimately, it's true, Gilda and her family do have more power over life and death than do the mortals. And in this universe along with that power must come responsibility or the vampyres are doomed to a soulless life. Those who recognize and meet that responsibility have "true" life, not the perverse terror that comes from preying on others. It's that balance that Gilda aspires to throughout her existence, making the novel, in many ways, a coming of age story.

Another element of the novel that grew out of my childhood was its Gothicism. Although I am no longer a practicing Christian, I have in the fabric of my life the sounds, stories and smells of my Catholic upbringing. The deep

red velvet and satin, the dappled church light and the unsettling Gregorian har-
monies all pointed me in the direction of vampyre stories. "This is my body,
this is my blood." How many times could I hear those words and not want to
create a world in which that transmogrification takes on new meaning?

Even though I didn't adhere to the sectarian teachings of my youth, the
passion and endurance of faith always stayed with me. To have faith in something and live your life keeping that "faith" is as important to me today as it was
when I kneeled to take holy communion. The faith today is in different things
than it was when I was a girl, but "faith" as a core element of progress, of
humanitarian action, of civil rights is the key. Without some kind of faith the
struggle is hollow. That's why the "bad" vampyres are bad. They believe in nothing except life for its own sake and at any expense. They are kind of like the
multi-national corporations that we read about everyday (see "Ultra Violet," the
British vampyre series for more of that view)—gobbling up family businesses,
polluting natural resources and destroying communities for the sake of profit.

For Gilda, mortal life is as significant as her own immortal life. Her journey is finding her place within the mortal community, learning who should
make the journey with her and understanding how she contributes to the lives
of others. This is what we're all learning.

There are several things that the publication of an anniversary issue makes
possible. The first is this chance to lay out the philosophical underpinnings of
the story more explicitly and, at the same time, know that it doesn't matter if I
do or not. The novel stands or falls on whether or not you care about the characters. My job is to avoid burying them under an avalanche of ideas and principles.

The second is I can acknowledge: yes, I am a bean counter. I tried to be
even handed about who was "bad" and who was "good." I didn't want to create a diatribe inadvertently. Once, a young man at a lecture observed that Gilda
seemed to take blood mostly from men and interpreted that as my dislike of
men. I was able to explain that in the time periods he cited it would have been
almost impossible for women to be alone on the street at night, hence taking
blood from men would be more natural. It was a societal proscription growing
out of sexism which he was unable to identify because he was such an unwit-
ting beneficiary.

My belief is that any good harangue should be carefully planned. When I
want to highlight my dislikes (self-centeredness, rape, economic exploitation)
it's pretty clear. My overarching concern was that most people be able to find
themselves in Gilda's story, to see a possibility for being changed and for chang-

ing society. I did not want the story to be a return to the simple comfort of "me good/you bad" nationalism. I wanted a novel that reflected the complexity of human nature as we know it while still holding on to faith in change.

I'm also afforded the luxury—in a new edition—of saying thank you to those who show up fully formed as themselves in the story. In some places I lifted characters from my life just as I lifted the photograph of my great Aunt Effie to be included. I loved the idea of having members of my community (the Gap Tooth Girlfriends writing workshop in Chapter Six, for example) recognize themselves. The interplay of reality and fiction helps create a bond within a real world community as well as giving fuel to the book. I also like being able to celebrate people in my family by giving them a walk-on role in their real context like my stepmother, Henrietta, in the Four Eleven Lounge in Chapter Four. These were small but emotional ways that I could pay homage to those who'd helped me create a book and a life.

Another privilege of this anniversary edition is that I'm able to reveal to aspiring writers how often I was told by mainstream publishers and by other lesbians that this story would never fly. I didn't give up and worked to make the story airborne. The manuscript went through a full year of intense rewriting and an untold number of revisions after it was first accepted by Nancy Bereano, the founder of Firebrand Books. And I am still working to make my writing better each day. As I look back at the novel I can see clearly where I would have rewritten or improved, including making it clearer that the story really goes in a circle.

The birthplace of one of the early main characters is exactly where the story ends. Sometimes it doesn't pay to be too obscure because I've been explaining that since the first reading. Editing is everything!

And finally, with this introduction, I get to say aloud how much it has meant to me that so many readers love Gilda. When I started writing I had no idea that there was such a large body of fans for vampyre fiction. Dracula and his brides spawned an entire generation of devotees, fascinated by the emotional and philosophical complexities inherent in discussions of vampire lore. Fans of the traditional Dracula movies, or of the erudite, historical vampires of Chelsea Quinn Yarbro's fiction or Anne Rice's brooding rebels were ripe for stories from a lesbian/feminist perspective.

The sense of community that I've always written about comes alive when I answer enthusiastic audience questions. We talk about the adventures women can have and the philosophical framework that Gilda represents helping to create that community among us as we are having the discussion.

I've read from Gilda at colleges, literary events and bookstores around the world and few in the audience have ever missed the point: Life is a romantic adventure in which we live fullest when we know we can each be a powerful force for social improvement locally and globally. And the more power we have, the more responsibility we have in our communities. At our best we do take blood, not life and leave something in exchange.

Jewelle Gomez
San Francisco
July 2003

JOE LOUIS WAS A HECK OF A FIGHTER

GILDA WAS MORE THAN ALIVE. The 150 years she carried were flung casually around her shoulders, an intricately knit shawl handed down from previous generations, yet distinctly her own. Her legs were smooth and mocha brown, unscarred by the knife-edge years spent on a Mississippi plantation, and strengthened by more recent nights dancing in speakeasies and then discos. The paradox did not escape Gilda: her power was forged by deprivation and decadence, and the preternatural endurance that had been thrust upon her unexpectedly. Her grip could snap bone and bend metal, and when she ran she was the wind, she was invincible and alone.

Tonight, hurrying toward home to Effie, she walked anxiously, gazing at the evening skyline. She glanced over her shoulder at the shadowed sidewalk behind her, where the light from the streetlamps was cast through shifting leaves.

She veered off of Broadway down to West End Avenue where grass sloped gently downward from the city street to the brackish river. The soft flowing of the water played in her ears, obscuring the city sound to her left and stirring her already bubbling uneasiness. She focussed her attention to steel herself against the discomfort of the running water of the Hudson River so she could enjoy the textured darkness of the tree-lined avenue.

Ahead of her, hidden from the streetlight by the shadows of a thick maple tree, Gilda saw a man leaning against the park fence. Her body tensed, but she felt no fear. This was a mortal, in his twenties, strongly built and obviously up to no good. He wore a sweatsuit several sizes too large, but that did not conceal his muscled arms from her. The cap pulled down over his brow, meant to hide his features, only exposed his vulnerability to Gilda. Gilda slowed her steps momentarily, then thought: he's just a man.

A surprise flood of anger washed over her. She'd only recently understood such anger could be hers. Her mother, Fulani features hemmed into a placid gaze, had not been allowed that luxury. She'd been a slave, admonished to be grateful. As a child Gilda had not understood: the master, who owned all and was responsible for everyone, never showed anger; his wife, whom he pampered and worshipped oppressively, was angry all the time. As was the overseer who regularly vented his anger on black flesh. But blacks were not thought to have anger any more than a mule or a tree cut down for kindling.

Gilda looked quickly behind her and saw several apartment dwellers moving casually past their windows, and a couple approaching a little more than a block behind her. The young man stood ahead of her under the maple, his intentions leering out from behind an empty grin.

Gilda's step was firm. She wondered what drove men—black, white, rich, poor, alive or otherwise—to need to leap out at women from the darkness. As she walked past he spoke low, almost directly in her ear, "Hey Mama, don't walk so fast."

Gilda continued on, hoping he would take his loss and shut up.

He didn't. "Aw, Mama, come on. Be nice to me."

The wheedling in his voice scraped and scratched at her.

We're connected by blood, Gilda thought, as she felt the young black man waiting. She understood that the poverty she saw around her ground people into hopelessness. This one reeked of his enjoyment of power over someone else he considered weaker, unworthy. An assault in the dark was the substitution for truly taking power.

Anger speared her, leaving a metallic taste in her mouth. Where were the words for what she felt?

Gilda stopped and turned to him smiling as she remembered the words of an irate Chicago waitress she'd overheard decades before: "I am not your mama. If I were, I would have drowned you at birth."

She walked on. He caught up. "Why you bitches so hard. Come on sistuh, give me a break!"

Gilda continued walking. She had no desire to let her anxiety about Samuel push her to end the night with angry blood.

"Come on sistuh, let me see that smile again." With that he seized her arm. His grip would have bruised another but Gilda shook free easily, leaving him off balance. In a smooth reach he snatched at her close-cropped hair, hoping to pull her into the darkness.

The image of Effie, waiting in their rooms, her sinewy form concealed in shadow, flashed through Gilda's mind.

A low moan sounded in the back of her throat. She could almost feel her slim fingers clenched around his neck, snapping the connection to the spine. She replaced that sensation with the memory of a hot night thirty years before—Florida in 1950. She'd been sitting in an after-hours club watching the fighter show how he'd whipped a Tampa boy who said boxing was just a "coon show."

Gilda smiled again as she raised her left fist in perfect form and smashed it into the man's jaw. He fell unconscious to the cracked pavement, half-sprawled on the thin city grass.

Gilda lifted him from the street and held him to her as the couple she'd seen earlier passed by. Once they were several paces away she lowered the man to the ground so he sat against the maple tree. She knelt low, hiding him from the street, and smoothly sliced the flesh behind his ear with her fingernail. His eyes opened in shock, and Gilda held him in the grip of her hands and her mind. He was pinned against the tree, its rough bark biting into his shirt as Gilda rummaged amongst his thoughts.

Confusion replaced shock, then rage followed. Unable to move, the young man bellowed internally. In his eyes she observed a coldness she sometimes saw in others hanging around street corners: they were always scavenging. They never really saw anyone they couldn't use.

Gilda pressed her lips to the cut. Blood had begun to seep out onto his sweatshirt. The flesh was soft, and smelled of sweet soap. Gilda could imagine the boy he'd been, when he was still able to picture himself a part of the larger world. She drew her share of the blood from him swiftly, barely enjoying the warmth as it washed over her. His anger began to swell inside of her, wiping away the sensation of his youth. She was engorged yet continued taking the blood, unable to stop, feeling no need to leave something for him.

At the final moment she pulled back, lifted herself from his neck, and looked into his almost dead eyes. She touched his nearly empty mind searching for a tiny space where there was no anger or hatred. She found too many places seared white with disappointment turned into rage. And then, a small moment where a treasured memory was hidden opened up. There she planted the understanding of what it could mean to really feel love toward a sister, and from that love find a connection to the rest of the world. In the shallow cavern of his thoughts she left him that one sensation to live for, to strive for as she held her hand to seal the wound. His pulse was faint but soon became steady.

She lifted him gently and rested him on the park bench, placing his arms casually behind his head, as if he were only napping. She drew the cap back so it rested on the crown of his head but left his dark face open and smooth in the dim light. His lips were no longer curled in a smirk but rested partly open, ready to finally speak. She could see the young man he'd been, the young man he might still be.

As she rose to leave, Gilda was glad she had such a good memory. "Yeah, Joe Louis was a heck of a fighter," she said aloud.